I0576312

Hebenon

Book 1 of The Scarecrow Trials

Tamara Brigham

Cover Design by: Tamara Brigham

Published by:
Tamara Brigham
PO Box 151
Clearlake, CA 95422

Printed and bound in the United States of America

First Edition

ISBN #978-1-7336708-2-1

For John Simm...

Whose talent gave rise to the Scarecrow.

We've never met...

But thank you for the inspiration.

❧*❧

...With juice of cursed Hebenon in a vial,
And in the porches of my ears did pour
The leprous distilment; whose effect
Holds such an enmity with blood of man
That, swift as quicksilver, it courses through
The natural gates and alleys of the body;
And with a sudden vigour it doth posset
And curd, like eager droppings into milk,
The thin and wholesome blood; so did it mine...
                    Hamlet: Act 1, Scene 5

❧CHAPTER 1❧

The slippery, vaporous, congested wasteland, the littered metal passages of perpetual darkness punctuated every hour of the day by the shimmer of alglamps and the pop of electric neon, teemed with life that never should have taken root here. The masked form, protected from the constant fog and mildew by mechanical breathing and sight apparatuses, peered down from the steel-platformed perch on which it hunched, watching the thin dregs of humanity pass back and forth at the other end of the alley. With more than an hour before shift change, this was the crawling hour, men and women either sleeping or working. There was little chance of Crow activity, though he knew they were there, their flat black eyes watching as surely as his own were. But they would not see him.

They never saw him. The day they did, he would be dead.

Or Vanished.

Thumping on metallic grating, a sound he knew well, magnified over the Falls' constant roar by the amplification units within his mask, turned his head. A tagger of indeterminate age, nondescript in a dark, wet slicker, stooped and ragged, hair damp and stringy around the uncovered head, glanced furtively about, familiar, erratic, paranoid movements suggesting an addiction to Heb and a recent usage that bordered on overdose. The wet wraith looked up at the corner of the building, outfitted, as most corners were, with a SCAM unit, but the tiny red flash that would indicate a working camera could not be seen, thus the tagger removed the spray can from the pocket of the tattered, oversized coat and began to spray.

There were other SCAMs, too far away or at off angles, that might catch the tagger but not offer a threatening image to whatever Crows were watching from their secret nests. But the SCAMs without a flasher whirred, its sensors detecting movement even if it was not transmitting, bringing its mechanical eye to focus on the delinquent who could not hear it over the hiss of the spray can, the rumble and growl of the four falls in the distance and the river below that accumulated the tributaries' spillage, and the drone and clunk of steam turbines within the building chosen for marking. The watcher heard it, however, enhanced hearing and his vantage point alerting him to the danger the tagger was about to face.

Even if the eyes on the other end of the SCAM feed saw nothing, the camera's effort to focus on something might be enough to warrant investigation. These days, nearly anything was enough.

Distance to the ground was judged. Muscles clenched and coiled as running boots, two pairs of them, thundered through the miasma of the alley, bearing down on the hapless tagger. Either oblivious to the clatter, too strung out to care, or determined in their stupor to let their outrage at the establishment be known, the tagger continued, abstract anger taking cohesive shape on the wall as the ones raged against drew nearer.

The watcher did not wait. When the black-beaked horrors, the tails of their long coats flapping behind them like wings as they ran, passed beneath him, he dropped, using the slick metal pole to swing around, leveraging his descent with practiced ease. His own black boots, designed as the Crows' were for running on wet surfaces, yet altered for stealth, caught the second Crow full on, one planted in his chest, the other across the throat to throw the figure, coughing and spluttering, into a collection of recyclables awaiting pick up. The Crow hit his head on the wall after a surprised squawk and lay still.

The tagger, hearing the tumult at last, dropped the spray can and ran blindly in the other direction, narrowly avoiding a fall into the fish pits teaming with the city's major food source.

Torn between pursuing the target and addressing the commotion behind him, the lead Crow spun mid-step, thumper swinging in the hopes of connecting with whatever threat was behind him.

The smaller figure, masked, head covered to be unrecognizable, dropped and rolled under the swinging black stick. The thumper clipped his shoulder, and then hissed through empty air. His roll brought him to his feet within inches of the Crow, mechanical eyes making contact long enough for the shorter individual to snatch at the vent line of the Crow's breathing unit with lightning speed.

Surprised, gasping to breathe, thumper falling as hands scrambled for the flailing end of the line attached to it, the Crow staggered back two steps and slumped to his knees. Breathing without the mask was not impossible: most in Hebenon did without such units every day. But great exertion required greater oxygen, less damp in the air…and for those unaccustomed to it, it could be a shock to adjust to.

If the Crow came from the Uppers, such an adjustment would be a necessity.

He dropped to roll again, snatching up the thumper as he moved beyond the struggling man's flailing grasp. His roll took him sideways, brought him to his feet, and after a single blow of the thumper to the Crows helmeted head, he was away again, a leap and a swing and a push off the nearest wall landing him back on an upper grated ledge. He disappeared down the path between buildings without being seen, without a second look at the protest the tagger had left behind.

He knew what the words would be.

Death to Kistama. Death to the lord of donkey balls.

Anyone in Hebanthe Falls viewing it knew exactly whom the message was for. It was the same all over the Levs. And if the moisture in the air did not erode it away within the next ten minutes, as it was already trying to do, bleeding the bright yellow paint down the wet wall of gray metal to drip into the churning river, so would anyone in the Uppers who saw it next.

❧Chapter 2❧

One note.

That was the only sound the abandoned cello made within its open case on the narrow hemplastic dining table, where it had rested for so long he no longer remembered opening it. Maybe he had not opened it at all. Maybe it had been left that way from before, before his life slid into an irreversible, mind-numbing, solitary nightmare. If he thought about it, he would remember that day, would count back to it as he had done every day since. Seven hundred and sixty-three. And counting.

He did not think about it now, though he inevitably would some hours later. Now he thought only of the purity of that note and the half-consumed bottle of Zaolei whiskey that had yet to numb the ache of the darkening bruise spreading across his bare shoulder. They were better things to focus on than the hiss and purr of heating and dehumidifying systems built into the walls, the whining wail of the shift siren beyond his door, or the false cheer in Soleia Ximenez's voice as she gave her usual early morning news report over the Echosys 235W on the wall. The computer was not the newest version, but it suited Rhyd's needs and so he failed to upgrade it.

The XCO 235W had been Venn's choice. Upgrading would have been removing another piece of Venn from his life.

Rhyd could not do it.

He did not want to watch the prodcast, wanted instead the relative silence of his home, but he could not afford to be tapped for failing to watch the requisite two of the eight daily fifteen-minute news reports or two of the eight daily five-minute Voices of Faith prodcasts available throughout the Levs. With each Echo networked to the rest, and back to the Hub somewhere on Lev 21, or Upper 21 as many called it, with the Hub and its connection to the SCAMs monitored eternally for dissidence, such a risk was too high.

Rhyd found it easy enough, most days, to ignore the voices on the screen by drowning in Zaolei. Or to simply tune them out of his consciousness with the earplugs he often wore to sleep.

His stomach churned, rumbled, eager for more substantial nourishment, but instead of appeasing it with the meal it desired, a meal that required movement and would take too much time and effort to prepare, he took another long swallow of whiskey and plucked another cello string. How many times, he mused absently, had Maemi urged him to sell the cello back to the Source? He could not play it, after all. It was not even his. And he could use the extra ticks. Not many people had the opportunity for extra income, to gain or save anything beyond the weekly stipend pre-determined by the Doctet. Ticks not spent month to month might mean a reduction in a person's stipend, if such thrift appeared to be a pattern, the Doctet's way, Rhyd was certain, of keeping anyone in the Levs from advancing.

On average, however, the Doctet did not cut ticks for income gained from the sale of personal property, or ticks gained for private transactions. But they could, at their discretion, cut anyone's income they chose. It was why he felt it smarter to hold on to material wealth if one had it. Save it for emergency purposes. Marked as the cello was with an owner data chip, no thief would be able to sell it without hacking the tag, and not many in the Levs were capable of playing it. The best place for the instrument was exactly where it was, in Rhyd's home, in its case, on the table where he could gaze at it and stroke its dark wood-stained surface with loving hands whenever he felt the need to reconnect to days long past.

Besides, there was still a chance, a hope, that someday Venn would come back through the door to pick up his life where it had been left, reclaim the instrument and make it sing again.

Rhyd looked at the dark shape of the front door, shadowed by the off-angled light of the Echosys, not noticing, in the turning of his head, the clothes that hung over the backs of chairs, the blankets and pillow haphazardly askew on the sofa, empty take-home trays on the coffee table, the vegetable boxes in the window with plants that drooped from thirst, or the boots and thumper tossed to one side of the threshold with the discarded mask. The odds were against his hopes ever seeing fruition; those who Vanished never returned, and those who had known them never saw their friends, loved ones, neighbors, or co-workers again. The Vanished ceased to be, and Venn, Rhyd knew, would not be an exception.

But hope kept the cello on the table. Hope and a stubborn reluctance to admit the truth, gave Rhyd the strength to rise from slumber each day and endure. Mulish hope, as cold and steely as it had become within his whiskey-laden gut, kept him fighting a fight most did not believe he could win.

Most days, he did not believe it either.

Yet still, he fought.

Movement out of the corner of his eye, or perhaps a word on the fringes of his perceptions, caused him to look at the Echosys where SCAM and ICD images taken not long before reported the assault of two law officers in an alley on Lev 1 near the fisheries. The two, their Crow masks replaced by breathers as med personnel took them away from the scene on stretchers, were reported alive but injured and unfit for duty for an unspecified number of days. Their assailant, believed to be the one known to the Levs as Scarecrow, had escaped unseen. On the wall behind the med units, smeared yellow dripped claws down the stone, left by an unidentified, unspecified individual during the night, the new markings left amidst the faded glyphs from taggers past, emblems of Faith, graffitied names of those seeking a degree of immortality, and a stylized spade and swords symbol.

Rhyd smirked wearily and dragged the cool bottle across his damp forehead. The mist had failed to erase the evidence in time. Good. Having seen enough, knowing those in power would see it too, he remotely switched off the screen to black and downed the remaining contents of the bottle. The burn of it, too much whiskey swallowed in one sitting, brought a rattling wheeze and cough into his chest and throat. Absently, he reached for the oxygen tank, put the mask over his nose and mouth, and lay his head on his arm there at the table, the cello case pressed against the top of his skull. He intended to rest until his labored breathing evened out, but as he stared across the room towards the cluttered kitchen counter, considering a shower and tidying the house, the whiskey took its toll on his deadened nerves and aching heart, dragging him swiftly into sleep.

It was better this way.

∿*∾

"Listen to your mother and study hard, Duncan," the dark-haired man chided warmly as he tousled the frowning boy's hair. The oldest child, a daughter of eight in a white dress with gold threads embroidered on each shoulder as if feathery wings, held the man's other hand, her blue eyes, much like her mother's, shining up at him with cool adoration. There were short arms wrapped about his leg, the youngest of the three, her short, brown locks held away from her cherubic face with pale green clips that matched the knee-length gown and soft cloth slippers she wore, giggled and pressed her face into his thigh. The boy's expression shifted from the frown into something more neutral at his father's touch. Anyone who knew the boy could see the conflict of annoyance and pleasure in his hazel eyes. He did not want to study…but he did want his father's approval.

"I will, Papa," he promised, as his younger sister tugged the man's shirt persistently.

"And then you will read with us?" she begged. "Just one? You promised you would."

"Papa is busy." The girl in white released her father's hand and took her little sister's instead. "Don't be silly."

The youngest girl's expression fell as she reluctantly released the man's leg and took a step back. "I am sorry, Papa…" she murmured, her voice barely more than a whisper.

Though he had been about to say something akin to what his eldest had said, the needs of duty never far from his heels, that sad, small face brought the man down to squat before them and he opened his arms to her. Eyes suddenly shining with glee, the four-year-old rushed into his embrace and wrapped her arms around his neck.

"I will do my best to see that I am free for a story this afternoon, Flora. I cannot promise you a time, but if you study hard and rest when it is time, I will do my best to be there to read to you."

"Yes! Yes!" she exclaimed. "I will learn everything Mama has to teach us!"

The man's eyes swept up to his willowy wife's cool blue-green gaze, a face that showed no warmth for him and only a little for the children they shared, but a look that gave him every bit of respect, honor, and obedience he could ask for. It was not the sort of marriage either had wanted, arranged as it had been by his father and her parents…although at the time she too had lobbied for the match with him that would better her own position. Their life together had afforded her luxuries and privileges that no other in Hebanthe Falls enjoyed and it had given him the heirs that he, and the city, so desperately needed if it was to continue. As long as she took care of the children and saw to their education, and as long as she performed whatever public and private duties her husband's position required, her life was hers to do with as she chose.

Compared to most in Hebanthe Falls, hers was a good life.

She meant to say something, words that came to her lips during the meeting of their gazes, but the chamber door opened and the imposing familiar figure of her husband's chief of security entered the room. He could not be accused of intruding here, in this office, but it was obvious in her gaze that she felt that he was. He paused just inside the door, hands clasped behind his back, and refrained from speaking as his employer extricated himself from the arms of his children.

"Come, children." The pale, strawberry blonde woman, her hair styled in a tapered bob that was the current fashion, gathered the three around her and herded them towards the side door that led into the rooms where the trio spent most of their daylight hours.

"Neoma, remember dinner this evening."

She glanced over her shoulder at her husband, an intolerant, barely discernable flash in her eyes, but she said, "I will be there, Haythem," in a cool but cordial voice. He loved her, she knew, in his own way, but the passion in their lives, if it had ever been there, had evaporated after the birth of Flora. Neoma had done her duty in giving him the requisite two children…and the expected male heir. The third child was an unexpected bonus. Duty done, she no longer had to feign affection she did not feel. Everyone in the Uppers knew their business. There was no need for pretending, for making a pretense of something that did not exist, so long as she showed him respect and continued to perform her public duties.

Haythem nodded and straightened his white Banyan with the palms of his hands as she and the children left the room. He chose not to acknowledge the distance in her expression, or the tone of her voice, that the other man may not have seen or heard. "Good morning, Captain."

"Good morning, Founder." The dark skinned man bowed, the gesture slight but acceptable. "Have you seen the prodcast this morning?"

"Should I have?" Haythem crossed the room and slid into the white, cushioned high-backed chair behind his desk. The wide, circular room housed few adornments and furnishings. Three empty white chairs were positioned near the desk, a long white sofa which matched the chair in which he sat rested against the wall opposite him, but the room held little else save the series of monochrome art sketches on the stark, white walls.

"He's back."

"Who?"

As soon as he asked, however, Haythem knew the answer. It had been nearly a month since the last reported sightings of the Scarecrow, and he had hoped, foolishly, that the individual had either been killed, had attained whatever goal he had been aiming for, or else had given up on his obsessive targeting of Hebanthe Falls' police force. This was not the first time he had disappeared and come back, however. Since his first appearance a few years ago, there had been occasional lapses between his attacks. Despite the rumors floating around the Levels, it suggested that this Scarecrow was as human as anyone else in the city, susceptible, Haythem imagined, to injury and illness…and…he hoped…death. For when active, the Scarecrow was known to incapacitate up to a dozen officers in a single night, a toll that made law enforcement difficult to maintain.

"How many?"

"Two. They were bagging a tagger when he struck. The tagger got away."

"Alive?"

"The tagger? Or the officers?"

"Both."

"Yes, sir. All survived."

Kemway snorted and distractedly rearranged the items on his desk. "Level?"

"One…near the fisheries."

Again, the broad-shouldered man snorted. "Increase patrols tonight. Find this quatsch and eliminate him."

Grainger nodded his bald head with a "Yes, sir."

It would not be that easy, of course. If it were, they would have caught the vigilante months ago. With nineteen levels of lower city to cover, three miles from the collection of four falls to the outer constructed wall and half a mile across between the earthen ramparts of the falls, and a mish-mash of crisscrossed layers of apartments, vindis, and maintenance tunnels, it was impossible to anticipate where the Scarecrow would strike. There was no discernable pattern to his appearances, and more frustratingly, there was no proof, yet, whether this Scarecrow was a single individual, a collection of copycats, or an organized host of people following the leadership of the original vigilante, a small, private army of sorts.

But Kemway did not care about those details. He only wanted the Scarecrow gone. Considering the matter dropped, since he said no more about it and seemed more interested in the stylus he was toying with, Grainger cleared his throat and continued, "We'll be opening East Four today. The hemp delivery should be good. I'm told it was a bountiful harvest."

"Good…Neoma wants a new dress…and the children are outgrowing their wardrobe faster than I thought possible." The hemp crop provided by the parah served a wide variety of functions in Hebanthe Falls, a resource badly needed once the population of the city had pushed the seams of what they could realistically provide for themselves. Birthing laws created since those years had caused the population to level off, even begin to show a decline over the last several decades, but still, the numerous uses for that one outside crop made contact with those unfortunate enough to live in the contaminated outer world, worth the risks. "Let me know if there is any news."

Grainger again nodded, murmured his agreement, and marched out of the room. There was no warmth between them, no sharing of words beyond duty, but there was no need for any. Grainger respected their positions as incontrovertible. Not once had he wished for their roles to be any different. Haythem Kemway was a Founder. No one questioned the word of the Founder.

☙*❧

Vibrant verdant spread to the east as far as he could see, the torrent of water behind him churning and clawing into the earth as it sought the lower elevation of the distant southern sea. To the other side of the ribbons of splashing dark water, thick trees, taller than any plant he could imagine, tangled boughs to wave at the sky, marching along the base of the regal white-capped towers far beyond the river's western-most edge. Trickling blue fingers wove their way between the trunks, intent on joining the western tributary, and on the banks, between the west river and the forest, the east river and the cliffs, where he looked on with a hand that shielded his eyes from the glaring golden sun, man-made channels had been fashioned to spread water to the tall crop surrounding him. Hand stretched forth, he dragged his fingers across the dark green tips and dainty cream-white petals, marveling at the textures as though he had been there before.

Then came the familiar crack and the scream.

He turned to face it, knowing he would see what he always saw.

"Venn!"

The cry escaped before his eyes laid sight on the dark-haired cellist no more than ten feet away. Venn released the cello, gaping as he stared at the red spreading across the abdomen of his pristine white concert shirt. Then his chocolate brown eyes lifted, his hand reaching towards the blonde in search of support. Vivid...so vivid...and wet, he found, as he reached Venn's side to catch the man as he fell. Liquid life came away on his fingers, his palm, as he tried to cover the rupture and keep Venn alive.

"Venn...don't..."

A gasp. A cough. A shudder.

"Rhyd...help me..."

Rhyd jerked awake as the Zaolei bottle on the table beside him crashed to the floor and shattered. In spite of the oxygen mask, he was gasping, choking, but not on the heavy air. He was choking on terror, though why that dream still frightened him after all of this time he could not fathom. The dream that had begun shortly after Venn's Vanishing, came to him still, a place he had never seen, a world that existed for the Levs only in holographic deks or as images viewable on the Echosys. An intangible place with intangible sights and smells, but a place, in that dream, where even the taste of the air and the symphony of sounds were as real to Rhyd as if he had lived with them his entire life.

It was not the same as the Van Gogh Venn had chosen to hang on the wall in the main room of their home, but it was real to Rhyd, and beautiful nonetheless. An idyllic dream shattered each time by the crimson of Venn's blood, of Venn's gurgling plea, of a man dying in his arms. Rhyd despised death, had seen too much of it, expected too much of it, but of those deaths, real and imagined, none frightened him more than the possibility of Venn dying in his arms. Venn would call him morbid, if he was here to hear of these nightmares, and Rhyd would have been tempted to agree with him.

But this was no simple nightmare. This, Rhyd was sure, as he pulled the mask off, turned off the oxygen tank, wiped his damp eyes and cheeks, and staggered towards the shower, was an omen. A plea from the Vanished for help. A cry in his heart not to give up hope, not to give up his search. Venn was out there somewhere. If he scoured Hebenon long enough, Rhyd would find where the man had been taken, would find all of the others who had Vanished over the last six years and set them all free, bring them all home. And no more, he promised himself again, would Vanish if he could prevent it.

The hot water loosened his tight muscles but also awakened the ache in his bruised shoulder. He groaned, massaged the area with his fingertips, and rolled his neck back and forth to allow the water to run through his short, shaggy blonde hair and over his face. A more serious bathing was called for, but he spent too much time allowing the hot water to beat on his skin and rinse away the psychological dirt he carried and the traces of tears that stained his face. The timer clicked and the water stopped flowing before he reached for the soap. He scowled but the failure did not trouble him. He felt clean enough. Tomorrow would be another chance for a proper shower.

He kicked aside the scattered dirty laundry on the floor while reaching for the towel on the nearby rack. Tainted gray from extended previous use and from lack of a recent laundering, it was at least dry and cleaner than the towels amidst the pile on the floor. Not that he noticed its condition as he cinched it around his waist. Within the sanctuary of home, those details meant very little any longer. He scrubbed his teeth with the worn blue brush, careful to leave the red one untouched, rubbed his chin only to decide against shaving today, then scrubbed himself dry. The invigorating roughness of the hemp blend fabric erased the traces of whiskey that fogged his thoughts, and outside the wail of the mid-day shift whistle told him it was time. On these days without work to do, this was the one thing he had to exist for, and if he could have gotten by with his day to day needs without work, this new life would have been the only one he lived.

❧Chapter 3❧

R hyd nodded at the stringy-haired blonde who opened the door of the adjoining flat as he was leaving his. The other, dressed in torn hemp denim and a sleeveless vest, seeming oblivious to the wet in the air, nodded in recognition but neither spoke. It was the same as every other day since Rhyd had moved into this flat with Venn. The man, known only as Lash, had been living in that apartment already, and in all of that time, they had never shared a verbal exchange of greeting. He had never heard Venn speak to him either. Rhyd only knew the man's name by a note someone had left on his door. He had yet to hear the man utter a word or a sound, except for a clucking noise he made to the numerous cats that loitered around his doorway waiting to be fed. It was rare for anyone to keep a pet, other than perhaps a fish or a small bird, but there were numerous cats roaming the Levs that often attached themselves to a caretaker in the promise of free and easy meals. With at least a dozen near his home, Rhyd never had to worry about pests.

It made him wonder frequently, however, what his neighbor did that he was able to afford to offer food to so many of them.

Not that the man lived a lavish lifestyle. Rhyd could not think of a single time coming or going that he had seen lights on in the flat, or heard the Echosys, just as neither were detectable now. He rarely heard running water either, but there were plenty of jobs to be had where showering in the workplace was allowed and encouraged, his own being one of them. And if his neighbor, like Rhyd, ate largely take away or in one of the diners or clubs available on each Lev, he would have no need to cook or clean dishes. There were XCO 237P screens located around the Levs for public viewing of prodcasts as well, meaning Lash could do his obligatory viewing somewhere else and only return to his flat long enough to feed the cats and sleep.

The man's clothes were inconspicuous, plain though at one time expensive, mismatched in design, color, and pattern, as though he cared little about his appearance, or what others thought of him. When Rhyd bothered to think about the lanky man, he thought nothing of his eccentricities, however, and, wary enough of the potential of being crowed, Rhyd kept his business to himself and left Lash to his.

The string of cats followed the man inside and a bare arm closed the door behind him. Rhyd did not look to see if Lash was watching him through the grungy windows. Where he was going was no one's business but his own, and his neighbor never seemed to care. Rhyd did not expect him to be watching now.

The cluster of dwellings here, some lit, some dark, many of similar dimensions though some were dual layered or double width to accommodate families, was left behind as Rhyd bypassed the elevator in favor of the grated stairs that took him up half a level to the nearest vindi tract. The kaleidoscope of neon signs in their myriad of languages did less to announce the contents of each vindi than the manned open-awning counters did. A gaggle of children, herded along by a stooped woman, squeezed passed him on the stairs, escorted home from the day's schooling. It was seven hours of social interface that was, for many, the sole interaction in Hebenon they received outside of their family and perhaps immediate neighbors. With few indoor parks or play places, and few sources of entertainment except for the virtual sorts that many parents denied their children until they were older, it was either the classroom, the children's gymnasiums, or home for the majority of Hebenon's youth.

The Voices of Faith building, differentiated by its sideways cross, its doors open as they always were, with the Echosys screen mounted on the exterior wall, attracted a collection of passersby to watch the midday Voices prodcast. Founder Kemway's face, the paternal smile always in place as though carved permanently into his features, was pontificating about the virtues of hard work, productivity, and cooperation. Rhyd paused at the back of the crowd to listen to yet another variation on a theme, the Founder's way, he believed, of keeping Hebenon's citizens to the daily drudgery in which most of them lived. When the prodcast gave way to a shimmering advert of a brunette stage dancer extolling the virtues of the Sources latest product, Deluxstra moisturizing crème, Rhyd shook his head and continued on his way. That made the third new crème in a month, as each attempted to outsell the others though it was a common, if unproven, belief that the same manufacturers made them all.

There were limited opportunities for manufacturing, after all, limited opportunities for people to advance or gain status.

The Doctet controlled most things the city needed.

Goods in clear cases for sale, though nothing frivolous. Clothing modeled on Echosys screens. Food displayed on scrolling belts to tempt buyers…and perhaps be snatched up by a hungry tinger. Rhyd passed them all, not interested in spending his ticks on anything other than a decent meal and a stiff drink. Grav pods and large dogs, goats, or men pulling carts had the right of way, causing the collection of shift-change pedestrians to weave and bob through the streets. A scantily clad woman, likely an andi as her pale blue skin was adorned with twinkling LED patterns, offered Hebbies from a beaded pouch that dangled around her waist to cover her genitals, an enticement to lure people into the club behind her.

Nerves already stretched tight from the press of people, Rhyd scanned the vicinity for Crows, half expecting a flock of them to descend on the club and arrest whoever had set the andi to distribution…and anyone within who had accepted the free offer of illegal drugs. It was not that they cared about the use of Heb in any of its forms; the illegal usage led to higher sales of the marketed form of the substance. It was, at its core, all about control, and Rhyd believed from his own experience, that to the Crows, and those behind them pulling their strings, control was all they cared about.

He passed the andi, disinterested in frivolous pharmaceuticals or artificial sex. His interests, his direction, pointed him onward through the cacophonous fog. A woman of Hispanic descent, her damp sleeveless shirt clinging tightly to her fit form, caught his gaze as he crossed the narrow street towards his destination. She almost smiled, a look he returned before she directed her young Chinese apprentice back to the task of repairing someone's old fashioned timepiece.

Race...nationality...no longer mattered. But in Hebenon, it was sometimes the only identity people had to separate themselves from others. Sometimes it was the only thing they had to feel proud of.

They did not need to speak. It was enough that Rhyd knew she would expect him later, after his meal in the club that bled music through its beaded curtain doorway, two doors away from her vindi.

He squinted as he stepped inside, adjusting to the lack of mist within and the strobing lights of red and blue that lit the catwalk and the center stage where a trio of topless andis gyrated to the pulse of the crushing music. For a moment he remained motionless, allowing others who entered to pass around him as he sought familiar faces...or threatening ones. But he had long ago chosen this club because those few co-workers he knew by name never came here, and because Venn had liked it here.

He also happened to like its atmosphere himself, despite the loud music and the mostly much younger crowd. A couple in their late forties seemed out of place, making them noticeable to him. Older than most around them, plain and average looking in too-loose trousers and work shirts, with dirty nails that suggested a stop on the way home from whatever manual labor they called their lives, sat knee to knee at the bar, heads bent together to converse over pale green drinks.

From her handbag, the woman drew something Rhyd could not see, but when her companion smiled and took it from her to pop into his mouth, chasing it with a long drink, Rhyd sighed and moved around them to the other end of the bar. Even Vapors was not immune to the shade cast by Heb, especially since, for a few hours at least, the couple would forget the drabness of their mundane daily existences. The mythos of a tiny blood orange pill changing anyone's quality of life, making the boring exciting, was absurd to Rhyd and he did his best to avoid it, and its users, at all costs.

With Venn, he had failed.

Had their life together been so bad as to require an infusion of that sort of excitement?

"What'll ya have, Whiskey?" the dark-skinned woman in an oriental dress, her pencil skirt hugging her curves down to mid-calf, asked from behind the bar, already drawing a glass from beneath the counter and a bottle from the shelves on the wall behind her. She wore pale green, a color that suggested that the hemp and algae fabric blend most wore these days had received minimal treatment beyond the addition of shiny dark green decorative threads that wove elaborate patterns across the shimmery surface. "Usual?"

"A double," he replied with a tap of two fingers on the bar.

Maemi did not scowl. She had known Rhyd for the better part of eleven years…or had it been twelve…since not long after she had inherited Vapors from the man who had been both adoptive father and father-in-law. His Chinese wife had been in no condition even then to run it, and illness had claimed their son, Maemi's husband, some years before, leaving Maemi as the only choice to secure Vapors' future. The choice of being a swiver at Vapors, to escape the life of a threader or a hosteler that might have been her future otherwise, had been an easy one to make. Maemi was too gregarious to accept a life hiding behind walls and great noisy steam driven machines.

She knew her regulars likes and dislikes, the tales of their day to days, the intimates they often could not share with anyone else. Rhyd Ballard was different. Whiskey, as she called him, was her special project, particularly since Venn's disappearance. If it was a double shot day, he had either had a bad one or else he was trying to drink away a hangover. Or both. She waved at the bony Chinese woman behind an open interior window at the side of the bar, and by the time the drinks were poured and placed in front of him, there was a steaming plate of grilled fish and cheese curlers to hand over, his usual selection on his bad days.

Perhaps not the healthiest meal, but at least he was eating. It was more than he usually did.

"Thanks, Maemi." He drank one shot, set the glass on the counter, then popped a curler into his mouth.

"Heard about the Crows at the fisheries?"

It was her way of trawling for information in the guise of small talk, since the latest assault on a pair of Crows was undoubtedly the gossip of the day and hence a safe topic to bring up in public if done discreetly. Rhyd nodded his head and muttered, "Yeah...ain't that somethin'?" around the fingers he was licking clean of fried cheese.

Maemi nodded but was prevented from saying more by the summons of other patrons back down the bar. It was just as well because Rhyd was not in the mood for talk this afternoon. He wanted to sit anonymously in this place, watch the dancers, eat, drink, and forget that there was any sort of world outside of Vapors in need of his help.

ȣ*ȣ

Crate after crate of hemp product, leaves and stalks and seeds for processing, was heaved from the flat wagons, wagons strung together and pushed by several large men through East 4 past the last of the sliding airlock doors that sealed Hebanthe Falls from the Outside. They were typically only allowed as far as the third door, rarely into the primary unloading zone. One by one, individuals in decon suits replaced the full crates with empty ones for refilling when the next harvest came. Those pushing the carts never saw beneath those ghost-like white suits and those in the decon suits never viewed anything without the protective filters of their goggles.

The possibility of contamination by exposure to elements from Outside was too high. The hemp and the entire room would be decontaminated after the parah were gone and the doors had all been sealed again.

For now, there were other goods to unload, leather, length blocks of precious wood that would be carefully tested for contaminants before use, a collection of Hebanthe seeds, buckets of salt and churns of butter, also to be tested and processed for decontamination, that was a rare and near priceless commodity within the great wet city in the falls' mist. Few words were spoken between the agents in their decon suits and the parah who brought the hemp for unloading, whether due to distrust between them or an inability to understand one another neither side could say. Hundreds of years of separation had taken its toll and neither side felt comfortable with the other.

But still the trading continued, as it had for centuries, both sides wanting what the other produced. The parah took a share of all goods manufactured from the processed hemp and an underhanded portion of Heb. The Source had no interest in what the parah did with Heb, as long as they were willing to trade for the innocent looking blood orange pills.

The process proceeded as usual, nothing out of the ordinary to report, until the end of the exchange, the decon-suited individuals retreating into the security of Hebanthe Falls and the parah returning to their life in the poisoned air of the Outside. As the airlock began to slide closed, a balding man in the midst of the parah train of wagons began to shout frantically, "Agnys! Agnys!"

The Hebenon security team, their bird masks swinging from side to side in search of the cause of the commotion, did not know if the word was a name or something else. With no commonality of communication, they had nothing to base a guess off of. As the man tried to scramble, hands outstretched as if reaching for something, from the midst of his companions, who tried to hold him back, the Crows presumed him to be a threat and began to beat the parah back with thumpers. When that proved insufficient, they fired into the group, their air guns hissing and popping as they hurled tiny hemp pellets intended to sting, to deter, but not cause any lasting damage.

A few shots, from a sharpshooter on a platform overseeing the exchange, fired darts laced with a more potent, law enforcement-grade version of the Heb street drug. The bald man and a handful of others immediately slumped to the floor of the tunnel. There was a noticeable skittering behind a pair of agents which brought the marksman's aim around to shoot between them at the small figure endeavoring to scurry for cover between stacks of crated goods. There came a tiny sound of surprise, but when the pair of agents rushed to grasp at the intruder, to apprehend and throw it back into the tunnel with the rest of its kind, it was gone. Gone into the vent shaft and the darkness of Hebenon's inner workings.

"Bring it to me!" the sharpshooter bellowed. The Heb that had subdued at least three adults within the now sealed tunnel would probably kill a child, if the fall into the vent shaft had not done so. But even a dead parah could be a threat to Hebanthe Falls, bringing in all manner of contaminants from the Outside and exposing the city to unfamiliar diseases and parasites. The intruder needed to be found and returned to the Outside, or disposed of, at once.

By the time the agents reached the bottom of the vent shaft, however, where the tiny body should have lain, it was gone.

*

The reedy redhead who sauntered behind the bar and wheedled his way around Maemi as if he owned the place, grabbed a bottle from the liquor shelf and came out from behind the counter to straddle the stool next to Rhyd. He was dressed head to toe in Level chic, with frills of lace at his neck and wrists, faux leather trousers, all brilliant reds and blues with touches of gold and silver on his waistcoat and blouson shirt, all finely fitted and tailored as if he was Hebenon royalty. People eyed him with amazement, even many who were familiar with his presence in this place, treating him with expected respect, with wonder and lust. To those who knew him, however, Skelter was anything but royalty. Still, Maemi allowed him the run of the bar, of the establishment, because he and his andis were good for business and because, despite his profession, or professions, she trusted him. As did Rhyd. To those who crossed him, the young man could be their worst nightmare. To those few to whom he gave allegiance, Skelter was one of the truest, most loyal men Rhyd had ever met.

"So…Whiskey," he drawled in a refined upper caste accent that was as fake as the figure he presented to the world. "Anything new I should know about?"

The blonde shook his head as he finished his meal except for one curler, downed a third shot that Maemi had obligingly filled for him, and pushed the glass away. No more tonight. Tonight was for business again, and he could not work if he was drunk. "Should there be?"

Skelter chuckled. "There never should be, but you know this city; always something I should know. I just don't know it yet."

The lights in the club shifted to pinks and purples and the music followed suit, bringing the sultry, long-legged blonde who drew both Skelter and Rhyd's attention to the dancing catwalk. Zara Peru, considered by many to be Hebenon's most alluring andi, preferred the old music, the jazz of trumpet and sax and guitar that was rarely found anymore in clubs throughout the Levs. With an angelic face, pouting lips and made-up blue eyes, some argued Zara to be female. Otherx, noting the lack of breasts or the typical feminine curves of hip and derriere, believed her male. Very few knew Zara's real story, and Skelter made certain to keep it that way. Despite what they all thought, she was no andi.

The mystique was part of Zara's draw.

Like many exotic dancers in the Levs, Zara also worked for sex, but the terms were always set by Skelter to protect the truth of the treasure he held her to be, to protect her life, her welfare, her dignity.

If her clients ever learned the truth, if that truth ever reached the ears of the Doctet and the Founder, Zara would surely be one of those to Vanish just as Venn had.

For that reason alone, and because he sincerely liked her, Rhyd kept everything he knew to himself. He held a great fondness for one of the few people who had saved his ass on multiple occasions. Zara was his friend, just as Skelter and Maemi were, and Rhyd would never turn his back on, or betray, a friend.

As she undulated against the center platform's pole, Skelter discretely slid his hand across the bar and then made a show of taking the last curler from the plate and eating it, licking his fingers clean, the sole action out of character with his attire that he had made since his appearance in Vapors tonight. Arms crossed over his chest, Rhyd used his elbow to push the plate back further, and with the hand that was hidden beneath his arm, he retrieved what had been left there on the table and pushed it into his pocket.

No one noticed the exchange. Their eyes were focused on Zara.

When the song ceased, to be picked up by a more modern tune that saw the previous dancers returning to the stage after a costume change, Zara slid off the stage and strutted to the bar. Rhyd uncrossed his arms to open them to embrace her as she positioned herself between his spread legs on the stool and press herself against him with a returned hug and closed-mouth kiss to his lips.

Others expected more from her. Rhyd Ballard, she knew, did not. But it was fun to tease and flirt with him. Thankfully, he took her attention in stride and never took offense at her actions. He slid his hands from her hips to her arms, then around to the small of her back, allowing himself a brief moment of physical longing at the feel of her secret pressed against his belly. But then he let her go and pushed those feelings aside. He would never take advantage of her, and she knew she was not the one he continued to pine for.

She backed away, fingers of one hand hooked into the waistband of his black trousers and crooked her finger, beckoning him to follow. The regulars in the club whistled in envy and appreciation, and though some muttered their disappointment that Zara had chosen him, none were surprised. After so many months, they assumed that Rhyd was either a well-paying patron, a personal friend, or a favored lover of Zara's…or perhaps that there was some significant agreement standing between Rhyd and Skelter. She drew him into the lavatory more frequently than she did anyone else, always under Skelter's watchful eye. They tried to be discreet, not to draw attention to those perceived trysts, and thankfully no one had yet thought to question them out loud or confront them about it.

Nor did they ever bother to find out why, five to fifteen to twenty minutes later, Zara almost always left the lavatory alone to take the stage for another dance…and Rhyd never followed.

Maybe they thought he snuck out the back door or was upstairs in Maemi's private residence.

Someday, he presumed he would have to change that pattern. After more than two years, someone was bound to start asking the questions he could not answer.

෨CHAPTER 4෨

She was not afraid of the dark. Dark happened when the sun slept, when the clouds came out and brought the rain. The dark did not hurt her. The dark just was.

It was the things in the dark that frightened her, things with fangs and claws and noses that could smell fear. Things that hid where she could not see them. Things her cousin had told her about every night as she prepared for sleep, things she had no reason to believe were fabrications of his imagination.

Those things had taken her father, after all, and he had never been seen again.

Here in this place, in a metal world she did not know, she pressed herself into the smallest crevice she could find and held her breath as the thudding, splashing, unfamiliar echoes grew louder, closer. Could they smell her fear, she wondered, one little hand over her mouth to mask her breathing and the other over her chest as if to keep her tripping heart from pounding too loudly. Did they have fangs and claws, or did they rely on the cracking shooting sticks and their long pointy beaks to tear trespassers apart?

Did they, like the eagles and the owls, shred their prey to be fed to their offspring?

Frantically, she blinked away the tears that filled her blue eyes. She had been warned many times. Never get too close. Never let the birdmen touch you. Never go beyond her uncle's care, never go inside the metal nest. If you did, you might never come out again.

Oh yes, she had been warned.

Even the strangers gave warning, reminding her people each time they approached the nest that inside was nowhere they wanted to be.

But curiosity, the vision of shiny white surfaces with buttons and levers and a glimpse of another dressed in blue and green and soft yellow, were too tempting to ignore again. Though she had no idea how to accomplish the childish goal she had set, she had been determined to try. A closer look. That was all she wanted. To know. To understand.

Stubbornness and curiosity would be her downfall. FaFa had always said it. MaMa had too. She tried to listen. She tried to be good. But now, as birdmen crashed past her hiding place, not yet noticing that the grate she hid behind was askew, she believed they might have been right. She was afraid and lost, with no idea where she should go now that she was inside the mysterious metal nest that extended down into the clouded depths of the falling water as if into the earth itself.

When the ruckus of the running birdmen could no longer be heard, she finally dared to move. Not back into the main shaft where there was a high chance they would return or that more would follow before long. Instead, she chose to crawl in the narrow conduit she was in, a space big enough for most adults to crawl through on their bellies, big enough that a child her size could maneuver the space with ease. With no idea where the tunnel would take her, as she followed one turn, one ladder, then another turn and another ladder, she knew she had to keep moving. Sooner or later she would find a way out. Somewhere she would find warm and dry, water to drink and food to eat. Somewhere there would be someone who could help her get back home.

She did not believe the old stories. There had to be more than birdmen living in this nest. Those in the bulky white decon suits did not have beaks, and those sometimes sent outside looked the same as everyone she knew. Both suggested that there were at least three types of creatures in the nest, although the birdmen seemed to be the dominant species. The ones to fear. But since there were men here too, men like her uncle and cousins and the other villagers, men like the one who spoke of music and hummed snatches of tunes she had never heard, there had to be others here too.

She was going to find them. All of them. She was going to find proof that what she believed was real. And she was going to find a way to bring more of the inside outside...if she could.

❧*❧

The panel to the heating shaft was closed behind him and Rhyd paused, back to the wall, heart thundering though he knew he had not been followed. He was never followed. He was safe here, and his knowledge of the maze of shafts, tunnels, and chambers that made up Hebenon's heating, ventilation, and dehumidifying systems meant that his C-Pass gave him access to almost anywhere in the Levs he cared to go. Once he had possessed a B-Pass, allowing him more extended access, and access to Lev 20, but he had lost that with Venn's arrest and, despite his clean job performance record and his personal adherence to all required check-ins, that Pass had yet to be reinstated.

He did not think it ever would be.

He rubbed the back of his neck with a bitter expression and drew the card he had been given from his pocket with the other. Odds were, his B-Pass would never be reissued, that some other bilger had been promoted to work Lev 20, or those in charge of such things had pulled someone down from the Uppers to handle that level too. No one who knew the Level as well as Rhyd, but someone adequate enough, someone not suspect. More and more the Uppers became insular, and more and more those in the Levels wondered what those men and women above them were hiding. What privileges they enjoyed that were not shared with the people who made their lives bearable.

Life must surely be better, a grand, comfortable, bright thing, in the Uppers. Few from the Levels were ever likely to see it.

Without turning on the light in the room, Rhyd found the reader that lay on the tabletop to his right, its flashing green light that indicated a fully charged unit giving away its position amidst the clutter where it lay. The card Skelter had given him was swiped twice to access the coded login, and then, after a quickly punched sequence on the keypad, it was swiped again and Rhyd hurriedly read its contents. It contained names, Lev designations, dates and times, of arrests made and arrests scheduled. Such data was difficult for all but a few to come by, but Rhyd never asked where Skelter got it. The redhead assured him time and again that Rhyd did not need to fear, that he had his source firmly in his pocket, firmly on their side, and to date, Skelter's information had never been wrong. If Rhyd was careful with his use of the data, there was little reason for anyone to link a series of coincidental circumstances to him, to Skelter, or to the redhead's source. Each of them seemed to get what they desired out of the bargain and everyone was happy.

The light came on with a press of Rhyd's palm to the wall pad and he squinted against the glare. He shed his standard leatherette coat and quickly began to rummage through the collection of gadgets, tools, and weapons on the table for those he thought he might need tonight.

He did not flinch at the sound of a panel opening on the other side of the room, as the entering footsteps were ones he knew well.

Tox did not speak. In her sleeveless tank with a waterproof shawl sewed at the shoulders, she looked less fashionable than functional, but sleeves got in her way when she worked, as did skirts and bustles and shoes with heels. She preferred the calf-length trousers and boots many schoolboys wore, but there was no mistaking her for a boy. The few who tried, of whom Rhyd was aware, had been carted off by a medi-unit for treatment of fractures, abrasions, and bleeding.

Seeing Rhyd, she pulled the long coat she had designed for him from the hook on which it hung and helped him into it, noticing the stiffness of his shoulder as he lifted his arm.

"Bruised," Rhyd muttered, knowing there was a question even if it was not spoken.

"Here." She slid her hands under the coat and expertly rubbed the stiffness out of the tight ball of bruised muscle. It hurt, but it was bearable, and Rhyd knew from experience that by the time she was finished, the ache would have diminished enough to get him through the night's work. "You got a schedule…or you libbing it tonight?"

He shrugged. "Both." He might hit one, maybe two of the targets Skelter had provided, warn others away from arrest if he could, for whatever period of safety they could find, but all other targets would come to him as the night chose.

Better that than to give away his foreknowledge of Crow activity. That was dangerous.

"He wouldn't want you to take these risks…" she reminded when he shrugged again, this time to be free of her hands to fasten the zippers, buttons, straps, and buckles that kept his coat and gear secure.

"He would want me to find him…to never give up." He chose to believe that, even though he suspected Tox was right about Venn. Even Rhyd was not certain any longer how much of his desire for action was what Venn would have wanted and how much of it was his own intractability.

It did not matter. Rhyd was not giving up. Tox knew that as well as anyone.

"Would it matter if I told you to be careful?"

He stretched out his arm and waited for her to place the head covering cowl mask in his hand before replying, "I always am."

More snaps and buckles held the custom-formed headgear in place, and as the sensors built within it touched his skin and the breathing filtration tubes were connected to the tubing built into his coat, they adjusted automatically to the room conditions to allow him to see, to hear, to breathe normally. There was no beaked breathing filter like the Crows headgear contained, but rather a smooth fitted hood with socketed metal mechanical eyepieces, sound amplifying earbuds, and a voice modulator that enabled him to speak in spite of the special breathing unit the hood contained. It was a heavily modified hood based on the mask he wore when he crawled through the ducts to repair, replace, or install dehumidifying equipment, a necessity that all bilgers, speners, skolpers, and most denki wore on the job to protect them from toxins, molds, and other hazards found in the overly damp environments they worked in. This hood was different, however, different enough to hide his profession from anyone he encountered on his nightly forays into the city's streets.

The C-Pass was secured in his pocket, the reader and Skelter's card secured in another, and the assortment of gadgets and tools he had begun to collect were either discarded in favor of others or else hidden in pouches, compartments, or pockets on his person. He rarely went out with much, just a few items that might be needed to get into, or out of, places, always a switch knife for emergencies, the thumper he had acquired earlier that morning, and finally his gloves. He needed little else. If he could not get by on his wits, his strengths, his own abilities, then he did not deserve to meet the Crows in battle.

For battle it was. Rhyd never lost sight of that, no matter how many nights he had been doing this.

The final glance at the reader imprinted the map data into the memory chips the hood contained and it took no more than a thought to map a path to his first intended destination of the night. This was one computer not linked into the Hub, an illegal standalone that had to be guarded and protected if he was to get away with what he was doing. Thank the gods, whichever ones were out there, that Zara's talents included more than dancing and sexual favors.

Back into the shaft, nimble movements belying his age, Rhyd hesitated long enough to glance back at Tox while waiting for his mechanical eyes to adjust to the change in lighting, and then he was gone into the darkness, leaving her to seal the panel behind him. They were the only two to know about this room in what had once been a bilger way-station. It had long ago been sealed off as an unused and unnecessary space behind her private residence, no longer paid any attention to by those at the top and the Crows who served them. With no known access beyond the vent shaft, it was the safest place Rhyd knew of to store the majority of his life's work. He had stashes elsewhere throughout the Levs, tools and equipment that might be needed should any part of his attire malfunction or become damaged, but the heart of his world was here. And Tox, friend and ally that she was, maintained it, and his equipment, with the utmost care.

Haythem had known the faces around him all of his life, had grown up with many of them, had been watched growing up by a few others. Women dressed in multi-colored layers of skirting, few having reasons to dress as men and thus discouraged from it. Particularly at events such as this. Men in waistcoats and top hats, as if they expected to be out in the elements when the Uppers never knew the extremes of weather. In the Uppers of Hebanthe Falls, there was no outside, was no weather. No wind, no rain, no hot, no cold.

In the Uppers it was always the same.

Layers of halls and rooms interconnected to form the labyrinth that had been home to the ruling class of the city for more than six hundred years. Fashion, like many other things, had grown stagnant, with such trivialities as hats and hairstyles and makeup changing from year to year to mark the passage of time. It was good, in Haythem's view, as it helped everyone remain on mostly equal footing. Everyone, that was, except for those in the Levs, and himself and his wife, both of whom wore the traditional banyan of their offices, a style adopted by the original Founder, clung to over the centuries as the one thing that connected them to the grandeur of a world destroyed by mans' folly and greed. Neoma wore blue, as she frequently did. Haythem wore white. Always white, accented with gold and blue threads but otherwise as clean and pristine of a vision as the walls of the Uppers were kept.

He believed in white. He believed in clean.

With the limited social circle of the Uppers, it was impossible not to know everyone of importance. They attended the same functions, worked within the ranks of Hebanthe Falls' governing body, scientific community, manufacturing control. They raised children together, passed each other in the corridors that served as streets. It had become necessary, within a few generations of creating the tall, misty city, to draw people up from the Levels in order to infuse new breeding stock into the gene pool, to keep the ancient lineages from becoming corroded, eroded. With the initiation of the whole of Level 21 into the ranks of the Upper Hierarchy almost two hundred and eighty years ago, however, a significant number of new families had been introduced into Society. Most on Lev 21 had been common folk, consisting largely of the actors, the musicians, the athletes and other scientists that the Founder and his circle relied on for entertainment and survival. It had seemed no far stretch to initiate those people, the best of the Levels genes, into their circle to keep the ruling class from destroying itself through extensive inbreeding.

Occasionally, a notable individual from the Levels, and their family, might rise to the top too, if their social contributions were deemed noteworthy, but that was rare. It required someone from the top paying attention to what went on beneath them. Beyond those who monitored the Echosys connections and communications, those charged with assigning passes and tick cards, or those who registered births and deaths and work assignments, people in the Uppers generally ignored the fact that there were any others in the world save themselves.

Haythem, however, wanted to know everything. About everyone. Or at least about those who might present a threat at a time when resentment was flaring and festering in the Levs. Without those in the Levels, he knew well that the city would not survive and he had no desire to lose the degree of comfort he and his family were accustomed to. He wanted to be certain that, when the time came, his children would continue to have a world worth living in, a life worth living. Regardless of the parah Outside, Hebanthe Falls, or Hebenon as those below called it…after the politicized drug of the same name…was the only world they had. The decay of the city meant death to civilized humanity.

It was that concern for survival that made his skin prickle as he circulated the room, shaking hands, making small talk with friends, colleagues, and ideological rivals, each time his ears picked up a tickle of some rumor that he had not yet heard. As the city's ruler by hereditary right, he believed he should be the first to know all things, or at least the second or third to know them since news of events had to come from witnesses to his security chief, before directly reaching Haythem. While Ulynda, his eldest daughter, played tunes on the antique piano under Neoma's watchful eye and the eyes of many of the guests, Haythem slipped to the rear of the room where Oliver Grainger maintained a wide view over everything and everyone present.

Grainger's family had come up with those from Lev 21, from a long line of security officers of whom Grainger was the latest. The man had no family of his own, a regrettable thing really, but it meant that Grainger could focus entirely on his work and that, Haythem believed, was worth the loss of a family name. Particularly now, with the Scarecrow running wild in his city.

A tilt of his head caused the darker man to follow. When they stopped by the door, out of earshot of others, Haythem was aware that his wife's eyes were shooting daggers at him for daring to disrespect their daughter's moment of societal introduction and triumph with business.

This rumor he was hearing, however, if it was true, was too important to wait until morning to verify. He would return to his daughter's side shortly.

"Is it true?" he muttered, the music and conversation of others meaning that no one overheard him. "There is a parah in the city?"

Grainger scratched at his goatee and his shoulders twitched as though he was suppressing a shrug. "It is under inquiry. I have heard a child slipped past the sentries while they warded off an attack but…"

"Attack?" That thought was chilling. Parah had never shown a penchant for violence or organization beyond farming, but perhaps this was some new result of the environmental poisoning those unfortunate souls endured. Perhaps they were beginning to go mad, turning into ferocious beasts. Perhaps, before long, the production and harvest of hemp would cease. What would happen then? With the parah twisted, misshapen, and hideous to look upon due to hundreds of years of exposure to the toxins and radiation that Hebanthe Falls protected the city's residents from, great care was taken to keep the populations segregated. One of those outsiders within the city walls, even if that one was a child, was a health risk of the most dangerous kind.

"As I said, the incident is under…"

"Tell me this child has been caught."

"I cannot." Grainger shook his head with a scowl. "She…at least it is believed the child is female, fell into the vent system when she was Hebbed, fell through one that was open for repairs during the attempt to apprehend her. There are officers scouring the shafts…"

There were miles of those shafts, perhaps more than there were miles of grated streets and stairways, used for circulating air into homes and vindis, housing water and sewer pipes, and containing the necessary dehumidifying ducts that kept those in the Levels, and the city's infrastructure, from crumbling beneath the decay of hundreds of years of water exposure. A smart person, a clever person, could live in those tunnels for years without being caught. Streeters were found in there all the time. Some, those trying to escape arrest or who had fallen off the Hub's grid, did live within them, making periodic sweeps of the ducts necessary by the Crows and by those who worked in them. But it seemed unlikely that a young child, a stranger to the city, lost and alone, could survive there for long.

That was not, however, a comforting thought either. A parah corpse decomposing in the veins that allowed the city's residents to breathe, to drink, to live comfortably, would introduce pathogens of a sort none had ever known.

"Find her before she contaminates the systems." Haythem was stopped by Grainger's expression and his worried frown deepened. "What? What are you not telling me?"

The dark man took a breath and exhaled slowly. "I did tell you. She was Hebbed. The marksman fired five Heb stingers. Three took down the parah who started the attack. The fourth was accounted for, found embedded in one of the crates. The fifth was fired at the child but has not been found. He swears he hit the mark…but that would only mean…"

Haythem took a step back, bumping into a stone statue behind him that he had to scramble to keep from crashing to the floor and breaking as his thoughts chewed on the implication of Grainger's words. If the child had been struck with enough Heb to fell an adult, she would have already been located, unconscious or dead. It should have incapacitated her immediately. It was possible that the stinger had snagged in her clothing, that she had never been injected, but Haythem knew that to be as unlikely as it was that there was a parah loose within the city. That she might have been injected and yet was immune to one of the city's primary peacekeeping devices was a troublesome thought.

This time when he spoke, Haythem's words were a growled hiss. "Find her. I don't care what it takes. Find her and take her to Lima and Tamner."

Grainger bowed to hide any expression that crossed his face. Rafe Tamner, in particular, did not have his father's or his grandfather's pragmatic, almost cold and ruthless demeanor. In fact, some considered him to be lenient, less concerned with the city's survival than he was with humanitarian measures. But he was a brilliant physician, surgeon, and scientist, and the top man when it came to understanding the effects of Hebenon on the people in the city. And Miguel Lima Junior was the primary voice in the production, testing, and manufacturing of Hebenon in its purest base form, though his primary skills were the same as Tamner's.

What happened to Hebenon after it left the lab, the manipulation that turned the product into Hebbies or Heb on the street or into the sleep-inducing mind control agent used in Grainger's line of work, while processes Lima and Tamner understood, were beyond their control. Despite their questionable affinities, if anyone could sniff out the potential root of immunity to something the Founder and his circle had grown to rely on to control the Hebanthe Falls population, it would be Lima and Tamner

❧CHAPTER 5❧

It was not an unusual sight, not the first time he had witnessed a roundup of streeters and tingers, those unfortunates hooked on the drug the government not so secretly supported, unable to maintain jobs, homes, families or any semblance of normal life. Convinced of Heb's promise to make everything better, make life more real, more enjoyable, more vibrant, many gave it all up for the drug. In the later stages of addiction, they even gave up eating in favor of spending what ticks they could borrow, trick for, or steal to get their next hit.

The effects, the need for a hit, could be seen in their ragged emaciated appearance, their shuffling, zombie-like state. On a high, they became erratic, hyperized and unable to remain still or focused. A few, at the very end, had to be strung out to sleep, and of the bodies he encountered during his secret trawling through the city's underbelly, some had wired themselves to the point of their hearts failing under Heb's assault or else their lungs imploded while they slept, congested and full of blood that seeped from every orifice when the organs shut down.

Those unfortunates did not deserve to live in alleys and tunnels, but frequently they had nowhere else to go. And the herpa who offered food and shelter, medical care and addiction-reversing medication for those who wanted it, men and women allowed to serve the marginal faiths tolerated by the government only as long as they did not teach anti-Founder, anti-Doctet dogma, did not deserve to have their chapels raided and cleared out of streeters on a regular basis. Some believed the government had created the streeter phenomena by the introduction of Hebenon generations ago, a twisted effort at population control when the city began to suffer the effects of severe overcrowding. In turn, the rise of streeters and addicts made it the Doctet's responsibility, the Founder's responsibility, to clear the city of undesirables. Most people wanted them gone, wanted not to see what the city was becoming.

Wanted addiction to be someone else's problem.

But as the streeter population grew to encompass not only addicts but also those unable to work, those the Founder and his ilk deemed undesirable, as people took to the streets to escape the oppression of the ever-watching eye of the SCAMs, the Vanishing grew to be an evil that the people wanted reversed. Gradually they had begun to seek help for those who filled the alleys and empty buildings. Gradually they wanted an end to the constant monitoring forced upon them and the cessation of abductions for the slightest hint of dissidence. They wanted more. More that they could never obtain.

Until one knew someone caught in Heb's grasp, until one saw firsthand what the drug did to friends, relatives, colleagues, how it took control, until someone close was rounded up by the Crows and taken away for reasons never explained, it was difficult to grasp the evil of that 'necessity'. Officially, men and women were taken for rehabilitation, treatment…reconditioning. For curing. But it was all a fallacy, Rhyd was convinced, a convenient tale without proof to support it. Never in his life had he seen one person come back, return to the lives they had been ripped from, rejoin their families. Streeters, addicts, and traitors who Vanished simply ceased to exist.

The number of those same living in the streets continued to rise.

Attempted hacks into the Hub and the Archives failed to reveal any mention of those faceless names, nameless faces, beyond a pickup date and the number of intakes in a day.

Sometimes there was not even that.

A Crow, injector in hand, pulled a seizing streeter up by the arm, prepared to pump his already overactive system with more Heb. It would not be a curing agent. It never was. The barred cart, curtained on three sides to prevent the curious from seeing the unfortunates who moaned or chirped or cried within, was open, two Crows blocking those inside from escaping as the third dragged the struggling, as yet unsedated captive to be added to the number of those already picked up. Grav carts could comfortably hold no more than six individuals, eight or nine if they were crammed in like pickled fish in a flat tin, but Rhyd could not tell how many were inside. A herpa huddled on his nearby doorstep, wringing his hands but not attempting to intervene. To do so could result in either the loss of his chapel and the ability to help others, or might end up with his Vanishing as well. For every streeter the Crows scavenged, another would eventually come to the chapel to take his place.

It was better if he did not resist.

But Rhyd was not a passive bystander. Not anymore. Tail of his coat billowing behind him, he leaped from the alley where he had observed the raid since stumbling upon it. He aimed in that leap for the nearest cart guard; a handspring allowed him to land a solid kick to the Crow's lower back, which sent the bird-masked lawman sprawling into his partner. The third Crow turned to witness the commotion, releasing his hold on his captive, the injector protruding from the fellow's arm though the plunger had not yet been depressed. The streeter landed with a yelp on the cold, wet metal and those inside the cart began to fall out in a hasty bid for freedom. Some looked around with confusion as if unsure of their location, others ran without caring. One of them, perhaps the most lucid of the lot, shouted, "Scarecrow!" as the herpa crossed himself and moved back into the shadows where he could watch, or disappear inside quickly should this chaos turn against him.

The Crows had weapons, thumpers, injectors, buzzers, and poppers, and the best training Hebanthe Falls could offer. Scarecrow had no more than his hands, his feet, and the confiscated thumper. But while his training did not come from a law-enforcement mindset, it did come from an eclectic group of skills, most of which he had learned as a child and had never imagined he would need as an adult. And his kicks, his tucks, and rolls, his leaps and thrusts of gloved fists, had things the Crows did not.

The need and desire for vengeance, retaliation, and freedom.

Three to one were good odds for him. Three to one was an ideal clash, enough of a challenge to break a sweat but not too much to overtax him or leave him on the losing side. Minutes later, the three lay silent, crumpled on the path, with the Scarecrow crouched in their midst, catching his breath as he listened for approaching threats and felt for signs of life on the fallen streeter. But the man was dead, his dirty, claw-like hand clenched around the injector, his thumb on the depressed plunger that proved he had been unable to resist one final high…or else he had chosen to hasten the end he had to know was inevitable.

It was either death or Vanishing.

Hearing no other Crows approaching, sensing no hostility in the eyes of those watching from behind nearly closed shades, the Scarecrow lifted his masked face, his mechanical eyes adjusting to the available light, and looked at the frightened herpa in the tag-wreathed doorway. The herpa's hand, clutching the door handle, trembled.

"Peace," Scarecrow said, his voice garbled and deepened into something unrecognizable from the voice of a normal man. He maintained his gaze with the frightened fellow until the herpa nodded, relieved appreciation on his face, and retreated inside. It would not matter if the herpa spoke of the fight to others. Scarecrow's identity was safe, and his efforts, no matter their success or failure in the end, were, to Rhyd, a satisfaction all their own.

❧Chapter 6❧

His free days past, his work week returned, a resumption of creeping through shafts, wiggling through tight passages, reaching small hands through small places in an effort to keep functioning the myriad of dehumidifying tubing, vents, and filters that allowed those on the Levs to live in dry homes, work in dry facilities, without the constant threat of the health problems that came from a relentlessly damp environment. Without bilgers such as Rhyd, the luxury of even dry sheets would be impossible throughout most of Hebanthe Falls. His father, his father's father and mother, and generations of Ballards before them had been bilgers, a duty once more respected as humanity appreciated those who allowed mankind to continue living in less than hospitable conditions, to survive when so many thousands of others beyond the walls of Hebenon had not.

These days, respect seemed something confiscated by the Founder and the Doctet alone and that was, at best, begrudgingly given. Most of those Rhyd knew did what they did without complaint, without demands from higher up the societal chain, but there was less and less joy to be found in living with each subsequent generation born. To combat the pervasive depression birthed in a realm of near perpetual darkness and continual dampness, music and plays, sports competitions and intellectual ones, gymnasiums and public reading rooms, dance clubs, and dining vindis were accessible to all, anything to get people's minds off of the mundane. Sunbooths had been invented, fashioned to give people access to sunlight they could not otherwise have. Simulated yes, but sunlight all the same, or at least light with the benefits that man's technology was able to infuse into it.

And there were deks, Echosys controlled virtual reality suites that allowed anyone to experience a world of grass, trees, oceans and mountains, ancient ruined places of earth, teaming old world cities bustling with life. They could enjoy blue skies, cloudy or not, or the black starlit beauty of true night, in a way that not one resident of Hebanthe Falls had ever seen.

It was no wonder, the doctors and psychs claimed, that joy was an emotion most of humanity no longer felt. It seemed no one knew how to be happy any longer, and as soon as they were, something, someone, conspired to take that away.

The way they had taken Venn.

But while there might be little joy to life, there was satisfaction to be found in a job well done, for Rhyd and for others. Joy he had lost the day Venn had Vanished. The closest he felt to it these days were the moments of exhilaration when Scarecrow took another Crow out of circulation, even if their absence lasted only a few days. His four-three schedule afforded him time to recover from injuries during the hours of slow, steady work, and those hours gave him time to think, to strategize, to design bits of equipment in his head, to ponder how he could improve himself and strive to make his efforts to help his fellow citizens more effective.

Hours after work were most often spent in the gym, when he was not hunting, on the mats, the rings, the bars, hours spent with his martial arts instructors, until he was too exhausted to do anything more than return home, devour a block of cheese and a shot or two of Zaolei before strapping on the breather and collapsing onto the sofa to the sound of a prodcast on the Echosys. As long as that played, and shut off when the timer ran out, no one in the Hub could tell if Rhyd was awake or not.

He doubted anyone other than the Founder cared.

❧*❧

Grainger's sole care, or rather one of his two primary cares, was the pursuit and apprehension of the individual the people called Scarecrow, the one who continued to harass the men and women he led, the one who persistently eluded their grasp regardless of their efforts. On the off chance that they could match the dates of his activities to another law enforcer's duty roster, or anyone's work schedule, Hub records and Pass activities were scanned and monitor, studied numerous times a week, but without success. Sometimes Scarecrow struck seven days a week. Sometimes he did not strike for a week or more. Some speculated the individual was a streeter, though not of the strung out, manic sort that Heb addiction created. No Scarecrow was no user. His actions, to Grainger's trained eye, were meticulous, too cautious, to belong to a man addicted to a mind-altering substance.

The possibility that he was a streeter, however, or was somehow connected to them, dovetailed perfectly with the full-scale hunt for the parah child who had found her way past Grainger's forces in spite of the odds and who, thus far, remained unfound. There had been no body at the base of the vent shaft, but all that meant was, if she had died of either the Heb in her system, injuries sustained in the fall, exposure to the city's hostile environment, or starvation, she had died in a place not yet scoured and secured by his teams.

Or she had doubled back on them and was someplace they had already been.

Perhaps she had fallen into the mighty churning collective river below the city. If that was the case, unless her body was caught in the nets and dredged, she would never be found…and might not be recognizable even if she was. The nets were periodically combed, but what was cleared away from them, a collection of rotting carcasses and plant life as well as lost tools and manmade goods, or rocks, branches, and logs carried over the falls from Outside, was rarely recognizable. It was impossible for anything living to survive there.

With no one yet reporting an outbreak of unusual ailments or symptoms, it seemed logical to Grainger that the child carried no pathogens likely to be a threat to Hebanthe Falls…or maybe she did not exist at all. Kemway did not agree with his assessment and argued that the lack of reports only meant that whatever she carried was a slow incubating sort of sickness, or that it was a disease that required direct contact with her…which it seemed no one had yet had.

Grainger's solution, therefore, as he looked at the frail things being escorted out of a grav wagon for interrogation, was a crackdown on streeters, especially children, throughout the Levs, in the hopes of finding the elusive child he began to believe more persistently was not real, and the hopes of drawing out the Scarecrow to put a stop to his vigilante tactics. For surely such a man was not targeting only Crows. How many innocent citizens, how many streeters found dead in doorways and alleys, had fallen victim to his assaults? When was incapacitating Crows not enough; when would it morph into the murder of Crows and the innocent alike?

And if he was attempting to be a champion of the downtrodden, how long would he allow the roundup of street children to go on?

Hebanthe Falls had never known anything like the reign of the Scarecrow, and Grainger, like Kemway, was eager to bring that reign to an end.

But his hunt again gained him nothing, not even reports of new attacks as one day turned into four. Grainger growled as another netting of streeter children was loaded into the now empty wagon to be released back into Hebenon's streets. The children, at least rarely Vanished.

With no hint as to what Lev the Scarecrow might appear on next, without any ideas wither his efforts to draw the man out were even reaching the attention of his prey, all Grainger could do was wait.

And continue to hunt.

❧*❦

The whir and schlick and wheeze of Rhyd's breathing, aided by the oxygen tank, was a familiar background sound, but one that always gave Maemi cause to worry when she came to his home to check on him and do the small chores he no longer did for himself. Partially a hereditary condition, from generations of exposure to the atmosphere of Hebenon's vent systems in which so many in his family had worked, partially a byproduct of Hebenon's perpetual damp, and partially from exposure to all of that vent work himself, Rhyd breathed well enough when awake, usually, though he wore protective gear in the vents and when he intended to be outside of his home…or experiencing great physical exertion…for any extended period. When his body rhythms slowed during sleep, however, he often needed the external assistance or else his lungs were in danger of shutting down…or at least in danger of inadequate intake that put the rest of his systems at risk. The alcohol, the overuse of it, did not help any more than Hebbies helped their users, but over the past two years, alcohol and vengeance had become the tools of forgetting, and she could not fault Rhyd for that. When her own child had been lost, Maemi remembered the pain that plagued her for the next seven years. It still surfaced at times, but she had moved past the worst of it.

She was not sure, watching Rhyd frown in his sleep behind the breathing mask, that he ever would.

Zaolei bottles were gathered from around the living area and kitchen and set aside for recycling. Taker containers, many from Vapors, were put in a separate pile, also to be recycled, and what eating utensils, plates, and cups she found around the place were cleaned and set aside to dry. Except for the collection of dishes in the left sink. She never touched those. Rhyd had forbidden it. She shuddered to look at them there, dusty and dirty, but again, she understood the sentimental value of a handful of dirty dishes and thus she did as he asked. Someday he would let them go. Someday he would have to.

Laundry was collected from the bathroom, laundry she would take for cleaning, and the clean laundry she had brought with her was left in a basket in its place. She would rather put it away, in the shelves and dressers where it belonged, but Rhyd would never look for his clothing in the closets and drawers. Not when he no longer entered that room. If not for her periodically taking some of his clothes from those drawers and closets and adding them to the clean items she brought with her to recycle what he wore or replace worn out items, he would be down to very few useable pieces of clothing. He never seemed to notice, never questioned, never seemed to care. As long as he did not see her in the bedrooms, see her opening storage spaces he avoided, he never said a word.

Now with the dusting done, the window garden box watered and weeded, Maemi having recently come back inside from leaving the recycling for pickup, Rhyd stirred to the sound of the door sliding open and then closed again. He groaned, blinking in the light at the silhouette in his kitchen, and shielded his eyes with his arm.

"Too bright," he muttered grumpily within the oxygen mask.

"Hush," scolded Maemi. "This isn't a cave, you know. A little light will do you good."

He growled as he removed the mask and switched off the tank, automatically checking the gauge to determine the oxygen level as he did so. She was right, he knew, that more light would help his mood, but it hurt his eyes and his head this soon after waking, and he truly did not want his mood helped. He was content as he was. Or as content as he wanted to be.

"Do you need anything in particular from the Source? Nessies? Soap? Toothpaste?" She opened the icebox, rummaged through the collection of limp algae leaves, stale crackers made from algae, chia and hemp seed, and dried berries, pickled fish, three discoloring eggs in a bowl, sour hemp milk, shriveled fruit and the remains of something green and furry. She removed everything that was not remotely edible for disposal on her way out the door. "Cheese?"

Sitting up, stretching, giving no thought in his shirtless state to her being there, he nodded with his eyes closed, "Yeah…that." It was the staple of his diet when home, one of the few things he ate with any regularity, but it would not be the only food she picked up for him. She had taken to managing his ticks since Venn's Vanishing, as she had taken up his housekeeping duties, and she would be sure he had food on hand.

He had not asked her to do either thing, and both knew he was normally not a sloppy man. Once he had been one of the tidiest, cleanest people she knew. Now, he did not care. He had other things on his mind, good things and bad things, and matters like housework and shopping were rarely given consideration. Half of his ticks went towards nessies and food, though a good deal of that food was set aside at Vapors for the meals he frequently ate there. He did not realize that, or did not care to think about it. Life, food, and nessies appeared when he needed them, life went on, without his thinking about it.

"I'll be back later. Clothes are in the basket...everything's wiped down. You're all set for another week." She bent over the back of the sofa towards his hunched form to kiss the nape of his neck in a motherly fashion. His elbows did not move from his knees, his face did not leave his hands, but he did lift his head just a little and sighed at her affectionate gesture. It was the sole form of tenderness, beyond Zara's occasional embrace, that he had accepted in more than two years. She was the only person allowed to try it. Not even Tox, for all of his closeness to her, broke that barrier, and when Maemi did, it was always obvious to her how close a breakdown was beneath his callous, calculating exterior, even after all of this time.

"Shower...I'll see you soon." Her hand rested briefly on his shoulder and then fell away.

A shower sounded like the ideal remedy for the stiffness and stuffiness that permeated his body and mind, even though he had taken one the evening before to rid himself of a work weeks' worth of filth and grime. He trudged into the bathroom, dropped his trousers onto the floor, and then swiped a hand across the mirror glass as if to clean it too. The shoulder bruise, he noted in the mirror, was fading, which explained why Maemi had not commented on it. He needed to shave still, but felt little compulsion to do so. Thankfully, he mused as he stepped beneath the heated jets of steam and spray, his facial hair did not grow fast.

'You're lucky…' a hand pressed against his face, rubbing down the pale, light stubble on his cheek. 'Lucky you don't have to shave every day…'

Aloud to the vision, the memory, within his head, Rhyd murmured, "You don't have to…you could let it grow…"

Laughter. A sound too long unheard. 'I'm afraid a beard wouldn't suit me…'

"How do you know? Ever tried one?"

'No…' Still chuckling, Venn asked, 'Think I should?'

Rhyd shuddered. Something, a note in that question, in the voice of the man smiling at him in his mind's eye, made his hand flex and clench against the shower wall, the memory of a smooth cheek beneath his hand making him whisper, "I'd like to see it…once…"

The sound of a door closing made him aware that the water no longer ran. His body was damp but no longer dripped, save for tiny droplets from his lashes that had nothing to do with the shower. He scowled, grabbed angrily at the towel hanging on the wall hook, and after quickly scrubbing his face to remove those traitorous traces of tears, he tied the towel around his waist and left the bathroom. If Maemi had come back and left, there would be whiskey. If she was still here, she would be a welcome distraction from the turn his thoughts had taken.

The dark-complexioned woman smiled at him from the kitchen where she stocked the icebox with several varieties of cheese, fresh eggs, chicken, and cherries. "They're back in season," she commented cheerfully, showing him the container of tiny deep red orbs. There were stories, spoken of by her customers and found on the Echosys, of fruits of great sizes, but here, where everything grew beneath artificial light, the citizens of Hebenon were thankful to have any fruit at all, no matter the size. Fruit was not easy to acquire, and expensive, but because of its nutritional value, additional ticks were allotted to each household strictly for the purchase of fruits.

"Thank you."

It was the tone, as much as the words, that made her smile falter. He was rough today. The mother in her wanted him to give in to the emotion, to purge the grief by encouraging those pent up tears to fall. But Rhyd was not that sort of man, and she feared that, if…when…he finally did reach that breaking point, there would be no returning from it. He would become a useless, blathering shell of a person, crouched in a corner, unreachable, unresponsive, helpless. No more Scarecrow. No more avenger of the masses. And selfishly perhaps, she believed that the citizens of Hebenon needed that from him as strongly as he needed to give it. No one else had given the city hope in a long time, in all of her life or the lives of her mother or grandmother. Hope was in desperately short supply. Hebenon needed Scarecrow…needed Rhyd. And he needed to act if he could not forget and let go.

"The Crows," she began, changing the subject to redirect his focus from his moroseness. "They're rounding up streeter children."

"Children?" Unconcerned about his state of undress, he trudged into the kitchen and took a handful of cherries from the bowl. "Mm…these are good." The pit was put down on the counter. Street children were generally ignored by the Crows unless they were caught in the act of theft or vandalism. He imagined they were not deemed worthy of the Founder's time and effort to help. "What are they doing with them?"

Pleased to see him consuming something that was not whiskey, Maemi set the bowl of fruit in front of him and found another bowl for the pits after closing the icebox. "No one knows. Questioning them…letting them go again…but that's all that's certain. Skelter says the Crows are looking for something…someone…"

"Who?" The most likely answer was the Scarecrow, as the Crows had been seeking him since the first night of his existence. It made little sense, however, for the Crows to think the children would know who he was, where he went, what he intended.

"A child…a girl of about five or six, he says." She paused as she picked up the pit from the counter and put it in the bowl. "A parah."

Rhyd stared at her. A parah? An Outsider? In Hebenon? How had that happened? Why had that happened? When had that happened? Doubting that Maemi had answers, but thinking that Skelter might, if he had been the source of Maemi's information, Rhyd muttered, "I need to see Skelter."

He did not know what he would do with whatever information Skelter might have. The Outsides were said to be deadly to human life, poisonous enough to mutate and twist any who breathed the unfiltered air, drank the unpurified water, ate the tainted, unprocessed food. Anytime anything was brought into the city from the Outside, even the fish caught in the river's rushing flow, it was tested for contaminants, treated and processed as necessary to make sure it was fit for use. A parah inside Hebenon would explain the increase in Crow activity he had noticed over the past week, would explain the half-heard reports of possible contamination of water and air supplies that had burdened him with extra hours of work…but afforded him extra pay…in a rush to upgrade, repair, or replace any possibly failing sifts or filtration units throughout the city.

That meant that the parah had been in the city for at least a week and no official statement had been issued by the Founder regarding her. Wondering what the Founder was trying to hide, or if he only meant to avert a citywide panic by keeping the news quiet, Rhyd wondered if he could, or should, find her first. Finding a threat, turning her over to the Crows, would throw them off his scent, protecting his identity as the Scarecrow that much longer. It might also, he thought grimly, bring him to Founder Kemway's attention, and that was not an eventuality he was prepared for. Soon, sooner or later, he intended to meet the man face to face, demand Venn's freedom and recompense for the damage he and his Crows caused too many people's lives.

But not yet. Rhyd was not ready for that.

Maemi put the abandoned cherries back into the icebox, hiding her creeping smile. As expected, that news was the sort of thing Rhyd sometimes needed to pull out of a slump he might never recover from if allowed to wallow too long.

"You know where to find him." She, like Rhyd, knew that if anyone had details about a rumored parah child, or any rumor at all, it would be Skelter or Zara. "When I see him, I'll tell him to expect you."

From the bathroom where he had disappeared to, in order to dress, Rhyd called, "Thanks, Maemi."

She smiled wider and closed the door behind her as she left. That was the Rhyd Ballard she liked to hear.

❧Chapter 7❧

E"ver wonder if the herpas are right?"

Miguel Lima lifted one eyebrow as he looked up from his experiments, but he took the question at face value. With Rafe Tamner, he always did. Even in the midst of Doctet meetings, Tamner spoke with the voice of the devil's advocate, always the man to challenge convention. Most thought him an agitator, a man who wanted to make them reflect and think, to keep the men and women of the Doctet, and the leaders of the science and business divisions, from becoming stagnant in their thinking. Few took his dissenting questions seriously and no one, Founder Kemway included, believed he meant any of the questions or viewpoints he argued.

Such questions came up every day in the lab where Tamner and Lima studied the conditions beyond Hebenon's walls through data collected from trade goods and fish brought in from the outside and from the assortment of sensors and disc arrays attached to Hebanthe Falls' skin. He was allowed to speak to none but Kemway about his findings, not even Lima, and this was not the first time Lima wondered if his co-worker's questions were rooted in the data he found. If it gave Tamner cause for doubt, surely the Founder would be aware of it. But no one, in Lima's company at least or behind closed meeting room doors with the Doctet and Founder, had expressed concerns over Tamner's comments.

Everyone knew that Haythem Kemway, like his father before him, did not tolerate dissent. If Tamner's questions and comments were valid, rooted in truth, meant as actual challenges to the status quo, he would have Vanished by now.

"Right about what?"

Tamner pushed aside his test slides and microscope and rubbed his eyes. "That Duncan Kemway wasn't the god and prophet he's touted to be? That his belief in our ability to return to the surface could come to pass someday? That we won't be trapped in here forever?"

Lima shrugged. "Trapped? I dunno. I try not to think about it. What does it matter? We'll not be leaving Hebanthe Falls in our lifetime. Our job is to make things better, easier, for those who live here now. The future will take care of itself." His petri dishes of tissue samples taken from the body of the corpse behind him were arranged in numerical order and he compared one after another as he spoke.

"I think," Tamner murmured, "he'd be dismayed, appalled, at that sort of defeatist talk…that we've turned him into some sort of deity."

It had been Duncan Kemway and his Kemway Consortium of scientists, theoreticians, and designers, who had warned of both natural and biochemical threats that would doom mankind to extinction if not faced head-on. It had been Kemway who projected the protective 'cure' in the waterfalls' spray, something about constant moisture, the minerals in the waters of the Four Rivers, that would keep the worst of the threat from reaching them, if his foretold apocalypse came to pass. His engineers had designed cities for several major fall systems across the rapidly changing global landscape, and world governments had spent vast amounts of wealth and resources to build them. Some cities housed the best, the most brilliant minds, and the wealthiest individuals who could buy their way in. Others, like Hebanthe Falls, the primary testing case for Duncan's theories, had understood that any long term settlement would rely on people from all walks of life, people with a wide variety of skills and abilities and a willingness to work hard, to get their hands dirty, that millionaires and bureaucrats would never have.

Some said Duncan had handpicked the families to colonize Hebanthe Falls. Some said there had been a great, worldwide lottery with every man and woman having an equal chance to escape the seemingly inevitable devastation. Some believed the city had been filled on a first come, first served basis, with chaos and slaughter and bloodshed determining the lucky few who made it into the city before her doors were sealed to an outside world already filling with strange, mutant creatures that could no longer be considered human.

Whatever had happened, tales relegated to myth rather than fact, those accounts were strictly guarded by the Kemway dynasty now…if they had ever been recorded.

Duncan Kemway, with no aversion to hard work and dirt himself, had helped design and build all of the basic systems, every nuance of the greatest city in the Falls. His son and grandson had much the same temperament, making changes and upgrades to the functioning systems honing it, perfecting it, but the city itself remained basically the same. By the fourth generation of Kemway leadership, Hebanthe Falls was running smoothly, like finely greased clockwork, with each piece, each person, having a place, a function. Everyone knew what was needed and expected of them in order to ensure the survival of successive generations. With no knowledge of how the other cities had fared, whether any human settlements Outside had hung on in a poisoned world, whether any other pockets of civilization survived, Duncan, the Grand Father, Grand Founder, had become the savior of humanity through Hebanthe Falls.

And with that perception, with no further goal to strive for beyond eternal survival, with no hope of change, or evolution, no chance to grow, hope slowly withered and inevitably, corruption set in. The notion of Kemway as the divine savior in this stationary metal ark bred the right of those of Kemway name and blood to lead and rule Hebanthe Falls. The Doctet of scientists, businessmen, and builders that was intended to become the ruling body of the city was relegated to a secondary, advisory position and the Kemway right to succession became set in the citizens' minds as the cornerstone of their faith and their lives.

They were all things Lima knew, understood, and accepted, and again his head bobbed. "You're probably right about that." In all of the texts he had studied, all of the accounts and treatises and journals of Hebenon's founding scientific minds and those who had gone before, Lima's impression was that his heroes were the same as most others. People who wanted to help, who wanted to better humanity, not be worshiped by them. That there were aberrations, those who thought themselves gods among men, he knew to also be true, but he did not believe Duncan Kemway had been one of those, no matter what the Voices of Faith or subsequent generations of Kemways had come to purport.

Tamner left his stool and stared at the cadaver on the table in the cold room. He and Lima had both been here when this fellow was brought to them, the same day, as it turned out, that it was rumored a parah child had fled into the bowels of the city. Neither of them had ever seen a parah before, only the dozen or more sentries chose to transfer trades in the shafts had…and they had been sworn to secrecy. Sworn or not, their tales were always of grotesque, misshapen forms covered with boils and rotting flesh, monstrous things more beast than human, who managed to cling to the rudimentary skills of farming and hunting, scavenging and logging but nothing more.

Tamner had long believed those were nightmare stories to frighten everyone, children and adults alike, into never considering a life beyond the walls of Hebenon. He had believed it, but there had never been visual, tangible evidence either way…until now.

This man was none of those things. Nothing about him, except for the strange, iridescent golden glow in his milky dead eyes spoke of the external deformities rumored to exist outside. Even the autopsy, performed jointly by him and Lima, revealed few differences within the corpse. A larger heart, larger lungs, lighter, but harder, bone density which both Tamner and Lima theorized reflected a thinness of air and atmosphere. Unless this man was a fluke, an anomaly among his kind, those were minor things, minor enough to suggest that whatever the parah were exposed to Outside, it was either not as harmful as the citizens of Hebenon were led to believe, or the people in the city were exposed to the same things and changing at the same rate.

They were not all that different from the things they feared.

As this was their first parah specimen in over a generation, Tamner, the specialist in things 'Outside', had been given the opportunity to catalog every detail of this male, down to the contents of his stomach, the diseases he had been exposed to, his blood type, the size and weight of his organs…anything at all he could study and learn about. What he and Lima were seeking today, however, was something specific. For more than the sentries had seen this corpse, and most who had seen it knew it to be the body of a dreaded parah. Given the Founder-supported reports of terrifying mutations in the Outside, it was imperative to keep their information contained…and to explain the similarities between parah and the city dwellers in ways that would continue to support the belief of the dangers Outside.

It was doubly imperative to determine what, if anything, in a parah's blood or body chemistry might lead to immunity against Hebenon. This man had not been immune, had succumbed to the injector in the attack and been trampled and crushed to death by his fellows dragging the carts hastily out of the shaft to escape the hail of popper fire. Hebenon had not killed this man. But he was still dead, and there was the chance that his blood would reveal something.

It had fallen to Lima and Tamner to find it.

Lima swore under his breath as the last petri dish was set aside with the others. "Give me a sample," he grunted, picking up a draw tube and pressing it to his own arm. It filled with blood as Tamner rolled up his sleeve and offered his as well. Fortunately, neither was squeamish when it came to using themselves as baseline test subjects. Tamner did not speak but watched his partner compare the differences in the three samples, until Lima leaned back on his stool, arms crossed over his chest in frustration.

"No differences?" Tamner asked curiously. He had seen enough already in his own experiments to know the answer, but he wanted Lima to voice his findings in his own words.

"Oh…there's differences. More red cells…carrying more oxygen… like they're living at a higher than normal altitude."

"That fits with the larger heart and lung capacity."

Lima nodded. "There's traces of antibodies I've never seen before, but beyond that…" He shrugged and scratched at his nose. "Nothing. Nothing to suggest immunity to Hebenon's compounds."

"In the antibodies, perhaps? Maybe there's a disease…something she has had that is blocking it…or she's…different."

"Obviously." Obviously the child was different. It was the why and how that the Founder wanted them to determine. Lima put his petri dishes into the storage case and sealed the box within the refrigeration unit for later usage. "Until we find her, we may never know."

Unless we find her, Tamner silently corrected. He glanced at his desk, at the holo of his son and infant daughter. The parah child, by all reports, would be about the same age as his son, all curiosity and adorable innocence. A capture would result in the study of her as though she was one of Lima's lab animals on which Hebenon was tested periodically to verify that the specimens were still viable and clean. Drawing blood and tissue samples was one thing. If it came to the request of an autopsy on a living child, Tamner already knew he could not do it. Not if the child was as normal in appearance as the man splayed open on their table. Unintelligent or not, animal or not, how could anyone who looked like his own children, of a stock who had survived the end of the world and continued to grow crops to survive, be subjected to such a fate?

Those thoughts, like many others, were ones Tamner kept to himself. He was willing to challenge conservative thinking, but not to the point of risking his life or his family's.

What he did say was a soft, "She's a child…" They were the only words that might give his feelings away.

"She's a threat," came the deep voice in the doorway as Captain Grainger's broad frame filled it, blocking the yellow corridor lighting that now hallowed him in amber.

If Lima had been about to speak, his words went unsaid.

"The Founder asks to see you both in one hour. He wants a report by the time he arrives."

The scientists glanced at each other but nodded simultaneously and said, "Yes, Captain," in one voice. The bald man looked back and forth between them, a faint touch of suspicion on his face, but he huffed and left without another word. This time, when the two looked at one another, it was with concern over what, if anything, Grainger might have overheard or read into their words…and what he might report to the Founder. Hopefully, if Kemway was told anything, it would be written off as the typical banter of inquiring scientific minds.

≈Hebenon≈

ᔰCHAPTER 8᠍

Nothing in Skelter's home suggested the dandy public façade he wore, which was the way, Rhyd thought as he bolted the shaft behind him, the redhead wanted it. Skelter invited few people into his home, allowed few to enter, gave few his address, which was why he and Rhyd had agreed on this particular point and mode of entry. It protected both men, neither of whom could afford public exposure.

The table to Rhyd's left was strewn with a variety of XCO bits, chip cards, tools, monitoring devices, and illegal hacking equipment that Zara was bent over, working deftly with thin, narrow fingers to piece together some gadget for another of Skelter's shady clients. Not shady in Rhyd's eyes, as most of those clients were fighting not against others on the Levs but against the perceived oppression of the Uppers. It was a cause Rhyd supported, the cause that fueled his own personal battle. That Skelter supported his cause fully, did not do what he did for the ticks, meant he could not be bribed by the Crows, an important detail that secured the line between success and failure.

"Good morning, Rhyd," purred Zara without looking up. It had to be him. No one else entered the way he did, and no clients came to Skelter's home. Rhyd was not a client; he was a friend. Their best friend. "Ivan will return shortly. Nessies day, you know."

"Yeah." Ticks were distributed weekly, with a different segment of the population assigned a different day of the week to avoid a rush by the entire city to purchase food and goods on the same day. It was why Maemi came to Rhyd's home like clockwork, and why he was not surprised to find Skelter gone now…why he knew this was the day of the week he would most likely find the man home soon enough.

Rhyd picked his way through the collection of discarded Echosys units that Zara scavenged for usable parts, towards the faded faux leather sofa and pushed aside the clutter there to create a seat for himself. Much like his home, there was a fair amount of taker boxes scattered about, but unlike his own, there was no clothing visible in piles on chairs and tables and the planter box at the window was devoid of living plants. Rarely home, Skelter found little time for growing and Zara's talents did not run the gambit to include gardening.

The gearwork of the wall clock whirred, ticked, and with a final click, chimed once to mark the top of the hour. He watched the second hand sweeping the face, using the sound to sweep his mind of clutter, relaxing more in those moments here than he often did at home.

"Tea?"

Rhyd shook his head. Zara had not looked at him when asking, knowing he would decline, but offered because it was considered polite to do so. It was warm enough in the room that her long legs were bare, and though she did not interest him in a sexual way, he found his gaze leaving the clock to stare at her legs as he waited. Showing skin was what she did for a living, he had seen it all before, but today, for some reason, it fascinated him as it rarely did.

"Want some of that, chushi?"

He blinked, scowled, and looked at the man who had entered the flat, not having heard him come in. It was either an indication of foolishness to lose track of his surroundings or else a product of how safe he felt in Skelter's flat. His eyes scanned past hand-drawn maps of the Levs on the walls, with points of interest tagged with colored spots of paper or ink, and when he met Skelter's gaze, he grumbled, "No, skolper…you know I don't."

Skelter laughed away the playful exchange of insults, jibes they often threw at one another without offense being taken. For Ivan Furrell, being called a sewage worker was not far from the truth. He did not work the tunnels and shafts, would not consider entering there unless his life depended on it, but he worked the underbelly of Hebenon, fed by the lowest tiers of society, feeding them in return with his own brand of 'service'. Technically, in the Hub archives, he was menasvodnik, a manager of dancers and sex workers, one of the few with a license to legally own andis. At one time he had managed two dozen andis, but over the years Rhyd had known him, that number had dwindled. There were still six who shared a flat near the club, who worked six-hour shifts each so that he always had one or two dancers on Vapor's stage. Rhyd did not know what had become of the rest. Those six were enough to allow him to continue to look legitimate in the records, kept him out of the Founder's and Doctet's scrutiny, while allowing him to pursue other interests.

The redhead took his armload of purchases to the kitchenette. "Don't suppose you've been to the vindi, eh?"

"No."

Skelter knew that Maemi had done Rhyd's stocking and cleaning since Venn's Vanishing; Skelter had been the one to find a drunken Rhyd two weeks after Venn was taken, in a filthy flat with no edible food, a man in need of a meal, a shower, a shave, a purpose. While Maemi and Zara had taken care of the flat, Skelter sobered him up, talked him out of the near psychotic doldrums he had sunken into, and introduced him more closely to Tox's work. Surprised that he had not known those details about the woman after all of the years he had known her and Venn, Rhyd listened to what they had to say, what they had to offer, and chose to take up the calling they suggested…just not in the way they anticipated. Soldiers against the Uppers came in all forms, and someone in Rhyd's profession could be a valuable source of intel. Before Rhyd, however, no one had taken it upon themselves to face Crows head-on, hand to hand, in the streets and alleys, in a fight for freedom from oppression. Skelter had thought he was recruiting a spy.

None of them had realized they had recruited a warrior.

Rhyd wondered still, sometimes, if Maemi had introduced him to Venn, who had, in turn, introduced him to Tox, Skelter, and Zara, with the intent of pushing him into the place he was now, or if Venn had been aware of the extracurricular activities of those closest to him. He wondered if the others had carried faith in him even then, in his personal abilities and strengths, in the hopes that he would champion those in need…even if Tox now frequently tried to temper his actions. Maybe she simply did not want to lose him too. He did not want to know. He did what he did for Venn, for himself. If it helped others, made a difference in the lives of the Levels, so be it.

"The talk's everywhere…"

"The parah child. Maemi mentioned it…"

Skelter grinned. Of course she had. That was why Rhyd was here. Both men knew it without having it said.

"What do you know?"

"Well, they say…"

"No rumors. Facts."

A bottle of Zaolei was tossed in Rhyd's direction; he caught it without blinking and cracked the lid. "Few facts to tell. Seems she got inside during the trade…got into the vent shafts. Word is she was hit with an adult level injector…but it didn't drop her. Didn't even slow her down they say."

"That's not possible…" No man, to Rhyd's knowledge, had ever walked away from an injector dart. The official governmental version of Heb was too strong, given in doses meant to incapacitate a man and prevent him from escaping arrest.

It was typically enough to kill a child or at least leave them intellectually, and sometimes physically, impaired for life.

"Apparently it is…or else the Crow who took the shot is a lousy marksman and a liar." Skelter shrugged, pulled a stool near to the sofa, and held out a glass for filling from the bottle in Rhyd's hand.

"Sounds more likely." It was easier to believe incompetence and falseness from the Crows than to think that anyone, especially a child, could carry immunity to Heb.

"They're scouring all the shafts…but you probably know that."

Rhyd nodded. It was impossible in his line of work not to notice the Crows marching to and fro in the most easily accessible shafts, sending streeters scrambling out of their way. Rhyd had thought at first it was an inspection, albeit a much more thorough one than he had experienced before. Strangely, none of the Crows had asked questions when their paths crossed; if they had, Rhyd might have known about this news sooner. A parah in the systems meant fear of contamination, and it explained why he had been kept busy with the filts.

"And now they've taken to rounding up streeters and tingers, the kids especially. I suppose they think she would be with them…like to like, you know…but a parah? Those kids would run screaming if they saw something like that. Guess they haven't found her yet though, so they're thinking she may have fallen…died…been netted…so they keep looking while they're waiting for the next dredge…"

Rhyd took a long swallow to fill the silence. Almost anyone falling into the river ended up netted, drowned or crushed by debris. It was normal to find three or four there a year, some falling accidentally, some intentionally either by their own hands or someone else's. A child surely would not survive that fall, the surging water's pressure, or the assault of rubble thrown at them against the nets.

"You'd think someone like that would be easy to spot…not like she could blend in," Skelter continued. "My ears tell me, however, that for a parah, she's no mutant…not on the outside at least."

"Not a…" Again Rhyd scowled. Every story passed through the prodcasts, through tales repeated from parent to child, written in journals and reports, spoke of the disfiguring horrors that resulted from living Outside, how those unfortunates no longer shared any recognizable features with the purity of Hebenon's remaining clutch of humankind.

"That's not…"

"Seems a lot of things may be possible that we thought otherwise. Even if she's not immune…if she's like us…"

After a low whistle and another swallow of whiskey, Rhyd handed the bottle to Skelter and got to his feet. No wonder the Crows were looking for her. They may not know that detail, if it was true, but the Doctet, or at least Founder Kemway, likely did.

Rhyd wondered how that made the Founder feel.

"How old?"

"Dunno...I've heard young...six or eight or so..."

So little. Biological or ideological threat or no, she must be frightened, hunted by bird-faced men in a dark, wet, foreign environment. A week it had been? Or nearly that long? How could she know what was safe to eat? Safe to drink? Where did she sleep? How did she stay warm?

"You gonna find her?"

Straightening his coat, Rhyd shrugged. Of course he would try. Venn would want him to help a child, and Rhyd was not the sort of man to allow a child to suffer if he could prevent it. If she carried contagion, it was undoubtedly in the air and water already, and nothing he could do would change that. Why subject her to the care of people he did not trust? Thwarting the Crows was what he lived for, and the sparing of a child's life was almost as worthwhile to him as bringing Venn home.

"We'll see." The vent was reopened and he hoisted himself into it.

"Good luck, Whiskey." This time Zara did look at him, blue eyes hooded to hide whatever she was thinking and feeling. Like most in Rhyd's circle, hiding feelings seemed to be one of life's essentials, and none of them questioned the others. Without expressing, without asking, each one knew and understood.

Rhyd nodded and closed the vent. It was time to hunt.

He did not talk to the streeters or tingers, not the young ones at least. Behind the mask, even though his reputation for fighting on their behalf had spread throughout the Levs, he knew he still frightened people, especially those strung out on Hebbies or liquid Heb, who saw him as some sort of beakless Crow. Knowing from years of familiarity with the shafts where groups of streeters tended to congregate, where they chose to escape from the mist and cold, it was easier to find them and remain in the shadows, to listen to their slurred erratic talk for cues and clues and details he needed, then to confront them and risk frightening them. As Skelter had said, none had seen a strange child, or a child strangely dressed; they did not even speak of her amongst themselves as if the possibility of a parah in Hebenon was nothing to be excited or concerned about. Maybe they did not know. With as much drug in their systems as most of them had, or as little in some cases, another kid in the alleys was no big deal.

He would not find the child this way, if he could find her at all.

But Rhyd could, by following street gossip, locate one, then two, then three units of Crows on Lev 4, above where he lived, three squads of four each that could be spied on, listened to, and prevented from making arrests. Twelve Crows was a good day's work; he rarely took out more than three or four in a night. His gloved hands left no prints, his travel through the shafts meant no Pass was required to move between buildings and Levs…if he took less common routes. Not one Crow lost their life; the most Scarecrow left them with was bruises, concussions, broken bones and a sense of embarrassment that a single man was able to outwit, and outfight, them.

The hours dragged by, bringing Rhyd his own collection of bruises, though no fractures and no chance of Heb injection through his carefully designed clothing. It brought the satisfaction of injured Crows, of men and women free a little longer to tag the walls, to hold their own beliefs, to live without fear for a few more days while they moved elsewhere or changed identities or found some other way to avoid the authorities. Once marked, it was almost impossible for an individual, a family, to hide from the Hub, from the Crows, for very long, and it was only a matter of time until the Crows returned for them. At least Rhyd offered them a small chance of autonomy and safety for however long it lasted, but he found no hint, not even a whisper, of a parah child inside of Hebenon's walls.

❧*❧

"We need a sample," Lima said, standing shoulder to shoulder with Tamner in the vast round room that had served as the Founder's primary office since the construction of Hebanthe Falls. In the background, a string sonata was playing, but neither man on their side of the desk could identify it. The barefoot Founder looked as if he wanted to pace, but instead, he perched on the nearest corner of the desk and stared at each of them as if he believed them to be lying.

Lima continued. "There's nothing in the male's genetic makeup to suggest a group immunity. We are running toxicology and antibody studies now, to learn what illnesses or allergies he may have had that could have developed into a Hebenon immunity…to determine if he has been using the product we export and if that has been a contributing factor…as well as judge if there is any reason to think his presence here is a risk to the…"

"Of course he's a risk," Kemway growled. "They both are…"

"It will take another few days for the tests to complete, for us to analyze them…" Tamner did not allow the Founder's interruptive snarl to intimidate him. "But we already know that he carried no specific immunity to it. His blood might give us more clues, and conjecture can be made if the child is in any way related to him, but without her…her blood…her tissues to sample, any conclusions will only be hypotheses. We cannot make policy based on guesses…"

"I," Haythem stressed, now studying his nails with fierce intensity, "can make policy as necessary. It has been proven that the Outside is contaminated. That is all we need to know."

His lowered gaze, as he continued to inspect his nails, meant he could not have seen Tamner's open mouth, or the grimace that immediately followed, but Tamner felt himself being studied regardless. Maybe it was the Founder's dark eyes peering from beneath lowered lashes. Maybe it was the SCAMs everyone knew to be positioned throughout the office, as they were in nearly every public area of the city, even when they were not readily visible. It was yet another way for the Doctet and the Founder, but primarily the Founder, to keep the population under control, to make sure that Hebanthe Falls did not implode under its own weight.

Not for the first time, the question of the legitimate need for such a stranglehold crossed Tamner's mind, especially since his analysis of the data he collected, examined, and gave to the Founder did not match the Founder's interpretation. What, Tamner wondered, was he missing in that data that Kemway could see?

"You will have your samples, gentlemen." Haythem stood up and rounded his desk. "Captain Grainger has promised results. And if he fails…there will be another source for your baseline. We will have the truth…and you will be prepared to fight for it."

Bowing together, both men muttered simultaneously, "Yes, Founder," though Lima's voice was the only one loud enough to be clearly heard.

❧CHAPTER 9❧

Three day's accumulation of bruises and welts did not prevent Rhyd from reporting for his expected shift, although his lack of success and depression over failing to find the child, or Venn, and failure to learn more about the situation in Hebenon, did. His Lev by Lev search convinced him of only one thing, one thing that he kept berating himself for as he clambered through the shafts around the Lev 20 sports complex replacing filts for the third time since the parah 'invasion', as his crew chief called it, had occurred. She must be somewhere above Lev 20, somewhere he did not have access to.

Wherever the child had ended up, without knowing her way around, she would be more likely to remain in the quasi-familiar realm of the shafts she had fallen into rather than risk venturing into the unknown alleys and metal streets beyond those unmarked walls. Or she was lost in them. At least in the shafts, the moisture was kept to a minimum by the filts, and the atmosphere kept warmer than outside by the hot air forced through the vents and pumped into homes vindis and public spaces.

What she lacked, however, was food and water. Without either, after so long, she might not even be alive.

Comments made about missing lunches by the second shift crew, while they dressed down and the third shift crew suited up in the locker room of the bilger Shed gave Rhyd the first glimmer of hope he had felt since his pursuit of this illusive parah had begun. It did not spark right away, but rather simmered and then ignited as he crept into the narrow passage containing his first filt change of the day.

Food. Of course. Nourishment was the key. There were rats in the shafts, yes. Specimens that escaped the labs, escaped the farms, or escaped some households' attempts at keeping them as pets. And rats meant the occasional cat. There were enough traps scattered throughout Hebenon that rats rarely survived long in the vents; most were caught within a matter of days of their escape, driven by the need for food in an environment where there was little to be found. Any source would attract them…as it would attract a hungry child. While it was possible that rats or a daring cat, had absconded with the workers' mid-shift meals, it was equally possible that the thief was the subject Rhyd and the Crows sought. With the Complex perpetually under use by a continual stream of events that were televised throughout the city, and food continuously available to the attendees, any streeter or tinger clever enough might make it here and scavenge a meal from the discards accumulated for recycling.

Survival was a natural instinct; it was surely the same for the parah. Why would not a child attempt the same survival tactics? For one reluctant to leave the shafts' shelter, the frequent ebb and flow of work crews in the tunnels around the complex meant that a sharp eye and a quick hand might snag a morsel here and there to stave off starvation and thirst.

Insulation kept most of the audience's roar for their favorite athlete or team out of the shafts but it was still enough of an increase, when added to the background noises of the steam-driven mechanical systems that operated here, that most working the shafts would not notice, or pay attention to the soft sound of fabric sliding against metal and plastic. To most, it would have been no more than the sound of their own clothing as they crawled about their day's work.

To Rhyd, his acute hearing amplified by the enhancements Tox and Zara had designed and installed into his bilger headgear, it was the sound of fate. He paused, held his breath, listened. Ahead of him.

Three yards. A filt grate slightly askew and ajar from its normal position. A filt grate marked out of service because the room beyond it was not currently in use. It was unlikely to be opened or tampered with until the room was put into service again, and thus the compartment, barely large enough for most men to fit into, would be an ideal hideaway for an observant, frightened child.

If she was there, Rhyd's respect for her intelligence had already taken root.

A muted hum of panic as he pried the panel open, a sound inside like a trapped, frightened animal, and then there was silence as man and child stared at one another. In this barely lit world of shafts, grates, filts, pipes, and tubes, color was mostly indiscernible. Even the enhancements added to his goggles were not designed to distinguish color, only to sharpen and clarify the images around him. Wires, tubes, and other mechanical parts were differentiated by texture, by design and shape, and the paths and shafts themselves contained no color beyond the dull grey-green and faded silver of the materials from which they were created.

But Rhyd did not need color to know that her hair was a paler shade of blonde than his own, her eyes some shade similar to Zara's striking blue. Her mouth, opened into a small, frightened O, held white teeth no different than any other child, and her skin appeared smooth, as flawless as anyone else he had ever met save for the smattering of pale pigmented spots…freckles he believed…across her nose and cheeks. He thought for a moment that she could be a streeter, nothing more, but years of experience in these tunnels and his gut instinct convinced him easily that she was not.

For all of her similarities to city children, she was different too. Too different to have spent her life in a world without the sun on her tanned skin.

Surprisingly, she did not scream, but perhaps that was because he had not reached for her and she understood that screaming would gain her nothing. If she was clever enough to have survived this long on her own in an unfamiliar, unyielding environment, she would be bright enough to know that screaming would not bring help but rather attract the bird-men who were seeking to capture her. This was no birdman, though he, like everyone else she must have seen within these passages, wore strange coverings over their faces that must make them look more like monsters than men.

Anticipating her fears by the quick, appraising movements of her eyes, Rhyd unsnapped the goggles and lifted them to reveal his own eyes. Eyes not so different from hers. Removing the headgear was too complicated for this confined space, but he could at least show her that their eyes were the same. He reached for her with his other hand and she skittered backward, as far away as the alcove allowed.

"Don't be afraid...here. Look. I have something."

He had not brought food with him, but food was probably easier for her to find than water. He unfastened a pouch from where it was strapped into one of his work uniform's many pockets and offered it to her. "Water; you open it like this." He showed her how it was done, but she expressed no indication that she either understood or trusted him. He expected the latter, given what little he already knew of her, but it had not occurred to him that any living beings...people or parah or whatever they might be...on the Outside, would communicate in a language other than what he knew. "Drink." He took a sip himself through the tiny tube to show her it was safe and offered it again.

His actions were enough to convince her to hesitantly take the pouch, and her thirst was sufficient enough to prompt her to drink greedily until the slurp of bubbles indicated the pouch was empty. She gave it back with a demanding glint in her eyes behind her fear.

"I don't have more...but I can get some."

He glanced at his wrist chrono. Halfway through his shift and far enough from the starting point that he would never get there in back in time to finish the filts he was required to inspect today. Another seven along this same shaft...but then what? He could check in ill; his breathing issues were well-documented though he never used them to his advantage, never reported sick unless he actually was...or was too injured from his other activities to work. And going back the way he had come, bringing her with him, would expose her to others. She looked normal enough, from what he could see, that maybe no one would make note of her unusual clothing and would mistake her for a streeter. Each of them had rescued stray streeters, or animals, from the vent systems before.

But he could not chance it. Not when the Crows were looking for a child in the shafts. Any thoughts he had given to finding her for the reward and recognition he might receive were gone. Washed away by those sad, round, frightened eyes.

"Stay here." He gestured with both hands for her to stay where she was while he backed away enough to put the filt grate into place. As an afterthought, he gave the empty water pouch to her. "I will come back. For that…for you." He doubted she understood, suspected she would escape this hideout as soon as he was out of sight and hearing distance, but he had to try. "Wait for me."

If she left here, he would find her again. He would have to.

Her head bobbed once as she mouthed the word 'wait' and then the grate was between them, blocking each other from sight.

Two and a half hours later, with the seven filts inspected, repaired or replaced as needed as hastily as he could work, Rhyd returned to the grate, a plan laid out in his head that ought to get her out of this dismal place safely. He had not yet given consideration to where he would take her, for nowhere within the boundaries of Hebenon would be truly safe for a parah. But almost anywhere had to be better than where she was now. He heard no sounds as he approached, expected her not to be in the alcove when he returned. The grate was as he had left it, intentionally upside down so that he would know if it had been moved…by the child or by anyone else who might find her there.

As he snapped the grate free, however, he heard the rapid breathing indicative of fear and the child scurried forward out of the chamber, attaching her arms around his neck as though she was grateful to see him or relieved that he had returned and not brought the birdmen for her. It was an awkward moment for him, causing him to freeze, but when she refused to let go, he sighed, wiggled her around so that he could put the grate properly into place, noting that she clutched the empty water pouch in her small fist.

Grate reattached, he stopped again. Listened. Heard only his own heartbeat, his own breathing, and hers…and the mechanical life systems of the city. So far, so good. He and the others in his shift were widespread throughout the Levs. There was no reason to believe he would meet any of them on his return to the Shed. As long as he did not take her there, and steered clear of the Crows, they would be safe.

Through shafts, down metal staircases, through hatches and past checkpoints where he made sure to keep the child out of view of the SCAMs he knew to exist at each one, he traveled with her clinging to his neck. He hid her arms and hands each time with his coat and repair pack, and turned his body so that her head was not visible, but it was not always easy. Twice the checkpoint systems hesitated, either in the reading of his Pass or because the SCAMs were trying to matrix an image they did not understand, but he was eventually buzzed through. He paused each time, the three seconds he knew it took the SCAMs to shut off after a successful Pass swipe, and as long as the child remained still and quiet, there were no other stimuli to give the system cause to click on again until the next Passcard swipe.

She seemed to understand the need for silence, for stillness, or else was paralyzed with fear as she waited to see where he would take her.

With two more levels to traverse, their progress slowed by sticking to narrower shafts when it would have been quicker to go through the larger ones or move into the streets, Rhyd stopped abruptly before reaching the final juncture that would take him home. Shaft workers did not always return to the Sheds at the end of the day; some opted to go straight home instead, if their home was nearer their day's posting than the Shed was. For Rhyd, the Shed would have been closer today, but more dangerous, and so he opted for home. At least no one would question his choice. His oxygen tanks were there, after all. This would not be the first time he had gone home to them instead of returning to the Shed after a shift.

But the desired juncture was blocked by the ascension of a single Crow, a sentry alone since no other footsteps were heard with his, and a quick peek around the corner showed no other Crows waiting at the bottom of the steps nor at the top. The Crow turned in Rhyd's direction but Rhyd did not think he could be seen in the shadows where he waited. Quickly he set the child down and pressed his finger to her lips, indicating the continued need for silence. She too could hear the familiar tone of those footfalls, heavy soles drawing steadily nearer, the filtered wheeze of mechanical breathing and she hastily looked around for somewhere safe to hide while Rhyd returned his attention to the approaching threat.

The Crow might not know he was there but he was a threat nonetheless. There was nowhere else for the officer to go except straight along the path or around the corner…directly into Rhyd's way.

There was nowhere to go except back down the dim tunnel through which they had come.

Knowing better than to cling to the stranger's legs now, as he crept slightly away from her, his body pressed against the shaft wall in the shadows, the child watched wide-eyed, mimicking his stance and stare, until he burst into the other passage, striking low, knocking the birdman off his feet and quickly popping up on the other side of him. If she had not seen him kick the birdman's legs, she would have thought their hunter had slipped in the accumulated moisture puddled on the floor at the center of this junction. There was the crack of bone as he landed on the hard surface and the birdman stopped moving.

Rhyd waved her forward, caught her hand at a run, and swept her onto his back as he started in the other direction. He could not risk those stairs now, could not risk swiping his Pass at the bottom, for the Crow would have done the same and Rhyd might too easily be tied to the fallen officer. There were few Pass points within the shaft system, and the ones that did exist were too easy to monitor.

But Rhyd knew other paths, all paths, from a lifetime spent in the tunnels, and the long arm of the T that branched to the right would also bring them to safety. He ran because he was not certain if his opponent would stay down and did not want to risk the child being collateral damage in a fight.

Up one level. Zigs and zags, grateful the soles of his boots muffled the sounds his steps made though the surface shuttered and shivered around him with each step, through a constricted set of shafts that forced him to slow. Then down once more, and down again. It brought him near to the city's edge, close to the widest and strongest of the falls, and the moisture in the air soaked the child's meager clothing and made his breathing systems and visual sensors struggle to function more efficiently, even here in the shafts. He could hear the roar, always the roar, the sound of water tumbling over rocks and beating against Hebenon's borders. The rush of the Four Falls was louder on this side of the city, loud enough to drive some men mad, loud enough that, even with earplugs, some men never adapted to the sound.

There was repair work to be done here, he noticed in passing, turning south, turning in the direction of home.

He wondered if anyone was aware of the needed work…and how he could report it without raising flags and questions about why he had been in these arms of the shafts to begin with.

When he set the child down again, it was to pull another grate from the wall, wiggle up into it, and then drop out of sight into the room beyond, where he held out his arms for her to come to him.

Whether she feared him or not, there was no hesitation to do as he asked. She did not want to be left in the tunnels alone, and he had saved her from the birdman. That was proof enough, it seemed, that he meant her no harm.

Though dim, the room she found herself in was better lit then the shafts, and, she concluded, appeared to be a home. His home, she guessed, as he yanked off his outer coat, dropped his work equipment wherever it happened to land, and quickly unfastened the straps and buckles that kept his headgear in place. Running had strained his breathing, and he fumbled for the mask attached to the tank that leaned against the nearest chair. He too, leaned against it, holding the mask to his face with one hand as he continued to remove anything work related with the other, dropping it onto the floor as well.

"Towels in the bathroom," he muttered without looking at her.

She did not move.

By the time his breathing came easier, his training with regulating its rhythm put into practice yet again, and his heart rate had slowed to its normal pace, he was startled by the tiny hand that touched the clear plastic mask covering his mouth and nose. He looked at her, surprised, and his abrupt movement made her freeze. She did not, however, jump away or flinch. It was the first time he was able to look at her closely, to see what she really looked like.

Definitely blonde, a color growing rarer as the conglomeration of humanity brought together by disaster interbred over the long years of isolation within Hebenon's borders. Rarer still were blue eyes, or even green, and redheads, which was why many andis were created to be blondes or reds with blue or green eyes. Even when wet, the child's hair was fairer than most, an oddity for which she would surely be noticed if she was out on the streets. He was not familiar with children, rarely interacted with them, but he guessed from her height of maybe three and a half feet that she was as Skelter speculated, somewhere between six and eight years old…unless those who lived on the Outside were somehow different in that regard.

The fabric of her clothes, dirty, torn and dripping on his floor, looked rough and scratchy, thick and thus possibly made for warmth, although her little shivering body did not look warm now. Her feet were bare, calloused and caked with dried mud from too much time without shoes, and the exposed areas of skin on her extremities were scraped, bruised and raw in places from crawling on hands and knees in her efforts to escape the Crows…and possibly from her life before, on the Outside. Was she constantly threatened there as well? Was she abused or mistreated? He could not tell beyond the wariness in her eyes, a wariness that likely had as much to do with the dangers she had faced in the last week as with anything she experienced Outside. Her nails were dirty too, as one would expect from one who spent a life raising crops. But she did not look underfed, only tired and lost.

"Let's get you clean," he finally said with a sigh. The sound of his voice made her drop her hand and step back. His words, his tone, did not suggest a threat. Rather they hinted at pain and weariness and she looked afraid that her hand on the mask might have hurt him. Rather than try to give her an explanation he doubted she would understand, he turned off the flow of oxygen from the tank and started for the bathroom, beckoning her to follow.

He did not make the mistake this time, did not assume she would know how to operate a shower, Instead, he filled the tub with his daily allotment of water, listening to the movement behind him but paying little attention to it. When he turned to instruct her to undress, he was surprised to find her already free of her scratchy, sack-like dress. He watched with further disbelief as she climbed into the water without hesitation. She flinched at its warmth, as if she had not expected that, but immediately began to rub the water over her skin to cleanse away the grime.

The corners of Rhyd's eyes creased. Did animals, monsters, bathe this way?

He thought not.

Feeling awkward about watching her, assuming she was smart enough not to drown, he left her to her bath and set his attention on feeding her. As he heated cooking water to sponge himself clean, he opened cupboard after cupboard, icebox and pantry, his frown growing deeper with each glance. What did one feed a child? Not whiskey, he knew that. But what did parah eat? How much? He had no idea. What if he made her sick? What if he gave her something she did not like…or could not eat? And what, he mused with a glance at the eternally dirty dishes in the sink, was he supposed to feed her on?

He settled on dried fruit and seeds and poured a handful onto the jar lid, which he left on the table where she would be able to reach it. A bit of pickled fish, a boiled egg, and, reluctantly, a piece of cheese were left as well, along with a short glass of goat milk still fresh enough from Maemi's last nessies expedition. Someone might as well drink it, he mused. By the time he got around to doing so, the milk would have soured.

Back to the living room and thus the bathroom door, he stripped off his shirt, dropped it onto the floor, and used a dishtowel to bathe with the heated water from the stove. Here in the safety of his home, it was easy to let his guard down, easy to forget the world outside of his walls, easy to forget that he was no longer alone…

…until a small voice behind him squeaked, "Ow."

He spun around, bumping the water pot, spilling the hot water over the floor and his still booted feet. He swore reflexively, regretting at once the outburst in her presence, and then stood there on one foot, shocked by the tiny creature dripping more water on the floor without wearing a stitch of clothing.

"Crucksake," he hissed, taking the dishtowel he had been washing with and trying to hold it around her waist. "Get dressed!" He hissed again when he realized that, even if she understood him, the only clothing she had to wear was too torn and filthy to put back on, and he had given her nothing else. And though she knew how to bathe, it did not mean she knew how to dry herself. Maybe parah did not need to but instead dried in the open air…the poisonous, discolored, open air.

"Come here." He caught her arm and pulled her back to the bathroom. She made no attempt to hold the dishtowel in place as she followed. He yanked the first towel he saw, his own hanging on the wall near the tub, and squatted down to make drying her an easier task. Hands that were usually precise and dexterous became awkward and hesitant as he wiped the moisture from her skin.

"It's not good to stay wet. It will make you sick. You have to dry yourself…and use this." His attempt to reach the bottle of moisturizer resulted in it falling, the lid popping open and the white cream within spurting across the floor. "Crucks…" This time he caught himself before the profanity slipped and he tried to cover his mistake with an attempt of applying the moisturizer to her arms.

She giggled at the touch and the cool substance rubbed on her arm, but she watched without flinching and willingly offered the second. That giggle took him back to another, to a sound he would probably never hear again. It was a memory that squeezed around his heart, prompting him to jump to his feet, thrust the bottle at her, and snap, "Finish. I'll find you something to wear."

But what?

He stormed out of the bathroom and looked around the living room at the various piles of clothing scattered here and there with no idea what might fit her. It was not until his gaze fell on the simple black undershirt he had discarded on the kitchen floor that a solution came to him, or at least a solution that would work until he found something more suitable. He dug through one pile, then another, until he found a shirt with sleeves, another all black one as most of his clothing tended to be black. He freed it from the pile as the still naked child emerged from the bathroom, no longer wet but now glistening from the neck down with a thick layer of white that she had not been taught to rub in, only to apply.

Rhyd groaned and behind closed lids, rolled his eyes, thankful he had never had children of his own. He was not cut out for this sort of thing. But at least she had the towel in her hand, dragging it along behind her. Rhyd sat cross-legged on the floor, took the towel, and began to wipe the excess cream away.

"Too much," he said. He swiped some off, put it on the back of his hand, and showed her how to rub it into her skin until it was no longer visible. "Only a little. This is too much," he repeated.

"Too much." She followed his movements and rubbed the lotion into her skin.

He could not tell if she was mimicking him or if she understood what he was saying, but he realized again that if she could speak, if she could mimic him even, she could not possibly be an animal or a monster. The parah had been human once…and seemed to every one of Rhyd's senses, to be human still. At least, she was; and if she was, then it was equally likely the others Outside were as well.

His head hurt too much to think about such things. He needed a drink. But a drink, tonight, was out of the question, so he pushed that need down and pulled the undershirt over her head. Once her arms were popped through the sleeves, he used a bit of string he had found, string normally used to tie plants to their stakes when his window garden became unwieldy, to tie the shirt in place about her waist. It drew the hem up enough so that she was not likely to trip over it.

Her bare toes wiggled beneath the fabric's edge and she giggled.

"That will do. Tomorrow Maemi will find you something better. She will know what to do." If not Maemi, then Zara or Tox. They would fix this. They would take this child out of his care and enable him to go back to the things he was supposed to be doing. He was not a parent, not a guardian, nor, he thought as he scooted her towards the meal he had offered on the table, did he want to be one.

There needed to be no words spoken for her to understand what lay on the table. She recognized the berries and seeds, the first things she attacked, devouring them within minutes while Rhyd used the lotion-slicked towel to wipe up some of the spilled water in the kitchen. She made a face at the pickled fish and pushed it to one side, but the egg and cheese, after closer examination, were eaten quickly as well. Glass after glass of goat milk was consumed until the small half-quart container was empty. She burped. Finally, Rhyd, who had been watching her out of the corner of his eye, looked directly at her.

She was full, content; he knew that expression on her face. And he could see how tired she was. Likely she had not slept fitfully while hiding in the vent shafts. It created a new dilemma, as they could not both sleep on the sofa. He refused to sleep in the bedrooms, nor did he want her in there. One was unfit for sleeping, having become more of a storage facility over the last handful of years, and the other he allowed no one to enter if he could stop them.

That meant one of them would have to sleep on the floor, and though he considered placing an extra blanket and pillow from the closet on the floor in the corner near the heating ducts, where she would be warm and out of the way, it was an idea he quickly quashed. She was not an animal. Not a pet. She was a lost, frightened child, who deserved the best treatment he could provide after everything she had recently endured.

"Wait here." He repeated the gesture he had used in the shafts, one she seemed to understand since she did not follow him into the bedroom. He hesitated at the doorway, eyes closed, heart thundering anxiously, and then went in, trembling, not looking at the array of down-turned holo-images on the dresser, avoiding looking at the bed, going straight to the closet with one thing in mind. He could not allow the past to distract him.

When he returned with the bedding, she watched him take the blankets and pillow from the sofa, toss them onto the floor, and in its place spread out the fresh blanket and a newly fluffed, clean pillow. He perched on one end of the seat and patted the middle."

"Come here…this is your bed tonight."

She crept forward, again as if understanding, and though she made sure to do so at the opposite end from where he sat, she did lie down with her head on the pillow and allowed him to cover her with a fold of the blanket. Her head bobbed sleepily, eyes blinking as they tried to stay open, the comfort of the long padded seat a beckoning haven for respite. But when footsteps rang outside, neighbors passing on their way to or from errands, a sound Rhyd was familiar with at all hours but which she was not, her eyes popped open with a flash of panic.

There were few options to block out such sounds. The noise filters built into the insulated walls dulled the sounds of falling water to a muted, constant roaring hum, but it did not always muffle footsteps and voices on the path outside, or the sounds of the neighbors above or too the side. And it would certainly not erase the wail of the shift sirens when they came. He could only think of a single remedy, one that made him shudder.

"This ought to help."

He was reluctant to try it. It had been too long since there had been music in his flat, too long since he had allowed the familiar recorded notes to blossom and fill the room with their fragrance. Venn's cello, a soothing, mesmerizing sound that had once calmed him, came to life over the Echosys speakers, without Venn being there to play a single note. It calmed the wide-eyed waif into slumber more quickly than Rhyd expected, for which he was thankful.

But hearing it again after so long, having someone in his care to protect and watch over as the memories of Venn tried to burst from his head, meant that Rhyd did not sleep for many long hours. He did not expect to sleep at all that night.

⮞Chapter 10⮜

The day began like any other, a day free of work, a day greeted at the rising by the sound of the cello in the other room. Rhyd rolled towards the sound shielding his eyes from the dim but intrusive glow from the living room, and listened until the urge to rise became too insistent. He pulled on the pair of sleep pants that lay in a jumble next to the bed where they had been discarded during the night and then padded to the doorway between rooms. There he stood, watching Venn play with eyes closed as he swayed, the instrument in his hands, the passion of the piece present in the way he drew the notes forth and in the set of his bare shoulders, the way he moved, the way his face twitched and smoothed, his dark hair hanging in front of his eyes.

Though tempted to close his eyes too, Rhyd did not. He stared, absorbing every nuance of the other man's melancholy passion with the feeling that something was wrong…the certainty that if he looked away the music would end and he would never hear it, never see the other man, again. On the table at Venn's elbow, a scatter of blood orange pills that made Rhyd scowl, pills he wished Venn would not take, pills they had argued over more than once in the past few months. Pills that were part of a growing addiction the cellist was having difficulty shaking. An addiction that worried Rhyd every minute of every day.

Am I not enough, he often asked. Why do you need those?

Venn had no answers.

Then it happened again, for the hundredth time since that day, and now, as then, Rhyd was unable to stop it, reverse it, unable to find the flaw in his actions that might have spared them both if the horror could be circumvented. Without warning, as his memory again failed to prepare him for the moment, the front door of their home burst inward and the Crows, four of them, erupted through the opening, black coats fluttering and flapping as they charged across the room, heading straight for Venn. Yet again, though the noise and suddenness of the action startled them, Rhyd thought Venn looked less surprised by the Crows arrival than Rhyd was.

He did not fight as their gloved hands latched around his arms like talons, wresting the cello from his grasp, allowing it to fall. The pills on the table scattered across the floor. Rhyd, already moving to stop the intruders, caught the instrument with one hand and Venn's wrist with the other. The cello was haphazardly propped against the sofa as the two men, clutching hands as though to serve as an anchor to the other, were dragged to the door by the superior joint strength of the Crows. There was no sound except for boots on the floor, and Rhyd screaming at the Crows to release Venn, shouting the Venn had done nothing wrong, that they had the wrong man. Rhyd would have traded places with Venn at that moment if he could, even though he had done nothing himself to warrant suspicion by the Founder.

But his words were to no avail, and when one of the Crows brought his thumper down across Rhyd's forearm, cracking bone as it connected, Rhyd yelped. His grip slipped. The thumper struck against his stomach, knocking him, winded, off his feet and his cry of the other man's name turned into a ragged gasp. The blow forced Rhyd to recoil, forced a separation of their hands as Venn was dragged into the street. Venn shouting back that he was sorry. Fingers dragged across the back of Rhyd's hand as he wheezed Venn's name one last time…

Rhyd bolted awake to that feeling of fingers on his hand, a touch, in his groggy state, he imagined to be Venn, and found himself staring into a child's blue eyes, her hand on his, seemingly comparing their sizes or assuring herself that he was not dead since he had fallen asleep at last with the oxygen mask over his face after giving in that morning and calling off work for the day. He could not work on two hours of sleep, and he knew today's agenda was going to be finding a more permanent place for the girl to stay. He looked at their hands, imagining it was the contact that had brought the nightmare back.

He knew he had small hands. Venn and others had commented on that over the years. Even his father had, degrading him for it as if it was somehow a fault or a failing. But it served his work well and had never prevented him from dropping Crows when the opportunity arose. He wondered if that was what she had been looking at or if she was simply looking for differences between herself and the man from the city inside the Falls.

"Good morning," he mumbled, removing the mask and switching off the tank. "Imagine you're hungry, eh?"

It was then he noticed something he had not before, several small somethings that added up to his total surprise. The chrono read noon, which meant that he had slept for seven hours instead of the two hours he had thought he would get. The blanket and pillow on the sofa were organized into a neat pile on one end, the clothes that had been haphazardly shed or scattered around the room were arranged in tidy collections…the dirty ones on the floor and the clean ones in sorted piles of shirts, trousers, socks, and undergarments all on the sofa where she had slept. His work equipment and clothing had been pushed over to the door and the towel from last night's bath was no longer on the floor. It was not, as far as he could see, in the living room either.

He got to his feet as his attention shifted towards the kitchen; he felt his breath catch in his chest abruptly enough to cause a stab of unexpected pain. Every dish in the sink had been cleaned and placed in the drying rack, and on the table, a plate with a meal, much like the one he had laid out for her last night, had been set. Correction: Two plates. Plates that had been in the sink for two and a half years. Plates he had been unable to bring himself to clean and that he had steadfastly refused to allow Maemi to touch.

He bit back the curses that flew into his mouth, swallowed the impulse to yell at the girl for interfering where she had no right to be involved. How could she have known not to touch them? How could she understand why he had not wanted them touched when most days the dirty dishes made him wonder why he left them there.

It was not like he needed them there to remember. Memory was all he had...and those memories held on without the vision the dirty dishes had represented.

Another deep breath and he turned in a slow circle, examining every detail of the room, noting a sort of tidiness that not even Maemi attempted. Maemi had been content, to a degree, to leave his flat the way he had it, knowing that even the arrangement of things was a reminder for him. And now, this innocent child, definitely not a barbarian or an animal, had inadvertently erased every reminder he could see from where he was. He wondered with dread if she had found her way into the bedroom and changed anything there.

He did not have the courage to look.

"Th...thank you..." he forced himself to say, to acknowledge her contribution, her repayment, perhaps, for saving her life. He sat at the table, thankful the cello had not been moved, and pushed it over far enough that they could eat together. He could at least give her that verbal token of gratitude for what she had attempted to do. Maybe, he thought as he took another look around, unexpectedly liking what he saw, it was time to let those little reminders go.

Surprised that she was able to accomplish all of that while he slept, that he had not heard her movements, that his internal alert systems had not gone off due to unexpected sounds in his flat, they shared fruit juice with their meal, the only thing other than water or whiskey to drink in the house. He would have to get something from Maemi, have her go to the vindi or go himself to pick up more nessies.

He shook his head and hid his scowl by shoveling pickled fish into his mouth. No. The parah would not stay long enough for that. He could not have her here, could not risk himself or her, could not take her out with him to work, to hunt...but leaving her alone and unprotected was also not an option. Having her in his life would mean missing work, would mean shirking his calling, and an effort to find care for her, to secure her an education, was going to mark her as exactly what she was. A parah. She could not even communicate sufficiently. Sending her, taking her, anywhere in public would be a huge risk, a huge mistake. Today she would have to stay with him; there seemed no other choice. But even that was a choice he was not comfortable with.

She finished eating before he did and got down from the table, disappearing to what he presumed was the bathroom. Being alone allowed him the opportunity for the drink he really wanted, the drink he had ignored since last night. But after a single, long swallow of burning liquid, he put the bottle away. He needed the drink, but he did not need to be drunk. He could not afford that today.

When she returned moments later, the object n her hands made him want to drink all over again.

The holo-image she carried, a shot taken during a dek session that had been a rare treat engaged in together when he and Venn had saved up enough ticks to do so, was a stretch of golden sand and a crystal blue sea, the likes of which no one in Hebenon had witnessed or enjoyed in more than six hundred years. He and Venn, caught mid-laugh, fighting over a colorful inflated globe of air. There were other holo-images on that short dresser as well, all turned down so that the happy faces on them stared at the dresser top. This one had been at the end of the dresser nearest the bedroom door; perhaps she had looked no further. But this one pained him enough.

"Venn." she whispered, pointing at the other face in the -image.

He must have called to the other man aloud in his sleep, Rhyd surmised, though how she could have guessed it to be a name he did not know. "Yes…Venn," he growled, snatching the frame from her and stomping away to put it back in the bedroom where it belonged. A cursory glance around the room told him that, other than that picture, nothing had been touched, a fact that made him feel better about her innocent intrusion on his memories. She followed as far as the hall, watched him put the frame back where it had come from, face down again, and then she backed up as he shooed her out of his way.

"Do not touch those. Do not go in there again. Ever," he growled. He closed the door firmly, a solid sound that he hoped emphasized that he wanted the room to remain closed and undisturbed, that he did not want her in there.

She stared, blinked, and then left him there to begin clearing the table. Rhyd remained still, breathing deep, calming himself, not wanting to be angry with her for honest mistakes. She could not have known his feelings about that room, about Venn, any more than she could have known to leave dirty dishes in the sink. Defeated by his own emotions, finding the anger draining out faster than expected, he moved piles of clothing to the coffee table where they would be out of the way but still accessible without going into the bedroom for them, and sank down onto the sofa with his head in his hands.

He must have dozed again, this time without the aid of the oxygen tank, for when he opened his eyes he was slumped sideways against the pile of blankets and pillow with a stiff, aching crick in his neck. The child sat on the floor before him, staring, watching him sleep in a fashion that he might have thought disturbing if she were anyone else. When he met her gaze, she smiled tentatively and pointed to herself. "Agnys," she said.

Rhyd blinked, stretched as he sat up, and stared again. Since he did not reply, she took his hand, placed it on her chest, and repeated the word, "Agnys."

"Agnys…is that your name?" Did animals name one another? Did animals attempt to converse with language beyond grunts and simple sounds? He blinked again when she did not reply but continued to look at him expectantly. He nodded, grunted, understanding that look, and pointed to himself. "Rhyd."

She nodded, smiling, clapping her hands before pointing at him and repeating, "Rhyd."

It was their first successful attempt at communication with more than hand gestures and commands, and it made Rhyd smile, pleased to have something to call her, and pleased to think that there might be hope of educating her, helping her fit in, after all. He did not recognize Agnys as a name, but she likely did not understand Rhyd either.

Beyond his walls, the air was shattered by the shift change claxon, making Rhyd blanch. He had missed last evening's prodcast…and this morning's as well. Someone was likely to sync his missing work due to claimed illness, to the failure to watch, but he did not want to risk it any longer than. He leaped up, turned the Echosys on, and motioned for Agnys not to move as the system calibrated itself for the day. Each system came with a built-in alert feature, used at turn on and at the beginning of each prodcast in order to log the viewer's identity into its system. Public displays had a broader scanning mode to record the number of heat signatures within viewing range. At the end of each twelve-hour shift, the audience numbers were tallied to determine viewership of each prodcast in an effort to give the audience what they wanted to see, to keep track of their tastes and gain approval ratings, and to make certain the populace was watching the obligatory two-a-day prodcasts produced by the Founder or a member of the Doctet. A single day missed might not mean much, but if the Hub managers thought the missing was suspicious, it could result in a Crow invasion, a confiscation of property, an effort to determine a person's loyalty to the city, and possibly arrest for no other reason than the suspicion of treason…whether warranted or not.

Rhyd knew how long the scan took, believed it could, even in private systems, detect the number of bodies in a room, and he made sure to keep Agnys out of the scanner's range long enough for the process to complete. The system would not recognize her, might not know the other occupant was a child, not an adult, would not necessarily find anything unusual about a second person being in his flat when Maemi, Tox, Zara or Skelter had been here before. But if it somehow did recognize her as a child, he did not want any flags raised in the Hub when he had no nieces or nephews, and few acquaintances with children who might be here.

Since he had never taken in streeters, or volunteered to care for anyone's children, he did not think he could afford for someone to question a child being here. He and Agnys could not risk it.

She climbed onto the sofa when he indicated it was okay for her to move and she snuggled beside him to stare at the moving images on the screen in awe. But he shut it off as soon as the Founder's prodcast, a series of admonitions and warnings and bribes, uttered for the finding, apprehending, and turning in to the authorities anyone suspicious, was over. With the viewing complete, he relaxed with a sigh, despite her expression of disappointment at the loss of the moving, talking pictures.

"Do not turn this on." Not that she could. The Echosys was coded to his voice, his print and retinal scan, and only another registered sys user could turn the unit on and off for him. Agnys could try, but she would not succeed. The only thing she might succeed in doing was providing the Hub with a log of a series of unregistered access attempts. Such activity might be ignored, might go unquestioned, or it might attract the wrong sort of attention and bring someone around asking questions.

Agnys nodded her head as if she understood, wrapped one arm around herself, and lay her other hand across the arm stretched out beneath her head. She yawned and fell quickly asleep where she lay, confident and comfortable in his care and company.

Rhyd, surprised by the pleasant sense he found in her trust, closed his eyes and allowed himself to sleep again too, assuming she must have eaten on her own while he had slept. This day, he decided, would probably be the most rest he had gotten since Venn had Vanished.

He had never realized before how much his body needed it.

☙Chapter 11❧

ong tether hoses anchored the four individuals in haz suits to the exterior of the dome, providing each with purified, filtered, breathable air through ports that connected them to the city's internal life support systems as they struggled with the jammed solar panel that had become cracked and broken and needed to be replaced. Normally the panels were retracted into Hebenon's shell where trained workers could safely repair damaged units before raising them again. It was generally deemed too hazardous to send anyone onto the shell to do the work as the risks of biological contamination and radiation poisoning were so high on the Outside. But on occasion, it was necessary to equip crews to go out, if the retraction system failed, to determine where the jam had occurred, and change whatever broken pieces needed to be replaced. The team, well-trained and well-drilled for such occasions, wore haz suits and visored helmets that helped them remain visible against the charred-looking surface of the world around Hebanthe Falls and kept them safe from immediate death.

Most systems in the city were driven by the never-ending supply of steam power the falls provided, water and steam that were converted into electricity that kept the city sustainable. There was power generated by a variety of waste recycling and repurposing plants too, a little more output then input to make the process worth the effort. In addition, the entire dome of the city and the rooftops of the three enormous factory complexes were covered with solar arrays that supplemented the system and gave Hebenon more power than she could ever need. Duncan Kemway's plan had accommodated growth for the city, with plans in place to stretch the limits towards the eastern coastline. But despite previous decades of overpopulation, that expansion had never happened. The city had grown a little for the first three generations and then had stagnated through minor growth, significant loss, the boom that had packed too many into too small of a space, and finally the now second great decline. After the last surge had pushed the current infrastructure to capacity, with the supplies intended for expansion having been used elsewhere in days long past, it had been deemed wiser to place reproductive limits on the population. Thanks to those limits and the losses sustained as Heb addiction took its toll, the population was now at a historical, if disconcerting, low. Still crowded below Lev 20, where the bulk of humanity resided, but dwindling nonetheless.

And still the power sources churned out their input, keeping the city alive with relatively little maintenance required.

One of the three holding on to another's tether, as the individual tried to climb the scaffold-like siding leading to the panel array in need of repair, stared absently across the horizon at the jagged peaks in the distance. The sky was bloody crimson, murky and rolling with a constantly shifting layer of clouds that spread across his entire line of sight. The density of contaminants in the air turned everything red, even the foliage, and the tiny buildings to the east, beyond the river's edge, looked like crumbling, decaying monuments to a forgotten history. Steam billowed from the stacks of all three factories, adding to the thickness of the air. The images were occasionally marred with bursts of static as atmospheric interference wreaked havoc with the suit's monitoring systems and created crackling pops of sound in the white noise of rushing wind caused by the conditions outside the suit's protective skin.

No one else in Hebanthe Falls possessed the opportunity to see what remained of the planet humanity had once called home, and not one of them, after their first foray into the Outside, wished to venture into that world without the protection haz suits offered. They had no desire to die the horrible death the red world would surely afford them.

How the parah could survive was a mystery and wonder.

A surprised squawk erupted through the comm unit, making the individual look up…and stagger backward at the impact of the metal wrench against the face shield of his helmet. He jerked away as the glass shattered, exposing his face, his lungs, to the poisoned air. He closed his eyes and held his breath after an initial scream…but not before he beheld a sight that no man in Hebenon had ever witnessed.

Not trusting his senses, he opened his eyes again, but it was too late. The noose of inflatable tubing built into the haz suit's lining around his neck began to fill, expanding quickly, cutting off the flow of oxygen into his body. He choked, coughed, spasmed, his hands around his throat clawing at the tightening there as he struggled for breath. Within less than a minute, he ceased to struggle and his body went limp, hanging from the tether as he slipped down the curve of the dome until he could fall no more, while his coworkers watched, horrified by the swiftness with which the Outside could rob a man of his life.

Haythem Kemway watched the tragedy through the open view screen, watched something fall, strike the faceplate of the other workman below, then watched the fellow flop like a fish removed from water against the blazing blue backdrop of sky. He sighed, perhaps a sound of regret, as he hit the button on the wall that drew the mechanical window covering closed and took away the view of that unfortunate person's fate.

In the doorway behind him, Grainger stopped, thinking for a moment that he had witnessed a twinge of blue beyond the closing panel, but he quickly shook off that notion, explaining away what he thought he had seen by convincing himself it was only the sun's rays refracting off the specially treated glass that had created the burst of blue, not anything that could exist on the Outside.

"The Doctet is assembled, Founder. They await your arrival."

Haythem snorted, wondering without asking what Grainger had seen. If he had witnessed anything out of the ordinary, anything other than what was expected, his expression did not hint at it and he said nothing. "Don't know why; they don't need me for their functions."

But he did know why they waited for him. It was protocol. The Doctet, regardless of what business they had to discuss or why they chose to assemble, was required to include the Founder in any meeting to which at least one-third of the members were attending. Once a week, on a precise schedule, the Doctet gathered to discuss business needs, concerns, and the state of each industry. Since those things did not tend to change quickly, and there were rarely any significant events or emergencies that required attention, the weekly meetings tended to be little more than an excuse to socialize, to break up the monotony of business. Often, Haythem did not object to such mingling. He found it a necessary evil to keep in touch with his council. But lately, he found such socializing to be tedious and annoying.

He would attend, however, because he must, and in truth, he had little else of importance to do until Grainger brought him news of the parah child's capture or that trouble-making vigilante's arrest.

With no news about either topic, Haythem was in a decidedly mixed mood.

"Tell them I'm on my way…"

"Father!" came a voice as his son and the heir to Hebanthe Falls' title of Founder bounded into the chamber alone. It was surprising to see him there, as most often the three children were together, with their mother or tutor, but Haythem liked to indulge his children, particularly his son, and beckoned him closer with open arms as Grainger started out. "Has anyone seen the girl yet? Has she been found?"

Face puckered in disbelief, Haythem asked, "What girl?" In the doorway, Grainger stopped to listen.

"The parah. The one who got in. Has she been found?"

"What do you know about that?" Haythem did his best to keep such troubling news away from his children's ears. At four, six and eight, they were too young, he believed, to understand or be burdened by such worries. "Who spoke of it?"

It was possible the boy had seen a prodcast, or heard other children talking about it, but Haythem wanted to be sure that no one was speaking to his children who should not be, about things they should not know.

"I saw her."

Grainger looked taken aback, and when the Founder looked at him, all he could do was shrug.

"Saw her? When?"

Duncan Kemway the Fourth looked between his father's face and the familiar dark one with all of the guile and innocence of his youth. "The day she came in…I saw her in the tunnel…helping load empty crates onto the wagons."

"What were you doing…?"

"Master Isaacs wanted me to see how it is done…how trade is conducted with the parah. He said it is important to understand such things if I'm to lead someday."

Haythem growled, a sound that made the boy cower but Duncan did not flee any potential wrath and castigation. He had already learned at his young age that trying to avoid punishment only made matters worse. It was better to face his father and take any reprimand that might be given.

But Haythem's growl was not at his son, nor at Grainger. Nor was it even at Dean Isaacs who oversaw the hemp exchange and processing facilities. Haythem had been the one to suggest and encourage such outings for his son. It was no one's fault but his own that his son happened to be there the day Hebanthe Falls was invaded by its first-ever parah…or that Haythem himself had forgotten that his son had been scheduled to be there that day. If there was any fault, it was that Isaacs had not reminded the Founder of this sooner.

If the parah had exposed his son to harmful contagions, it was the Founder's right to know.

"I'm sorry you had to see that," Haythem said sympathetically as he brushed off his annoyance and lifted the boy onto his hip. "It must have been frightening…"

"I'm not afraid of a girl," Duncan said indignantly, "as long as I don't have to dance with one." He grimaced at the repulsive thought.

"Not afraid? But you saw her…"

"A girl with yellow hair…littler than me but not as little as Flora."

Haythem's scowl grew deeper, but this time rather than direct it at his son, he looked again at Grainger. The security team was looking for a monster child, someone with obvious deformities and afflictions from a short lifetime of exposure to the Outside and generations of genetic mutations caused by that same exposure.

What if they were wrong? What if the child was no monster, as was initially assumed? What if, despite their beliefs and everything they knew, the child appeared normal, like every other child in Hebanthe Falls? How were his officers to find her? And if she, and the body in Lima's lab, were the norm for parah in the village near East 4, then was the Outside as toxic as the Founders touted? Could the Founder continue to make that claim if there was proof to the contrary?

How, Haythem wondered, was he supposed to counter that?

Grainger feeling the dilemma of a question he too would like to have answered, a question which immediately brought to memory the fleeting glimpse of blue he thought he had seen through the window, cleared his throat and said, "Founder…the Doctet is waiting."

Relieved for the disruption, Haythem put Duncan down and ruffled his hair. "We will discuss this later, yes?" Later might give him the opportunity to come up with answers for the boy, especially if his counselors demanded answers for that same questionable rumor.

Use to such interruptions though no less disappointed, Duncan nodded obediently and said, "Yes, Father." He skipped across the room, then realized at the last moment that skipping was undignified, and forced himself to exhibit a statelier pace as he went out.

Haythem wondered, for the briefest moment, if he should allow the boy more freedom to be a child while he still could be.

∾Chapter 12∾

Taking an indirect path to Vapors meant spending twice as long as normal to get there, but Rhyd had to keep track of Agnys, to make sure she stayed close without anyone noticing them. He did not think she looked suspicious, despite being dressed in one of his undershirts, but he did not want to raise questions among those who might recognize him, did not want anyone to be too curious about the child with the blonde-white hair who had never been in his company before. He did not have answers after all, nor was he successfully coming up with any as they paused now and again to adjust his shirt around her or to allow him the chance to listen and look for potential threats at intersections and vindis where he knew Crows to frequent.

Thankfully, he encountered no one he knew or recognized except vindi owners, not even the fellow Lash when they left the flat, and though he needed to drag Agnys away from the horde of cats, there were no significant delays, nor a sighting of a single Crow.

That, in itself, felt off, and he wondered fleetingly, as he pushed back Vapors beaded curtain door to usher the child into the dimness, if perhaps the Crow he had encountered in the tunnels, or another of their number, had died. A dead Crow often meant a gathering in whatever place they called home in order to mourn their loss.

He did not want a death on his hands. If it was too late for that, it could not be helped.

He stopped abruptly at the sight of the trio of mostly nude andi dancers on the platform and then shielded the girl's eyes as he quickly herded her to the bar and placed her onto a stool to sit with her back to the stage. It was a useless effort. He could not keep his hand over her eyes the entire time they were here, and the wall of liquor shelves contained a mirrored back that reflected the performance for the enjoyment of those seated there. No matter what Rhyd did, Agnys was going to be subjected to an environment of leering people, loud music and voices, the pungent cloud of alcohol and smoke, and dancing andis she would never have seen before.

For the moment, at least she seemed more fascinated with the flashing, multicolored lights than anything the dancers or their audience were doing.

Maemi took one look at Rhyd and the child at his side, opened her mouth to say something scolding, utter some admonition, but she refrained long enough to wave Skelter to the bar from across the room where he appeared to be engrossed in some sort of deal-making with three others, a young mop-top of a fellow, a dwarf, and another whose long gray jacket had its' hood pulled up to hide their head, their face, and hair.

Might have been three men, might have been two men and a woman. Rhyd only knew, by the cut of mop-top's figure, that he and the dwarf, at least, were male.

He shook the distracting vision of them out of his head.

It appeared Maemi's usual help was not here, but Skelter had enough experience behind the bar, mixed in with his many other talents, to manage Vapors for a short time. It took her serving several more drinks to escape duty, but when Skelter was in place, his visual assessment telling the redhead all he believed he needed to know about the situation, Maemi squeezed past Rhyd, her hand on his arm, and muttered against his ear, "You…with me. Now."

Not about to leave Agnys alone in a sea of strangers, even if he could have pried her off of his arm to escape her, Rhyd followed with the child in tow, through the kitchen full with the smells of cheese curlers, burgers and vegiburgs, and chips. Up the short set of stairs that it took to bring them into the flat Maemi shared with her nephew, his mother, and her mother-in-law. The elder woman was downstairs cooking, the other woman about whatever work she did for a living, and Xiaodan was passed upon the stairs. He gave Rhyd and the child a curious glance before Maemi scolded, "Get on with you…don't keep Tox waiting."

"Yes, Yima," he said politely and hurried the rest of the way down the steps, around the corner, and out of sight.

Maemi closed and locked the door of the flat before speaking in a strained, terse tone. "This her then? The par…" She knew she had to be right. What other child would be in Rhyd's company?

"Parah," Agnys said in a near whisper. She had heard the word many times, spoken by the birdmen during the trades, and knew it somehow applied to her though she seemed to have no idea that it carried negative connotations and was not meant to be a compliment.

"This is Agnys," Rhyd corrected, finding the word parah offensive for the first time. It had been one thing to use it as an anonymous label when he had no experience of those on the Outside it applied to. It had been drilled into them from infancy, an easy thing to believe the communal knowledge of hideous mutated things, once human, who lived beyond Hebenon in the poison air. Agnys, at least was not one of those things; calling her anything other than human felt wrong.

Looking at the girl, he pointed at the dark-skinned woman and said, "Maemi."

Agnys hesitantly touched Maemi's hand, then examined her fingers, as if expecting the pigment to come away on her skin. When it did not, she smiled tentatively and repeated, "Maemi."

"She doesn't understand most of what I say…at least I don't think she does," Rhyd explained, "but at least we've gotten to names." His tone hinted at surprise that she could speak and communicate at all.

"You shouldn't have brought her…"

"Nowhere else to take her. I don't have food…or clothes…or any other nessies a kid needs…and I can't leave her alone at the flat.

Already missed shift today because of her. She can't be there alone, can't be anywhere alone. It isn't smart…or safe."

Maemi sank into a cushioned chair, studying the girl, and then held open her arms to her. After a glance at Rhyd as if seeking permission, Agnys presumed an embrace was safe and accepted the offering of lap and hug without a word. She might not understand their language, but some gestures, it appeared, were universal. "I don't think it's gonna be safe for her anywhere," Maemi crooned as she stroked the girl's hair. "What'll you do?"

"Dunno." He raked his hand through his hair and began to pace a few steps back and forth. "I don't think getting her back Outside is an option…getting up to any of the trade shafts is damn near impossible. But I'm gonna look into it." There was little other choice, but they might have to make do with second best until then. "Right now, all I can do is…"

"All we can do is feed you, Qinai…something more than fruits and nuts and pickled fish and cheese." She gave him a teasing grin that barely masked the tension behind it. Asking anyone for help in this situation was asking them to take a huge risk, but if it was not one he was willing to take himself, one he had accepted the moment he had begun looking for the girl, he would not have asked.

But as he had said, he was not, Maemi knew, equipped with either food or clothing, or the emotional strength perhaps…to manage a child. Maemi was already surprised by how comfortable he appeared to be with the girl hanging against him the way she had been. Rhyd was not the sort of man to welcome others into his physical space. Not anymore. Not since Venn.

"She likes it," he protested half-heartedly. Admittedly, she had likely been starving, and any food was better than no food, but she had not seemed displeased with what he gave her. After a skeptical look from Maemi, he shrugged and added, "Except pickled fish." He was not a fan of that himself, but it was something he could keep in his icebox that did not spoil so quickly, and so he kept it on hand for those times when he was hungry and had nothing else to eat…and was too tired to make it to Vapors. Emergency rations, he called them.

"You should cook her a proper meal."

He glowered at her scolding, though he knew she was right and meant well. But other than an occasional omelet, Rhyd had not cooked since Venn had Vanished. And he had not had anything on hand to cook. Asking it of him now was no casual thing. "I need to go out...I need recon...news." Skelter might have some, but it was unlikely to be enough. Rhyd looked at Agnys, glad now that she could not understand what he was saying. "She can stay here? With you?"

Maemi's scowl went unseen behind Agnys' head. "I have to get back down..."

"Tox then. Hell...Zara..." He ignored the woman's incredulous look. Zara was lovely, trustworthy and kind, but a child's caregiver? And given her connection with Skelter, and her assorted careers, was placing this particular child in Zara's care a safe and proper option?

Maemi sighed, however, got to her feet, and went into the kitchen where she removed a pot and pan from her cupboard, intending to cook something more substantial then what Rhyd had yet to offer Agnys. When it got down to it Zara and Skelter, in their circle of friends, were likely the safest caretakers Rhyd could find. Given Skelter's known propensity for taking in occasional streeters for jobs, as dancers, as an odd bit of charity or for a favor here and there, no one would think twice about a child in his care.

"Talk to Skelter...if he agrees..."

Rhyd nodded. Squatting in front of the chair where Agnys now was, where she had been left when Maemi went behind the kitchen counter, he took both of her hands in one of his and tucked a wisp of blonde behind her ear. She had been watching back and forth between them as if trying to understand their conversation, but it did not appear that she did. "I have work...I have to go out..."

She might not understand his words, but her trembling pout made it appear she understood his intent well enough. "I'll be back with someone...you stay with her...with them...until I'm back, okay?"

As her skillet sizzled with heating oil, Maemi observed the interplay discreetly, hearing the words, particularly the last few, that spoke of either a sense of obligation from Rhyd or else an attempt to assuage the child with promises he did not mean to keep. Because she had never seen him interact with children, she was uncertain which was his intent.

"You come back for her," she scolded, less for her own sake and safety then for the child's…and for Rhyd's peace of mind. Say what he would about it later, it was Maemi's opinion that having the child to focus his attention on, having someone other than himself to think about, would do Rhyd a world of good.

Rhyd grunted as he lay his hand on Agnys' head and then disappeared through the door before she cried and changed his mind, intending to first talk to Skelter, to Zara, and then to take care of business. He needed to know what the status of the parah hunt was. He needed to know how safe Agnys might be with him. Or how unsafe. Perhaps he should take her to a herpa. Perhaps a man or woman of faith and conviction, someone who commonly served streeters and tingers, would be the best caretaker for her. Such a choice would keep his friends safe.

But having witnessed and intervened in chapel raids and the roundup of the youngest streeters on the Levs, the Scarecrow of Hebenon suspected that the chapels were one place he could never leave her. She would not be wise enough to keep silent about where she came from, and the odds of anyone, particularly inexperienced children or some streeter hoping for the reward of enough ticks for another hit, betraying her to the Crows, was too high.

No, Agnys was safer with Maemi, Zara, Skelter, and Tox. There was certainly enough of them to keep an eye on one little girl, which was something Rhyd could not do. He was not cut out to be a parent. He wanted to be alone. Far better, he believed, that she be somewhere with caring, affectionate, stable people…not an emotionally stunted vigilante no longer fit or suited for sharing life with another person.

☙*❧

"We found something, Founder."

Haythem rose from his lounge chair, prying himself from between his two oldest children and setting the youngest, and the handheld XCO 237T2 device they had been reading from, down where he had been sitting, to join Captain Grainger near the door. Neoma, her expression languid where she lay by the narrow, shallow pool, gave Grainger, or perhaps her husband, a cool glance of perusal, and then lay her head down on her arms again and closed her eyes to continue enjoying the warmth of the UV lamp and the cool artificial breeze blowing across the water's surface over her skin.

"I want good news," the Founder growled, his back to his children and wife to keep them from seeing his stern expression or hearing his hard-edged voice.

"Perhaps. In the shaft, where the parah fell, we found this snagged on a loose bolt." He offered Haythem the gold musical note pendant. While the flat surface was smooth, save for a pronged setting where some sort of stone had once nested, the back contained an engraving. Haythem rubbed his thumb over the infinity symbol and a stylized letter R.

"A worker's?" It was unlikely, though not impossible, that this could belong to one of the Crows or one of his sentries. They were forbidden to wear jewelry or identifying personal items while on duty.

Grainger shook his head. "There have been none scheduled in those tunnels since she came, to avoid contaminating the scene or…finding her…themselves. We are examining the Archives to determine who might have worked there in the weeks prior." The pendant could not have been there any longer than that. It was not tarnished enough.

Turning the gold note around several times in his hand, Haythem pondered its significance. Perhaps someone, one of his sentries, one of the Crows, had disobeyed command and worn this…losing it in the shafts and never making a report so they would not be punished for the mistake. Or perhaps it had been dropped there to hide it when the guilty had realized they had not removed it before duty…and though they may have intended to return for it, had not. Perhaps it was a relic from Earth's ancient past, found by a parah, polished and worn or kept as some sort of trophy. Most troublesome, however, was the possibility that the parah themselves had created this.

Haythem quickly set that thought aside. It did not fit into the nature of the Outside world he envisioned. It was impossible that a parah could have made this. Could have used a letter of their written alphabet. Could know what a musical note was.

The final possibility was one he was even less inclined to consider. If it held any validity, then this parah might not be a child at all…and might be a spy or saboteur sent to make contact with someone inside the city. The possibility of a conspiracy between the Levs, or even someone in the Uppers, and the parah horde, sent a chill up his spine.

"I want all of your people questioned…investigated. Find out if any of them own this…or could have. And question anyone who has access to those vents." The pool of workers with access to the Uppers systems was small. Questioning them, at least, should take less time than questioning every Crow in Hebanthe Falls.

"Yes, sir." Thinking himself dismissed, Grainger turned to go.

"And Captain…"

The darker man looked back into the fanatically flashing eyes of the Founder, surprised that the man had caught his arm when he rarely touched anyone except his children, unless it was a handshake or some other expected public gesture.

"I want a thorough search of the Uppers. Every home…every business. Every corner, every drawer, every crevice. I want that thing's owner found. I want anything suspicious confiscated and brought to me…only me. And I want that child," he shuddered at the use of the word, "brought to me at once."

The frown he felt reached Grainger's eyes but his expression remained otherwise neutral. Such a search and seizure in the Uppers had never been carried out in his lifetime, and he could not recall when the last one might have been. If there had ever been one. The Doctet and their families, as well as the rest of Hebenon's elite, would be understandably displeased by this invasion of their privacy…as if they were lowly Lev residents.

It would not be an easy task to undertake, an easy duty to fulfill, but Grainger would do his best.

He nodded and said again, "Yes, Founder," before gratefully retreating from the man's presence. Sometimes he wished he better understood this man. Most days, however, like this one, he was thankful he did not.

≫*≪

He had unintentionally fallen asleep on the sofa with the Echosys still running through the day's recorded prodcasts and was abruptly jarred awake by a rare knocking upon his flat door. A quick peek at his wrist chrono revealed he had slept no more than thirty minutes, since he recalled the official Founder prodcast ending and that had been nearly thirty minutes ago. Yawning, surprised he had slept as much this day as he had, the most sleep he had gotten in over two years that had not been alcohol induced, he shuffled to the door and spied through the peephole in case whoever was there had not come for social reasons but rather to arrest him.

Not that such people would knock politely.

They had not done so the last time.

He groaned and opened the door, unable to ignore the two people who waited in the cold damp outside. As soon as the door was open, Agnys, now dressed in a plain green dress, dark leggings, and tiny black boots...much like any other little girl in Hebanthe Falls, flew through it and clung to his waist with a sound that might have been a sob of relief...but he could not believe it had been.

Zara closed the door with a sympathetic, apologetic, shrug. "I'm sorry; she insisted on seeing you. Maemi thought it best. She tried to come on her own when you did not return. I thought it better to bring her, to come in case you were not here, to show her you were not."

And here he was.

There was no condemnation or judgment. Whatever Rhyd had been out doing that evening, with a day of work scheduled the following day, Zara knew he was not likely to be out all night. He needed to be rested and clear-headed.

Where he took that rest, however, was none of Zara's concern.

Hand on Agnys' hair, stroking through it as one might a cat's head, Rhyd shook his head and tried to hide his frown. "She can't stay here...it isn't safe..."

"Safer than her being out there, looking for you," Zara pointed out. "You saved her life. I think you're stuck with her."

"I don't want to be..." The thought made him glower. He could not be stuck with the girl. He was not her family. Not a parent. He could not take care of a child. He could barely take care of himself. "She has nowhere to sleep!"

Toying with the ends of her long blonde hair, Zara studied the room in which they stood, as much of the flat as she could see. She had only been here a few times, attempting to avoid the public possibility of being seen here when Skelter's clients knew she never went home with anyone. Tonight, however, there had been no choice.

"There looks good enough...where she slept before, I assume? Good enough for now at least," she added as she pointed at the sofa with its blankets and pillow that suggested someone had slept there recently. She did not seem to realize that it had served as Rhyd's bed of choice for more than two dozen months.

Or maybe, Rhyd thought, his scowl deepening, she did.

"But I work..."

"And I'll come in the morning," she promised with a grin down at the child and an offering of the long, feathery yellow scarf she wore. Agnys giggled and let go of Rhyd's waist long enough to snatch the offering from Zara's hand and wrap it around her neck. "Lock her in...feed her before you go. Maemi's bringing nessies tomorrow...so she'll have what Agnys needs...and I'll bring puzzles and games. She'll be okay. No one will think twice about it."

No one would think twice unless Zara's visits appeared to be a habit. Skelter's clients...her clients...would question it, even if no one else did.

His sigh, tangled with a groan of temporary defeat and surrender, hissed out between his teeth as he unlaced the girl's arms from around him again and directed her towards the sofa. "She better be," he grunted. "If I come home…and she isn't…"

Zara smiled understandingly and embraced him, kissing one cheek and then the other. "She will be. I promise." She waved at Agnys, blew her a kiss, and murmured, "Goodnight, little one," and hastily retreated before Rhyd could make further protest and find some way to get out of the duty and responsibility he had undertaken. As much as she enjoyed the company of unassuming children, as much as she enjoyed playing with them and teaching them, this time, Zara agreed with Maemi. Agnys might be what Rhyd needed to get back into living again…though hopefully not at the expense of Scarecrow.

❧Chapter 13❧

The room was white. It did not need to be; there was no rule written anywhere to dictate the décor in the Uppers. But the Founder's home, the collection of rooms surrounding his office where his family resided and where he sought refuge when not tending to city business, had always been white. The earliest images of the first Duncan Kemway in the place where Haythem stood now, smiling with a mixture of melancholy regret and pride in the rooms that were to be his home when Hebanthe Falls sealed its doors against the rest of the world, showed the walls to be white, and not one Founder since that day had changed it. The furniture changed, some of the bedrooms and other personal rooms changed according to the tastes of the ruling Founder and his family, or when they were replaced for disrepair, but this particular room never did.

It was always white.

Haythem's father, a man of contrasts, had sported black furnishings against the white of the walls, ceiling, and floor. Haythem, however, preferred white, from the lamp fixtures above his head down to the plush hemp carpet that spread across the middle of the room in front of the holo-fireplace that flickered and glowed against the far wall. The children, none of whom shared his preference for white, had shuffled off to bed, their bare feet trudging sleepily away before his wife's guidance, leaving Haythem at the fireplace, staring at the counterfeit flames with his hands clenched behind his back.

There was no conscious thought, no mulling over the issues facing Hebanthe Falls tonight. Use to matters of economics and population control, health concerns and petty crimes, such major issues as the vigilante haunting the Levs and the infiltration of the city by a single parah child were sapping Haythem's strength. He was weary, tired of thinking, and tonight all he wanted was to sleep and forget.

He did not hear Neoma's return, did not know how long she stood behind him before she spoke, but he recognized the low tone of her growl as she said, "You have gone too far this time."

"Too far?" he hissed through his teeth, not knowing precisely what she was referring to but able to make an educated guess.

"Mandatory searches of every home in the Uppers? Really? All of this for what? Your paranoia has gone too far this time…"

"All of this to find a parah," he snorted, noting with triumph the horror that crossed her face. As much as she might side with the others of their station against his invasion of their privacy, his reason was entirely justified.

"A parah? In the Uppers? How?"

"In the city…somewhere. Got in through East 4." He did not explain how she had gotten in, or when, or that the parah was a child. That did not matter. "The only clue we have demands that I search…"

"But our homes, Haythem! Surely none of us would harbor…"

"She did not vanish? She is not invisible. She is here, somewhere, and I will find her. The diseases…the toxins…the contaminants she must have brought inside, Neoma! This is the single greatest threat Hebanthe Falls has ever faced. She must be found. Immediately. Whatever it takes."

Normally calm and collected, Neoma's hands were trembling when she clutched Haythem's and pulled them to her chest. She was not seeking comfort but she was, he knew, forcing him to look at her by that action. She could not believe their friends and acquaintances would knowingly harbor or protect a parah threat, but being a staunch believer in the horrors of the Outside, and those who lived there, she had no doubt about the sort of danger such infiltration would present to all of them, the Uppers and Levs alike.

"You will find this parah…eradicate her…won't you, Haythem? You will not fail us?"

The corners of his mouth twitched. There was a tick at the corner of one eye and his jaw clenched. Those words were a challenge, but they also revealed, in the fear his wife expressed, that she expected him to do precisely that.

To fail.

"As I said, whatever it takes. I will find her. You and the children are safe."

Neoma kissed his hands without breaking his gaze, a rare gesture meant to seal his words between them as a promise. Her expression warned him of retaliation, if he failed, and then she stalked from the sitting room without another word.

Haythem's fists balled at his side and he growled.

His hands clenched and unclenched in his sleep, an act of frustration or disquiet that Agnys could read though she did not know what it meant. She did not understand him, this stranger who had found her, who cared for her, who had taken her in. Who knew how to fight and yet hid here, in the dark, alone the rest of the time. And his words, those she did understand, made little sense without a context to put them in.

What she did understand was that, in spite of every warning she had been given about what lived within the metal nest, this was no birdman. He could be trusted. He said as much, the stranger taken into the village, one of many who had joined them over the years, but she had never imagined actually seeing this man's face. Or any nest-man's face. She was the first of her village, her kind, to come into the misty fall city, to prove that the birdmen were not alone here, were not the majority. The first to see that there were good people, normal people, in this damp place, pale people, dark people, people she believed would be happier, better, if they could see the sun the way she had. Not one face seen in her few days here looked honestly happy. They seemed trapped, but she had no idea how, why they could not leave. Perhaps, she mused as she got up from her cross-legged position, the birdmen kept them from escaping. The birdmen certainly controlled what came in and out of the stone and metal tunnels.

It was a fluke that had allowed her to get past them. She would be lucky if she ever got out.

Wrestling. Laughter. Damn, it felt good to laugh.

Though slighter of build by a fraction, he was stronger, and his childhood training meant that he quickly had the dark-haired man pinned beneath him in the synthetic dek field of knee-high grass. The scent of earth, of grass, of ozone in the air that suggested an impending storm, was a heady perfume more intoxicating then any Zaolei Rhyd had ever consumed. Venn curled his hands around Rhyd's to push him up and off, but the effort was halfhearted…and ended with Rhyd collapsing to one side where he lay staring at the clouds in the blue sky above, still laughing, his head against Venn's shoulder.

"So that is what a cloud looks like…"

Climbing onto the back of the sofa, Agnys sat with her feet dangling, staring at the painted image of a field that hung on the wall. She had never seen anything like it, a field where there was no field, grass and flowers where there were none, a static, stylized, flat display showing a world she missed. She missed her cousin, her uncle. She missed the people in her village. She missed the sun and the soil between her toes, missed scented flower petals and wet leaves and the fur of the animals, missed being able to run and play with others her age. She missed not being afraid. As young as she was, however, she understood that getting out of the metal nest would not be as easy as getting in had been.

Reluctantly, she was coming to terms with the notion that she might never leave this place.

One of many performances, Venn was supported by the small Hebanthe Falls orchestra for which he had fought hard for the title of lead cellist since he was a child. Last night's celebration of the appointment, and too much Zaolei, had not hampered his ability to perform, and the audience, the first of many Venn Weyer was to entertain in his new role, was smitten. Men and women alike gathered around him as the music bled away, absorbed into Hebenon's walls, people who felt lucky, privileged, to share those moments of near divinity with the bearded darling of Hebenon's premier orchestra. There was talk already of being asked to play in the Uppers, for the Founder, a dream come true that might, Rhyd knew, lead them both to the chance of advancement in society, if they were lucky, if those above were fortunate enough to hear Venn play.

But none of them were as lucky, Rhyd thought as he watched the other man with pride, as he was.

She sniffed and wiped her nose on the back of her fist. It was her fault she was here, that she had made her cousin and uncle and others worry. She should have listened, should not have let her curiosity win the battle against wisdom that day. But she had needed to know what was inside. Needed to know that the stories were true. She needed to know what the elders were hiding from her, from so many.

The metal stairs were slippery, slick with mist and fall spray, the way they always were. No one in Hebenon expected anything else.

Everyone was careful, yet sometimes accidents happened. A turn, a playful grab at Rhyd's arm, and a pulling away by the blonde who, in a fit of pique had not wanted to be touched, and the other man tumbled, cello in its case the first to hit, to bounce down the stairs, to the landing below, stopping outside the apartment door at the feet of the stringy-haired blonde man who looked at Rhyd with confusion and reached one hand down to help the dark-haired man to his feet.

Rhyd did not trust him. The fall had been his fault. He should be the one helping…

"Venn!"

The cry startled her and she fell back onto the cushions behind her. She stared and tried to climb carefully away, not wanting to wake him. He did not stir beyond calling out that name in his sleep for the second time, his head moving back and forth in denial. His fists were clenched tight, his chest began to heave and flush red as he gasped and wheezed. That much, his struggle to breathe, she understood, and though she did not understand how the tank worked, she knew from observation that pushing the button and holding the mask over Rhyd's nose and mouth would allow him to breathe more easily. She turned the tank on, climbed onto the arm of the chair where he slept and pressed the mask to his face. Almost immediately, his body began to relax as the effort to take in oxygen lessened.

He did not wake…and she wondered why he would not sleep in the other rooms…why he chose to be in this uncomfortable position. Was it just to watch over her? Something about those rooms frightened him, seemed to hurt him. Perhaps it was because of the faces in the pictures he had turned down so they could not see him…and so he could not see them.

But why, she thought with concern, did he still not wake?

He could hear him, hear the voice, the weeping, and feel the stirring of the cello strings from where it rested, though the instrument's owner was not to be seen. Frantically he searched the flat but knew he was alone without doing so. Beyond the open door, in the dimly lit steam and spray, the voice continued to beckon, but what he saw there were shadows and vague amorphous forms. A step into the street and the door slammed behind him. The tonal hum of vibrating strings grew louder, and though he tried to open the door, feeling certain Venn was there when he had not been before, it would not budge. Through the window he could see the instrument, upright, leaning against the table, vibrating and swaying as if in the hands of its master, but no one was holding it. There was an image with long blond strands of hair in the window to his right who, at Rhyd's pounding, peered at him with a distant, vaguely irritated expression.

Rhyd stumbled back against the rail that kept him from tumbling from one Lev to another, surprised by what he had seen and not understanding it. Then his own face in the window, hands splayed against the glass with an expression of horror as booted footsteps stole upon him from the right without the door there ever opening.

The long-haired man again, looking on with concern. Rhyd opened his mouth, coughed, choked, and spit blood into his open palm. He wiped his aching, swollen nose with the other hand, feeling as if he had been struck, as if his nose had been broken when he could not remember it happening. More blood. The blonde was staring still, offering a handkerchief without a spoken word and with no other indication that he could be trusted.

How could he be when he was intruding in private dreams where he had never been before?

Rhyd could not breathe. His visage in the window was sliding, melting, fading with the sound of the cello. Venn's distant voice had ceased. The world was turning red. Another cough, and his knees buckled.

Hesitant fingers slid down the gold chain around the man's neck, though her eyes were focused on the scars and bruises scattered across his torso. The corners of her mouth drooped into a frown. So much hurt there. And too sad, she thought again, as she lifted the pendant with its tiny white stone from the hollow at his throat. She did not know the symbol, did not comprehend it or its significance, but she had seen it before.

When he felt, from the depth of his sleep, fingers against his flesh, felt the ever-present weight of that slight pendent lift from his skin, it was enough to jolt Rhyd out of the perplexing series of disjointed dream images. He caught her wrist, a reflex even in sleep, and as his vision cleared from the dream-red to the normal dimness of the room, he and Agnys stared at one another. Her mouth opened to speak, but fear kept her from it, the first fear she had shown of him in some time. He counted slowly to ten, breathing deeply of the oxygen he had not put into place himself, even before realizing that it was her other hand that held the mask to his face. Calm again, and grateful for the unexpected act of assistance, he released her.

Only then did she relax.

"Venn?" she asked, tugging on the necklace lightly as if to indicate the word she spoke was connected to the symbol between her fingers.

"He gave it to me, yes…we bought them together."

He remembered that day as if it was yesterday, the celebratory day Venn had passed his first audition to Hebenon's primary orchestra. It was an expensive bit of celebrating, but one Venn had insisted on.

Rhyd had never learned where the ticks had come from to make the purchase. The claim that they were a bonus from the orchestra for completing, passing, the first audition had never seemed right to Rhyd.

"Venn." She nodded, slid off the arm of the chair, and disappeared into the bathroom. Moments later, she returned with the soiled sack dress she had worn when he found her, her hand fishing in the pocket as she stared at him. What she brought forth, what she offered in the palm of her hand, made his heart skip. He shook his head, refusing to believe what he saw.

A gold chain could belong to anyone. Not many in the Levs owned such luxuries it was true, but Venn's bonus had been enough for the purchase. The purchase was made a mere three months prior to his Vanishing, and Rhyd had been unable, unwilling, to take it off since.

He shook his head again. It could not be.

"Venn," Agnys repeated. This time, she put the chain into Rhyd's shaky hand.

Despite the clutching, squeezing ache in his chest and the pounding in his temples behind his eyes, he took the time to study the chain in the relative darkness of the room, hoping at least she would leave him be with her persistent repetition of the other man's name. After a few moments of his thumb and forefinger rubbing against the gold ribbing, he got up, turned on the light in the kitchen where it was brightest, and slipped his own necklace from over his head for the first time. Side by side, beneath that brighter lighting, the chains were exactly the same linkage pattern. The clasp on the one Agnys had given him, however, was broken as if it had been yanked free, and the pendant had been lost, but what were the odds that this chain was the same, the twin?

The one Venn had worn?

"Where…?"

Maybe Agnys understood the word. Maybe it was the look on his face or his tone of voice that she understood. She pointed at the ceiling. Pointed up. Rhyd's breath caught again in his ever-tightening chest.

The Vanished had to be moved to the Uppers. It was an obvious truth that everyone believed because there were not many other possibilities except for the mythical Core that no one knew for certain existed. If the Vanished were held anywhere in the Levs, Rhyd would have found them by now, and if the Core was real, he would have found that too. He knew where every shaft, every pipe, every filt line in the Levs ran. But his C-Pass would not allow him into the Uppers, most from the Levs never got beyond Lev 20, and so somewhere above that was the logical place to take those who had been arrested for treason…or suspicion of treason. Or the streeters. Or any other people deemed undesirable to live amongst the normal population.

What happened to them there, however, was unknown.

"Did you see him? Where? Where did you find this? Did he give it to you?"

Agnys could not answer in words, in any way that was helpful, but instead, she continued to point at the ceiling. Rhyd growled in frustration. It was unlikely she had seen Venn, even in passing, or that Venn could have given this to her to give to a man she did not know, had never seen, would find impossible to locate. How could he have communicated any of those desires to a child in fleeting moments of contact when their languages were incompatible? How could he have told her who Rhyd was, how to find him, where to find him? It was illogically insane and yet now that he held the string of gold in his hand, it was a dream Rhyd's soul latched onto with fervent hope.

What seemed more likely was that the necklace had been lost during his arrest, that it had fallen into the vent systems through a grate and that Agnys, in her days there alone, trying to stay alive, had found it. That she could have found it, and then found Rhyd, to give it back to him seemed a chance too full of coincidence, and yet she had found it…and had returned it to him. He held it now.

Maybe some sort of divine fate had brought this to him. A sign. For hope? For remembrance? For a chance to make peace and let the past go? Or something else?

The shift change siren punctuated the silence with its startling shrill sound. Rhyd looked at his chrono and frowned. "I have to go," he grunted hastily, shoving both chains into his pocket as he scrambled about the house for his work clothing. "You have to stay here."

Zara had not arrived yet, but Rhyd trusted that she would soon enough. She had promised she would be. "You know where the food is…take what you want. Don't touch the cello…stay away from the windows…stay inside."

His words littered his actions until he threw on his coat and opened the door. He turned, used both hands to gesture for Agnys to stay inside the room, the same gesture he had used in their first meeting, but this time he was greeted with smoldering terror on the child's face.

It was exactly the same, the same terror he had seen in Venn's eyes as the Crows dragged him out of sight.

As in his dream, though without the blood or the ghostly echo of the cello or Venn's distant voice, Rhyd dropped to his knees. Awkwardly, he opened his arms; Agnys closed the distance between them before Rhyd's knees touched the wet metal ground and she hugged him hard.

"I will be back. I promise. Zara will be here soon." He still did not believe Agnys belonged here, in his home, still intended to find her a better, safer place then he could offer, one with parents, if possible, who were capable of raising a child, but he admitted he did not like to see her frightened. "Stay here, where it is safe. Wait for Zara…please."

Agnys knew Zara's name. That helped to calm her. Fifteen feet away, his neighbor's door opened and the man and a host of cats came into the street. The man paused long enough to glance at them before sliding past and down the stairs towards one of the lower two Levs. Afraid of what the man, an unknown to Rhyd who had lent a menacing flavor to his dreams, might do now that he had seen an unfamiliar girl in Rhyd's home, Rhyd shooed her inside with a desperate, "Zara will be here soon. Stay inside until then. Please."

"Please."

Rhyd, accepting her repetition of the word as confirmation, understanding, and agreement with his instruction, got to his feet and closed the door. He was going to be late, but having taken an ill day the day before, he hoped his tardiness would be attributed to some lingering degree of ill health and overlooked. He was rarely late. He was one of the most skilled, punctual, steadfast bilgers Hebenon had.

❧*❧

The nine adult test subjects, men and women from the Levs, all of differing ages and ethnicities, were line up within the cubicles, immobilized by binding straps and slabs on either side of their bodies that made escape an impossibility. Some were former streeters, taken before they could endanger themselves or others further, were incapacitated by their own Heb use, but such were needed as a control, a parameter in the search for how, or why, an Outside child could be immune to a drug specifically created for population control.

The serums, concoctions of antibodies taken, synthesized, replicated from the blood of the deceased parah, had been given to another nine subjects, kept in identical cubes across the room, while others, now being secured into place on a third wall, were exposed to whatever elements, toxins, or parasites had been on the parah's skin, in his stomach, in his lungs. Later, they too would be tested with various levels of Hebenon to learn their reactions to it, to try to narrow down the elements that might serve as an inhibitor for the drug's effect.

The process would take time. The best scientific research always did. Tamner knew this, even though he and Lima were being given no opportunity to refuse this rushed duty or to argue its illogical approach beyond Tamner's one feeble protest. Founder Kemway wanted answers, wanted assurances of the city's health and security, and he wanted them as quickly as possible. That it was assurance the two scientists could not legitimately, accurately give in the time frame it was demanded did not matter. They would give the Founder what they could, accurate, complete, or not, and Kemway would do with it as he would. When, if, their assurances proved faulty, as Tamner feared they would, they too would endure the fate of the Vanished.

Whatever that fate happened to be.

Tamner let the injector hiss against his subject's arm and looked at Lima to his left as the other man did the same to someone else. They were running out of time to protect themselves. But what else, Tamner thought grimly, were they supposed to do?

❧*❦

"Tsk…you should not be out here, child." Zara did her best to keep fear and anger from her face and voice as she descended the stairs nearest to Rhyd's flat to find Agnys sitting cross-legged on the grating in front of the door with a gaggle of cats around her as she petted them happily and fed them bits of pickled fish. The door behind her was closed, and Zara guessed she had been locked out in the cold and wet, long enough to have accumulated the sheen of moisture over her skin that had soaked into her hair and clothes. How she had gotten out to begin with, since Zara assumed Rhyd had locked the door when he left, she could not guess. Maybe he had forgotten to lock it. Or perhaps Agnys was clever enough to have undone the lock herself.

From the inside, it was not so hard to do. She would not have needed a key card to accomplish it. Only an understanding of locks and nobs and handles.

Using the spare card Rhyd had given to Maemi when the woman began to do his nessies shopping for him, Zara reached over Agnys and opened the door. The sound brought a similar one from the flat next door, and the child waved to the blonde who peeped outside. Zara caught the man's face too briefly in her rush to get Agnys indoors.

"You should not be out here…or talking to strangers," she scolded. "You don't know them. People want you. It is not safe."

If Agnys had been taken, it would have been as much Zara's fault for being late as it was Rhyd's for leaving her alone. But Zara had been sidetracked by a group of complimenting Crows and had, dutifully, stopped long enough to briefly entertain them with conversation as they desired rather than risk angering them or prompting them to follow her. Leaving Agnys alone briefly had seemed preferable to leading the Crows directly to her. Even now, Zara was not certain if she had been followed or not, and thus she locked the door and kept the lighting in the flat low to give the appearance of an empty apartment as she put the bags she carried on the kitchen counter.

"Change…" She handed the child a collection of clothing she had procured from a herpa. "And then you and I are gonna play a game."

A game called how quiet can we be, she thought to herself before putting the food contributions she and Skelter were able to spare into the icebox and cupboard. She would send a message to Skelter as soon as she could. He would make sure they were safe.

Skelter always did.

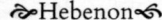
Hebenon

❧CHAPTER 14❧

T he day felt longer than any he had endured in a long time as Rhyd worked hard to atone for his tardiness, his previous day's absence, and in the hopes of squelching any suspicion that might be pointed his way after finding the Crow in the shafts two days prior.

If felt as if it had been so many more days than that.

Apparently, there was no suspicion to be thrown, however, since the joke of the day amongst his coworkers in the Shed was about a clumsy Crow who had slipped and hit his head. With slipping always a hazard in the Levs, even in the protected environment of the shafts, and since it was standard practice to protect against it…and against the moisture in general…anything that made the Crows look clumsy, foolish, or incompetent, was a welcome relief and good for a laugh.

Particularly when it appeared that the official account by the Crows was of an accident, and not an attack, as well.

Rhyd used his lunch break to gather information from the streeters hanging out near where he worked this day, listening in the shafts instead of questioning them directly, avoiding frightening them with troublesome intrusion or leaving them a face that could be described to the Crows in exchange for Hebbies or ticks. The search was still on for the parah, although it appeared that the focus had moved away from the tingers and streeters and back to scouring the tunnels and shafts. Rhyd wondered if that would make the streets safer, if he could get Agnys into the hands of a trustworthy herpa for safekeeping. That idea, despite its flaws, kept coming back to him as the most viable, even though he was also confident he would never do it.

He could not. Not if it meant putting Agnys into the care of people he did not know well enough to fully trust. Herpa were generally trustworthy, but he knew none enough to trust them with her life.

He felt awkward, off balance, out of his element and off his game since that embrace that morning, and knew he needed things to be different. He could not continue as the Scarecrow with a child at home depending on him. Something needed to change.

He also, before that noon break was over, took the time to visit Tox, to give her the gold chain and ask her to repair the clasp. She seemed peculiarly stressed when he spoke with her, but she swore it was nothing, a bad day nothing more, and told him not to fret.

But he did fret, the entire time he combed the streets and shafts during his lunch break, and the entire remainder of his day as he replaced and repaired more filts and repaired the dehumidifying generator in a home. The possibility that Tox's side activities had been discovered by Crows, or that some gadget she and Zara had devised had been used in a crime that was being tracked back to her, was a very real fear for them both.

Tox would never crow him, would never turn on him, at least never intentionally, but suspicion on her might bring suspicion on Maemi, on Skelter and Zara, and on Rhyd. Her heels-dug-in insistence that everything was fine rubbed him wrong, like sandpaper in his shoe, the entire rest of his shift.

He would go back for the chain after work, he decided as he clocked back in for the second half of his shift. He would question her deeper when he did. He would have the truth and then he would go home to Agnys.

That thought brought an unfamiliar, not uncomfortable but still unwanted, flutter of anticipation.

Not good at all, he thought with a frown. Not one damn bit.

❧*❧

After trying to entertain a child whose single interests were the cats outside the window and Rhyd's return, Zara decided, when it was time to return to Vapors and there was still no sign of Rhyd, to bring Agnys with her to the club, where she might be able to distract her with music or the shiny spangles of her costumes. Leaving Agnys alone again was to end up with her locked out on the street with the cats, in the open where the Crows or anyone who might recognize her differences…anyone interested in a few extra ticks from the Source, could grab her. Zara would never, if she could help it, put someone, particularly a child, at risk. There was a risk moving her across town, but of the options she had, it seemed the better choice to make.

Besides, there were still errands to run for Skelter before the night's show. She left a message on the Echosys screen that Rhyd would see when he arrived home to find the prodcast still running, and herded Agnys in the direction of the club, making sure she was covered with the shawl Maemi had procured for her. Not only did it help protect the child from the damp, it also hid her blonde hair and shielded her from the curious gazes of others.

"Stay near me," she instructed, holding the girl's hand as they wove through the end of shift crowd.

Agnys bobbed her head and followed close. Maybe she did not understand the words but she was beginning to understand the dangers that existed outside of Rhyd's home. She watched the array of dark cloaks and coats, glistening wet beneath the sheen of colorful neon, the splash and spray of water beneath boots on the grated metal surface, noted the graffiti on the many walls they passed, and tried to pretend she could not hear the constant roar of the falling water surrounding them in the distance.

How could they tolerate that sound the way they did?

That was another good thing about being inside of Rhyd's home, or inside any building. They were constructed to filter noise, as well as moisture, dulling the fall's rumble considerably. But it was always there, below the surface of every person's subconscious. How Rhyd could hear the things he did, as he had shown within the tunnel when he had rescued her, Agnys did not know.

This wet world was frightening and she wished she could go home. Staying close to Zara was the only way to remain safe.

Curious girl that she was, however, when Zara stopped at a vindi at the corner of an intersection, at a place where Agnys could see the club which she and Rhyd had been in before and guessed that was where they were going, and Zara released her hand to offer the seller her tick card, Agnys scooted across the intersection to inspect a glass-encased shelf containing a variety of gadgets, tools and widgets, things with tiny gears and crank handles, tubes and wires, more intricate then she could imagine. There were many people around them, but their destination was close. What harm could there be in so little distance between them? Zara would certainly see her there, know where she was. Agnys inched gradually sideways, studying the unusual, unfamiliar contents, not realizing in doing so that she and Zara were growing further and further apart…or that anyone else was near enough to step between them.

"Something interests you?"

Agnys had no idea she was being spoken to until a large hand clasped her shoulder. She stared up at the tall stranger's face with surprise and alarm.

"I did not mean to frighten you."

This was not the first time Captain Grainger had been to this Lev. Though a resident of the Uppers, duty took him throughout the city and he went wherever that duty beckoned. While the noise, the smells, the damp and cold, were bothersome, they troubled him less than they did many of the Uppers residents. Off duty now, stressed by his unsuccessful hunt for a child he doubted he would ever find, one of his officers had suggested the club Vapors as the ideal place to relax and unwind. There were some amazing andis there, the officer had said, especially the one with the long blonde hair. Enough to make you forget your troubles for a while. He had been heading there when, like this child, he found himself engrossed in the eccentric collection the repair tinker offered for sale, items hawked by others, some bought and paid for but never retrieved, things built by someone with a keen eye, deft fingers, and a creative mind. Someone he might be able to utilize for the force, if that individual was interested in that sort of contract work.

Not many in the Levs were.

If the urchin beside him had an interest in such things, perhaps it would be possible to apprentice her…and groom her towards the security force…if her parents did not already have her future mapped out for her. Always thinking about Hebenon's future, the idea was worth consideration.

The young man of Chinese descent behind the counter had just asked him, "Can I help you?" when the small figure bumped into Grainger's leg without noticing she had done so. Grainger did not realize her gender until she looked up at him in that turn, revealing the dress and her shiny black boots. Expensive clothing, expensive at least for the Levs, so she was no streeter…unless she had stolen those clothes. But her face and hands were clean, so he dismissed that thought too.

She was no tinger, even though her paralyzed rat in a flashlight gaze was filled with fear.

Given the reputation of the Crows and his imposing size and the expression that many of his officers called fierce, he was not surprised by the way she stared.

What did surprise him was her blonde-white hair and the blue of her eyes. Not unheard of; there were at least a dozen natural blondes that he knew in the Uppers, the Founder's wife being one of them…though her hair was more reddish than true blonde. And the dancer he was here to see was said to be blonde. But this was the first truly blonde child he had seen up close, face to face, and her remarkable features fascinated him.

When she did not speak, he looked around them with concern. "Where are your parents?" He did not see anyone who looked to have lost a child, no one frantically searching, no one who seemed to be of expensive enough dress to be…

No, he thought. That woman there. The blonde cattycorner across the street buying skin care products. Her hair was nearly the same blonde. That must be the girl's mother.

"Hey…miss…" he shouted, his deep, commanding voice cutting through the crashing of water and the constant chatter of haggling voices around the intersection.

With no intention of visiting Vapors tonight, only passing by it to check in with Tox and retrieve the chain he was now obsessing over, Rhyd headed straight there after his shift. It would only take him an extra handful of minutes to do what he intended and get home. Despite his preoccupied thoughts, he paid attention to his surroundings, always keeping watch for the enemy he wanted to destroy. Though Grainger was not wearing his duty coat, the Crow uniform minus the bird's mask hood the officers on duty wore, Rhyd recognized his stance, his height, the shape of his bald, ebony head.

He did not think the chief security officer was there, in front of Tox's vindi, on official business as he was neither officially dressed nor had he brought other Crows with him. There was other business he could be on, however, perhaps trying to win over the residents, sway them to gain their trust in order to wheedle information from them. Perhaps he had heard rumors about the Scarecrow's identity and it had brought him here.

Or perhaps he had heard something about Agnys.

Rhyd ducked into an open doorway from where he could observe and listen when Grainger shouted at someone across the intersection, waving and starting forward with his hand around a small child's arm. The shawl over the child's head fell away as the youngster dragged her feet, resisting being taken anywhere.

Agnys!

Across the street, directly in line with Grainger's diagonal path, was Zara.

There was little thought to his action, when normally Rhyd would have hesitated long enough to formulate a plan. The man's face, that voice, flashed through Rhyd's memory, echoed in his head, a warning embedded in memory that filled him with fury. This man had been in his home, had come for Venn, had taken Venn away, had hit Rhyd with enough force to keep him from interfering in the arrest or following them. This was the man Rhyd had been seeking for months, a man whose face was rarely seen since his orders were primarily delegated to lesser officers while he managed things from behind a desk.

Now that Rhyd saw him again, remembered him fully, he wanted vengeance.

Without a sound, he charged, no protective clothing or gear to shield his body, to help him see or hear or breathe, nothing but raw training to his advantage against a larger opponent. Periphery senses told him the streets had cleared, people driven to shelter by the shout of a man they recognized from endless prodcasts and his years of duty.

It was possible they were also driven back by the smaller man with the insane audacity to attack the leader of the Crows.

At the last moment, Rhyd roared, seeing Zara begin to turn towards the voice at last as she noticed that those around her were clearing the street. His martial arts training allowed a kick to the man's side and the time to spin away before Grainger could turn and react to the surprise attack. Grainger released Agnys' arm as he turned and the girl was quick enough to duck to the side to avoid the ensuing fight. Faster than Grainger, small enough to duck the punch aimed at his head, Rhyd's next kick caught the man in the thigh, causing Grainger to stumble and start to go down.

Zara sprinted across the street, grabbed Agnys' hand, and yanked her away, disappearing with her into the first open doorway she could reach. Vapors. Agnys began to shout Rhyd's name, but Zara clamped her hand over the child's mouth to protect the identity of the man who might just have revealed his alternative identity by an unprovoked, but understandable in the circumstances, attack on the captain.

Hoping the man would continue to fall, would go all the way down so that Rhyd could more easily reach his head and knock him out, a third kick came, this time catching Grainger in the chest. It sent the large man sprawling backward into a metal street pole with an alglamp affixed to the top, but this time, Grainger was ready for the attack. He caught Rhyd between the legs with his big fist, which made Rhyd double over and fall awkwardly against the nearest staircase railing. The pain of the blow and the sideways landing on his wrist that twisted bones, ligaments, and muscles, gave Grainger opportunity enough to draw his injector…

…as Agnys broke free of Zara's hold and dashed to Rhyd's defense.

One shot. It should have been one. But one became two when something heavy and unexpected crashed into the back of Grainger's skull and dropped him to the ground.

The first dart poked out of Agnys' neck, the other caught Rhyd in the stomach. In Vapor's doorway, Zara stared in momentary horror, as did Xiaodan from behind the counter where he had not yet moved since the altercation had begun.

"Give me his coat."

That was Skelter's voice, the redhead pushing past Zara into the street as the warning sirens blared. Within minutes, Crows would be swarming this place. Skelter tore off his own velvet waistcoat and tossed it to Tox, but the woman, though she caught it, held it back out to him as she shook her head. "I'm closer to his height…let me do it."

Skelter did not argue, though he was not sure they had the same plan in mind. Instead, he helped peel Rhyd's coat away and hastily put Tox's coat on him. It was not a good fit, but it would have to do. Tox, in turn, pulled Rhyd's coat around her shoulders. Thus far, Rhyd had not fully succumbed to the drug in his system, although his efforts to stand and walk were unsteady and he clutched the handrail he had fallen against in an effort to remain upright.

Agnys, however, appeared unaffected by the needle protruding from her neck and was determined to help Rhyd walk as Tox was trying to do.

"You gonna make it?"

Rhyd nodded to Skelter, not sure what had happened except that his stumbling first step nearly caused him to trip over Grainger's prone body on the street. "I do that?" he slurred, his determination and experience with intoxication enabling him to point himself in the direction of home despite his off-kilter senses.

The siren's wail was beginning to throb between his ears.

"Sure did," Tox assured him, content to let him take the credit for her first violent anti-Crow act. Running footsteps could be heard now, hard soles on wet metal that reverberated throughout the floor beneath their feet. "We've gotta go."

Agnys pointed the way, though Tox did not need the direction. The woman, supporting the majority of Rhyd's weight, followed.

Skelter, meanwhile, dutifully bent over Grainger and tried to rouse him with gentle slaps to the face and light shakings of his shoulders. He would rather have left the man in the street. As the Crows began to spill into the intersection, six of them, Skelter cast the still-gaping Xiaodan a threatening look, willing him to silence, and then tried to appear as normal as he could.

By the time the Crows reached them, Grainger was beginning to come around. His memory of what had happened was hazy, and the back of his head burned and throbbed from the blow. He remembered a fight…possibly the girl's parents wanting to protect her from Vanishing. Understandable, but insanely ill-advised to attack a Crow. He had fired at the man…hadn't he? But there was no one close by except an elegantly dressed redhead and the streets around them were empty of the teeming activity of shoppers that he remembered.

The little girl and her mother were gone.

"What happened?" the filtered mechanical voice of one of the Crows rasped as he pushed his way between Skelter and Grainger to help his boss.

"Someone hit me…" Grainger rubbed the back of his head lightly and scowled.

"The Scarecrow?" The Crow looked at Skelter, but it was impossible to say whether the face behind the mask was expecting an answer or was directing his suspicions towards Skelter.

It was all the redhead could do not to laugh at the apprehensive tone of the masked officer's words. Obediently, with an appropriate degree of fear, he shrugged, neither confirming or denying the questions, and in anticipation of the next one, he hesitantly pointed…but not in the direction Tox and the others had gone.

"After him," Grainger muttered, trying to make it sound like a snarl but the effort was undercut by his pain. Three Crows ran in the direction Skelter indicated as the sirens continued to drone. Another helped Grainger to his feet as the last two took off in the direction Rhyd had been taken. Again, Skelter threw another glowering glare at Xiaodan, thinking the young man must have given the Crows some sort of clue. But Xiaodan, in his shock and amazement, had not moved, so perhaps it had been something in his eyes that had alerted them.

Or maybe the Crows were simply intending to circle around and cut the Scarecrow off.

"Why don't you come inside, sir…sit…have a drink…" Skelter offered, gesturing to the beaded curtain, hoping he could distract the Captain with the pleasures inside Vapors.

Grainger did not think twice about accepting the honest offer, despite the pounding in his skull. The bleeding had not yet stopped, but he pressed the cloth the redhead offered to it and followed the fellow's friendly smile. All he wanted was to get the drink he had come for, and try again to forget about duty for a few hours…or at least until his officers returned with the Scarecrow in custody.

He lacked a hood, thus would not have the advantage of respirator and night vision goggles, which would make finding the escaping vigilante in the dim layers of the Levs more difficult. To join the pursuit when he was unsteady on his feet would be futile. His officers could handle it.

Although, he grunted silently as he leaned against his escort to stumble into the club, if it was the Scarecrow they were after, they might not be as successful as he hoped.

To hell with success. Grainger wanted a drink. Everyone else could go to hell.

Despite their headstart, it was not long before the sounds of running footsteps, familiar to Agnys despite the lack of echo the shafts produced, began to resonate behind them. Thus far, Rhyd had not collapsed under the assault of the government grade Hebenon in his blood, but Tox could feel in the rate of his pulse against her, in the weight of his staggering steps and the growing glaze over his eyes, that the drug had fully taken hold, but it did not appear that he was at risk of an overdose. She did not think he needed the anti-serum, did not think he risked coma or death, but he needed to get off the street. Tox was surprised he was still trying to walk. She was more surprised, however, that the child showed no symptoms of Hebenon exposure.

Was it true then? Were parah immune to Hebenon?

"Can you make it the rest of the way?" Tox asked as they reached the steps that led to the housing sublevel where Rhyd's flat was. She was reluctant to leave them but felt confident she could lead the Crows away from Rhyd and the girl and escape them as well.

Rhyd's effort to nod was more a side to side bobbing of his head as he groaned, "We'll make it." Tox waited only long enough to be sure Rhyd's weight was supported by the handrail on the staircase, and swung up to the upper sub-level, leaving the pair alone. Agnys frowned, trying to manage Rhyd's weight as he held fast to the rail and tried to will his legs down the first step without her assistance.

What his bleary, fading vision saw, however, did not coincide with what his motor skills could manage, and that single step resulted in a tumble the rest of the way down the staircase, much the way Venn had fallen in Rhyd's dream. Agnys avoided falling because his hand slipped from her grasp, but she ran after him in the hopes of breaking his fall. Tox did not come back to help; she was already out of sight.

Rhyd's door was more than twenty feet away and the thundering of boots was now too close for Agnys to try to pull him inside of a door she could not open. She did not even think she was strong enough to pull him into the crevice beneath the steps before the Crows closed the distance. They might continue after Tox, who made enough noise in her escape to draw their attention, or they might stop to investigate the fallen man and the child with him at the bottom of the stairs.

Unsure of what else to do, hoping they would be ignored, Agnys bent over the man's body and tried to cover it, hide it, with her own.

A door opened. Eyes peeped out from the darkness, listened, and after a quick assessment of the situation, the gaunt form slunk outside long enough to pull the man and girl into the dark beneath the stairs. There was not enough time to move them anywhere else. The Crows stopped above, may have glanced down though Agnys could not see them, and then they continued to run in the direction of the fleeing steps that continued to move away from them. Finger on his lips, the man with the dirty blonde hair kept the girl and delirious man still until the sound of running boots could no longer be heard or felt.

"Card?"

Agnys looked at the man without fear but it was clear she did not understand. He started to roll his eyes, stopped himself, and muttered, "afatottari," beneath his breath as he rummaged through Rhyd's pockets. When he eventually found what he sought, he muttered, "Stay here," and left the alcove.

Again Agnys stared at him but she would not leave Rhyd, and could not pull him after her, so she remained beneath the stairs as the man slid the Passcard through the reader and pushed the door open with the toe of his shoe.

"Come here." He waved to her but she did not budge. "Hold the door. I'll bring him inside."

His hand gestures, the way he held the door with his foot, were easy enough to interpret. Agnys nodded and squeezed Rhyd's hand.

"Go…" he slurred. He might not be entirely aware of his surroundings, his situation, but getting Agnys indoors, to safety, was still his priority.

It was enough to ease Agnys' mind and she ran.

It was easier for the long-haired man, despite his thinness and age, to hoist Rhyd beneath his arm and maneuver him into the flat, out of the ill-fitting woman's cape he wore as Agnys closed the door behind them and the cats that had followed them inside. When Rhyd was lying sprawled on the cushioned sofa, the blonde saw, at last, the injector needle protruding from the man's stomach. He was surprised the end had not broken off. He scowled, glanced at the girl now cuddling the smallest of the three cats as if to find comfort in the animal's warmth, and noticed the same protrusion at the side of her neck.

She winced when he pulled the needle free and held it to her in his open palm so that she could see. "So you're the one the fuss is about. Don't look like no monster to me."

Agnys blinked at the odd sound of his words and pointed at Rhyd.

The small man's body had grown rigid and began to shake with random tremors as the Hebenon in his system interfered with muscle control. It appeared that this was a more potent dose of the drug than what the Crows usually used, for while they wanted prisoners incapacitated, they rarely gave them enough to overdose or kill them. That was the sort of mistake that could get a Crow banished from the force, for it would bring down the wrath of every man and woman on the Levs. Killing someone in plain sight, killing anyone in Hebanthe Falls' meager population, was heavily frowned upon even by those in the Uppers. It was bad enough that people Vanished. The citizens expected that now, and the threat of it was typically enough to keep most in line. Killing them outright, however, was another matter.

Rhyd's propensity to alcoholic numbness might have been the only thing that had warded off the Heb's effect as long as it had.

"I'll be right back." Keeping Rhyd's Pass in his hand, Lash left the two alone, trusting that the child would be safe enough for just a few minutes. He could not count on Rhyd having on hand what was needed to reverse a too-high Heb dosage and there wasn't time to look. Lash knew what he had in his own cupboards, however, but he needed to hurry if he was to administer it before the damage to Rhyd's system became irreversible.

Not knowing where the stranger had gone, whether he would be back, Agnys did the only things she knew how to do. Having watched her mother die of fever, having seen how others cared for the sick, Agnys moistened a towel and put it over Rhyd's forehead. Then she removed his boots and covered him with a blanket. He was muttering nonsense words and his skin was growing an odd shade as his hands clenched again and again as though he was trying to grasp something he could not reach. When his jaw tightened, making her think he would break his teeth; she remembered something else she had seen done to a man in her village and quickly struggled to pull Rhyd's belt free. Awaiting her opportunity, when his mouth opened in a struggle for air, she pressed the leather-like material into his mouth for him to bite on. Lastly, she dragged the oxygen tank from where it rested near the chair he had slept in since they met, worked the strap around his head to keep the mask in place as much as the belt in his mouth would allow, and turned it on to help him breathe.

Her ingenuity impressed Lash when he returned with the needed ingredients loaded into a hand injector, and he patted her head.

Upon seeing the needle, however, Agnys frowned and tried to slap it out of his hand with a stern "No."

"It will help," Lash said with frustration, knowing she did not understand. When she again shook her head and pushed protectively between the two men, he snapped, "Get him some water." But still, she refused to move.

Lash had two choices, and gauging by the increasing spasms in Rhyd's body, the first choice was becoming less of an option by the second. To hold off on the counter-serum meant the man's heart, diaphragm, and lungs might seize and refuse to relax again. That would mean certain death.

He had to risk losing the child's trust to save Rhyd's life.

With one arm he pushed her aside long enough to press the injector against Rhyd's neck and depress the unit. The pale amber fluid within was dispersed into his bloodstream without further interference. Agnys opened her mouth to scream at him but the stern, scolding stare Lash threw at her made her scoot backward in fear. She did not move far enough, however, to lose her hold on Rhyd's hand.

"Needed doing."

He looked at their joined hands, seeing for the first time the discoloration, the evidence of bruising that indicated a break beneath the skin. This time when he scowled, his gaze traveled up to the Echosys. He could not risk summoning medical help as there would be questions and a record of Rhyd's injury, his identity, logged into the Hub archive that might allow the Crows to track him to his home.

No…if the break was to be mended quickly without an extended medical absence from employment, mended in order that he could continue to do the more important work he was doing to protect this child, Lash knew what he had to do.

But he did not consider moving until some hours later, when Agnys slept seated on the floor, her head against Rhyd's leg and two cats curled on her lap. Rhyd's muscles had ceased twitching and the blue-gray of diminished oxygen in his blood had faded to leave the man wan and still. The rapid eye movement, the grinding of his jaws, the sweat that had broken across his face and forehead, were evidence of the Hebenon still in his veins. He was not beyond the effects yet, but he was far enough out of danger that Lash chose that moment to leave the flat in search of the medical aid needed.

Neither Rhyd nor Agnys heard him go.

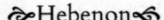

❧Chapter 15❦

As offices went, his was not much of one. Even in the Uppers, room for such things was limited. The cubicle size space was big enough for his chair and desk, and for the two chairs opposite that were necessary on the occasions he had to speak with any of his officers privately. But there were also interrogation rooms for that, the primary offices where all of the force could gather together on the rare occasions when that was necessary, and there were even smaller cubicles, with smaller desks, where officers could file their reports. That sort of work could also be done at any Echosys in the city, since they were all connected to the primary Hub, but for those uncomfortable with, or otherwise hindered from giving verbally detailed reports, sitting down at a terminal in the office was often the preferred way of doing things.

And it was white. Everything was white…or varying shades of metal grey, black or silver. Kemway white, as many called it.

He hated white. He would have settled for anything else, no matter how obnoxious, so long as it was not white.

Grainger sat in his little cubicle of an office, his own report from the previous night's escapade staring back at him on the Echosys screen, the words feeling inadequate because of his team's failure in capturing either the Scarecrow or finding the man with whom he had fought. He was less concerned about that man, to be honest, counting the skirmish as a reasonable mistake, although there was, by decree, a fine required to be paid for assaulting an officer of the law. It was a fine Grainger was inclined to forego, and might still overlook if he could find the fellow and explain that he had not been attempting to take the child away. With the number of streeters and tingers rounded up for questioning of late, many of them children, it was easy to explain a man's fear for his child, even though Grainger had no children of his own to have experienced such fear first hand.

Losing the Scarecrow again, however, was more irritating, particularly when coupled with the relentless reminder of it that came at the back of his skull every time he turned his head too quickly. Every person he had spoken to, inside the club or out, had either not witnessed the skirmish and attack, or would not admit to it, or swore that the attacker was the Scarecrow, sworn to defend anyone in the Levs about to be taken or assaulted by the Crows. A man? A woman?

No one knew. Or no one would say.

His officers lost the vigilante in the falls' vaporous belchings, and with no clues to follow, no leads to be had, they had been called off.

Perhaps, he mused, rubbing the welt on his head and wincing again, the man and child had seen something. They must have, given the direction they had been facing and the direction from which his assailant had struck. Though he regretted it now, he was sure he had shot at least one of the two, and since they had escaped unseen, someone in that street must have taken them for help. But there were no reports from any of the clinics of Heb victims matching the description of man or girl, and he did not want to conduct a door to door search of the Levs to find a man he felt had done no wrong.

To catch someone who had, however, he might. Frustrated, he punched send and the report disappeared from the screen. Founder Kemway would have it no other way, and it was time for the Scarecrow's reign to end.

≈*≈

Lash returned to the flat with a pudgy, balding man with dusky skin and dark hair and eyes who carried an armload of medicinal supplies and equipment as he puffed and panted along on Lash's heels. The door opening and closing caused Agnys to open her eyes but Rhyd did not stir. Her anger and fear of Lash had faded during the night with Rhyd's improvement but she watched the unfamiliar newcomer warily. Too many people knew where they were, and she was smart enough to know what dangers that could bring.

But she also knew by the dark mottling of the skin around Rhyd's wrist that something was wrong, and she did not have the knowledge to make it better. The stranger spoke not a word but pulled the coffee table over to rest Rhyd's arm on it after pushing the clean clothes aside. Those that toppled to the floor, Agnys picked up and stuffed onto the chair where Rhyd normally slept without bothering to fold them. She wanted to be closer to Rhyd, to see what the stranger was doing, but Lash held her back so that the medic could apply another injection and set to work.

It looked to Agnys to be something to deaden feeling, for after a scan of Rhyd's wrist with an Echo T2, creating a picture of the fractured bones on the tiny screen she could see from where she stood, he took out a set of injectors, different from the rest, and pushed them through skin, one by one, down to the bone in multiple locations, front and back. Whatever was inside of the opaque tubes was injected to the breaks, gradually changing the Echosys image, erasing the tiny fractures and fissures visible on the screen. The process took nearly fifteen minutes, and when it was complete, another small device was used to treat each of the external punctures.

As the pudgy man wrapped Rhyd's wrist with heavy fabric that would hold the joint rigid, he said, "Should take it easy for a week while the bioplast fully sets and everything heals."

"I'll tell him," Lash promised, though he doubted Rhyd would be prone to heed that advice. "See Skelt about payment…"

The doctor nodded expectantly. "Does he need a medipass?"

"Not for a few more days. He's got sick hours to use. He'll be in touch when he does."

"Send him to Skelt." A forgery obtained through Skelter meant protection for a doctor not wanting to be accused of misconduct, or not wanting to be accused or caught helping fugitives or streeters off record. He did not know which of those things Rhyd was, and he did not want to know.

He never even asked the patient's name.

"Course." Lash did not need to say it or agree to know that Rhyd would bypass a medic and go directly to Skelter for what he needed. Rhyd did not know it, but Skelter was one of several links he and Lash had in common.

❧*❧

The room behind the repair shop that the young man's tip had brought him to was filled with a conglomeration of gadgets and tools, most of which Grainger could only guess as to their purpose. Though it had been hidden behind a disguised panel at the back of a closet, and locked with a passcode that took too much time to decrypt, there was nothing, at first glance, that looked as suspicious as the young man's message had led the Captain to believe there would be. Some of the devices might be questionable for the average man or woman to possess, but he presumed they had uses in trades he was unfamiliar with. There were tools to read and adjust vent systems, goggles and respirators that would protect those who were exposed for too many hours to the vapors of the Four Falls, and bits and pieces that might protect one from falling debris…or from falling themselves, in the course of a variety of manual labor positions. Nothing seemed noteworthy until the youngster thrust into his hands a leather hooded, goggled, cowled mask that Grainger recognized all too well.

"Whose is this?"

Xiaodan shrugged, his face beginning to show additional worry as soon as the mask was out of his hands. "I don't know…it's not hers…"

"Whose? Who is she?"

Many on the force had assumed the Scarecrow was male, had doubted that any woman could be powerful or well-trained enough, to bring down so many proficient officers. There were women on the force, but they, too, did not believe another woman could take on multiple Crows in one fight and win. Even Kemway referred to the Scarecrow as male.

Maybe that was why the vigilante had not yet been caught.

"Tox would not…she's anti-violence." Or she had been, Xiaodan believed, until last night. He knew she was fit, that she spent time in the gymnasium with the boxing gear, but he had never seen her fight, never known her to fight until now. The blow she had given Grainger was unexpected, even if she had been trying to protect an acquaintance and frequent customer. "She doesn't know how to fight."

A Crow picked up a thumper from the midst of the table strewn with parts and equipment and showed it to his captain. Grainger frowned. "Apparently," he mused, "she does."

It was easy to assume that this had been the instrument to knock him out last night. Knowing how to fight was not necessary in order to use a thumper, but the two fit hand in hand well enough.

He ordered two Crows to confiscate everything in the room for analysis, hoping for prints, fibers, DNA evidence…anything that might reveal who the Scarecrow was.

"No…she would never…"

"Your spouse? Sister? Mother?" Not likely a daughter, for this young man was little more than a child himself. "Where is she?"

"Mentor," Xiaodan murmured defensively in mounting distress. "But she would not…she makes things…fixes things…she is not…"

"Then who else comes here? Who else does she bring home? Who has access…and where is she?"

"This isn't her home!" Yes, it was attached to her home, but Xiaodan did not live here and had only discovered this hidden workshop by accident when trying to find where the absent Tox had gone. "I don't know…no one…I have not seen her since…"

It was the sole reason he had made the report. Out of worry for her welfare when she did not come to the vindi that morning, he had searched every inch of her place in the hopes of finding a clue about where she might be, where she might have gone. He did not know how she spent her nights, it was true. Tox lived alone above the vindi and spent most of her hours, to his knowledge, in the shop instead of her home. He never saw her anywhere else, or with anyone other than Maemi and those she shared the vindi with. But he knew she had not returned, as he had waited for her long after his shift had ended.

Someone else could have access to the room where she slept, the other fixers and apprentice that covered her twelve-hour off shift, or the older fellow who came to cover on days when no one else could work. A twenty-four hour, seven-day-a-week operation meant that she could not always be behind the counter. Who knew who came in her off time, who had keys to her flat, who these things could belong to. Xiaodan assumed they belonged to someone else, and that someone had done something to Tox. It had not occurred to him that the authorities might suspect her for this shop's proximity to her home, and Xiaodan now felt sick about accusations he had not foreseen, and the trouble it would create for the woman he admired.

"Since?"

"Last night," he replied weakly. She had gone off with the man and child and never returned. "She took a fellow away…the one you injected…"

That was news worth hearing, regardless of what the contents of this room revealed. "Where? Where did she take him?"

"I don't know." Xiaodan shrugged. "Maybe she stayed with him…but I don't know where." Having served as Tox's apprentice for less than two years, he did not know the relationship between Rhyd and Tox, had not known Venn except in passing, did not know Rhyd's name or that he was more than a client to Tox, more than a casual acquaintance. He did not socialize with the man his Aunt Maemi called Whiskey. It was all Tox ever called the blonde in public as well.

He decided against revealing that, against revealing that his aunt might know who the man was or where he lived. If there was any chance such information would result in further charges against Tox, or against his aunt, his mother, or his grandmother, or the Vanishing of any or all of them, the less he said the better.

"If he comes back here…if you see him again… tell me. Same if she comes back." They were not questions. Grainger had a lead now, possibly two, and he intended to run with them. The news, however small the details, ought to bring him a hint of Kemway's favor.

What it brought Xiaodan, however, as he watched the contents of the room, the tools and devices and clothing, vanish out the door in the hands of the Crows, was fear and self-recrimination. What, he wondered, had he done? For the first time since last night, he began to hope that Tox never came back to the vindi. Never learned what he had done.

At least the Scarecrow, whoever that was, could no longer put Xiaodan or Tox in danger if he had been using this room without Tox's knowledge. He did not believe Tox was the Scarecrow and hoped the Scarecrow's arrest would remove suspicion from his mentor fully.

❧*❧

Rhyd groaned and worked his tongue around his dry mouth, disgusted by the bitter taste and acutely aware of the cotton-headed dizziness that plagued him. He remembered the early evening's details well enough to recall the injector biting into his belly and knew that to be the cause of the all-over body aches, chills, and lingering disorientation, even though he had never experienced the effects of Hebenon before. It was his first exposure to the drug, not the recreational variety but the full-fledged official version, and he was not sure why he was not dead…or why he was, he mused as he cracked his eyes open to the sound of the prodcast running in the background, in his own home.

If he had been drugged, surely that meant he had been Vanished just as Venn had been.

Vague recollections of Agnys, of Tox, came back to him, and then one of Lash, and the last realization brought his eyes wide open as he whipped his head to the side in the hopes of seeing the girl safe, in the hopes of defining the source of the noises from the direction of his kitchen. For several minutes he saw nothing but darkness, a deep burgundy shade of it tinting the edges of his vision as pain and dizziness avalanched and took its time bleeding away. That sudden vertigo brought panic in its wake, but it was an emotion that was eased by a small hand on his wrist and another on his forehead. The touch on his arm brought fire, but the other gave comfort, and he impulsively reached with his other arm to pull the small body against him.

"You're safe."

She sighed and embraced him back.

Tox must have come back. She would have kept them safe. No one else had been there to do it. Few others knew where he lived.

"How do you feel?"

A stranger's voice, lisping and odd, gravelly and deep. Not recognizing it, responding only to the knot of fear in his stomach, Rhyd forced his eyes open and looked directly into the face of the speaker through his still crimson vision.

Lash. His neighbor. His neighbor, of all people. Wasn't the guy a crower? Hadn't every instinct in Rhyd's body warned him to keep his distance from the thin, blonde-haired man, particularly since those troubling dreams of…a day ago? A week?

Rhyd did not know how much time had passed since he had been dosed. He did not know the day, or the hour, and he did not know how Lash had gotten into his flat.

Uncomfortable with the trapped feeling that tried to bind him to the sofa, Rhyd slowly sat up after releasing his hold on Agnys, though he pushed her slightly to the side as if to put himself between her and the man he had no reason to trust. If Lash was a threat, in his home, it was time for Rhyd to get his senses back, time to get on his feet.

The pressure on his wrist as he pushed himself up, however, sent flames of agony racing up his arm, up the back of his neck, into his spine and skull and he hissed.

"Got you these…for the pain."

Lash set two pills and a glass of hemp milk on the coffee table. Rhyd eyed them suspiciously, with no intention of taking what might be more Hebenon, despite its deceptive yellow coloration, or might be something far worse. But Agnys picked the tiny yellow tablets up and pressed them to his lips, urging him to take them. Had he taken them previously? Why did he not remember that? Had he been lucid enough at some point to swallow them without choking?

He must have been. It was the only reason he could think of for Agnys to trust them. Reluctantly, only to ward off the still seething pain, he accepted both painkillers and milk.

"Damn lucky," Lash said over his shoulder, having returned to the kitchen and the sounds and smells of whatever he was cooking. Whatever it was smelled good, Rhyd admitted, realizing that he had not eaten in a very long time. He glanced at the corner of the Echosys screen, with its still playing prodcast, to judge the date and the time.

Eighteen hours since he had eaten last.

At least he had not lost too much time.

"Thanks," he grunted. If he was lucky of anything, it was that this man appeared to have brought him in out of the cold and damp, away from the Crows, but he was not yet confident of his safety. He fingered the bandaging around his wrist, wincing again as Agnys, seated on the sofa beside him, played with the cats that had come into the flat with Lash's comings and goings.

"Nothing you wouldn't've done, Ballard." He did not know Rhyd, did not know the reasons Skelter had asked him to keep an eye on him, but the act of finding and sheltering the parah child proved to Lash what sort of man Rhyd was.

"How do you know my name?"

Lash ignored the growl. "Been neighbors long enough."

That was true, though they had never spoken or been introduced. During all of those years, however, even back before Venn's Vanishing, someone had to have spoken Rhyd's name at least once within Lash's hearing.

Two plates of steaming garlic potatoes with cheese on them were brought to the coffee table, then the third and the carton of hemp milk. "Lash, by the way." The older man, barely taller than Rhyd, though leaner, offered his hand as he settled onto the chair he had pulled over. Agnys slid down to the floor to be better able to reach her plate.

That time as Lash spoke, Rhyd noticed what he had not before, the reason for the other man's stilted speech. Lash had what Rhyd had never encountered before: a prosthetic tongue. He had heard of such things; they were very rare, most often gotten through unofficial channels because those who required them had access to some knowledge the Doctet and Founder did not want to have known. Removing a man's tongue could not stop them from sharing secrets, not while the individual had hands to type or write with, but the violent act was most often enough to discourage anyone from revealing whatever they knew.

Or the man was a Crow plant, an agent of the Doctet altered to make those he interacted with sympathetic…prompting them to give him their trust. The hair on the back of Rhyd's neck stood on end.

"I know."

Seeing that increased wariness made Lash shrug as he watched Agnys draw shapes in the melted cheese on her plate with the tines of her fork. His secrets were his own, never shared with anyone, not even Skelter, but he was willing to wager that if Rhyd considered the matter long enough, his level of trust would change. A man who lost his tongue to the Crows, to the Founder, and took the risk of a prosthetic, would not likely bring himself to their attention, not even to act as an informant. And no man Lash knew would willingly give up something like that just to act as a spy. Of the three others Lash knew, one had later been killed when caught, one had died of a Hebbie addiction, and the third had disappeared off the grid as Lash had done. It was either live outside of the Hub's, the Archive's, data stream, survive as a streeter, or risk Vanishing or death. Lash had no death wish.

He wanted to live.

He also believed that the truths of the world deserved to be known. But he was not yet certain, despite what he had seen thus far, that Rhyd Ballard was the man for the job as Skelter claimed.

❧CHAPTER 16❧

Enough hours had passed, dodging through streets from one Lev to another, long after the sound of following Crows had been lost, that Tox felt it safe to return home. She took her time, her pace leisurely, in order not to draw attention as she walked, smiling at passersby, waving at children, even appearing to enjoy the water spray and mist in her hair. She stopped at one vindi after another, a morsel or trinket or tool bought here or there so that her absence from her own vindi would be less likely questioned by any except Xiaodan, who was nosy enough to grill her on where she had been all night. She could always claim to have a lover and that would, she believed, silence his questions. She did not worry about the operation of the vindi. Xiaodan and the others could manage it without her, and repairs he could not yet do himself would wait for one of her coworkers or until her return.

After stashing Rhyd's coat where she would instruct him to look for it later, assuming he survived the Hebenon and had not been arrested or Vanished, she descended the final staircase to her vindi level, hands full of sacks. She could see Xiaodan at the booth, leaning his elbows on the counter the way he had been instructed not to do many times. His expression was one of alert caution, however, with no customers currently on hand, so she knew something was wrong.

When their gazes met across the distance between them, his eyes grew wide and his mouth opened as if he would speak. Tox's own senses immediately snapped to alert seconds before hands closed around her arms. Her packages dropped, their contents spilling over the wet surface, some falling through the grate to clink and clatter as they descended to some lower level or into the river. Though she struggled to be free, the Crows held her fast. At their side, guiding them, was a face behind a breather that no one in the Levs, especially this deep, ever expected to see.

Not Captain Grainger.

Founder Kemway himself.

The last thing Tox saw, as the injector in someone's hand jabbed her arm, robbing her of coherency, was a look of guilt and horror on Xiaodan's face as she was dragged away, purchases abandoned.

Xiaodan did not know whether to retrieve any of the fallen items or leave them be.

☙*☙

"Take it easy on that thing for a week, doctor says...don't work if you can...or be cautious if you gotta...and it should heal alright."

Rhyd grunted. He could take the time off of work if he had to, as the injury was easy enough to prove, but he might not be able to afford to take it easy with Agnys needing his protection. Wondering again what he was going to do to ensure her safety, he glanced at her; she looked up with wide, adoring eyes as if she knew he was watching, and smiled, relieved that he seemed to be doing better than he had been the night before.

"Little fighter saved your ass. That's a keeper...unless you can get her home."

"Get her...?" The words escaped before Rhyd could stop them and prompted him to scowl. "What do you know about...?"

"The needle in her neck when she got you here...that stuff dropped you and didn't touch her one bit. She's gotta be the one the Crows are talking about...the parah with immunity..."

"You were…" Frantic hands roamed over the girl's exposed skin until he found the red welt where the needle had pricked her. Her body did react to the Heb, enough to produce the welt, but not enough to affect her in any other way. Parah or not, no wonder the Crows wanted her. Something like that, such an immunity, could be a gift to her, to many if it could be synthesized, but it would be considered a danger to the elite in the Uppers.

Of course she was hunted.

"Bound to be medics…scientists…in the Levs that'll want her too…could give immunity to all of us."

"No!" Whatever the future held for her, Rhyd was not going to subject Agnys to a battery of scientific tests and experiments. She was a child, a human…not a laboratory animal.

"S'what I thought," Lash continued, pleased, by Rhyd's response. If the man had been willing to subject a child to something like that, Lash would have thought twice about whatever came next. "That's why you need to get her out…she'll never be safe in Hebenon."

Rhyd said nothing, but he already knew Lash spoke true. It was something he had thought about numerous times the day before, something he knew Venn would have agreed with too…although making it happen was as likely as Rhyd becoming Founder. He knew of no good way to get into the Uppers. He knew of no good way to get into any of the shafts to get her to the Outside where she belonged.

"That can't…that's not…"

His thoughts and their meal were interrupted by frantic pounding on his apartment door. The men looked at one another; Rhyd pushed Agnys in Lash's direction, showing a willingness to trust him with her safety in spite of whatever misgivings he had about his neighbor.

"Who's…?" Rhyd began.

"Whiskey…it's Zara…"

It took effort for Rhyd to get to his feet and what Heb lingered in his body made his balance unsteady and his movement jerky and erratic as he struggled towards the door.

"Whiskey," came Zara's desperate plea.

Rhyd opened the door, leaning on it heavily as Zara slid inside. When he closed it, he lost his balance and collapsed against her; she caught him but almost fell as well under his unexpected weight.

"What...?" She had not been aware of the injector hit he had taken, had not realized he had been wounded beyond the hit he had received between his legs, though seeing him now, his injuries were obvious. She made note of the food on the coffee table and the other man in the room and nodded to him as she helped Rhyd sit.

Instead of answer her aborted inquiry, Rhyd asked, "What's happened?" Something had, some sort of bad news that he imagined was going to require an abrupt evacuation of his home. He was already making plans for that eventuality in his head.

"They took her...Founder Kemway...they took Tox...they think..." Though she knew Lash from his association with Skelter, she did not know what he knew about Rhyd and his extra-employment activities. She settled on, "they think she's you..." expecting that Rhyd would understand the exact implication of her words.

He did.

His stomach sank.

"But I can't..."

He could barely stand. How could he pursue a squad of Crows, who now had a several minute head start? Moreover, he was no closer to knowing where they took those who Vanished or were arrested, beyond disappearing into the Uppers, so how could he hope to find her when he had spent more than two years looking for Venn to no avail?

Head in his hands, he groaned and struggled against an almost unbearable sense of despair. Perhaps, with both Agnys and Tox' lives at stake, as well as Venn's, it was time to take that one risk he had resisted since he had first donned the Scarecrow's mask.

"Quatsch...I might be able to get you there..." Rhyd eyed Lash over his fingertips. "You get a Pass...I can show you where they're...a lot of them at least...are held..."

Rhyd held his breath. With help, with the right tools, with fortune on his side, Rhyd might get into the Upper shafts without an official Pass, though it was a dangerous risk he had never dared to undertake.

The shafts of Upper 20, having originally been part of the Levs, had never been sealed off from the level below it the way those above 20 had been, and they were rarely staffed by Crows as the change in Pass credentials was generally sufficient to keep the unwanted out. He had once worked the Lev 20 shafts and knew his way around them without knowing what sort of rooms existed outside the walls…except for the sports complex and the supporting rooms connected to it.

The levels above that would be trickier; they had always been part of the Uppers from the time of Hebanthe Falls original construction. He had never been in them, though he knew they required either an A or B Pass to gain entry. If he was careful and lucky, he might be able to get around the security protocols without one, but only if he could bypass security between Upper 20 and Upper 21. He could hide in a crowd of sports-goers, but not as the Scarecrow, the only way he felt confident of facing the dangers there, and as he knew all attendees bags were searched, anything other than food being forbidden and confiscated, he could never sneak his gear in that way. But there obviously had to be ways, else Agnys would never have made it from the Uppers into the Levs unnoticed.

He wondered if he dared take her as his guide, if she would understand what he wanted to do, wanted to know, and was willing to take that risk. Would she trust him enough for that?

Did he trust himself?

What he did not know was where on those levels above 20 prisoners could be held, as there were no easily accessible schematics in the archives, and Skelter had not, to Rhyd's knowledge, found anyone willing to part with that information. A hack into the Hub, into corners of Archival data that were heavily encrypted and protected, was more difficult and costly then hacking into private records and lower level archival stores of Lev data, thus Rhyd had never asked Zara to try. He did not think her knowledge of Echos extended that far and he did not want to endanger her by pushing her into some clumsy hack any more than he wanted to endanger Tox or Agnys.

He had, until now, been content to seek information the slow way, at the end of his fists, venting his wrath on the Crows. But he had suspected it was a risk he would have to take if he was ever to see Venn again, and it was that knowing, and his guilt over not attempting it sooner, that contributed to drowning in Zaolei night after night.

"You know where they take people?" Had Lash known all this time? Had he not told Skelter…or had Skelter not told Rhyd? Had Lash held the key to finding Venn all along?

"Upper 21 East…or the Core…but no one gets into the Core. No one knows how." Rhyd frowned at his mention of that believed to be fictional place but Lash continued, "Upper 21 is where they took me when they…"

He did not finish that sentence and Rhyd did not push. Rhyd knew what he intended to say.

"I didn't see them…any of them…but I know there are labs there. Test facilities and medical units…not far from the East trade shafts." There were shafts to the west as well, but as the parah did not, to anyone's knowledge, live or harvest on the west of the sprawling central river or its western-most tributary, it made little sense to think that Agnys had come from the west.

East it had to be.

Rhyd resumed rubbing his face, favoring his sore hand. "Even if I could…" Could he? He was a fighter, yes, but did not consider himself a tactician. Getting into the Uppers, getting to one of the east shafts, getting into the labs and getting Agnys out, was going to take more planning then he was used to. "I'm not…it will be days before I…" He absently fingered his wrapped wrist. "They could be…"

They. Venn and Tox. He had never come so close to admitting to himself or anyone else that Venn might be beyond his help, might already be dead.

Sensing his despair, Agnys climbed onto the sofa and knelt at his side, arms around his neck. A few moments later, she tugged lightly on the chain that was again around his neck and whispered, "Venn."

She did not know what they were discussing. He believed that. But something, the pitch of her voice, the look in her eyes, begged him to have faith, not to lose hope, to fight even if he felt he could not. Sighing, he pressed his forehead to hers and closed his eyes.

Zara looked away from that intimate moment, her own quandary pounding like a tiny hammer inside of her skull, creating an ache between her eyes. Not even Skelter knew all of her secrets, but she felt that one of them, at least, should be revealed now if it would help.

"I can get the schematics and the Pass...and maybe a location...a cell number or..."

She and Rhyd stared at each other for many moments, he with a measure of disbelief and uncertainty, she with a touch of apology for not having said so sooner.

"You can do that? Isn't it...?"

"You put your life in danger almost every night, Whiskey. Just because I haven't tried...I think I can do it...with the right equipment and a little time. With you...Tox and Venn...maybe Maemi and Ivan in danger too..."

"He won't let you." Skelter might benefit from her dancing, from the sexual favors offered to others, but he adored her too. He would never want harm to come to her because of a breach into the Hub. Such a breach would likely bring down the full hand of the Founder's wrath. Skelter might be a more significant obstacle than software and hardware firewalls.

But Zara trusted him not to overreact, and with some coaxing, from her, he could be persuaded to give in. Particularly since they all shared a common goal. If she discovered she had to hide such activity from him, so be it. "He won't have to know...but if he does..." she shrugged. "I want to do this. I need to help. I think he does too."

Twisting and flexing his wrist despite the pain, Rhyd frowned. "A few days of rehab...I can get this up to par." He did not want to wait two days, was afraid of what two days might mean to Tox, what two more days might mean to Venn, but he could not move beyond the limitations of his body. He had two more days before he was due for shift again. Time in the gym, instead of on the streets hunting Crows, would tell him if, when, his arm would support such covert activities properly. If necessary, he would put in to use some of the vacation hours he had accrued and not used since Venn's disappearance. Five weeks' accumulation ought to give him more than ample time to do what needed to be done…or for him to die trying.

"I'll put in for the time…include it as medical if I have to…if you're sure you want to do this, Zar…"

"I'm sure," she replied. It had been a long time since she had been so sure of anything. "Do you need anything in the meantime? They took everything from the shop…"

That news made Rhyd frown deeper. How could anyone have found that workshop? Until now, he had not thought anyone else knew of its existence except him and Tox. "I've got backups…" Not of everything, but enough that he could make it work. "Painkillers. Serious ones…not the weak quatsch." What Lash had given him had barely taken the edge off. If he was going to push his body's limits, Rhyd was going to need something more potent…but something that would not leave him incapacitated and unfocused.

"And you…" He glowered at Lash. "You need to protect Agnys. Someone needs to stay with her. I can't bring her to the gym…and I don't want her in Skelter's place." He might have trusted that to be a safe place before, but since he assumed that Zara would be working from home, doing whatever hacking she believed she could do to get into the Hub and the Archives, Rhyd would not risk Agnys being caught in a raid should the Hub directors discover a security break. "Here…next door…I don't care which. But you will keep her out of the Founder's hands."

If Lash had lived without detection, without Crow notice, for at least ten years, he should be able to keep Agnys safe for a few days. "If they've taken…and tell Skelter I'm gonna need more oxygen."

Both Zara and Lash nodded in agreement, the older man not inquiring about what had been taken, and Zara not pressing the matter further. Rhyd either had what he needed stashed elsewhere or he would make do without. What he chose, how he decided to proceed, mattered less than a successful plan of action. In this case, the ends would definitely justify any means necessary.

❧CHAPTER 17❧

The metal chair was the least of her discomforts, the gag and the clasps that bound her hands behind her bearable compared to the pain of what they wanted from her. Above her head, the dark grey ceiling was lined with tiny pinpoints of light, reminiscent of the stars she had seen on Echosys images once when she and Venn had visited the deks as children. There was no pattern to the placement of the lights that she could determine, as if the designer had intentionally created an arrangement to produce vertigo in the unfortunate individuals who ended up confined here to stare at them for too long. But she found a focus in that pattern, something that enabled her to tune out the worst of the tortures the Founder ordered inflicted when she refused to reveal if she was the Scarecrow. She did not even speak under the influence of Heb.

Morenski, the Doctet member in charge of weapons design and manufacturing and the head of criminal interviews of those suspected of treason, wanted to inject her with more, but Lima, present for much of the interrogation at the Founder's insistence, lobbied successfully against it. Occasionally an increased dosage meant a successful extraction of evidence from captives, but with the current batch of Heb in use by the security force seeming to be stronger than in the past, the danger of overdose was noticeable as soon as the woman had been brought into custody.

Haythem did not want to risk her death. Not yet. While the items from her workshop were inspected for trace evidence, he hoped she would admit, one way or other, if she was the Scarecrow…and if she was not, that she would reveal who the Scarecrow was. She knew the answer, Kemway was sure of it. He was determined to have the information, but they could not get it if she was dead.

Morenski's fist, the object of torture at the moment, stopped mid-swing as the interrogation chamber door crashed open and Captain Grainger stormed into the room. The Captain stared at the woman in the chair, whose arrest he had ordered, but who had been caught and brought in without his knowledge.

Then he stared at Haythem, who returned the taller man's furious gaze smugly.

"Why was I not…?"

"Tut, tut, Captain. You should be proud. Without your legwork…"

"My…why was I denied the honor of this arrest…?"

"Because," the Founder spat, detesting the challenge from a man who had been loyal and respectful all of the years they had known one another, "it is not yours to have. It never was. Your place is duty…obedience. Honor is mine…and I will have the truth from her without your interference. Me, Captain. Not you. Is that understood?"

Grainger, his eyes flashing and his fingers twitching as if his hands wanted to clench into fists and swing at the other man, neither moved nor allowed his feelings to otherwise alter the expression on his face. The size of Kemway's ego was a long known, well-established fact. The Captain should have expected this turn of events, but he had always believed the Founder respected him, appreciated his work, and would be willing to give him the credit he felt was due him.

That Kemway instead undermined him to take the credit for himself was a bitter pill that stuck in the back of the Captain's throat and refused to dislodge. "Yes…Founder…" he grunted in as neutral a tone as he could command despite the current of disdain he felt for the man for the first time.

"There, that wasn't so difficult, was it?" asked Haythem cheerfully, offering his white-gloved hand to his security chief. He watched Grainger swallow further indignation and stiffly accept the reconciliatory gesture. "You are welcome to join us, to stay, to help. Who knows, you might learn something useful."

Grainger weighed his options during the time it took Morenski to strike the woman twice. How long, he wondered, before she choked on blood behind the gag? Whether the Founder admitted it or not, Grainger recognized the defiance in the woman's eyes and suspected she would die before she broke. Some people were like that…and he had no desire to watch anyone die.

There were better ways, though he doubted anyone in the room was willing to listen to hear them.

No, he was more likely to get the information he needed from the labs, from the examination of the items confiscated from her, particularly the cowl and its breathing apparatus which was likely to contain all of the defining markers needed to identify the wearer.

"No, sir," he said, showing no visible distaste for the torture nor his belief that the efforts were futile. "I have reports to submit."

And evidence to examine. And, if his suspicions were correct, the real vigilante to catch. Whatever this woman's crimes, assaulting Crows was not one of them.

Haythem did no more than wave him away, not watching Grainger depart in favor of witnessing another blow that knocked the woman and chair backward with a crash…making sure to remain far enough from the torture that the spray of her blood never fell on his pristine white suit.

❧*❧

A day and night of sleep and painkillers, the attentive care of both Agnys and Lash, and a quick visit by Maemi with what appeared, to anyone watching, to be nothing more than an unexpected delivery of nessies, brought Rhyd to the gym and into the sphere of his trainers, old men and women who had schooled him as a boy and now as an adult in both gymnastics and martial arts. The opportunities for physical sports and activities were limited in Hebenon, with fields and large arenas in which to play them sorely lacking. Most physical activities were limited to those that could be conducted in small spaces, by individuals or two to four-person teams. Such limits to activity made it imperative that children be coached and given every opportunity to develop strong, healthy bodies. Rhyd's small frame and predilection for climbing the sides of stairs, hanging from railings to flip down to the ground, had caused his mother untold worry that he would fall into the river and led to her decision to enroll him in gymnastics training. His father, thinking such a sport to be unmanly, had insisted his son take up the fighting arts as well, little knowing how the two disciplines would one day combine when their only living child reached adulthood.

But it was less actual training that Rhyd had come for this day then it was to test, to strengthen, to adjust to the pain and limitations of his injured wrist so that when he entered those shafts next, he would have the ability, the capacity, to do what needed to be done.

He was thankful, as he pushed through hours of drilling and exercise, for his high pain tolerance and the additional painkillers Skelter provided. He was also thankful for his foresight, for the collection of tools and weapons he had secreted across the city over the past few years as well as the additional coats and masks created and hidden away. Each was in locations that, to his knowledge, no one else had stumbled on during that time, as none of his gear had been removed or rearranged. He checked on each stash before and after his gym visit, and began to strategize, as he worked out, about what he might need to do when the time came to initiate his developing plan.

There was no way of knowing when it could be put into effect. Zara needed time to work, to find a hack into the Hub's primary system, to locate the schematic and blueprint information needed. An A or B-Pass would take time for Skelter to procure, but that would be easy compared to what Zara needed to do. Despite his need for physical therapy and recovery, which he intended to be as short a time period as possible, Rhyd hoped they could act quickly. Tox could not wait. Venn could wait no longer. Now that the mission had sprouted, Rhyd was anxious and ready to begin. He had wasted two years on fear, self-pity, and procrastination. If Venn was still alive, he prayed the man would forgive him for having taken so long to come for him.

Waiting for news to be sent to his card, convinced that the roots of the Scarecrow still lay somewhere on the Lev where he had been assaulted, where the woman being questioned under torture had been found and arrested, Grainger hunched over the polished, worn bar and ordered another mild ale as he pushed his empty glass away. Drinking on duty was forbidden, but he was technically not on duty, having been placed on medical furlough after the blow to his head, so he chose to drink. It was a useful cover that allowed him to observe those who frequented this establishment without seeming to do so. The other patrons still suspected his presence; he could not blend in or be anonymous after his fight in the outside street, after his shouted orders to Crows who rushed to obey him had marked him, giving away his out of uniform identity.

Vapors patrons gave him a wide berth, moving away when he sat down, making sure to stay as far away as they could when they came through the door. The swiver, however, seemed friendly enough without plying him with unsolicited drinks or obvious questions about why he was there.

His primary reason for being there they already knew, or at least could guess, and was enough to hold them at bay. His more personal reason, however, still prompted by the remarks of one of his officers, was the blonde dancer who had just finished her performance and was leaving the stage as he watched her in the mirrored reflection behind the bar. She was undoubtedly the woman he had seen in the street, the one he had believed was the child's mother.

She was no mother…and no andi. She was flesh and blood alright, but not old enough, he believed, to be a mother. In Grainger's eyes, she the loveliest creature he had ever seen, in spite of her flat-chested figure. She called to the swiver to have whatever Grainger was drinking as she stopped close enough to be within touching distance, without actually touching him, and he felt the first smile creep in that he had felt since the parah invasion had occurred.

"You look like you need someone," Zara purred, her heart thundering at the prospect she was presented with in this one person's fortuitous visit…and his obvious interest in her. This was the Captain of the Crows. Maybe he recognized her from that street encounter and was hoping to glean information; maybe that was why he was here. But she hoped she too could extract information from him. At the very least, if she offered some of the attention he seemed to be seeking, she might be able to delay him from whatever he had come to the Levs to do…and at the most she might be able to take him out of play, eliminate him as a threat to whatever Rhyd planned.

"Need?" Was that what he felt? His smile faltered as new drinks were put on the counter, one for her and one for him. He had not asked for another, but as it might be Vapors' policy to provide a free drink to someone one of their dancers approached, he decided to accept it. One more drink was not going to hurt him at this point and he had enough ticks available to pay for them both if that was expected too.

"If you have the time, of course," Zara murmured. "There's a room…if you're looking for a short one? Or a proper upstairs…cost you a bit more but…"

She let the words hang between them, glad that Skelter happened to be scouring the Levs for anything, news or tools or weapons, that Rhyd might be able to use, as well as a few things Zara herself needed to continue her hacking efforts. Skelter discouraged clients from sharing her bed, wanting to protect her as much as he was able, and she knew that the secrets she kept could place her at risk from the Captain of the Crows. But sex was her best tool at the moment, it seemed, or at least a friendly, sympathetic ear would be useful, and so offering whatever he needed was a risk she chose to accept.

Grainger did a mental calculation of the ticks he had to spend, the time he had to kill as he waited for the lab to send the requested information, the chances of missing his quarry if he took the blonde up on her offer. He had almost talked himself out of accepting when she laid her slight hand on his. Expecting to see in her face that she read his reluctance and was trying to sway him, that she had been able to tell that he was leaning towards declining the invitation, he saw nothing in her eyes but sympathy and a touch of warm comfort. He lost the will to resist her.

Without a word, he downed the drink, got up, and waited for her to lead him.

Maybe he should have married again, he mused as they started up the stairs at the rear of the club that went to a sub-level consisting of several closed-room doors, rooms where the music from below throbbed up through the floor into his feet. A decision to remarry would have kept him out of such places, places he seemed to visit too often when his willpower was at its weakest. But his work precluded the possibility of meeting anyone suitable, and as work had become his life, it was all he lived for now. Work and moments such as this.

Inside of the room she chose, a plush room decorated in red and blue and gold with its age and wear masked by the flash and burn of neon through the window outside, she held out her hand for his tick card and, without realizing there was anything unusual about her actions, slid it through the debit reader so many in her profession used and handed it back to him after the briefest of hesitations to make sure the transaction went through successfully. The device, a mixture of tech she and Tox had designed and cobbled together, made the expected tick transfer between accounts, but it also made a duplicate image of both sides of the card and recorded every morsel of data the read-strip stored.

Zara would not have to craft an A or B-Pass now. An exact forgery of Grainger's Primary Pass, which gave him access to anywhere in Hebanthe Falls, would get Rhyd anywhere he wanted to go.

"There now…" She began to unbutton the man's coat with a leisurely, comforting expression of seductive grace. "Why don't you relax and tell Zara what's troubling you?"

"Zara…that's your name?"

Hers was an innocent and fair question, as those in her profession often served as private confidants, holding confessions as well as any Talker or herpa, often better. She knew it. He knew it. But there was also a risk in telling her too much, a risk that it could later be used against him. Still, as he began to relax beneath her skilled hands that eased the tension from his muscles, and eventually beneath the skill of her mouth as well, he began to talk.

❧Chapter 18❦

Her head lolled to one side, swollen eyes appearing closed as she thankfully accepted the respite between torturous periods of repeated questioning. The pinpoint lights above her had long ago blurred into tiny glares, nothing more, and any detail on the walls of metal plating reinforced with dingy soundproof materials had grown distorted, flat, and featureless. Only the SCAMs, one in each of the ceiling corners she presumed as she could see one in each corner in the direction she currently faced, were discernible. No windows or mirrored glass, only the door she knew to be behind her, now that her chair had been turned this way and that enough times she had lost count. She had no idea how long she had been in this room without food or water.

Hours? Days? In the near darkness, it was impossible to tell, and her body, clawing inside with pain, hunger, and thirst, was no reliable indicator. She refused to talk, refused to break, and suspected that her obstinacy would result in her death. With Venn's Vanishing, she too had felt dead inside, a deadness that allowed her to support Rhyd's quest for vengeance…even assist him…as he broke the laws of treason in search of equality, fairness, and the return of those taken from the Levs for no reason beyond suspicion alone.

She would never willingly betray either of them, her cousin or his partner. She would keep Rhyd's activities, his identity, his secrets safe until the Founder and his Crows stripped the life from her bones and the breath from her lungs. The persecution of the Levs had to end. And it had to begin not only with Rhyd Ballard, but with Tox and everyone else in Hebenon willing to stand together to make it stop.

&*&

Arm around Zara's shoulders as she lay, eyes closed, breathing deep and soft as if sleeping, Grainger hissed at the buzz of his chrono, not wanting an interruption now. The uncovering of Zara's hidden assets, the ones she revealed to so very few out of the fear that the Founder's quest to purify Hebanthe Falls' genetic pool would lead to her extermination, had startled him. But surprisingly to them both, it had proven less of a bother for him than expected.

Maybe, he mused, as he nosed through her tousled hair and ignored the buzzing that had ceased now, he had not objected because he had suspected from the start that she was something more than female, something more than male, while at the same time being wholly human and not an andi.

With traces of pollutants in the air, the food, the water…none of those things completely filtered out of their atmosphere despite Duncan Kemway's attempts at designing an almost entirely enclosed city for mankind to survive in…it seemed reasonable that people like Zara…different people…were more common in Hebenon then anyone realized. If the parah who had disappeared into the heart of Hebenon's 'society' was normal in appearance, despite what poisoned her and her people on the Outside, was it so strange to find that there were 'monsters' within? Was Zara any more a monster for her unusual sexual traits than anyone else was without them?

Not to Grainger.

With the comm silent at last, Grainger shut his eyes, intending to drift back to sleep, intending to forget there was another world outside of this room, outside of this bed. It was tempting to remain here and let Hebanthe Falls take care of itself. But a few deep breaths later, when the fog of sleep started to tug at the corners of his waking mind, the buzzing began again.

He groaned.

Though she did not move or open her eyes, Zara murmured, "You should get that." She felt no attachment to the man at her side, saw him only as a gateway to needed information, but she was grateful that someone had looked beyond her peculiarities to the person inside, who even seemed to relish her differences, and accepted both without making her feel like the aberration she was sometimes called.

Grainger grunted, flailed one hand about until he found the comm on the bedside table, and after tapping the smooth surface, tapped the bud in his ear. "Grainger," he said in a sex-roughened tone.

The voice on the other end, speaking directly into his ear, caused him to sit, rubbing his eyes with the back of his hand as he listened. Zara rose to her knees behind him, pressed her head against the back of his, and slid her arms around his torso, hoping that proximity would allow her to overhear what the person on the comm was saying while trying to appear simply affectionate. She could not, however, but through that contact, she could feel Grainger's mounting excitement.

Enjoying the last vestiges of physical closeness he suspected he would feel for some time, Grainger patted Zara's arm. "You're certain?" he asked into the comm. "No possibility of error?"

She lifted her head, hoping to catch a single word, a phrase, or something helpful, but there was nothing.

"Good…run the program. Yes, that one. He will get it when his aides log in. Send the details to me; I'll take care of it."

"Send what?" Zara asked innocently, kissing between his shoulder blades as she raked her nails lightly over his abdomen. She knew he was on this Lev hunting the Scarecrow, hunting Rhyd. She knew he did not yet have the evidence needed to find him, or the resources required to mount an assault or make an arrest. And she knew he had not yet found the parah child he had been commissioned to locate. He would have other duties too, of course, other investigations and problems to solve, and the call might pertain to any one of those.

But it might also be the call that targeted Rhyd and Agnys for arrest or death.

"I must go."

"So soon?"

"The Founder beckons…and he does not like to be kept waiting."

"Mmm…" The call had not sounded like that sort of relayed request, not from the words he had spoken, but Zara could not pry too deeply without raising suspicion. He rose and dressed beneath her watchful gaze and she pulled the sheet up around herself like a shield. "You will come again?"

She allowed herself to sound interested, hopeful, as if his company meant more than it had. It might have been a standard ploy intended to hook a repeat client, but Zara did not seem that sort to him. Everything about her felt more sincere than that. And if she was hoping for details about his work, she did not pursue them, and Grainger appreciated that. He had no time to talk. He had what he needed, peace of mind and a level of physical calm and centering he had not recently felt, as well as proof that the Founder was wasting time torturing a woman who might or might not know anything of use. The real culprit, the man he had been searching for all along, had been right under his nose that last night in the Levs, and Grainger had not even realized it.

He had a face now, rough though it was in his memory, and a name, and within minutes he would hopefully have a residence as well, so long as his target was not a streeter. With a flash of spite, Grainger had deliberately ordered the corruption of the data at the Hub level to make it difficult for Haythem to follow him, should the Founder and Morenski ultimately give up on the woman and decide to investigate the gathered evidence instead, the way Grainger had done.

It gave the Captain the lead he wanted, as he was already in the target vicinity, and as soon as his Crows rallied to him, he would suit up in preparation for the raid. Though the target had, to Grainger's remembrance, been injured and drugged, might even be dead if he was one of the unfortunate few to suffer adverse reactions to Heb, Grainger was taking no chances. The Scarecrow was known to single-handedly take out entire squads and teams of Crows. Grainger's instructions to his team were explicit and detailed. If he called for them, they were to take extra precautions and once they gathered, he would do the same. The Scarecrow was not getting away from him again.

And Zara, worried about his intentions as he strode from the room without replying to her last question, would not waste time either. She allowed enough time to pass for him to leave, to see him through the window of the room when he looked up and down the walkway expectantly. Then she dressed, snagged the Pass reader, and headed home to make use of what she had gleaned from Grainger's Pass…but only after sending a message to both Lash and Rhyd so that they would not be caught off guard should Grainger be heading their way.

ᷤ*ᷤ

Agnys, surrounded by cats on the sofa, looked at the buzzing panel on the wall and then towards the door. She was alone, except for the cats, but she knew Lash had not gone far, only to the flat next door that he called home. She did not know what the buzzing meant, but when it stopped on its own, ending with a single beep, she went back to playing with the cats. Whatever had been making the sound, she trusted that Lash would find it when he returned, just as she believed his return would be any moment now. There was nothing to fear. She was safe and Rhyd would come back for her soon.

ᷤ*ᷤ

Workout complete, one final check made on the stashes of supplies he had created…now that he was more worried than ever about them being found and confiscated, and Rhyd started for home, noting an increase in Crow activity in the streets when he left the Shed. Their abundance made him withdraw into the first doorway he reached, and after several minutes of watching their swarming, he retreated into the familiar territory of the shafts.

It was no coincidence they were there. Tox's arrest, the impounding of his equipment from her workshop, Zara's promised attempts to hack the Hub's archival data in the Uppers, any or all of those things might have pointed fingers at him. Wearing the pair of vision goggles he typically used in the shafts and the filt mask that kept molds and contagions from being inhaled into his already compromised airways, Rhyd sprinted in the direction of home.

If his identity was blown, his home was no longer safe for either Agnys or Lash. He had to get them out, take them somewhere secure.

He believed he knew just the place.

❧CHAPTER 19❧

His Crows did not bother with protocol. Not this time, not with a matter as sensitive and important as this one. Knocking would serve as a warning, and Grainger wanted to allow the Scarecrow no time to arm himself, no time to flee. Nor did they take the time to open the door with a Pass or with explosives that might compromise the infrastructure of Hebenon. The storming of the flat, two simultaneous kicks against the latched side of the door, popped it open; it swung back and crashed against the shelving behind it, knocking the planter box to the floor. The act was enough to draw attention as it was, a regrettable thing but the quickest way inside with the element of surprise.

A girl within the room, the child Grainger had seen before, screamed in terror and tried to scramble beneath the table beyond their reach. She was not their objective, Grainger did not care about her being there, but one of his two dozen Crows, someone from the middle of the cluster, unable to see clearly who was moving, fired an injector with the intention of hitting the individual they were here to arrest. The dart luckily hit the moving target and not any of the other Crows who surged into the building first, upending furniture in their search for the Scarecrow.

Grainger growled, intending to have words with that officer later.

The cello flew from its open case with enough force that the impact with the kitchen counter snapped its neck and popped strings under the strain.

Rhyd froze in the shaft, his sensitive ears split by the snapping of cello strings and the screams of a frightened child that reverberated directionless off of the mostly metal surfaces around him. Crawling through narrow passages, prepared to drop into his living room to fight, to kill, however many intruders had broken into his home where he was certain the sounds originated, he was stopped by a tight hand on his ankle. He kicked and twisted, intending to cut down whoever dared to hinder him, to see Lash waving him frantically back with a determined shake of his head. Rhyd growled, hoping that meant that the child he had heard was someone other than Agnys, hoping the girl was safe with Lash as he expected her to be. The sounds he made were unheard by the invaders, masked by the still screaming child, a voice his gut knew to be Agnys' despite his hopes to the contrary, and he scurried back to where Lash waited.

Whatever the man knew, whatever was happening, he would demand answers for why Agnys was alone as soon as he saved her.

Her screeching would not stop, despite the injector fired at her, the normal-looking, beautiful blonde child with brigh blue eyes who showed no reaction to the Heb except for an initial surprised squawk before she yanked the dart from her shoulder and threw it to the floor to crush it beneath her foot. She darted away to elude the reaching hands. For a moment, none of the Crows moved. Grainger stared.

She was the one? She was the immunity?

She was the parah?

Not a monster, not a mutant, but a normal child like any other in the whole of Hebanthe Falls?

How could he have been so blind?

Yet how could he have known? Nothing Grainger had been told, nothing he had learned growing up, nothing he had passed on to his officers to assist in the finding and capture of this child, permitted her existence to be real.

What was inside of her, however, what could not be seen, could be as deadly as anything on the outside, and if she carried an immunity to Heb, then Founder knew what else she might carry that could infect everyone in the city, if they were not infected already.

A gesture and the two Crows closest rushed to catch her, eliciting a louder pitched scream for only a moment before a hand covered her mouth and someone else rapped her across the head with a thumper.

Only then did the screaming cease.

"What…?"

Lash frantically shook his head, demanding silence now that there were footsteps and voices on the other side of the wall that separated Rhyd's flat from Lash's.

The bedroom. They were defiling Venn's space.

Rhyd began to surge out of the shaft into Lash's dark home but the lanky blond blocked him and grunted, "Stay."

"No one, sir." The mechanical, inhuman-sounding voice created behind its bird-beaked mask faded as it passed from the bedroom back into the living room.

"Next door."

That was a voice Rhyd knew, a voice that made his skin crawl with fury. That man, on the orders of the Founder, had robbed him of one person, likely two now, was about to abduct another. Someone he had sworn to protect, who was too small to protect herself.

Together, he and Lash pulled the vent grate into place and Rhyd scooted back to the nearest junction to prevent anyone from finding him should they shine a light through the grate in the search for spies, stowaways or contraband. He could no longer see Lash and so had to trust him as the door of the man's apartment was kicked open.

Instead of crashing against the wall, the door broke free of its hinges and fell to the floor.

The Crows at the front of the force stepped into what appeared to be an empty flat, one littered with clutter and debris and a flurry of cats that scattered in every direction with yowls and hisses at the crashing of the door and the flashing of the light sticks in their direction. Because one window was broken, slightly ajar and cracked on one side, it made an ideal entry point to allow felines and rodents to seek shelter from the city's damp. The sight was not an unusual one; none of the Crows were shocked by what they saw.

A Crow's beam crossed over a cowering, emaciated man in a corner behind a well-worn, barely padded chair, and had to come back to him to verify what they saw. The man wore shabby clothing, not rags but not decent either, and he trembled and shuddered and tried to hide from the light by raising his spindly bare arms to shield his face.

"Where's the man next door?"

Lash shrugged, still cringing, shaking his head side to side so that his long hair swayed in front of his eyes. Dissatisfied with the non-verbal response, one of the Crows yanked him to his feet, thrusting him against the wall with his other hand around the man's throat and the point of his mask's long-beaked respirator inches away from the streeter's nose. He had to be a streeter.

"Where is he? Have you seen him?"

Lash, still shaking his head as much as the hand around his throat permitted, opened his mouth, revealing a cavity devoid of tongue. Each Crow knew what that meant, knew that the man had once held high clearance in the city, higher than any of them would ever attain, and had been silenced to protect what he knew, what he had seen or heard. The rumor that such men still had access to the Founder, or at least to members of the Doctet, for whom they had once worked, was enough to make the Crow holding him drop him to the floor.

"Search the rooms…then let's go," he grunted. He was not going to take the risk of this pathetic man either turning him into the Founder or being called a colluder for interacting with a traitor.

He did not expect to find anything in this neglected rubble. As timid and fearful as this fellow was, if anyone else was here, the officer felt certain he would have turned them over to protect himself. They, a large unit of Crows acting on the Founder's behalf, were surely more fearsome than a single vigilante acting without authority.

Lash waited, watching with the terror they expected to see, until they vacated his 'home' and rejoined their captain in the street. They could eject him for vagrancy, but their fear, or perhaps respect, of whatever his position in Hebanthe Falls had once been, caused them instead to choose to ignore his presence and leave him alone.

They were on a mission they deemed more important. Lash's being here was inconsequential.

Grainger snarled at his newest failure, having anticipated bringing the Scarecrow down and proving himself to be the captain the Founder seemed to have forgotten he was… the captain he no longer believed in. But the child slung over one of the Crow's shoulder was a prize worthy of as much respect as the Scarecrow was. Perhaps more, since the parah threat was to all life in the city, not only to the Crows the Scarecrow persistently harassed.

"Take her to Lima and Tamner. You," Grainger pointed to two Crows, and then to another two. "He has to return sometime…for her." He looked at the girl again, her face angelic in the blow-induced sleep. As protective as Ballard had been of her in the street, daring a public attack without his usual masquerade, Grainger knew the man would come for the child from wherever he had gone. The four officers chosen were the largest of his unit, the best trained. If they used both size and skill and the element of surprise to their advantage, he hoped they would be enough to take the Scarecrow down, bring him in.

The broken door of the adjoining apartment, however, was a regrettable strike against the element of surprise.

"Bring him to me when you have him. No delays. Directly to me. He glowered down at them with a snarl. If they had any thoughts of taking their captive to the Founder instead, Grainger wanted it known how much of his displeasure they would incur.

Fortunately, most Crows were more loyal to their captain than to anyone else in the city.

From within the shaft, Rhyd listened, counted footsteps, knowing from their tone and count their distance from the flats, and when, at last, they were far enough away for him to emerge without fear of capture, Lash pulled the grate open. By now he had reattached the prosthetic tongue without Rhyd knowing how it was done.

They waited to see if the movement of the grate attracted the attention of the Crows left next door. When none came, Rhyd dropped out of the shaft and hissed, "What the cazzo…how did…?"

"I came for milk…that was all. Not even three minutes." Lash felt miserable, guilty about what had happened, as if he was somehow responsible, despite the fact that, if he had been there, he would have been no more able to protect her then he had been able to from the flat he claimed as his. He could have insisted she come with him for those few minutes, but how could he have known what was so near at hand? And as the Crows had come here as well, looking for Rhyd in Lash's apartment, bringing Agnys here would have made no difference.

"I've got to find her…I can cut them off…"

"You can't…you're not equipped…and there are too many…"

"They're going to kill her!"

Lash caught Rhyd's face between his hands to still him, quiet him, force him to focus. "No, they won't." At least they would not right away. She was too valuable a specimen to the Founder and his science teams to risk her immediate death. "They need her. We can find her, save her, take her home, but we need a plan."

"I have a plan. I'm going up there. Now."

"Not without a Pass, not without your gear…and not without me."

Rhyd stared at him incredulously.

"This happened on my watch…I know those halls. Those levels. You get a Pass; I can take you wherever you want to go, whether Zara gets the blueprints or not." He had no desire to go back to that world, had never intended to, but time was short now. It had to be done.

Rhyd caught a breath and closed his eyes. Maybe Lash had a fair point. Maybe taking him would be best. But he was not convinced.

"I need you to get some things out of there for me…"

"But there's…" Anyone looking at him knew Lash would be no match for four Crows.

"I'll lead them out of there long enough for you to get in." He shoved his Passcard into Lash's hand. "Take the oxygen tanks…the cello. Take them to Maemi. Might be Crows watching Vapors…in the streets…so I can't do it. You'll have to be careful. I'll meet you there."

Believing that Rhyd could avoid the Crows as he said, though not with oxygen tanks and a cello in tow, Lash reluctantly nodded in agreement. If the Crows were watching the streets between the flat and Vapors, watching the club, it would be difficult for Rhyd to get there by any route other than the vent system. Lash, however, if he changed his clothes into something more respectable than typical streeter attire, would not raise an eyebrow as he passed.

He did not need to remind Rhyd about his injury. There were three lives at stake, two adults possibly dead and one little girl who, for the foreseeable future, would be kept alive and studied, examined as a laboratory specimen in the hopes of learning what made her different from those in Hebanthe Falls and, it seemed from those on the Outside as well. That wrist injury was the least important thing to Rhyd now. Finding Agnys, Venn and Tox was all that mattered.

❧Chapter 20❦

Agnys opened her eyes to a view of a man's backside, a birdman's, she recalled once memory began to return, and she began to struggle as they traveled upwards in a glass and metal box driven by a hiss and whirr that pushed steam through tubes and lifted them higher in the city. Panicked thoughts…where were they taking her…why…what did they want…what had she done…pushed through her head, encouraging her to break free, escape, even though she saw no way out of the box from where she was held.

But the grasp around her legs was too tight and a smack across her thighs by a gloved hand stung and burned enough to silence her and force her to be still. There were Crows all around her, more than she could count, the tallest being the one with the voice she recognized, a voice she would never forget.

How could this have happened? Where was Lash? Where was Rhyd? Where were they taking her?

She knew birds of this sort. She had watched their big black beaks peck apart the carcasses of animals in the fields, ripping out eyes and flesh and devouring them until more ferocious predators came to drive them away. She had been warned about the birdmen in the metal nest who must surely be the same, warned by her cousin, her uncle, the newcomers…indeed everyone in the village. The birdmen were not to be trusted, no matter what they offered in trade. Not with their bent sticks that shot air and hard round pellets, not with their needles that sickened men and sometimes killed them. Their eyes could not be seen behind reflective sheen that covered them, and she was warned never to trust anyone whose eyes she could not see.

Eyes were windows into who someone was.

She had not trusted them, but her curiosity about what lay inside the nest had been her undoing. She had discovered the truth, that the nest was not filled only with birdmen but with people like her, people who were kind and wanted to help even though neither they, nor she, knew how. People like Lash. People like Zara. People like Rhyd.

Rhyd would come for her. She had to believe that. Somehow, he would find her. Rhyd was looking for Venn still, he was making a plan to look for Tox; he would not give up on her either, any more than he had given up on Venn. Rhyd did not give up.

She had to believe he would come. She had to cling to that hope and have faith in him. Squeezing her eyes shut, she blocked out the dizzying effect of movement outside the transparent-walled box and held on to hope as she felt her blonde savior growing further and further away.

෨*ක

Though she was not entirely surprised to have Rhyd squirm through the vent and drop into the apartment, the noise of his opening the grate, and her fear that he could be someone else, were startling enough that, when he straightened on his feet, Zara had a popper aimed at his head, pointed between his eyes. Both hesitated, neither moving or breathing until she released a long sigh and lowered the popper.

"You have no idea how close you just came to a hit, Whiskey," she muttered, setting the popper down on her workbench and leaning against the edge with relief.

"Think I do," he snorted, emptying the packs he had brought on a different table to rummage through their contents. "With all the activity out there, you'd better keep that thing handy."

"That bad?"

"They got Agnys…they think they'll corner me…but it ain't happening. Lash make it by?"

She had not spoken to Lash other than to learn what Rhyd had just hinted at, that his home had been raided and Agnys taken. She nodded with a grim, sour expression as she pulled a warm, plastic coated card from the programming device near her hand. "He's helping in the kitchen downstairs…blending in. Seemed the safest place until things cool down."

"Don't think they're gonna…not til they noose me…or I end this."

"End this?" She did not like the way that sounded. Inevitable. Final.

Weapons and tools were strapped to his legs, his arms, into the pockets and pouches of his gear, his coat. It was nearly everything that remained in his arsenal that Grainger had not taken, everything brought into this fight against the Crows and the Founder. There would not be another fight after this one. Not for Rhyd. He was either fighting his way to the top, freeing Agnys, Tox, and Venn…and any other prisoners he could find, or he would die trying. Perhaps he would accomplish both.

"Long as paranoia rules in Hebenon, there won't be peace. No one's gonna have a better life. It can't happen the way things are." It did not matter what the Talkers and herpa said of Duncan Kemway, the original founder of Hebanthe Falls. All that mattered was what the Kemways had become in the centuries since then. And what they had become, in Rhyd's opinion, was unfit to rule those they did not appreciate. They, and those of the Doctet around them, had no empathy, no concern, no understanding of the largely invisible supply source of the Levs, those in the great body of Hebanthe Falls who the Uppers parasitically sucked of life.

Though inclined to agree, as most men and women in the Levs did after experiencing the eroding conditions in which they lived, like many, Zara wondered if there was really an alternative. Fighting for something better was her way, but she admitted often she could not fathom what 'better' would mean from where she stood. There was nowhere else for them to go, no one else to lead them, and no easy way to change the minds of those eternally in charge. Hebenon was the only home any of them had known, the Outside a poisonous wasteland, leaving them few opportunities for improvement.

Was Rhyd's suggested solution of removing the Kemways from leadership really the best, the only, answer to ensuring the city's survival? Or did their hope for survival revolve around the little girl Rhyd hoped to rescue?

It was not the time to argue the point. Now was the time for action, of any sort, to bring home those they loved.

She put the card in Rhyd's hand. "A duplicate...down to the programming codes...of Captain Grainger's All-Pass."

"How...?" Rhyd paused as if afraid to accept it, and then shook his head dissmissively as he stuffed the Pass into his pocket. "Never mind." It was better he did not know how she had come by that card.

"It should get you through most of the access points."

"Most?" He knew there would be at least one exception. There were always exceptions. Grainger was the Captain of Security, but likely only the Founder had a true All-Pass.

"Lash says there are a few coded keypads that require spoken or typed codes. You'll have to avoid voice codes...unless you can imitate Grainger or one of the others imprinted into the system. For the others, I'm giving you this."

The miniature earbud was slid into Rhyd's ear and he looked at her quizzically as a second piece was retrieved from the table, a morsel no bigger than a grain of rice which she affixed to his chin, below his lip, with a round dot of adhesive.

"You'll be able to hear me, and I'll be able to hear you, across the Echosys. I know the model they use...or used. I should be able to work you through." It was possible the Uppers had upgraded their hardware since the last time she had studied such things. Then again, very little in Hebanthe Falls changed quickly. "You'll still have to swipe the Pass, but once you do, it'll give me access to the unit and I'll be able to decrypt the passcode. I don't know how long that decryption might take. I've hacked similar systems, but it depends on the length of the sequence they're using. Lash doesn't know. Once you swipe…"

"Be ready to run." Fortunately, running was something that all of Rhyd's coaches had pushed on him in addition to his other training.

"I'll be right here, with the Echo…and I'll hear everything you say. You need help…anything at all…"

Rhyd nodded, understanding what she did not say. By the time he reached the Uppers, he would be too far away for anyone he knew to be able to help if he needed it, but the offer was comforting.

"Lash said he was…" she started again.

"I'll be faster alone."

It was Zara's turn to nod. Rhyd always worked alone. This time would be no exception. Lash was expecting Rhyd to summon him, to include him, but Rhyd had no intention of doing either.

"By the time you're at 20, I'll be tapped in; I can guide you if you…"

"Too much talking." A thought came to him as he picked up his hood. "Can you tap into my visuals? Send me a schematic overlay?" That, he hoped, would be a simpler thing than her trying to talk him through each turn, passage, and doorway. The heat sensors, the infrared and night vision sensors, all were computerized, a system designed in collaboration between Zara and Tox. If anyone could tap into the design, make it happen, its creators should be able to do so.

Zara nodded. Seeing what he saw through a shared electronic connection was not impossible, but it was a breach into Scarecrow's world she had never planned to make. What he did was none of her business. She did not want to see the world he saw, the way he saw it. But she had his invitation now, and the ability to do so.

"Should only take me a few…" She plopped down with her Echo T2 on her lap, and several minutes and keystrokes later motioned for his hood. The sensor chip came out and Rhyd watched anxiously as she plugged it into the chip burner built into her system for such work. The sequences of letters, numbers, and symbols on the screen meant nothing to him, but moments later the chip was again in place and the hood back in his hands. "Put it on…let's give it a test."

He felt better with the hood in place, a mask that disconnected him from the man he was and turned him into the man he wanted to be, the Scarecrow, the protector of the oppressed in the Levs of Hebenon. The sensors went live in response to his body heat, and on the screen in her lap. Though the images looked distorted to Rhyd through the goggles, he could make out his own visage looking at the laptop. Turning his head meant that he could not see the screen, but Zara's grin and tiny sound of elation when he looked at her proved that much of the test was a success.

"I'll work on an overlay," she promised. She should have time to do that as he started up through the vent system. "First…" she said as she set the Echo aside and got back on her feet, "Let's get you wired."

It was easier for others to help attach the tubes and wires that enabled all of the protective features of his suit and coat to work together, and as he did not have time tonight to waste, he welcomed her help. New equipment designs were constantly in the works, efforts by Zara and Tox to make his gear more self-sufficient so he did not need assistance to get out into the city to do what he did. There was no more time for any of that now.

When everything was connected, the microphone and new earpiece she had given him working as flawlessly as the new visual system was, Rhyd caught her wrist and held her there, near to him.

"Zar…"

She shook her head with a little smile and extricated herself from his grasp. Whatever he had been about to say, it was better left unsaid. "Be careful," she murmured.

"Tell Skelter…and Maemi…"

Tell them what? Even Rhyd, at that moment, was uncertain what he would have said if he could have continued. He was not a man for flowery speech, for romantic or emotional words. How many times had Venn chided him for that very fault? But he felt it, the emotions behind the failed words, emotion that translated through the mechanical voice modulator and that caused Zara to nod again.

"I will." She would think of something to say, something appropriate, in the event that he did not make it back. Each of them would know the words were not Rhyd's, but they would also know that the sentiments behind them were very much his.

"And tell Lash…thanks…and I'm sorry."

Not sorry enough to include him, but sorry nonetheless. Those words, at least, he could say. Would the man despise him for denying him the chance to help or would he understand? Rhyd did not know the man well, but he wagered that Lash, the survivor, would understand why Rhyd needed to do this alone.

At least, he convinced himself as he hoisted into the darkness of the vent shaft where the goggles made his vision perfect, he told himself that Lash would understand. They all would. They had to. He owed this to Agnys and Tox. He owed this to Venn.

He had to do this alone.

Zara replaced the vent grate and returned to the desk with her Echosys setup in front of her, murmuring, "Good luck," into the silent air, forgetting for a moment that he would hear her.

Or more likely, Rhyd thought darkly, she had not forgotten at all.

Lima already had the child strapped to a padded table by the time Tamner entered the sterile room, the summons to the lab coming amidst a family dinner that he had found tedious and was happy to get out of, though he did not know the purpose of the summons when he arrived. He still wore his formal dinner attire since he had taken no time to change, and was pulling his lab smock over it as he passed through the whoosh of the sliding doors. There was a pair of officers guarding the door, positioned inside the room rather than outside, and that made him immediately suspicious rather than merely curious.

"A patient?" he asked, wondering why there was no medical staff on hand if that was the case. The child, a girl he guessed from the length of her blonde hair. He could tell nothing else about her yet. She was alive, breathing, but she did not look to be a streeter, and she was not, as far as he knew, the family member of any of the Doctet or their usual Upper entourage.

He did not know everyone in the Uppers, however. This child could be anyone.

Tamner approached the gurney, visually examining her as he came nearer, noticing that the straps were too tight, that there was a red welt on her shoulder as if something had stung or bitten her. It was impossible to miss the terror in her eyes.

"The parah," Lima muttered under his breath, finding that he hated the word as much as he had ever hated anything. It should be just a word. Right now, it was much more…and much less.

Tamner's face paled, but the knowledge did not keep him from reaching to touch her with an ungloved hand. Lima caught his arm with a look that warned against contact and muttered, "Protocol," but it was a look, an admonition, Tamner ignored. He, more than any man in Hebanthe Falls, knew what was outside, what the sensor data, temperature readings, air quality instruments and pollutant detectors revealed every time he checked them. The Founder might proclaim one thing, but Tamner believed something very different.

Since the day his father had taught him to read the instruments and compare the data they offered to the centuries of records the Hub and Archives contained, he had known…as his father had known. Had known and Vanished because of it, having disappeared under the guise of some contagious ailment that required him to be held in isolation until his passing. Tamner's mother, his sisters, other members of the Doctet, and the community in which they lived, might have accepted the official story at face value, but Rafe had not.

It had been that story, and his fear of a fate similar to his father's that had caused Tamner to never challenge the 'official' reports on Outside conditions that Founder Kemway gave to both the residents of the Uppers and the Levs. Neither had ever seen a parah, after all, except the old man dissected and studied days earlier. But now there was this child, this seemingly perfect living specimen of humanity, and inside Tamner, his heart and will were crumbling. He could not remain quiet and idle much longer. If what he was seeing was real, was true and not a hoax, he needed to speak out.

But who, he wondered, would listen?

"Ssh…" he murmured to the child, hoping his tone, the sounds he used to soothe his own children, would calm her as well, as might his gentle, ungloved touch on her bare skin. Her expression did not change, but she did utter a soft, pleading whimper that he barely heard.

It was enough to tear at his heart however.

On the other side of the gurney, Lima was prepping a long needle and an array of vials to begin the process of blood and tissue collection. Tamner glared and hissed, "Miguel," below his breath.

Miguel glared back at him, rolling his eyes in the direction of the unmasked Crows at the door, who thankfully could not see the look. But Tamner did not care if they could see, if they could hear. He did not care if they might report him to the Founder. This was not right.

"We can't do this…this is a child…"

"A parah," Lima pointed out, although Tamner knew the man well enough to see that he was opposed to the battery of tests they were expected to run on a living child no more than seven. Tests that would, ultimately, likely end in death for a final, comprehensive autopsy. He was conflicted about what he had to do, but he was also afraid. Drawing blood, he could do. Experimenting on political prisoners or those too defective or addicted to notice or survive, he could convince himself was harmless and even necessary. If this parah had been what they had all been led to expect, the path laid out before him and Tamner would have been passable. Now, however, he, like Tamner, was uncertain he could follow through.

Which was precisely why, they both thought bitterly, Captain Grainger had left his officers here.

Whatever their reservations, the Captain expected fear would keep them on course.

"We take blood," he said as evenly as he could.

Tamner held his breath, held eye contact with Lima, and then let out a long hiss of capitulation. They drew blood.

By the Founder, he hoped that would be enough.

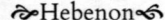

Hebenon

❧Chapter 21❦

It was slow going through the first Levs of shafts that Rhyd traveled through, with Crows alone or in pairs tromping through the larger passages in search of him. He doubted they expected him to be there, since they made enough noise to alert anyone in the area of their approach. Or else, he thought with amusement, they were fearful enough of confronting him that they wanted to warn him away to avoid conflict. It seemed they were covering the most obvious exits in and out of each Lev vent system. He did not know if they knew his identity, if they were searching the Shed for him, grilling his coworkers. He did not know if he would have any life to go back to once this night was over. But the presence of Crows in the shafts was enough to cause Rhyd to take indirect routes through crawl spaces and cubbies that the Crows were unlikely to enter in their cumbersome attire. Unlike Rhyd, they would not know their way through the smaller passages. He doubted any of them were familiar with the shaft system. If the Crows knew anything about them, they knew the access points intended for repair teams to enter, and those that were often used by streeters to build nests safely away from moisture and harassment.

But Rhyd knew every passage, every way in and out of each Lev, and although it took too long, by the time he made it to Lev 7, he no longer heard the footsteps of Crows echoing through the tunnels. They were focused on the Levs closest to his home, closest to Vapors, which was to Rhyd's benefit. It was the first obstacle averted.

He expected there to be many more, however, as he zigzagged through the dark from one entry point to another. Lifts were avoided. He could not get caught in one, should someone determine where he was, where he was going, what he intended to do. It was better to run, to take stairs or upshafts that no one would expect him to take. Safer and thus, he hoped, faster.

Maemi sent her mother-in-law home with Xiaodan, not wanting the young man or ancient woman to be caught in the crossfire that she sensed was brewing, that would likely descend on Vapors if the manhunt for Scarecrow, for Rhyd, brought the Crows to her door. The Captain's earlier appearance in her club had served as a warning, even though it afforded Zara a useful connection, and the gossip about the capture of a parah inside of Hebenon, the parah the Crows had been seeking for several days, had come to her through a handful of patrons after Lash's arrival brought the cello, oxygen tanks, and the same news from Rhyd's flat. The items were carefully hidden, the tanks placed in Skelter's care where Rhyd would be able to get to them if he needed them and the broken cello securely stowed in a compartment upstairs with the older woman and Xiaodan.

Maemi was struggling not to be angry or bitter with Xiaodan's unfortunate choices. He was young, naïve. He had never been entrusted with the secrets Tox kept, the ones she and Rhyd and others protected from the city. He did not know who Rhyd was, did not know that the events of the past had come full circle. He had been sheltered from all of it, by his grandmother, his mother, his mentor, his aunt. He could not know that his choice would have grave repercussions.

His naiveté had shielded him from the dark underbelly of Hebenon. Until recently, he had viewed the Crows, the Doctet, even Founder Kemway as distant benevolent rulers of their claustrophobic world. While many grew up feeling the yoke of oppression, there were always those who never seemed to feel it, see it, who never noticed or refused to believe that things were as grim as others made them out to be, whose optimism never allowed them to see anything but the best in their world. Venn's arrest, as young as Xiaodan had been when it occurred, had not impacted his life. He had only met Venn in passing as he had not been apprenticed to Tox until after the man Vanished.

There was gossip, things spoken about in hushed tones, about Venn and the others who disappeared, allegations of anti-Founder, anti-Doctet, activity, insinuations of Heb addiction, inferences of treasonous opinions, things that were often all it took to prompt an arrest if such rumors came to the attention of Founder Kemway.

Xiaodan had not been able, for whatever reason, to understand that there was nothing criminal in either addiction or thoughts.

Even for someone who shared those treasonous opinions, however, finding what appeared to be a criminal's hideout, a secret room in another's home, might have been cause to raise flags, make a report, the way Xiaodan had done. He wanted to protect Tox. How could he know that such a stash was not meant to harm him or Tox? How could he know it was not a threat? He could have asked, but in his inexperience, asking Tox…especially since she had been missing at the time…had not crossed his mind. He had not anticipated that his efforts would backfire and result in the arrest of the very person he wanted to protect most.

Maemi could see the regret in his eyes every moment since Tox's arrest, see the pain and horror and the birth of understanding of the opinions and views of his elders. Maybe they had been right. Maybe Hebanthe Falls was not the haven, the paradise, he wanted to believe it to be. But the damage had been done and there were few ways he could begin to atone for that mistake.

If the Crows were now seeking the Scarecrow, however, that meant that Tox was innocent…and yet still she had not come home. Maybe she was in league with him and he was going to rescue her. Or maybe the Crows were merely stomping around Hebenon using fear to drive the populace back into submission.

The Scarecrow had been fighting on their side. Xiaodan saw that now. If Tox was indeed the Scarecrow, he thought, and there was no one else to fight for their cause, who was going to save her?

He did not know what Maemi knew. That Rhyd Ballard had a plan. He barely knew who Rhyd Ballard was.

With the old woman absent from Vapors, there was little food coming out of the vindi's kitchen, only the fried fish and steamed cabbage her unexpected helper was able to prepare on short notice. Maemi did not know Lash, though she had seen him occasionally in Skelter's company, but she was certain she had served him a few times in the club over the years. She might have been reluctant to trust him with the Crows on the prowl in the streets and alleys beyond the beaded curtain doorway, but the cello he had brought, broken as it was, and Skelter's willingness to vouch for him, was enough to give Lash a temporary hiding place in her kitchen until Rhyd's mission was complete. Until he returned.

If he returned.

Maemi was not the only one to believe they might never see the blonde man again.

She was in the kitchen too, most of her customers steered away by the overactive Crow patrols, trying to determine what else they could serve for food to the patrons brave enough to come in or stay, when shouts of surprise and fear pushed through the serving window. Through it, she could see them, Crows in their long black coats and bird-beaked masks, erupting into Vapors by the dozens. They grabbed men and women, andis and human alike, knocking over cloth-covered tables to prove that no one was hiding underneath, poking beneath the dance platforms with the staves some carried to flush out anyone there. Some thundered through the vindi to the dressing rooms where they rounded up more people, andis and clients, while others crashed about behind the bar, knocking over bottles in their carelessness, shooting poppers and injectors into the crowd as some of the patrons confronted their bullying assailants head on.

Maemi was about to storm from the kitchen into the main room, to demand an explanation for their destructive raid, when the kitchen entrance flew open. Her first thought was more Crows and she grabbed an empty pan to throw, the only weapon at hand. But it was Skelter, not Crows, frantically waving for her and Lash to follow. Behind him on the grated platform, Zara waited, anxiously watching the stairs above and below, her Echo T2 clutched to her chest.

"Gotta go," Skelter demanded, his voice barely heard over the chaos in the room behind Maemi.

Concern for the vindi that had always been her home, the legacy her family had left for her, might have been enough to draw Maemi back, enough to compel her to stay. But Lash's grip on her arm, tighter and stronger than expected, and a healthy dose of self-preservation, proved enough to make her do as Skelter asked. Expecting that the Crows would soon follow, since at least one had to see the movement in the vindi kitchen, she paused long enough to set the door code and lock it so that the kitchen door would have to be broken or hacked by a tapper in order for the Crows to come this way.

"Where…?"

Skelter gave Maemi a boost to the platform above them where Lash knelt with an offered hand to pull her up. Zara had already made it halfway up the staircase, but noises in the kitchen behind the locked door left them little time to dally or talk.

"Up…anywhere…" Skelter hissed. "Lash will lead…get us to safety…" He was starting up the slippery metal stairs himself, following the others. "Move. Go."

They did not wait, not even Zara, who looked back over her shoulder as they ran, to be sure Skelter was still there, was behind her, joining in their flight to safety. Perhaps not safety, she mused, knowing how hard life could be to get by without ticks, without a Pass, without a home to put down roots in if they were being forced to leave their old lives behind.

But the Crows she had seen in the streets, the ones Rhyd had warned about, the ones Skelter was now shooting at with the first of three poppers he carried, were determined to find associates of the Scarecrow in order to find him. Whether Tox had broken and given away Rhyd's identity or whether they still believed that she was the

Scarecrow, those who knew them both, and especially those who claimed to be friends, would be at the top of the wanted list for a long time to come. It would not be difficult for the Crows to extract names from those they were terrorizing.

Running was their only chance.

∂*∾

In spite of the triple-layered breathing filt built into his headgear, his well-trained nose, in addition to the sensors incorporated into his gear, registered the rising level of methane contaminants in the shaft as he neared the junction that would bring him up to Lev 14. He was making adequate progress, unhindered by heizers, speners, skolpers, other bilgers, or Crows, and avoiding passages that would require the use of his Pass or Grainger's. If workers had been recalled from these levels, there was a reason for it, something other than luck, which had cleared his way.

Their total absence made Scarecrow leery, wary and when the shouts erupted in his earpiece, Skelter's voice and voices from somewhere further away down below, he froze, straining to form a mental picture based on those sounds. The incessant clack-clack of the Echosys keys as Zara continued her efforts to break the Upper's security codes stopped abruptly with those shouted voices, and Rhyd scurried into the first narrow panel cubby box he found. It was an alcove where shaft workers were allowed to relieve themselves, tight quarters but private enough for his needs.

Hand pressed over his ear as if it would enable him to hear more clearly, he hissed. "Zar?"

There was no answer and the comm went dead. He assumed she had closed the Echo feed, possibly the Echo itself. The likelihood that she had been caught, captured, or even killed, was not worth pondering. It would paralyze him into inaction if he gave into such wildly whirring thoughts. It was more calming to believe she was too smart to be caught, to believe that if she was forced into a quandary, felt she was about to be discovered, she would kill the feed and protect herself, protect them both.

But Crows in the streets around her home, pursuing Skelter, was a real possibility, a likely threat she would have to guard against, and he hoped that if that was what he had heard, what the two of them faced now, that they would make it to safety.

Unless he returned below when this night was over, he would never know.

That smell again pulled Rhyd back to his surroundings and when the possibility of the source being inside the alcove where he hid proved negative, he was drawn back out to the juncture where the strongest concentration of fumes was detected. Searing steam spewed from a punctured pipe that ran along the base of the wall, and with it dripped a viscous fluid that corroded the surface upon which it fell and glowed with red heat to the sensors in his mask that gave Rhyd clear vision within the city's vent system.

Though he could not repair the corrosion damage as he had brought nothing with him that would allow that, he could wrap and repair the puncture to prevent any further contaminants from escaping the pipe. He was not a spener or a skolper, but he had experience with pipes. To ignore the damage was to risk poisoning the Levs, and his mission, while important, would be for naught if their home fell into toxic decay and the residents died because of it.

He swore beneath his breath, pulled out a small tube of pipe caulk and squeezed some into the stylus-sized puncture, doing his best to avoid getting any of the leaking fluid onto his gloves lest it eat through the reinforced fabric and his hand. As the steam thinned, the filling decreasing its output, Rhyd could better examine the damage before wrapping it with repair tape.

This was no ragged puncture, nor the result of natural wear. Accidental, perhaps, if the last repair crew through here had been careless with their tools, but any proper spener or skolper would have realized the problem at once, or would have turned to see what they had hit, look for damage. In the shafts, being careful was a necessity.

This, to Rhyd, looked intentional, and it, and the continuing silence in his earpiece, increased the rawness of his nerves. The amount of fluid spreading across the floor, drying now in contact with the heavy air, indicated no more than an hour and no less than thirty minutes of drippage. He had been in the vent system that long. Whoever had done this might still be near, might have set this as an ambush point of a sort Rhyd had not expected. He stayed crouched, listening to the familiar creaks, pops, groans, and shivering of the shafts, the whirring and hissing of systems heating, cooling, sucking and belching, cleaning the air, the water, and the waste of anything that could potentially poison the residents of Hebanthe Falls. The steam-driven mechanical symphony yielded nothing unusual, no footfalls or voices or glimmers of light stick beams.

For now, he was safe, but lingering was inviting trouble. Zara's presence had not yet returned, but Rhyd could wait no longer. He was going to have to rely on himself now, the way he always did.

But he readily admitted that this time he wanted her company inside his headgear. He did not want to face his end alone.

ॐ CHAPTER 22 ॐ

T he men glared at each other across the glass and metal table, the thing one believed was protecting him, the thing the other believed was preventing either of them from assaulting the other. Perspiration glistened across the taller man's dark-skinned skull and face, but he did not wipe it away, even when it threatened to trickle into his eyes. To do so would break gaze with the fire-shooting scrutiny of the other who gripped the edge of the desk hard enough that his knuckles were white.

Grainger had started the hunt for the Scarecrow with the break-in of Rhyd Ballard's flat, a hunt that had failed in its primary objective but which had produced the sweet fruit of the parah who had evaded capture for too long. The news of that had barely come to Haythem's attention when the Founder, the moment Grainger's was otherwise distracted, demanded a full-on assault of Lev 3 to find and arrest the Scarecrow. The Founder did not have a face, but he had a location, and that was enough for him to prompt action. He demanded the stationing of Crows at every stairwell, lift and shaft of those bottommost Levs, sending officers door to door, through the streets, questioning everyone, searching everywhere, with the intent of pinning down the vigilante by leaving him nowhere to hide.

It was, to Grainger, an admission that the woman held captive and brutally tortured was not the one they were looking for, was possibly, likely, entirely innocent of wrongdoing.

Rhyd Ballard was no one, a man without a face to Kemway as the Founder had not yet scoured the Hub archives for his identity. Even when Grainger had tried, he peculiarly found most of the data missing, redacted, firewalled, but the Captain, at least, had seen the man's face. He knew who he was looking for, though he did not know why that information was protected…or by who.

Founder Kemway knew none of those things.

But the Founder believed he had enough to find and capture the man, and he was going to prevent Scarecrow's escape by sending an overkill of Crow presence into the Levs that Grainger feared would create a backlash that would generate additional problems.

So determined was the Founder that he wrenched the hunt out of Grainger's control and was directing it himself, the constant stream of messages scrolling up the Echosys screen to his left serving as a reminder of that to them both every moment he and Grainger glowered at one another. With neither of them below to directly oversee the manhunt, however, the reports Grainger could make out through the garbled voices were of disorganization and chaos.

"Get down there and sort them…"

"I did not start that!" the Captain spat, thrusting a finger at the Echosys screen.

"Your search brought us…"

"My investigation consisted of a dozen officers…the rest returned with me and the parah. I gave no orders for that mess."

Insulted by the word mess, the Founder hissed, "They are your officers, Captain…and you are mine…you will do this or be stripped of your rank and I will find someone who will, is that understood?"

Grainger growled in frustration and anger, his gaze never wavering from the Founder's face, his pointing hand not lowering from the ever-changing view of messages and reports. A jumble of thoughts tumbled through his head, thoughts he had never entertained before, things that frightened and troubled him and darkened his already black mood. But from that fear came purpose, a decision, and with that decision came the slow, controlled lowering of his arm to his side. Gaze remaining steady, shoulders drawing back in defiance, though it probably appeared to be a gesture of respect to the Founder, Grainger said flatly, "I will deal with it."

No 'sir'. No 'Founder'. No name or title or rank. Only the admission that he would do something, with no hint of what or how.

"Good." Haythem refused to break the stare either, a strong enough man, firm in the conviction of his power and control, to not back down against a man he viewed as his lesser. He did not react until Grainger was forced to look away by turning to march out the door.

Then Haythem collapsed more heavily than intended into his tall-backed chair to stare at the Echo screen.

Moments later, minutes, perhaps as briefly he lost track of time, he switched the Echo off and stood again. He trusted Grainger to do as instructed. Men in the Uppers always did what the Kemways asked. Haythem's real interest and concern were in seeing this parah child for himself, and leaving the mess in the Levs for his Captain to sort out.

She had started all of this. He wanted to find a way to blame it all on her, for there was no one else to blame.

No one except the still-illusive Scarecrow.

❧*❦

The Crow-instigated violence was spreading. Skelter could see it around them as Lash led his companions this way and that through the grated streets and alleys from one stairway to the next in the quest for each way up between the Levs. They had made it to Lev 5 before more Crows began to appear as if from nowhere to take up stations at each landing in an effort, Skelter guessed, to contain the violence to the lowest Levs and let it play out.

For violence it was. They could hear it as they fought to leave it behind.

But playing out was not on the immediate horizon, Skelter realized, after popping two Crows on a platform to Lev 6 as he and those with him sought someplace safe to rest and rethink their strategy for a few minutes. Crows came down each lift and poured into one Lev, then another, to find their brothers fully engaged in the fight with men, women, children and andis, people who had once cowered in the city's shadows, staying clear of Crows out of fear and begrudging respect. As some citizens teamed together and rushed the Crows in the streets, fighting with everything they had within reach, more than once Skelter heard the cry of "Scarecrow," lift up through the mist, echo through the metal maze, and erupt from somewhere else.

Whether a plea for help or a rallying cry, Scarecrow was no longer combatting oppression alone. Hebenon was striking back amidst a hail of stinging pellets, burning injector needles, sizzling buzzers and the bludgeoning of thumpers.

A hunk of stone, errant or not, flew across their path and caught Skelter in the lower back as he turned from his companions to shoot at a pair of Crows they had not yet shaken. He yelped, arched forward as the force thrust him against the staircase rail. Maemi reached back, caught his wrist as his knees buckled, but when a popper burst rained down on them from somewhere above and one member of the team Skelter had been shooting at got off a lucky injector shot, Skelter's body twisted in such a way that Maemi lost her hold.

"Ivan!"

Further up the stairs, Zara saw him spasm with each hit his body took, and when a needle caught him below his right eye, he twirled, bucked and slid beneath the lower rung of the guardrail. They saw him hit the edge of one platform, the impact coming below his ribcage, and after a brief last look into Zara's eyes, he disappeared into the mist.

"Ivan!"

Zara's shriek was cut off by Maemi's battle cry as she leaped from the step where she stood and planted one foot into a Crow's chest. The injector, his popper, and his thumper dropped as he sprawled backward from the platform and tumbled down the flight of wet stairs. She scrambled to gather all three weapons, as well as the popper Skelter had dropped as he fell, and raced up the stairs following Lash who continued pulling Zara towards safety.

Zara wept, though the spray of the Four Falls on her face made tears unnoticeable, but there was no time for words, for grieving, for hope. If Skelter survived the fall, did not end up in the river to be tangled in the nets, it would be a miracle. Miracles were all the three had to hold on to as they ran and climbed, but Zara, no matter what miracles might come, knew better than to believe she would ever see Skelter again.

Something, a jolt, a shock, a glitch in his sensory and respiratory systems, the loose panel beneath his feet that unexpectedly threw him off balance, brought Rhyd to a halt again, this time with such abruptness that he nearly tumbled headlong down the incline he had entered. His arm flew out to steady him against the curved shaft wall with enough unexpected force that the contact sent searing pain the length of his arm, along his spine, into an eruption of multi-colored light behind his lids. The pain made him swear and slump to the floor with his back to the wall, his aching wrist cradled in his lap.

His gloves came off as he tried to listen for some sign of danger that might have prompted him to stop, but all he was aware of then was the shattering pain in his arm. Fingers beneath the sleeve of his tight black undershirt, he winced as they probed around his wrist and up and down his arm as far as he could easily reach to assess what damage, if any, had been done. He felt no rupture, and the internal dressing felt to be in place, but the pain was undeniable.

Perhaps there was no further breakage, but something had happened in that hit, a tearing of ligaments, another hairline fracture, or impaction of the joints. Favoring his arm, he fumbled with his good hand through his multitude of pockets until he found what he needed: one of the injectors full of some variety of painkiller Skelter had acquired. Something powerful, Rhyd thought with a gasp as it flowed through his veins and momentarily blurred his vision. He had two more, and a small vial of pills, none of which he planned on using any more than he had planned on this dose. Brought in the event of debilitating pain, to keep him going when he might otherwise fall, the narcotics could slow him down, dull his senses. He did not want to risk those things, but without something to ease the worst of the pain, he would never be fit enough to fight any enemy that crossed his path.

Hearing nothing, still not sure what had brought him up short, he staggered to his feet when the searing ache subsided enough to allow him control of his limbs. But his legs felt heavy, his steps sluggish under the initial influence of the painkiller. Progress was slow, his vision now a vivid dark purple around the edges, but he kept moving. Those initial side-effects would diminish over time. He could do this.

He found his way into Upper 20 without difficulty, taking advantage of passages he had once frequented that did not require a Pass to enter. How easy it would be for any of those in the Levs to have trespassed into the now largely forbidden twentieth level of the city. Those from below could attend sporting events in the arena, but were otherwise discouraged from being on Upper 20, the lifts and stairwells protected and monitored at all times, and the workers from below no longer worked these shafts without the proper Pass.

There were no physical barriers, however, to keep Rhyd or anyone else out of the vents. How easy it would have been for Rhyd to come here, in his search for Venn, to rule out any chance of his being there. That he had taken the Shed manager's word for it, that the Upper 20 shafts were off limits, that with his Pass permissions for 20 revoked he was unable to go there, made him now feel like a fool.

Clear this level and he would reach the entrance to 21. He would need all of his strength and focus by the time he got there, and prayed that the slowness of his movement now would give his body enough time to bleed those side effects away. There would be no fight in him if it did not.

❧*❧

"What do you mean?" Haythem snarled at the man before him. "How can they be fighting back? How dare they!"

Barefoot, he had been on his way to see the parah for himself when a courier found him and summoned him to Ximenez's suite of offices from where every prodcast in the city was aired. What the Founder discovered there was a maze of panicked staff flitting this way and that, scurrying between desks, between XCO Archive and maintenance systems, correlating streams of data, SCAM recordings, and field reporter's comments in a push to make sense of what they were hearing and seeing.

To his credit, Kenneth Ximenez, director of media and prodcasts, a man whose lineage stretched back as far as the Founder's, did not flinch beneath the tirade though his eyes read of stress and concern.

"I did not believe it myself at first…thought the reports from Lev 3 were exaggerations, a misunderstanding of events, a result of false data or hacks into the Hub. But the reports are the same, coming in from other sources on Levs 1 through 7…and now 8, 9, and 10. The Levs are rioting, Founder…and the riot is spreading up."

"Where is Grainger? Get those men…"

"I've spoken with Captain Grainger, sir. Everyone has been deployed that he can spare…save for those serving the Uppers and those in recovery…"

"Send them, all of them."

Ximenez's brow arched on his paling face. "All of them?" Sending every officer to the Levs would leave the Uppers unprotected and if the effort failed to stop the momentum of pushing protestors, and they found or forced their way through code, voice, and Pass protected doors, there would be unprecedented destruction where there had always been security. It was a difficult concept, an impossible situation to imagine, something the original Founder had never envisioned.

"All of them," Haythem growled. The Uppers defenses would hold. No one would get as far as Level 21, and if, by some twisted fate, they did, they would never bypass the measures that barricaded the top two levels of Hebanthe Falls. "Shut down all B, C, and D passes and get Ibarra for me. Now!"

❧Chapter 23❦

Anything that could be used as a weapon, furnishings, cooking utensils, and work tools, were wielded against the bird-faced beings that had long tormented the Levs with arrests that the majority deemed unwarranted and unnecessary, arrests of friends and loved ones for no other reason than bearing dissenting voices or addiction to a substance the city hierarchy provided. Though many fell beneath the thumpers blows, the bitter euphoria of Heb-laced injector needles, or well-aimed pellet shots from the poppers, the Crows who had begun this fight the earliest had now run out of ammunition, leaving them no better equipped than the people they fought to subdue. It was hands and thumpers and feet against tools and utensils and broken chair and table legs, and though their protective gear offered defense against the horde of assailants, they were vastly outnumbered now so that protection did little but prolong the Crows inevitable fall.

A new level reached, drawing fresh bodies and the weapons of fallen Crows with them as they rose, the masses surged on, cutting down officers before them, swarming over those they subdued with no intent beyond ridding their world of the invasive, oppressive heel that held them down. If the Crows were incapacitated, caught and rendered helpless, the Uppers would lose their hold on the Levs, and with no enforcers in place, the staples and goods necessary to sustain life would be denied to them. The Uppers would have hemp, and the sources required to turn the plant matter into useable substances. They would continue to have the great structures used to process steel and stone, but they would, most believed, lose much of their manufacturing force, the manpower to operate those factories.

They would also lose access to food and drinkable water, which was grown and filtered in the Levs they subjugated.

The masses were not thinking that far ahead, however, thinking about what they themselves might lose. They were not considering the repercussions of their actions, what would come after. They were only striving to end tyranny and segregation.

Lash did not stop running, pulling the pair of women along in his wake, until he reached the nearly deserted Lev 19. Any Crows that had been on 19 must have migrated below, it seemed, or they had been herded there by the occupants of the Lev since the streets and vindis were deserted of everyone except the very old and the very young. Many homes were open and appeared empty.

As if he knew where he was heading, Lash found an empty flat at the edge of the city, against the sturdy south wall, its door ajar, making entry a simple matter. The flat looked to be in use, someone's home, but it was empty now, and with the unlikelihood of anyone returning except looters until the fighting ceased, it was a safe enough haven.

"Should be good for now," Lash muttered between gulps of air as Zara collapsed at the desk in front of a small Echosys screen, knocking a scatter of crystals and stones from the tabletop onto the floor. Rather than immediately turning on the flat's unit, she opened her own in the hopes of reestablishing communication with Rhyd.

"What do you think is…?" Maemi began, pacing from one side of the room to the other, watching through the door and window, unable to sit still with so much nervous energy racing through her blood.

"Ssh," scolded Zara as Lash emerged from the kitchen with three bottles of beer. Someone would miss those later, but if that was all that was missing by the end of the rioting, the flat's owners would be lucky. Maemi took one gladly but Zara waved hers away. She could not drink now. She wanted to be clear-headed to tend to the job before her.

Within moments, she had interfaced her system with the Echo on the desk, avoiding traps and pitfalls in the software that would notify the HUB moderators of unlawful use. Then she turned on her portable unit and once more hacked into the heart of the Hub and Archives in the hopes of reestablishing connection with Rhyd. The prodcast now playing on the apartment Echo allowed them to view Hebenon's panic as the familiar, normally steady voice of Vittorio Oslo, once a respected athlete but now a sports commentator, narrated the playing SCAM footage, images that flashed in rapid succession across the screen. His voice was tense, uneasy as he tried to talk over what sounded like chaos from within the prodcast recording room. As Zara worked, Maemi and Lash watched in fascinated horror until the sight of a Crow's severed arm flew in front of one of the SCAM units, at which time Lash turned the apartment's view screen off.

The dark screen had no bearing on whatever work Zara was undertaking on her Echo T2.

She did not look up from her smaller screen and her efforts to patch into Rhyd's system. After losing Skelter, Rhyd, at least, had to be alive. The thought gave her a shred of desperate hope, hope that stretched thinner with each second it took to reconnect to his signal.

"They're fighting back," Maemi murmured in awe and pride. "Finally did it…got them to fight back."

"About time," snorted Lash who made another trip to the kitchen, this time in search of something they could eat. He had no intention of fleeing again until they had somewhere to go, but he wanted them to have enough strength to move as long as they had to, if it became necessary to do so again.

"Scarecrow…that you?"

A crackle erupted over the Echosys, the sound of footsteps and a distorted echo of breathing, before the shaky image of the interior of a vent shaft came into view.

"Nice of you to join me."

His voice was off, his steps unsteady, giving the view presented by the cam a degree of vertigo that made Zara blink.

"Are you…?"

"Fine. I'm fine. You safe?"

Zara was not convinced he was fine, but arguing would be unproductive. "For now…yes…"

"Good. Coming up on Upper 21…might need a boost."

Surprised that they had been running for so long, or that Rhyd had progressed as quickly as he had, Zara nodded, though he could not see her doing so.

"Tell him."

Zara shook her head, thinking that Maemi wanted her to tell Rhyd they had lost Skelter. She was not about to burden the man with that bad news while he was focused on survival.

"Tell me what?"

With the mic more sensitive then she expected, not thinking he would have heard Maemi's voice, Zara answered quickly to keep either Maemi or Lash from saying something she thought they should not. "They're fighting back…everyone. Everyone in the Levs. Shouting for the Scarecrow…fighting in your name. We saw it…on the streets, on the prodcasts just now. They're pushing up the Levs towards the top. Overpowering the Crows…"

"Kill the feeds."

"What…?"

"Do it, Zar. Don't let them see what's coming."

Understanding then, Zara nodded and began to hack into the prodcast system, a much simpler task than digging into the heart of the Hub. Seeing the horror, the encroaching onslaught from below was bad enough. Having witnessed a taste of it, and then losing the feed, left unaware of the progress the throng of Lev inhabitants might be making, would be much worse for the residents of the Uppers. The more panicked they felt, the more afraid, the more mistakes they might make and the easier, Rhyd hoped, his job would be. The chance was worth the risk of having stopped now, and with Maemi at the door on watch as Lash scavenged the flat for food, usable medical supplies, weapons, or other defensive items, there would be time enough, they hoped, for Zara to work magic on Hebenon's Echosys eyes to blind those who believed they lived in security in the Uppers.

❧*❦

"He isn't responding." Ximenez nervously cleared his throat.

"Isn't…how can he not be…?" Only a sleeping man, or one physically indisposed, was excused from avoiding communications and summons from the Founder. Ibarra knew better than to ignore Haythem. Everyone did. "Get him! Cut all the feeds into the factories except his line. And get me Grainger!"

Another communique was entered into the Echosys, encoded to Ibarra's private system, but a push of the send button saw the entire Hub, every terminal and screen in the room, go dark. Not a power loss, for the lights in the room, dim though they were, still flickered. But the familiar underlying hum of the Hub's Echo terminal was silent, and without the previous deafening chatter of reports pouring in from the Levs, the sudden silence in the room was shocking.

Technicians swarmed to the backup systems, to the ports of the main Hub and the power lines in an effort to determine the cause and scope of the problem and decide how to repair it quickly.

The abrupt silence cut Kemway's tirade short, and the buzzing of Ximenez's comm kept it from starting again. Hoping the message was from Grainger, Haythem snatched the comm out of Ximenez's hand and barked, "I told you to get down there and…"

"You wanted to speak to me, Founder?"

Ibarra sounded breathless, and in the background, a myriad of other voices could be heard, some with a crisp echoing quality as they gradually faded in the distance. It sounded like a man speaking from one of the corridors. The Founder scowled. "Where are you?"

"West One…evacuating to Factory One as per orders…"

Haythem's face began to burn a furious, deep red. "I ordered no such…"

"No, sir…the Doctet voted and…"

"The Doctet!" Haythem glared venomously at Ximenez, who shook his head and shrugged with confusion. Though also a member of the Doctet, he had been trapped here since the chaos began; like the Founder, he had no idea what Ibarra was talking about.

"I've been here! I attended no such...I was not summoned..." Ximenez mumbled apologetically.

Again Haythem growled. "Get back to..."

"I'm sorry, Founder," muttered Ibarra. "West one is sealed." Sealing the passage meant that nearly one third to one-half of the Uppers residents had been evacuated, without Haythem's knowledge.

After a furious howl, Haythem stormed out of the prodcast room, into a corridor glaring with the alternating red and white of emergency backup lighting. The Doctet had no right to convene without his call, could not vote without his approval, and his vote alone could overturn any decision they made. Maybe Ibarra was a liar and there had been no convening, no vote, only he and however many others with him who had seen the prodcast, panicked, and fled into one of the three havens available to the Uppers in an emergency situation. Such an emergency had never occurred before.

Haythem was determined to have the truth, and heads and hearts, of any who had dared to defy and undermine his God-given authority.

And he would find out what had happened to the damned lighting.

❧*❧

From the corridor beyond the shaft, Rhyd could hear noises, thumping in a disjointed rhythm, mutters and murmurs of voices, the clatter and jangle of things falling and skittering across the hemp-vinyl floor. To his mechanically enhanced ears, the sounds meant people, a lot of them, hurrying in the same direction. He wondered if he dared wait for them to pass or if he should attempt a different route to the next paneled opening. Upper 21 had sounded surprisingly empty as he worked his way to the one exit Zara was confident they could open, but as he was not aware of any scheduled entertainments or prodcast events at this hour, and it was mid-shift for any work crews, he decided that most people were either on shift or else at home on the levels above. He did not think anyone lived on Upper 21. If 21 housed medical and lab facilities, if prisoners were held there as Lash suggested, it seemed unlikely anyone except perhaps the staff those jobs required would be here.

Now that Rhyd was poised at one of the many vent openings into Upper 21 East, hearing what sounded like a small heard of people passing, he fleetingly wondered if the mass movement was in any way connected to what was happening below.

Were they afraid of the violence spreading here?

Waiting to enter, however, came with its own risks. It meant either a delay or continually dodging the SCAMs as he sought other entrances into this level if Zara had not yet disabled them, or if the Hub managers had found some way to block and disengage her hacks. Zara and Lash's instructions thus far had helped him avoid Pass points, helped him reach this particular shaft, and it seemed his best choice if he could make it out unnoticed.

Doubling back would be a waste of time too, particularly since the effect of the analgesic in his blood had begun to fade enough to grant him a decent pace and acceptable vision and hearing while still managing his pain at a bearable level. If people in the Uppers were migrating away from Upper 21, Crows being deployed or residents fleeing the chaos of which Zara had spoken, the chances of finding a usable entrance elsewhere were little better.

He was here now. He might as well hope for the best and prepare for the worst.

When the footsteps receded and none could be heard in the distance any longer, he popped open the shaft cover and gingerly dropped into the corridor, favoring his wrist as he worked. Pressed against the wall, he looked left and then right. To his left, where the hurried footsteps had gone, the corridor was long and empty, with several open doors in his field of sight from which he imagined the people had come. There were no sounds within any of them that he could detect. To his right was much the same, except that the corridor was blocked some seventy-five yards away by a sliding panel door that spanned the width of the corridor. He could not read the poorly lit writing from his position.

Frowning, he whispered into the hood's comm, "Schematics, Zar...now."

"Lash." Zara waved the man away from the door, away from the sudden downpour of moisture that splattered against the flat's window where Maemi was keeping watch. When he stopped beside her, Zara pointed to the schematics on her screen, where a single small red pulse of light waited in a corridor that would take Rhyd into the eastern medical wing of Lev 21, where few from the Levs had ever been.

"Cazzo...he's making good progress," Lash muttered with surprise. He had feared that, without his guidance, Rhyd would lose his way, but the bilger apparently knew the shaft systems well enough to have gotten to Upper 21 without significant delays. "He needs to go through that door...into that hall..."

He pointed to a spot on the screen that coincided with the door blockage Rhyd could see. Zara nodded and whispered back to Rhyd. "Right. To the door. I'll get you through."

The clacking of Echosys keys began again.

Some of the side doors he crept past, pausing at each to be certain there was no one within who could ambush him, led into other corridors with other doors, dwellings or offices, Rhyd could not tell. Each passage was hauntingly silent, suggesting that all of the occupants and employees had abandoned this area. Still, he continued with caution, not knowing what he expected to find. At one time, as with the Levs below, there had been a collection of vindis and flats separated by interconnected short stairs and grated platforms serving as streets and footpaths. But Lev 21, like Lev 20 below him, had been incorporated into the Uppers long enough ago that the streets had been closed into hallways, the outside moisture of the falls sealed out, the grating replaced with white hemp panels, the alglights and neon replaced with typically white light that glowed in a rhythm mimicking night and day.

Night and day were never differentiated in the Levs. It was always night there.

Here, in this corridor now, the world was red. Red and white.

The sterility, the emptiness, seemed disjointed from the jostle of humanity he was accustomed to in the Levs. Maybe it was because this passage was less used than others, only by the medical and scientific staff Lash hinted at.

Or maybe, since this passage was near the city's outer edge, the sterility was indicative of all life moving upwards and to the center.

Maybe fewer people lived in the Uppers than those below imagined.

Once Hebenon's sports arena had been here, located at the city's center. Decades later, a century or more into the city's life, as the level of the four falls had shifted, Lev 21 was lifted higher out of the mists and annexed into the Uppers to allow for the growth of Upper population. Or so it had been said. The sports arena had been relocated to Lev 20, as Lev 1 had been deepened to keep the fisheries near to the surging river. Many had been displaced from Lev 20 in that relocation, forced downward to crowd into already crowded conditions, but the residents of the city had adjusted.

There was no other choice.

And with Lev 20 undergoing a similar enclosure now, there was once again discussion about the necessity of relocating the athletic complex into Lev 19, as the forces of nature outside lifted that level out of the mists as well by eroding the world around it.

It would, Rhyd knew as he struggled to adjust to the flashing emergency lighting, become much the same as Upper 20, what Upper 22 and above had been at the time of Hebanthe Falls' construction. White and clean, at least he guessed it was white since it was difficult to tell beneath the flashing lights, with tiled floors and bright lighting and the absence of mist and steam that those in the Levs lived with every day.

Below, his gear helped him blend into the pervasive shadows. Here there was no blending, no hiding possible, only slow, steady, movement as he crept closer to the corridor barrier.

Rhyd was not sure what he expected here, but this was not it. If Tox and Venn lived, he hoped he would find them somewhere beyond that panel before his inability to hide proved to be his downfall. And he hoped Agnys would be there too.

What he did not anticipate was the unexpected opening of the sliding doors before he had the chance to run the Pass in the hopes of getting through without setting off alarms. His initial thought was that Zara had opened them without notice, or that he had been unable to hear her warning, but the lone figure on the other side of the door, silhouetted by the bright red and white light was like a mountain against a bleeding sky punctuated by bursts of lightning flares.

Rhyd dropped into a crouch, a flat, circular metal throwing disk ringed with razor-sharp spikes was held at the ready to throw should the man come at him. This was the fight he wanted, or one of them, but Rhyd was in no condition for this confrontation. He knew it. All he wanted right now was to find those he was looking for.

Grainger stared at the crouched individual, the mask, the attire, the stance, indicators that his quarry, the Scarecrow, had come to him. His hand was inches from his holstered popper but he wagered that, by the time he drew it, whatever the Scarecrow held would have found its target. It was a standoff, tempered by the slight side to side weaving in the other man's posture. Would that unsteady movement give him an advantage, the Captain wondered? Did he even want to try?

Hours earlier, the quest to apprehend this man who had caused the Founder, and all of Grainger's officers, so much grief, had been one of his primary priorities, had been a priority for more than two years. Now, with the discovery of the vigilante's identity, the chaos he knew to be enveloping Hebanthe Falls from the Levs, and the recent face-off he had shared with Founder Kemway, Grainger found he had little interest in Rhyd Ballard, in his past, his present, or his future. The threat below, and the Founder's ego, felt to be far greater dangers to Hebenon than one man trying to protect civilians.

Perhaps, at the heart of it, Ballard was right. Perhaps the Scarecrow was exactly what Hebenon needed, and perhaps, for now, at least, his agenda, whatever it was, coincided with Grainger's.

"Where are they?" Scarecrow growled, the mechanical breathing device masking his true voice. "The ones you've taken? The girl? Where do you keep them?"

Grainger pointed to the corridor behind him, the direction from which he had come, the direction in which the Scarecrow was facing.

Scarecrow growled again.

❧Chapter 24❧

Philipa Underwood, long-time member of the Doctet and a cornerstone of the original family who had designed, manufactured, and directed the installation of the solar panels on Hebenon's outer shell, caught the Founder's arm as he barreled past, ignoring the outrage on his face. "Where are Neoma…the children? Is it true? Are the Belows breaking into the Uppers?"

"They are not…" Haythem caught himself. Did he know they were not? He had viewed the rioting on the Echosys screens at the Hub and knew that, if he had seen those prodcast reports, others in the Uppers would have as well. Then the system had shut down, either a malfunction in the Hub, an interruption in signal from the Level reporting stations, or else because someone had hacked the Hub and was blocking the feeds. Any of those possibilities could indicate the upward progress of the rioters. Or they were coincidences. He did not want his people to panic, did not want to admit that whoever had initiated the evacuation, had brought the Doctet together, had done it without his command or knowledge. That would undermine the authority he had been born into.

The Uppers needed his authority now.

He cleared his throat and forced a comforting smile into place. "There is minor rioting on the lowest levels but it is being contained.

Evacuation is strictly precautionary in the event of a loss of power. This is a preventative drill. Of course Neoma and the children are joining you. They may already be evacuated. I will be along as soon as all systems are secure."

Like the captain of old maritime ships, it was his responsibility to remain until the last moment, and there was still adequate time to evacuate. There was no need for panic.

His words seemed to allay her fears; she no longer wrung her heavy hands and the tremulous corners of her mouth and around her eyes grew still. "Very good, Founder. Thank you. Thank you for seeing to our security. Bless you."

She bustled away after her family whom Haythem could no longer see, down the long corridor, her wide bulk bumping into others as she passed them. Her words of gratitude had a similar effect on him. The Doctet should not have acted without him, and Grainger, or whoever had spread the news of invasion, should have come to him to have the report approved for sharing. But with the comm systems down, potentially compromised before their failure, if Grainger or someone else suspected danger due to the reports from officers stationed below and had chosen to act instead of delaying as he searched for Haythem, the result might save many lives. Or at least it might prevent chaos in the Uppers should action come too late.

Grainger was no fool, nor, Haythem admitted as he continued down the corridor, were most members of the Doctet. His control of Hebanthe Falls had less to do with a belief in the strengths and failures of others than it did on the belief of entitlement by birthright.

Someone had been right to protect the people of the Uppers. But Haythem still felt the someone with the final say should be him.

No longer concerned with locating Grainger, assuming the man was doing the job he had been ordered to do, Haythem reached his originally intended destination and stopped in the doorway. Lima was huddled over a view scope, examining slide after slide of blood samples, while Tamner recorded blood pressure, heart rate, reflexes, and gathered samples from the stationary child's nose, mouth, and ears. They, at least, had either not received the evacuation notice or had chosen to disregard it.

Those where things Haythem noted on the periphery as he gawked at the girl on the lab table, strapped to it with leathery cuffs around her wrists, ankles, neck, and waist. Warily he approached, ignoring the men who stopped what they were doing to watch him. A sheet of reusable sterile cloth covered her from shoulder to upper thigh and she appeared to be either asleep or unconscious. The shallow rise and fall of her chest proved that she lived.

Haythem did not know what he expected to see when he lifted the cloth to view the first parah child to ever be examined in Hebanthe Falls. A monster, a thing that logic dictated should exist in a world poisoned and destroyed when the fortunate portions of humanity were forced into Hebenon or cities like her, and the unfortunate had perished. Parah were either ill-fated survivors of global disaster or else were those who had lived elsewhere, in some other perhaps failed fall-city who had migrated into Hebenon's orbit but had been unable to get inside. It did not matter which was the case, but decades of belief in the logistics of radiation science said that this child should, by all rights, be a monster. The same as every parah with whom Hebanthe Falls did trade.

What he saw, however, what he heard from her throat made him look into the parah's now open eyes, should not be. He dropped the cloth and stepped back, more horrified, he was sure, then if she really had been a monster.

"Finish as many tests as you can in the next thirty minutes…then destroy her and evacuate yourselves."

"Evacuate?" asked Lima over Tamner's "Destroy her?"

The Founder was already hurrying away, having seen enough, his complexion green, his fists balled at the end of stiff arms. Tamner and Lima looked at one another, at the child who might not understand their words but understood their sudden distress, and then one another again with expressions of confusion and horror.

❧ * ↩

With the star still poised to throw, Rhyd pushed to his feet, masking what vertigo the movement prompted with the removal of his popper from his coat with his empty, injured hand. He flattened against the wall and began to slide cautiously towards the open panel, watching the man on the other side. If he could get through without needing to swipe the Pass, without needing to rely on Zara's hacking skills, it would be a fortuitous turn of events, but there was still Captain Grainger to deal with. He did not know if Grainger intended to attack or if he was allowing him to proceed. With the warning light on the panel at the side of the door flashing orange, an indication that the door was about to close or an alarm about to fill the air with screaming, he was running out of time to decide.

"If the door stays open, the alarm'll sound; they'll come looking."

Grainger did not know who would come. The majority of his officers had been sent below, save for two dozen deployed throughout the Uppers to assist in the evacuations of the remaining citizens into the land-based factories. The factories stored enough food and supplies to feed all of the residents of the Uppers for a year or more, depending on how carefully they rationed what they had, stashes originally created by Duncan Kemway as emergency stores for the whole of Hebanthe Falls.

But those in the Levs did not know they existed, had long ago forgotten, and thus the stores had become a prize for the Uppers alone. The smallest group, the families of the Crows who were overseeing the evacuation, any stragglers who were not able to reach the other factories in time, and a few selected others, would have Factory East to themselves. A smaller group, a larger supply, a longer opportunity for survival, until the violence in Hebenon was subdued and a chance for peace could be arranged for whatever remained of the city.

If it came to that.

"You want to pass?" The Scarecrow cocked his head towards the corridor he had come through. Grainger did not seem interested in hunting him, likely had another duty, even in the Levs, or else he had been following those who had hurried down the corridor earlier.

Whatever his business, Scarecrow decided to let him get to it, so long as the Captain did not interfere in his agenda.

If forced into a fight, he would do so, but he was not as confident of his chances as he typically was.

Grainger nodded.

"Then let me go. Let me find them."

The deal was considered briefly before Grainger nodded again and sidestepped towards the still open hall door. Slowly, though now with more determination, Scarecrow did the same, each man easing in the direction he wanted to go, assessing the other, continuing to anticipate an attack as they neared a face to face stance.

With Grainger no longer in the doorway, however, and Scarecrow having not yet reached it, the steam-driven mechanical doors began to slide shut. There was no time to think about his next action. Scarecrow dove between the closing panels, intending to roll to his feet, letting the star fly as he did so, in an effort not to kill the other man but rather to stave off any attack the Captain might make.

Grainger, too, whipped sideways enough to catch hold of one of the exposed hoses on the side of Scarecrow's mask and yanked one end free. Scarecrow stumbled and fell backward, landing on his ass, while Grainger slid on the corridor's slippery floor and fell with a cry, the star protruding from the palm of the hand he had grabbed the hose with. As the door closed, the last they saw of one another was each sitting on the floor, Scarecrow grasping the disconnected hose and Grainger gripping tightly to his bleeding hand.

There was panic when Grainger's grab dislodged the breathing hose. Rhyd doubted he would need it here, as the Uppers were rumored to have more efficient filtration of air and water than the Levs, and being above the fall's spray, they lived without the constant moisture that plagued those in the bowels of Hebenon. Of course, those here lived without natural atmosphere either, rarely stepped foot into the 'outside' air unless they made a trip into the Levs for some reason, where the city was not as well insulated from the Outside. Here they were protected by thick walls that shielded them from the harshest conditions and were fed water and breathable air through the processing systems spread throughout every level of the city.

The air would be safe, but Rhyd did not trust it enough to remove the mask. Nor did he want to remove it and reveal himself to anyone he encountered. As long as the hood remained in place, his breathing would be labored unless he reconnected the hose. It took several minutes of fumbling with his injured hand to reattach it and secure it in place with the binding tape he had used earlier. He expected to be found there at any time, exposed, his position given away by the Crow's Captain.

Between the side-effects of the pain-killers and the panic of stolen air, his breathing came no easier until the hose was repaired. Once done, he took several moments of deep, calming breaths as he listened to the sounds of the level around him. The door had not opened again. Grainger had not returned and from the distant retreating sounds of his footsteps, he assumed the Captain had gone about his business.

They would meet again. Grainger was not going to allow a potential enemy to roam the Uppers any longer than necessary. Whatever pressing business he had, the Captain would eventually return for him. In the meantime, Rhyd had business of his own. It was time to take the opportunity the Captain permitted him and get to it.

☙Chapter 25☙

"Where are we going, Papa?" Flora asked, her arms clinging to her father's neck as Haythem ushered his family as far as the entrance to West 2. West 1 was, as Ibarra had indicated, already closed, having filled with the majority of the Doctet and their families as well as many of the top scientists, builders, and thinkers who called the Uppers home. The Underwoods, slowed by the medical needs of their youngest child, had been slow in making preparations and thus were forced into West 2 and Haythem had seen the Ximenez family disappear past two Crows in front of the tunnel's entrance that he and his own family could not yet see. At least, Haythem thought with a huff, he would have people of class and breeding, not just entertainers and athletes, to share his evacuation time with.

"It's a drill, Flora darling…how to evacuate in case of an emergency," Haythem said sweetly, kissing her hair as they muscled through the crowded antechamber towards the guarded door. Though some complained and swore at him in muttered tones, none tried to stop him when they saw who had pushed towards the front of the slowly proceeding line. Whatever their feelings at this moment, he was still the Founder.

He still had the rights of office and position he had been born into.

The guards, their filtered bird masks in place though they were not needed in the Uppers, spoke directly to him when he was within hearing distance at the front of the queue. "Founder," they growled simultaneously.

At least it sounded like a growl to Haythem. Their tone caused him to stop. Neoma and the older children, after several forward steps, did the same.

Perhaps it was their perceived manner, and nothing they had actually done, that carried implications. What Haythem heard and sensed, however, was an order not to proceed, not to enter the tunnel, to leave his family and remain behind. He began to scowl, to growl low in his chest, to demand the rights his office afforded. At the last moment, however, as Neoma turned a scathing look upon him, warning him not to put the rest of his family at risk, he lowered his well-practiced, easy, diplomatic smile into place. It was an air Neoma knew well, and thankfully one their children could not see through.

Haythem put Flora on her feet and again kissed the top of her head. "Go with mama, Flora. Do as she says."

"Aren't you coming, Papa?" Duncan asked.

People continued to jostle past, bumping them with packs of clothes, nessies, and items of wealth they deemed important to take on the off chance that this was a real evacuation and not a drill. Neoma and the other children were forced to step to one side, out of the line, as they waited for Flora to join them. The line's progress was slow as the Crows checked credentials, and there were some further back in the line who were beginning to push and elbow closer to the front out of fear of being denied entrance.

Haythem did not squat. He rarely lowered himself to anyone's level except Flora's, and though he wanted to embrace her, to embrace all of his children, he felt it more important to retain an air of dignity on his feet, to further the illusion that they had nothing to fear, that this drill would be over soon and they would be reunited.

He was also, secretly, concerned that the pushing crowd would knock him over and trample him.

He put a hand on Duncan's head, and one on Ulynda's. "I must see to it that everyone is evacuated, Duncan. It is the responsibility of the Founder to see that his people are safe."

"Those below too? Is that why people say they are coming up? To evacuate with us?"

Haythem took a breath, not having expected such a question from his cool-eyed eldest child who had a frustrating habit of asking difficult questions. But he was spared the need to answer by his wife's intervention. "It is time. Kiss Papa goodbye; we shall see him soon."

Husband and wife's eyes locked over the children's heads as one after another embraced him and kissed him farewell. Neoma did not know what was happening Below, beyond the initially reported rioting shown before the Echosys feeds went dead, and she did not know what the outcome of these events would be. But she did understand duty, understood what the guards had not said in that single spoken command, and understood that, when they passed into the factory without him, it would likely be without looking back.

She felt no grief because of it, save over what distress the children would experience if their internment persisted, if they emerged to find their father gone. But she did wonder, as she scooped Flora up and started towards the final evacuation door, what sins she, Haythem, and Hebanthe Falls had committed to condemn them all to this.

❧*❧

There would not be time to open every cell in his search for Tox, Venn, and Agnys. There were too many doors in this corridor and, for all he knew, there were more elsewhere. Grainger's Pass allowed him to open the first eight he reached, some to emptiness, some to people strapped to gurneys kept alive by IV fluids fed into their arms, some to cramped rooms of bodies swaying on their feet, moaning with glazed, vacant eyes. When the doors were opened, they were unresponsive to the brightness of the corridor's irregular lighting. Here and there, bodies could be seen at their feet, having fallen where they stood without notice. What Scarecrow saw was not the result of

Heb addiction, at least not any level of addiction Rhyd was familiar with. Emaciated, nude and hairless, they were more dead than alive, no more than skin stretched taut over a skeleton, kept upright by the others packed tightly around them. Only their genitalia distinguished them from one another. Those at the front who had been pressed against the door fell forward when the door slid back, but not one who fell made an effort to get to their feet or move from where they lay in a groaning heap, as if it was a relief to no longer be standing.

"Bozhe moy," gasped Maemi, looking away from the screen on which Zara and those with her could see what Rhyd was seeing. Even from where she stood to keep watch at the door, what she saw there, what Rhyd was seeing, was recognized in all its horror.

Zara wished she could not see it either. She did not understand how anyone could treat another human that way and felt deeply sorry for both the victims and the perpetrators of such horrors. "Do you see them? Venn? Tox? Agnys?" She could not, but her view was doubly distorted by the filters on Scarecrow's lenses and by the interference caused by the distance, metal, and electronics between them.

"No."

Tox would not be here. She had not been held long enough to reach the weakened state these unfortunate souls were in. If Venn had been held like this, Rhyd thought grimly, he would be dead by now. No one could survive in this state for more than two years.

Typing furiously on the Echo keypad, Zara muttered, "I'm opening them all. Find them." It would take too long for Rhyd to get to every door, to open them all with Grainger's Pass. Better for Zara to do it and free them all at once. Better to hope that, by doing so, Rhyd would find those he sought…or they would find him.

Scarecrow's head bobbed and he continued to stagger forward.

Outside the apartment where the trio hid, the distance sound of fighting, of dozens of feet pushing towards the heavens, was growing more noticeable, less of an echo, more immediate as the mass migration of people caused the foundations of Hebanthe Falls to shake, to creak, to groan and shudder. The city bore its weighty burden of life well, but it had never been designed to hold the majority of its residents condensed into fewer and fewer levels.

Lash scowled and drew the blinds. One hand over the mic on Zara's Echo, he muttered, "Got to go."

"I have to finish this or he'll never…"

Lash knew Zara was right, that what she was doing, the risks they were taking remaining in one place, were necessary if Scarecrow was to reach his goal. He also realized more and more too, as the horrors Scarecrow's eye cam was transmitting reached them, that even if Rhyd found those he was seeking, he would never be able to free them from the Uppers by working alone. If what they saw was any indicator, Tox and Venn, if they lived, might be in no condition to flee, let alone fight for their lives. Agnys could be carried but she could not fight.

There might not be anything below to return to by the end of this night, but whoever survived was going to need leadership. That leader, Lash thought, ought to be Ballard, but the man was going to need help if he and those he found were to make it out of the Uppers alive.

"He needs us up there…and they're getting too close. We go now…or we won't be any good to him."

"What about through there?" Maemi pointed at the vent shaft above the table where Zara worked. Thus far they had relied on streets, alleys, and Lash's knowledge of them to avoid the Crows and the fighting in the streets. That reliance had cost them Skelter. Lash might not know the vent systems well enough to find their way up through the Levs, but perhaps Zara, with the Echo T2, could manage it.

They looked at one another as Lash continued to cover the Echo mic with his hand to keep Rhyd from hearing them. "We go up…we find Rhyd, we help any way we can."

The women, of the same mind regarding the likelihood of Scarecrow's survival, particularly with potentially ailing or injured loved ones in his wake, nodded without speaking.

"We're gonna move again, Whiskey," Maemi said after pulling Lash's hand from the mic. "They're too close." She did not tell him where they were or what their intentions were. There was no time for the argument that information was likely to generate.

The movement of the cam image indicated a bob of Scarecrow's head. "Stay safe," he admonished as Zara climbed onto the table, removed the grate, and crawled into the shaft first. Once she was inside, she rigged the Echo to serve as a map of the vents as well as a monitoring system to continue to track Rhyd. By the time the Echo was ready, the other two had joined her and she pointed the way to go.

Staying safe was possible. Being careful was less of an option.

⟌*⟍

"I'm not staying here." The mention of evacuation had prompted an abrupt quest for information which revealed that the Hub was down and that the comms were only working in sporadic, barely intelligible bursts. It was little wonder the Founder had brought them the command himself. As soon as the first good connection was made, Lima's son brokenly explained that there were reports of rioting in the Levs and that the Uppers were being evacuated, doomed to invasion. Evacuation was the sort of precaution, the sort of action, that had never been attempted in the centuries Hebanthe Falls had existed, as far as Lima or Tamner knew, the sort of precaution talked about behind closed doors at Doctet policy meetings but never expected to be implemented. Drill or not, invasion or not, the fact that evacuation had been ordered sent chills down both men's spines and Lima quickly began to fumble around the office collecting records, tools, and equipment, anything that he thought might be useful, should the Uppers sustain significant damage and the evacuees be trapped in the Factories for weeks to come.

"What about them?" Tamner pointed at the people restrained in chambers around the room, the test subjects of their most recent experiments with parah samples, research that could continue to bear useful data even though they now had the child. "What about her?"

Agnys no longer twisted in her bindings, too afraid of the prodding, poking, swabbing and robbing of fluid the two men had been doing to consider fighting back. The restraints forbid it, and struggling, she believed would bring about great pain. Lima, moving wildly about the room, speaking in a tone of fear she understood, even if she could not discern his words, frightened her even more.

When Lima did not reply, Tamner barked, "They'll die, Miguel!"

"They're dead already."

A quick glance around the room at the majority of their subjects made Tamner sigh in frustration. Addicts, cripples, the ill and the weak, most had already begun the slow decline into death as Lima asserted. Tamner could unbind them, set them free, but he imagined they would collapse to the floor and probably die before ever trying to get to their feet.

But the child was not dead, in no danger of dying except at their hands if they followed the Founder's orders. Abandoning her here to an uncertain end was no different than killing her themselves. Maybe the invaders would set her free, spare her life. Maybe they would not.

"She's not."

Lima shot him a disgusted look that suggested Tamner had lost his mind. "You can't take her into evac…that would get you both killed. They'd never let you in. You've got children to think about, Rafe. Best to let her fend for herself."

"She can't do that strapped down like an animal." Decision made, Tamner began to unbuckle the straps, starting at her waist.

"What are you doing?" But Miguel already knew, and after an irritated huff, came to the table to help. He did not want to be guilty of the child's death, regardless of what the Founder had ordered.

"We take her to a shaft…she survived in there once, she should be able to do it again. If Founder asks, we disposed of her before anyone found her and started asking questions." It was not an ideal solution, but it was the best Tamner could think of that would allow her some hope of survival. Maybe she could make it back into the care of whoever had been watching over her when Grainger found her.

Lima nodded but said nothing. He was satisfied with freeing her, felt it necessary, and lying was going to be equally necessary whenever they faced the Founder next, or returned to an empty lab of nothing but corpses. The lack of cremation paperwork would be easy to explain; they were not going to take time to file protocol papers under a pressing evacuation order. Lima was not, however, risking separation from his family by taking the unnecessary time to help the parah find safety. Freeing her was all he was willing to do.

Let Tamner take the risk if he wanted.

When she was unbound, Tamner helped her sit and bent down to her, fingers to his lips to indicate quiet, gesturing with the other hand to stay where she was. They were gestures she appeared to recognize as she remained silent and still.

"Wait here until we're ready." He had precious few minutes left to pack for himself or else he would never join his family in time. He assumed they had already evacuated.

Agnys nodded and stared, too frightened and confused to budge.

By the time Tamner, who tossed an examination gown in the girl's direction, turned towards the sound of the whooshing door, where the guards had left their post sometime earlier, Lima was already gone.

❧Chapter 26❦

Tox!

The word was a cry in his mind as he charged through the open door towards the battered woman strapped to a metal chair. His search had been made easier by Zara's efforts to unlock and open every door on this corridor and elsewhere. Some, those capable of lucid thought and movement, had wandered into the corridor where the white lights had ceased flashing, leaving the world now burning beneath flashes of crimson in the darkness. Some were too afraid to leave their confines, believing this to be some new trick or prelude to some varied form of torture or experimentation, but as those now free shuffled past the open doors, without seeming to have a destination in mind, some of those others chose to follow. Rhyd could not direct them to freedom; he had no idea where freedom could be found.

Instead, he focused on his own mission and left the others to their fortune and luck.

Wire cutters cut the zips that held Tox's cold arms behind her and bound her bruised legs to the legs of the chair. She lifted her head groggily, confused and disoriented at first, but there was no mistaking the mask, the mask she had helped design and create. Her composure broke in a gasping sob as she caught his head between her hands and pressed her forehead to his with tears of joy.

Rhyd did not object, but nor did he take time to indulge her relief the way he should. Time for emotional displays would come later...if they lived until later. "Venn?" he asked as he helped her stand on unsteady legs, not sure she could support her own weight.

She shook her head and Rhyd scowled within his hood. Of course, she had not seen Venn. She had probably seen no one in this room except her tormentors. Since he had not yet seen Venn either, he knew the odds of finding him had grown slimmer with each open door. There were another dozen or so cells on this wing, according to Zara, their doors already open. There might be other holding facilities elsewhere, actual prison cells and not medical experimentation rooms; there were too few people freed thus far to account for the numbers taken every day, every week, every month from the Levs. Unless those taken were executed, an end that contradicted every official report of rehabilitation for traitors and convicts, they had to be somewhere else.

Other corridors. Other rooms. Maybe other levels.

"You there!"

The voice behind Rhyd surprised him, his focus on Tox preventing him from hearing anyone's approach. Scarecrow spun, pushed the tortured woman back through the door behind them with enough force that her weak legs buckled, and he ducked, crouching low at what he expected would be the hiss of a popper or injector aimed to stop him. The Crow, not wanting to risk a stray shot in the middle of the shuffling hallway herd he had stumbled upon, did not take a shot, however, but he did run forward, hoping to knock the intruder off balance since he already seemed unsteady in his stance and step.

An inexperienced or arrogant Crow, Scarecrow mused with a snarl, launching upwards to catch his shoulders beneath the attacker's ribcage. A Crow whom, it seemed, had either not heard of the Scarecrow or else had no inkling or concern about what the vigilante was capable of. Both flew across the hall so that the officer was pinned between the corridor wall and the momentum of the Scarecrow's weight, hitting with enough force to crack ribs and wind him. The Crow toppled sideways, his grip around Scarecrow dragging Rhyd to the floor with him. As Scarecrow struggled to his feet, struggled to keep his balance, he could not tell if the officer was unconscious or disoriented and unresponsive since he could not see the eyes within the bird-beaked helmet. He thought he should kill the Crow, avoid a potential problem, but to his knowledge, the Scarecrow had never killed anyone and he was not prepared to start doing so now. He slid sideways, away from the Crow after snatching the popper from his grasp, grabbed Tox's hand when he reached her in the doorway she had used to pull herself to her feet, and after thrusting the popper into her grasp, he pushed her along in front of him towards the remaining dozen doors ahead.

If he reached the end of this corridor and there was no sign of Agnys or Venn, he did not know what he would do.

It took a single moment of split concentration and a failure to disarm the Crow fully to become aware too late of the melodic pneumonic hiss of a popper's mechanism and the snap of the trigger release. The bewildered Crow's aim was wild and the pellet ripped through the palm of Rhyd's already injured hand. Due to the lingering pain and stiffness, he had not bothered to put his glove back on when he had removed it in the vent shaft earlier. Scarecrow's cry within the helmet sounded like a feral, ghostly bellow but as he turned to strike back, there came a second pop. This time when the Crow crumpled to the floor it was with a trickle of blood flowing from his exposed throat beneath the edge of his hooded mask.

He might not be dead yet, but he would bleed out if he did not receive prompt medical attention.

Beside Scarecrow, Tox lowered the popper she carried. He nodded once in appreciation; while he did not kill on principle, he had no disrespect for someone who did. Tox had saved his life…and after everything she had endured at the Crows' hands, he decided she was entitled to strike back.

She shrugged, ripped a strip of fabric from her tattered shirt, and tied it around his palm, binding the wound in the hopes of staunching the blood flow. Satisfied, they began moving again, following the prison horde, checking one room after another for Venn, for Agnys.

Splatters of red on the clean white tile followed in their wake.

☙*☙

"There."

Zara pointed left ahead of them, to yet another dark sloping passage that looked like every other they had fled through. They each wondered how Rhyd could find his way in this maze without some sort of marker or map to guide him. There was none that they could see. This last tunnel would lead them to Upper 21, leaving the last level they would be able to traverse through with ease. On Lev 19, from within the vent shaft, they could hear occasional shouts and popper fire from the world outside, but the sounds were sporadic, sparse enough to suggest that the rioting in the lower Levs was not progressing upwards as fast as they were. Undoubtedly, the Crows, any who remained capable of fighting, were realizing they were running out of terrain in which to fight and were doing their best not to be pinned down with nowhere to retreat to. Many were likely congregating to a rallying point from which to make a final, concerted stand. Eventually, if the momentum of the people in the Levs held, the Crows would run out of manpower, a dilemma that would result in unprecedented chaos when the fighting petered out.

None of the three in the shafts looked forward to those days, provided they lived long enough to experience them.

Zara's hacking skills had gotten them into the area of the deserted sports arena on Lev 20. Though they heard no signs of life, detected no activity in the rooms and corridors beyond, they remained in the shaft system, as Scarecrow had done, feeling it safer than the halls could be. They doubted they would encounter Crows here, but anyone seeing them would know from their attire that they were not residents of the Uppers. It felt safest to remain out of sight as long as possible.

With one of their confiscated poppers in hand, Lash led the way, listening to Zara's instructions as she followed the computerized schematics to keep them moving forward, upward. She did her best to direct them as well as lend her eyes and ears to Scarecrow who was somewhere above them. She was also preparing for crossing into

Upper 21, for they had no duplicate Passcard to use as Rhyd did. There had been no thought given to the need for making a second duplicate of Grainger's card.

How could she or anyone else have anticipated what was to come?

Intending to exit the shaft in the same location Rhyd had, to find their way to the same hallway door, they followed the route he had taken, knowing there would be no one to help them through it. They would have to rely on Zara if they were to continue unimpeded, as quickly as possible.

At the rear, Maemi watched over her shoulder, unwilling to believe they were safe just because no one had come for them yet, crabbing along behind them with both poppers she carried drawn and ready. Thus far, however, they had crossed paths with no one else, no Crows or shaft workers or streeters or anyone considering using the vents as a safe means of travel out of reach of the violence.

Their luck, as they had feared, ran out when they reached the shaft exit they wanted, the one Rhyd had used, to find two Crows at the ready, guarding the corridor and the barricading door. Neither Crow appeared to want to be there, nor to be paying attention, when Lash popped his head unexpectedly through the uncovered vent opening.

The Crows were startled, caught off guard, with little time to draw their weapons. Lash got off a single shot, but the pair of Crows was too distant for accuracy and the pellet missed its target, ricocheting instead off the left-hand doorframe and embedding in the wall on the right side of the corridor.

The Crows scrambled to avoid the shot, expecting more to follow, shooting back as they sought safety in a hallway that offered none, but Lash had withdrawn into the shaft and their shots stuck in the wall.

"I'm out," he hissed before darting up long enough to throw the empty popper at the nearest Crow. It hit with more accuracy then Lash's shot had, producing a yelp but doing nothing else to remove the impediment from their path.

"Here." Maemi handed over one of her poppers as she pushed past Zara to the front alongside Lash. One of the Crows had crept nearer, intending to fire into the shaft. As one, Maemi and Lash fired at the bird-masked face that appeared in the opening before them before he could take his shot. One pellet punctured the black beak that housed the mask's breathing filtration unit, the other shattered the tempered plastic piece over the Crow's left eye. His scream was aborted and he toppled forward, following the single shot he managed to make, a shot that nicked Lash's shoulder, drawing blood before it whizzed past Zara's head into the wall beyond her.

The voice of the second Crow, filtered, mechanical, distorted, began a desperate plea for reinforcements. Maemi drew up, jerked back to avoid the officer's shot but got off a shot of her own. It caught the Crow in the knee with enough shattering impact to cause him to fall. He fired again, but Maemi was out of sight.

When the echo of that shot died away, Lash took the risk of emerging fully from the shaft, dropping to the tiled floor as the Crow attempted two more shots. But the trigger's click yielded no result, either a jam or a lack of ammunition thwarting his efforts, and Lash ran forward to kick the Crow's popper out of his hand. He kicked him again, in the head, for good measure.

"Zara...do it!"

With his popper pointed at the Crow's head and no idea how much of the officer's message had been transmitted and understood, and who might respond to the call, Lash did not want to risk firing again. They had made enough noise. Conserving what ammunition they had made more sense. Zara scrambled out of the vent opening to race to the control panel on the wall, followed by Maemi who confiscated the first fallen Crow's weaponry and then frisked the one at Lash's feet.

More weapons meant a higher chance of survival.

Fifteen seconds. Thirty seconds, Forty-five. Ninety passed before the clear signal on the console flashed and the metal gears within the walls turned to pull the doors open to the continuing corridor beyond, filled with cycling red light and darkness and at least a dozen staggering, emaciated forms dressed in soiled rags or nothing at all. Lash gave the Crow at his feet another kick to be sure he was unconscious, to prevent a second message for help, and then he pushed through the opening, catching Zara's hand as he began to run.

"Come with us," he called to the lost souls without knowing if they could hear him or if they would listen. "We'll get you out."

None of them knew how they could do that. But the more bodies in the corridor with them, perhaps the better their chances for survival, even if those other bodies could barely keep up with them as they ran. But neither Maemi or Zara had any idea where they were running to.

They were simply following Scarecrow and Lash's lead.

ᕲᐦCHAPTER 27 ᐦᕲ

T here was still no sign of Venn in any of the rooms he and Tox passed, only a host of other barely surviving test subjects, some diseased, covered in boils, scabs, and the scars of unknown medical issues either natural or inflicted on them. Many showed signs of Heb addiction, the ticking and twitching of muscles and the occasional trickles of dried blood from ears, nose, mouth, and eyes. Rhyd wagered they were mostly streeters, people that few, if any, would miss after their capture, after their deaths. But Venn had been no streeter, despite his blossoming addiction; it, and the length of time he had been gone, explained why Rhyd did not find him here.

But it gave no indication where the man could be. If, by any miracle of fate, he was still alive.

So what had become of all the others who had Vanished?

"Are there others elsewhere?" Scarecrow asked into the rice-sized mic secured below his lip, knowing Zara would not likely have answers but hoping Lash might.

But he received no reply and from the nearness of the exchange of popper fire behind them they could hear, he guessed that Zara and the others had reached Upper 21 and were being pursued. Shot at. Perhaps she could not hear him. Perhaps she was in no position to reply.

He considered briefly going back to help them but decided it made more sense to the mission for him to continue forward, though he had no idea where he was going. Perhaps the junction ahead would lead him to more rooms, or else a lift or stairs that would take him to the top where it was claimed the Founder resided. Maybe Lash did not know what became of the rest, but the Founder surely would. He would know where Agnys and Venn had been taken. He would know what had happened to everyone else who Vanished from the Levs. Scarecrow would find him and the Founder would be his guarantee of survival, and the survival of those he loved, those he sought.

The continuous circular path, however, brought him instead within sight of a tall, dark-haired man in a lab coat, bearded and alone except for a child he was hastily steering along with a hand tight on her shoulder. The child was barefoot, wore a medical gown that hung loosely from her shoulders and dragged on the floor. It did not matter what she wore, however. The blonde hair that tumbled down her back gave away her identity and filled Rhyd with a flush of relief.

"Agnys!"

He reached for her, realizing only then that his hand still bled as the red dripped between his outstretched fingers. Tox aimed the popper at the stranger in the lab coat, but Rhyd held his other hand up to stop her from shooting. He would not risk the girl being injured in a shootout and he guessed, from the other man's grip on her and his now terrified expression at the visage before him, the form that fit the description of the mythical vigilante Scarecrow, that the stranger had no wish for harm to befall her either.

It was true, Tamner thought with an anxious swallow. Those below were infiltrating the Uppers…starting with the Scarecrow.

Agnys did not recognize Rhyd's voice, altered as it was by the modulator and the respiratory system in his mask. She had never seen this mask, this coat, and the visage it presented, not the same as the birdmen but frightening all the same, made her hesitate despite hearing her name. But still, she knew him, knew his height, knew the bandaged hand that reached for her. She knew the beaten woman at his side. She reached for him but they were too far apart.

"Please," Tamner stammered, as Agnys cried, "Rhyd!" and tried to yank free to run to the masked individual. Tamner's hand on her shoulder, however, held her back.

"Let her go."

Scarecrow advanced, closing the distance between them, with Tox to his left and slightly behind, using the wall for support but steady enough, he hoped, that her aim with that popper would be true if they needed it to be.

"I intend to…but not here. If they find her…"

"They won't." Scarecrow was not going to allow that to happen. "Agnys," he said again, feeling his outstretched arm weaken under the strain of his reach. His hand throbbed, his wrist ached, and the nerves stretching up towards his elbow were tingling as if on the verge of going numb. He needed more meds, but not here. Not now.

"Your hand…"

Scarecrow's eyes narrowed inside of his hood at the man who was changing the subject without releasing Agnys. He growled and the stranger, visibly shaken, abruptly let her go.

"Yes…of course…"

Showing no fear of the man whose face she could not see, trusting him to be the one person in the metal nest who would protect her, Agnys ran to him and clutched tightly to his leg. Scarecrow pressed his good hand to her head, the exhilaration he felt at finding her alive and unharmed, and seemingly in good health, sapping some of his strength and energy with a heavy breath of relief.

But his job was not yet finished, his primary mission still incomplete. Tox knew it too and kept the popper aimed, waiting for Scarecrow's next decision. The man had his weaknesses, but he had found her, had found Agnys, and he would continue to search for Venn, though the likelihood of finding the cellist, alive or a footnote in a record of the dead, was much smaller.

"Where are the others?"

Tamner twitched. Were there officers in pursuit of this man? Didn't he know he risked his life standing here in the corridor asking questions? Or did he know, perhaps, that the majority of residents and workers in the Uppers had already evacuated, allowing him free run of these levels to do as he pleased? Tamner knew if he did not hurry, did not leave now, he would never make it to the last Factory shaft before it was sealed...if it had not closed already...and he would be trapped here with the masked vigilante and the hordes of rioters he believed would soon follow.

"What others?"

"Others you've taken; not the streeters, not the tingers, the others."

"Cells are back..." he pointed in the direction Scarecrow had come from and the black-clad figure snarled.

"There are more! Where are they?"

Swallowing harder this time, Tamner's twitching included a shrug of his shoulders. He was not a fighting man, had never held a popper or thumper, knew nothing about combat that would allow him to win against the Scarecrow, even though the vigilante was bleeding onto the white corridor floor. Deciding that he had nothing to lose by replying, that he was likely to die anyhow, as might Scarecrow if the Crows caught up with him, Tamner croaked, "Some are in the factories...laborers...some are sent to the Core."

Scarecrow growled again, a strangled sound of hope, relief, and frustration. There was still a chance then, that Venn was alive. Those in the Levs had only rumors and wild tales of how the Factories worked, who ran them, how they produced everything Hebanthe Falls needed. Sending those arrested there to work, a form of slave labor surely, at least allowed them a chance to live, a better chance than the test subjects behind him had been given.

But the Core. The Core was not real. It was even more fabled than the stories about the Factories. Yet here was another voice, a man of learning and science, who professed the place to exist. The thought that it could be real struck Rhyd with a sense of horror and finality.

If it was a place where people were sent, it was also a place from which no one ever came back.

"Where is the Core?"

"I don't know; I don't have clearance to…almost no one does…"

"The Founder has clearance."

"Yes. Yes…but from what I…few are ever sent there. I don't know why…how. Most they bring up are laborers…as I said…"

"Three factories. There is a roster of who works in each?"

Tamner nodded, sounds in the corridor behind Scarecrow filling him with a higher level of anxiety. "Yes, I expect so. Pass records in the Archives if nothing else."

"Then find me a terminal…you will help me find who I'm looking for, then you are free to go."

"We can't!" Tamner glanced at his chrono and tapped it, holding it up as if to show Scarecrow the numbers though he was not near enough to see the reflective surface. "I don't have access to that data, don't have clearance, and even if I did…" He tapped the chrono again. "They'll be closed by now…or will be closing soon." Or they would certainly close those exit points the moment Scarecrow reached one of them.

He did not expect the wounded man, slow and unsteady on his feet, to charge and pin him to the wall with his good arm across his throat. There was no seeing the eyes behind the mask, but Tamner was no idiot.

Those eyes were flashing with anger as Scarecrow barked, "What do you mean closed?" the distortion of his voice filter breaking the words into static.

In the corridor far behind Scarecrow, Zara winced at the feedback in her earpiece.

"They've evacuated…or they are…everyone on these three levels…into the Factories…"

"Why aren't you with them?" Scarecrow had no reason to disbelieve him, except for the fact that he was still here, a level below the three factory exits. Rhyd only knew there were three tunnels, three factories, by the word of others who had been there. East Three was said to have been destoyed centuries ago, cutting off access to what had once been Factory East One.

As none alive had ever been there, had ever seen it, no one knew if that tale was true or not.

"We were...examining the par...the girl..." Tamner began, correcting his stammering words in the hopes that the vigilante would not be offended by the slip.

"We?"

The word made Tox scan the corridor, now expecting an ambush.

"Lima and me...when he came...the Founder. He told us to dispose of her before we evacuated...to kill her and..." He shook his head as best he could beneath the increased pressure at his throat. "I decided to release her back into the vent system, where she might be able to hide...from whatever's coming. Lima's already gone. There's only me. Is it true? Are those from below...coming here?"

Scarecrow snorted and dropped his arm. "I don't know." He glanced at Agnys, whose hair he was stroking with his bloody hand, and then at Tox, who nodded in reply to his unspoken thoughts. It was comforting to know she would agree to anything as long as he kept them safe.

Her trust, after the torture she had endured on his behalf, meant a lot.

"Take us there."

"Where?"

"The shafts. The Factories. Whichever's closest."

"But..."

"Do it!"

There was no reason not to go that far. If the shafts were not yet sealed, Rhyd could get inside. The Founder had to be in one of them, and the Founder had the answers he needed. If the tunnels were closed, then he would wait for the violence in the Levs to calm, wait for Kemway to emerge, or wait for Zara and her Echosys to reach him; together they would find a way inside. Not with Tox, and not with Agnys, but at the moment he did not have a plan to keep them safe.

Sending them back to the Levs, or to join Zara and whoever was following, would likely mean condemning them to death.

If Zara and the others were even still alive.

The shuffling sounds in the corridor gradually drawing nearer proved that someone was coming. It did not prove who.

Tamner shivered again, but nodded warily and led the way as commanded. They were on the east side of the city with a chance of evacuating to Factory East if the west ones were already closed as he suspected. Having seen no one traveling in this direction, they had either all crammed into the West Factories or else East was closed as well. They would not know which until they reached it. The East was less desirable to many, too close to the parah on the Outside to make the majority of the Upper residents comfortable with evacuating there despite the larger abundance of survival supplies stored in the East. But Tamner was not afraid, of the East, of the Outside, of the parah who lived there. Not anymore. He trusted the data he had spent years gathering, data that contradicted what the Founder proclaimed in every city-wide prodcast.

He trusted the evidence this child standing before him offered.

He would willingly go East, but his wife and children might not be with him.

"I could tend that for you," he offered cautiously, indicating the man's injured hand.

Scarecrow snarled and Tamner fell silent.

By Zara's calculations, they should be within sight of Scarecrow's position, but they had yet to find him in this disorienting, red-lit hallway. They had seen the horrors he had seen, the dead, the dying, those rotting from the inside, infested with a Heb addiction that devoured their brains and organs. Though many spoke of rumored horrors that existed in the Uppers, most in the Levs refused to believe it could be true.

Now that they had witnessed it with their own eyes, how could they ever doubt again?

Maemi was the one to spot the blood on the wall, the dripping trail made where a Crow had fallen and continuing ahead of them. As long as the trail lasted, Scarecrow was alive, and that gave them impetus to continue at a quicker pace. Those rambling along behind, the shuffling mass of struggling humanity, did their best to keep up, although, at the back of the crowd, stragglers dropped now and again and did not resume following.

A larger accumulation of blood splatters indicated a place where Rhyd had stopped for a considerable amount of time. A quick survey of the area offered no explanation, although they knew Tox was traveling with him now, and that her health was not good. Her blood, perhaps, some injury they had stopped to tend before they continued on. If they had stopped to bind the injury, the efforts to stop the blood loss had failed, since the trail continued, and so the three followed, concerned now about what effect that injury, whoever it belonged to, would have on Scarecrow's ability to proceed.

They thought to be hindered by the access panel to the lift where Scarecrow had stopped again, but found the door to be open, its wiring yanked free and gears jammed so that the door would not close. The blood trail turned here and continued up the incline nearby.

The three looked at one another. If Rhyd had done this knowing they were behind him, or if he suspected they were, or even if he had disabled the lift to keep Crows from following, then they could not likely be far behind him.

The shuffling crowd continued their pursuit.

❧Chapter 28❧

amner's Pass gave them access through most doors, onto any level, into most areas they might need to go, which meant Scarecrow did not need to rely on Grainger's duplicate Pass and thus expose any secrets of how he had gotten into the Uppers. Scarecrow made note of every grate, every vent duct, every access panel they passed as they moved steadily in the direction Tamner promised the Factory tunnel to be. Agnys, hand in his uninjured one, and Tox with the popper aimed at the back of Tamner's head in case he entertained any heroic notion about trying to get away, turn on them, or somehow alert the Crows to their presence here. Upper 22 was more deserted then Upper 21 had been, with no trace of medical patients and test subjects.

As below, the lights flashed red in the darkness, but Scarecrow noticed something else as well. Tox, Tamner, and Agnys were all slowing, their steps dragging, their breathing becoming thinner and more labored. He paused their progress to listen for proof of his suspicions, and inside his mask, he frowned.

Evacuating the Uppers, preparing the Factories for additional individuals, had meant shutting down most of the systems here and redirecting water and air into the Factories. Not only had the lighting been switched to emergency levels, but the air circulation and filtration had as well. Invaders from below would not last long in an atmosphere devoid of breathable air; attackers who could not breathe would not be attackers for very long. Such a precaution would force them to retreat, unless someone amongst them was proficient in the electronics that controlled life support systems in Hebanthe Falls.

Someone like Zara. Or Scarecrow.

Soon Scarecrow would be forced to share his oxygen tank, or else he needed to find a control switch or hatch from which he could manually restart the air systems. Without doing so, even the people he had freed were going to die.

If they could make it to Upper 23, Tamner's gaze seemed to suggest, they would survive. The Founder's offices and suites would be the last place deprived of life support. Whether the Founder had evacuated or not, his chambers would continue to have all needed systems for as long as possible. But how much further, Scarecrow wondered as he hoisted the wilting child in his good arm and cradled her against his chest and shoulder, did they have to go to get there? It felt like they had been trekking through these corridors for hours, though it was likely that perception was complicated by his flagging physical condition, and the random flashes of pain in his arm and hand.

He resisted using pain killers again, not wanting to give Tamner any moment's advantage. Soon, however, he would either have to kill the pain and hope he could trust the dark-haired man not to attack them, or else risk being overpowered in an increasingly disoriented state. The way Tox was leaning on the wall, dragging her shoulder against it as she steadfastly moved one booted foot in front of the other, was another warning that Scarecrow could not continue to ignore.

By the time they reached a door that Tamner opened to another inclined passage, marked Upper 23, even the scientist was struggling to remain upright. The sliding open of the door allowed a whoosh of cool air to flood over them and both Tox and Tamner slid to the floor, one against one wall, one against another, gulping in relief. Agnys lifted her head from Scarecrow's shoulder at the sensation, her mouth open, gasping at the much-needed air like a baby bird awaiting its parents' nourishment.

Here, behind the wall panels, the ventilation system throbbed more loudly as the sensors of Upper 23 detected the sudden pressure decrease presented by the opening of the passage between levels. So long as the system monitored that drop as oxygen from one level bled into the lower two, it would struggle to compensate for the lower density and feed what was needed through the systems. As long as the system worked correctly, no one in the Uppers was going to suffocate.

Those behind him would live.

The popper was no longer aimed at Tamner, but the man was not going anywhere. He did not have the strength or will for it. He had nowhere else to go. He was stuck with these people. Cooperation ensured his survival.

"How far?" If Upper 22 was vacant, it made sense now for the others to remain here, where they were, recovering strength, awaiting the reinforcements that could not be so far behind, while Scarecrow went ahead to find either the Factory tunnels, Founder Kemway, or the Founder's office to gain access to whatever records his Echosys could provide. By the time Rhyd found any one of those things, he hoped he would have regained communication with Zara. He could not hack into the Hub, into the Archives, without her.

Chest still heaving as he gulped the cool air, Tamner squeaked, "At the junction…at the end of this hall…left leads to the West Factories and…" he hesitated but added at last, "the Founder's antechamber. Doctet offices…meeting rooms…goods storage and distribution…Straight will take you to living quarters…banquet hall and concert chamber…recreation areas. But…" he coughed and wheezed. "First right…more storage and processing facilities…for the hemp…and access to Factory East."

Unseen, Scarecrow glowered. Unlimited choices, but few that would benefit him. He began to nod, his decision made, and he set Agnys down next to Tox. He knew what Tamner was thinking. They had taken too long to get this far. Night was passing, dawn would arrive soon, and the West evacuation routes were certainly closed. Tamner could try to reach them, but it would likely be an effort wasted.

If there was even a small chance to enter Factory East, it being closest to them, he needed to take it.

"Go east; take them…keep them safe…alive…give them medical care…and you will see that she gets home." He pointed to Agnys.

Tox grabbed his uninjured wrist. "No…"

With a long breath, Scarecrow squatted before the woman and child and slowly removed his hood. It exposed him to Tamner, but he no longer felt that it mattered. Whatever came next, he doubted he would ever need the suit again.

"I have to do this. I have to find Venn…to know…whatever it takes. I don't know what will happen, but you'll be safer with Agnys…and she'll be safer with you. You have to do this. You're the only one…you have to make sure she's safe." He did not fully trust Tamner. Until the others caught up, there was only Tox. He trusted her to do this, just as he had trusted her with the secrets of his identity.

To the child, who was now touching his damp hair, exploring with certainty and relief that he was who she had believed him to be, he murmured, "You stay with Tox…she will make sure you get home…"

"Home?" Her eyes brightened but a frown tugged at the corners of her mouth. "Home…Rhyd."

Rhyd shook his head. "Can't take you home, Agnys. It's not safe down there with me anymore." Grainger knew his face, his name. Now Tamner did too. It was only a matter of time before the Founder likely did as well. "You have to stay with Tox."

From around his neck, he removed the chain he wore, the duplicate of the one lying amidst Tox's possession far below, unable to be retrieved now, lost forever. "Keep this. I'll be back for it."

He could not make that a promise; whatever awaited him, he doubted he would ever be reunited with the child who had saved his life in small, barely perceptible ways. There were no photos, no trinkets, nothing to remember her by, but nor were there any of Venn left to him either, and if he was honest with himself, by the time the new day dawned, he expected to be beyond needing reminders.

He would probably be dead.

Agnys' small hand closed around the gift and when she looked into his face, it was with the sadness of understanding in her eyes. She knew what goodbye meant, without knowing his words. She hugged tight around his neck, crying against his stubbled chin, refusing for many moments to let him go. He stiffened, awkwardly brought his arm around to return the embrace, feeling a cracking inside of the walls against emotional pain he had fought so hard to build and keep strong after Venn's Vanishing. He squeezed his eyes shut, thankful Tamner could not see his weakness, even though Tox could, and fought against the tears that trickled free.

It was Tox, sensing an impending emotional break by the slight movement of Rhyd's shoulders, who gently pried Agnys away and allowed Rhyd to get to his feet. She picked up the headgear from the floor as she got up, temporarily ignoring Agnys' renewed attachment to Rhyd's leg, and positioned the hood and mask on his head, connecting every wire and tube that had popped loose when it had been removed. He bobbed his head, thankful for her support, untangled Agnys from his leg, and crossed to where Tamner rested. He was surprised, since the man could breathe freely now, and there was no popper aimed at him, that he had not seized the opportunity to escape during Rhyd's distraction.

"I'll see to it," Tamner said to the vigilante, extending his hand to seal the bargain he was agreeing to now that he had experienced a small taste of who this man was. "They will be safe. I'll do my best to make it happen."

"Yes…you will." Or Scarecrow, provided he lived, would hunt Tamner down and make him pay the same way the Founder would if he did not produce viable, valuable, accurate information about Venn. If he had in any way been instrumental in Venn's death.

"How will you…?"

Anticipating the remainder of the question, Rhyd snorted but did not reply. He took two steps into the inclining passage, was stopped short by Agnys' wail, and turned long enough to look at her. One hand was raised into the familiar signal for 'stay', the other, bleeding enough that he refused to put his glove back on, was splayed across his chest, over his heart, leaving a red stain there as well.

Agnys covered her heart too, copying the action without fully understanding it, and continued to cry as he disappeared from sight.

꧁*꧂

"You're back." Whatever Rhyd had done, the visual connection was reestablished by the time Zara had her own technical difficulties sorted and she could now see that he was moving up another incline. In hearing him again, she also heard a seldom heard hitch in his breathing that made her pout. "Where are you?"

After a delay, as his breathing returned to something more controlled, he replied, "Entering Upper 23."

"Twenty-three." She whistled low beneath her own ragged breath. "I suppose we have you to thank for the air?"

"Just opened a window." The life systems from Upper 23 were doing all the work; he had only made it possible for the air flow to stretch down into the other levels of the Uppers.

"Where are the rest? Did you find…?"

"You're in the Uppers?" he asked, ignoring the question.

"We're on 22…following a trail of blood…Tox's…or yours?"

"Keep moving. You'll find them. Tell the others to go with Tox. But Zar…I need you to come up here."

She bit her lip. The thought of traveling through the Uppers alone was a frightening one, but she believed Rhyd would not ask her to do it if it was not safe, if his need for her was not pressing.

"Anything," she murmured.

"We've gotta get your Echo to the antechamber; we need access to the Founder's records."

"Will any console work?" They had passed others, wall units and open residences with Echos on desks or mounted on walls. She could see Scarecrow's location on the Echo screen she carried, but she did not know how long it might take to reach him or how long they had. If interfacing with another console might work, it would be faster.

His shoulders shrugged; she could not see it but she knew him well enough to imagine that gesture in the momentary pause before he spoke. "Don't know…don't wanna chance it. Wanna do this right."

Lash and Maemi could not hear Rhyd's voice, could not pause to view the Echo images as they rushed forward in pursuit, but they could hear Zara and her words made them look back with concern.

"What is…?" Lash began.

"Where…?" asked Maemi. She, like the blonde, was anxious about their progress and what Scarecrow had planned.

Zara did not have the chance to answer. A childish squeal erupted from the hall ahead of them. The echo of it continued through the corridor as the girl, her face red and wet from crying, threw herself at Lash and held tight to his legs as she had done to Rhyd earlier. Tox and the stranger with her scrambled to their feet, the stranger with an apprehensive expression and Tox with her popper aimed in the group's direction until she recognized the approaching faces.

"Rhyd?" Maemi asked breathlessly, assessing Tox's condition with horror and hurrying forward to offer support.

"Quincy?"

He was the last person Tamner expected to see. He did not know the man well, they had not traveled in any of the same social circles in those distant days, but they knew each other in passing from the day Edgar Quincy had been exposed to the Outside, the day Kemway had issued his declaration on the man's fate, the day he lost his job, his tongue, and anything resembling the normal life he had once had.

"Tamner."

Tox pointed up the passage, ignoring the man she knew only as a face, an acquaintance of Skelter's, ignoring the fact that he and the man next to her knew one another. "Gone ahead. He's leading the way." She pointed her finger and her narrowed gaze at Tamner, who shakily nodded his head, aware that he had been thrust into something much larger than a single vigilante and a parah child.

Tox's glance over the group revealed the absence of Xiaodan and Skelter, but she did not ask where they were. Safe or not, it was irrelevant at the moment. "We're getting her to freedom…sticking together…until he gets back."

Until. Not if.

"Then let's go," Lash grunted. The throng behind them, those who had not dropped away due to the decreased oxygen, had nearly caught up. Tamner could see them, the evidence of Rhyd's earlier efforts, the proof of all of the work he, Lima, and the other scientists undertook at the Founder's and Doctet's insistence to improve the lives of those in the city, primarily those in the Uppers, further proof of the efficiency of the Founder's number one weapon against dissension.

With two additional poppers in the group, the bargain he had made swelling to include three more under his protection, Tamner nodded and began to trudge up the incline the Scarecrow had previously followed. Perhaps the entire population of the Levs would not be invading the Uppers, but these people behind him were enough. Quincy, after all, knew a truth that very few in Hebanthe Falls knew, proof that Tamner suspected, believed, but had never been able to expose. The loss of his tongue to silence him, to keep him from speaking, had not prevented Quincy's survival. Whether the others, save for the girl, knew that same unexposed truth, Tamner could only guess, but the precipice of some great revolution stretched across his horizon as he never imagined it would.

He would have no choice, he knew, but to step off into the void of knowledge and truth and watch the whole of history change.

☙Chapter 29☙

With Tamner no longer accompanying him, Grainger's duplicate Pass allowed Scarecrow into a realm that few in Hebenon ever saw. Certainly, to his knowledge, no one from the Levs had ever been here. The two levels beneath him had been sterile, pristine white beneath the flashing red, with tile floors that filled the corridors with the sound of heavy footsteps as people passed through them, and tall ceilings unreachable without a ladder. But here, in the topmost level of Hebanthe Falls, the corridors were adorned with a softer, less hostile shade of white and his steps on the floor were muted as though the tile was insulated to reduce noise. There were no flashing red emergency lights and the systems still ran to provide both circulating oxygen and a soft warm glow of pale amber in the corridors. The lower half of the walls, instead of smooth paneling that contributed to the sterility of the previous two levels, were lined with sound absorbent material as well, while the upper portion portrayed colorful murals of the antiquated cities of Earth's history, the world that none in Hebenon had seen. The paint had faded over the centuries, as if no one had bothered to brighten it, touch it up. Rhyd wondered if there was no one in the Uppers with the talent to restore it.

Anyone in the Levs who might have been able to do so went unnoticed by those living above the falling rivers' mist.

The images were distracting, too easy to get lost in as he passed, the fingertips of his gloved good hand brushing over the outlines of majestic buildings, scenic natural vistas, and an ever-changing night to day back to night again painted skyline.

How Venn would have admired this, Rhyd thought bitterly.

Into the mic on his lip, he hissed, "Which door?" There were at least four he could see ahead of him before the corridor divided right and left and continued ahead.

Zara, also finding the view Rhyd was showing her to be a pleasant distraction in a sea of unpleasantness, tore her eyes from the images long enough to study the open screen window of city schematics. She had to stop walking in order to focus and it took her companions several moments to notice they were leaving her behind.

"Hurry, Zar," Maemi called, beckoning the blonde to follow with a curling hand.

"No." She looked up from the screen in the direction her friends were going and then down the hall where she knew Rhyd to be. "I can't."

"Zar…"

"He needs me."

The two women stared eye-to-eye, assessing and expressing intent. Zara had lost much with the loss of Skelter, had lost the center of her world. They might not have been a couple in any romantic sense, but they had been a team, their mutual need of one another binding them in a tight relationship from the time both were very young. With Skelter gone, there was no going back to the life that had been, even if Vapors stood unscathed.

Zara needed to be needed.

Wherever they were going, whatever lay ahead, the more independent Maemi and Tox, and the survivor Lash, would push through and prosper. Zara's heart was somewhere else. Even if it meant facing death as Skelter had done, Zara had the three things Rhyd required most: her Echo, her skill, and her trust. As long as that was true, she would go wherever he beckoned.

Behind Maemi, between Tamner and Lash, Tox understood what was not being said and nodded her head at the woman she had worked with for so long. Having survived what she had, not knowing yet of Skelter's fate, not knowing the extent of what was transpiring in the city beneath their feet, she had little reason not to cling to the hope of reunification. "See you soon, Zar. Hurry back to us," she murmured before pulling Maemi along. Zara watched them move, forward and then right, disappearing quickly out of sight, leaving her alone and unarmed in the Uppers with nothing but her Echo and the short knife Skelter had insisted she always carry with her.

Into the mic, she said shakily, "Last on the right, Whiskey…then the door directly across."

Scarecrow heard her fear. It was impossible not to. "Hurry, Zar."

The sooner she caught up to him, the sooner he could offer protection, but he could not afford to wait. He had to secure the Founder's Echo while there was time. Before anyone found him here.

There was no reason for Tamner to care about the blonde's decision to leave the group. He did not know her, did not know any of them, and what he did know about Lash…Quincy…was enough to set his nerves ajangle. The man was not tall, was unimposing save for the intensity of his eyes, but a man with a secret could always be a danger. It was a secret Tamner suspected and had kept to himself, having never truly challenged the Founder, or anyone else, with what he knew. He had been too afraid of suffering his father's fate to take the risk. But these people, whatever their fears, possessed a conviction that had brought them from the bowels of Hebenon to the realm of the Uppers, and if they shared the vigilante's mission, and believed it, if they shared any of Lash's knowledge, he assumed they would stop at nothing to bring down what had taken centuries to build, uphold…and undermine.

He did know that their primary goal was to see Agnys to safety. He knew his duty was to see that they were all safe, regardless of whether Scarecrow completed his unspoken mission or not. Scarecrow was looking for someone, that was all Tamner knew. That search, and

≈Hebenon≈

a parah child, had brought them all here and now those with him were trusting his leadership. Lash trusted him, and the group's faith in Lash meant that they were relying on him to do precisely what he had promised Scarecrow he would.

His path felt so predetermined now, that Tamner moved as if it was the most logical, natural, thing to do.

Whatever was on the women's minds, whatever was going through Tamner's, Lash had his own agenda, one that involved the parah child and meant proving himself sane and sound, proving that his memories of his last day in the Uppers was accurate and not the twisted, faded threads of a too-often reoccurring dream.

And Agnys, clinging to Lash's hand, tripping along as near to his leg as she could, ached to be home. To see the sun, feel the wind and rain, taste the air and see her people again. She did not know precisely where home was compared to where she was now, did not know how the path they were taking would fulfill that desire, but Rhyd had indicated that home was this way. Home was where she was going to go…and maybe the new friends with her would come too.

≈*≈

"Don't move."

Zara froze midstep and then hesitantly set her foot down to keep from stumbling in that one footed stance, trusting that the command was not meant to keep her from doing that simple thing. She trembled from head to toe, terror threading through her heart and drawing tight, squeezing so that each beat burned within her chest and forced what little air her lungs held out with it.

The Uppers had been evacuated. Grainger had made the order himself, with a few exceptions, and he had seen to it that the residents, except for those few, were safely stowed away in the West Factories without communications or prodcasts to inform them of events in the whole of Hebanthe Falls. He had not anticipated the cutting of communications, had not called for it to be done and had not done it on his own, and thus he felt a wealth of gratitude to whatever tapper in the Levs had the skill to accomplish it.

The disadvantage had been, however, that he was out of touch with his officers and had no way of knowing the status of the situation in the Levs. The inability to communicate left him with no other officers in the Uppers except for a dozen he had sent to the Factory East tunnel, along with their families, and the two he had stationed where he had last seen the Scarecrow in order to defend the Uppers from anyone else who breached there. Or if not defend it, they might at least bring him word of an incursion. Not that he expected anyone else to enter there, or anywhere in the Uppers. The stairwell doors and lifts were sealed with the shutting off of the main power and would require force to get them open. Scarecrow had been lucky. Nothing short of a properly coded Pass should let anyone else through.

There were prisoners here too, people in the Core, people in medical stasis and in testing rooms from which the med and scientific staff drew their subjects, but to Grainger's mind, they did not count. He could not save them, and he feared to expose the city to any contaminants those people might be infected with. The ones in stasis or in holding were beyond saving by his reckoning, and only the Founder had the code key to the Core. There was nothing Grainger could do for any of them, even if he wanted to.

That should only have left him the vigilante roaming Upper 22, trapped without access to Upper 23, nowhere to go but back down, maybe a handful of roaming officers or individuals who had either not received the evacuation orders or who had not been able to carry them out before the Factory exits were sealed. And, if his officers had done their job, it would be the one individual that he had decided, over the course of the day and night's events, needed to be replaced.

There should not have been this beautiful blonde figure that he found before him now. Her presence here was a puzzling and unexpected surprise.

"Zara?"

She turned slowly to face him, her eyes wide with the fear he expected to see from anyone caught in the Uppers without proper authorization. But regardless of her reason for being here, he did not want her to be afraid, not of him, not of being here. Some small part of him hoped she had come for him. He touched her cheek and though she flinched as though believing he would strike her, she did not make a sound and did not jerk away from him. She cautiously closed the link on the Echo with a flick of a finger to hide what she had been doing before his fingers reached the bud in her ear.

"Who are you talking to? Why are you here?"

She did not speak. Only stared.

He growled softly, a sound of frustration, not anger. He did not have time for an interrogation, but he was not going to leave her here to be found by either his Crows or by Founder Kemway. "Never mind," he muttered, deciding not to press for an answer she would not give. He gripped her upper arm a little too tight so that she could not escape and continued in the direction they had both been going. If her destination was this way, he would see her to it…after he reached his and did what he now believed should have been done by someone a long time ago.

The Kemway dynasty had ruled Hebanthe Falls long enough.

❧CHAPTER 30❦

He stood alone, barefoot, in the center of the barely lit chamber, staring at the brilliant pale blue of dawn through the open skylight, the fringes to the east still bearing pinks and oranges, and to the west, the fading traces of the purple of vanquished night. Head thrown back, hands laced behind his skull, he pondered what the morning air must feel like, if it smelled as clean and fresh as claimed in the old accounts his mother had read to him often. With his father's words drilled into his head, centuries of warnings dating back to the birth of Hebanthe Falls on the tail of global catastrophe that left the world humanity had known contaminated with pollutants, viruses, toxic poisons, and radiation, he could not imagine air any cleaner than that which was filtered and fed through the myriad of purification systems scattered throughout Hebenon.

But the shifting light levels in the Uppers, programming meant to separate night from day in ways that those below had lost, could never simulate what he saw above him. Inside was artificial at best, cold and indifferent despite the efforts made to shift the light hues in accordance to someone's predetermined idea of what the passing hours of the day had been like in centuries past.

Hebenon

None of those programmers had ever seen this, save in dek simulations or historical images that remained in the Archives. Until this morning, neither had Haythem Kemway.

He tried to comprehend the events he had been hurled into, the sudden changes in Hebenon that had spiraled out of his control with the arrival of one small parah girl. When he closed his eyes, he saw her there behind his lids, a perfectly normal child, on the outside at least, strapped down on a cold, clinical table, no older, he imagined than his son Duncan. A child with wide innocent eyes like Flora's and a depth of wisdom and soul that mirrored the look Ulynda sometimes gave him when she questioned the why of the world inside of Hebenon's walls and without.

Not a monster at all, not a thing disfigured and disgusting as centuries of tales held true. And not, he had seen in those frightened blue eyes, a soulless thing devoid of humanity.

That was what frightened him most when he had looked into her eyes. The possibility that perhaps parah were still human…and that perhaps the outside world was safe once more. Perhaps it had always been safe.

If that one small group of humans had survived the apocalypse that had driven so many into Hebanthe Falls and cities like it, how many others had too. And if the world beyond was safe, how could he ever keep those within his city from leaving?

A wisp of cloud, the only one to be seen, drifted slowly across his field of vision, from east to west, its white amorphous fringes ever-shifting until it disappeared from sight, like a puff of smoke after a candle was blown out. He wrinkled his nose as if to smell it, but there was nothing to smell but the sterile city air.

No, he realized when the sky was an unaltered blue again. The parah child had not been the start of Hebenon's decline, but rather the marker at the beginning of her final spiral into chaos. The beginning had come…when? He squinted as he tried to remember. Not with the passing of any law. The laws of treason, the laws of borders and boundaries, had been in place long before Haythem had come to power as a boy of nineteen. Nothing had changed, no new laws had been enacted. There was only the tightening of them, an effort to keep things the same as it seemed the residents of the Levs grew ever bolder with their criticism of Hebenon's age-old policies. The tighter his grip had become, the more control had slipped between the fingers of the hand of law.

Now his people, those within his circle in the Uppers and those who designed, developed, and created the prototypes that kept advancing the lives of every resident in Hebanthe Falls, had left him. Maybe not deliberately, for the order to the officers that had kept him out of the Factory with his family must have come from Grainger, but they had shut him out all the same rather than disobey that order as they should have.

He was the Founder. His command should have trumped that of any other. He believed it should, at least, as it had for generations of Kemway Founders before him. They would return, once the SCAMs were operating again allowing them to see that there was no invasion, that those from the Levs could never penetrate the Uppers, that there was no one remaining to protect them except their Founder who remained steadfast at the seat of his power, warding off societal collapse by remaining strong in the face of this threat.

They would come back when they saw that the violence was over. And then Haythem was going to have words with each individual who had chosen to abandon him. Starting with Captain Grainger…and Neoma.

The true beginning of the end, however, he began to narrow within his head, came back to the rise of the vigilante called Scarecrow for his habit of targeting the bird-masked law officers those in the Levs had dubbed Crows. Scaring them from doing their duty efficiently. Haythem had no idea what had brought the vigilante to the fore, prompted him into action. Perhaps it had been an arrest of someone of significance. Perhaps it had started after seeing too many friends or family members poisoned by Heb and then taken away. Perhaps it had been nothing more than one fed up individual deciding to take control for those whose lives had little meaning beyond survival.

Hadn't Haythem tried to give them meaning with his prodcasts? Hadn't the Talkers with their Voices of Faith done everything in their power to give Hebenon's citizens something positive to hold on to? What more, Haythem wondered, could he have done…besides opening the doors to the Uppers and eradicating a status quo that had existed since the city's founding?

Whatever the case, the two-year battle between Scarecrow and Crows, neither side winning…unless one considered the Scarecrow's constant evasion of capture and persistent ability to hospitalize the Crows he fought to be winning…had brought Hebanthe Falls to where it was this morning. The people in the Levs fighting back, rising in search of a better way they did not even know existed…all because of the capture of one child and the chokehold search for the Scarecrow as soon as identification had been made.

Haythem was not to blame. The child was not to blame. If any one man was to blame for all of this, it was Scarecrow.

The gears in the wall snapped and groaned and the door slid open behind him. Thinking himself alone in the Uppers now that the West and East factories were sealed by a passcode he could not override until the threat was contained, he spun in surprise and shock to stare at the masked figure silhouetted against the brighter light of the corridor.

Rhyd, however, stared not at the man he had not expected to find here, despite his hopes of it, but rather at the open portal above their heads, the solar panels retracted, the metal skin of Hebanthe Falls peeled back to reveal the sky. Not a dek image, not a program projected by an Echo on the room's ceiling, but the actual horizon to horizon gradually bluing sky of morning. Behind the mask, he gaped, but with his head tilted slightly upward, it was not clear if he was staring at the unanticipated miraculous vision or looking haughtily at his prey across the vast circular room.

Scarecrow. It had to be. Haythem had seen enough SCAM footage of this individual, watched it too many times to count in the hopes of finding some identifier, some means of capture. Too much footage of this masked vigilante disabling his armed Crows with feet and hands as his sole weapons more often than not.

Haythem took a tentative shifting step to his left, towards the desk at the side of the room where his weapon was hidden. He had never had to use it, no Founder had, but it had remained hidden there for just this sort of occasion. With enough distance between them, Scarecrow would be no match against a taser, even though Haythem had no idea how to use the thing. When the Scarecrow did not shift focus, did not appear to notice his slow movement, Haythem gauged the distance he had to cross, studied the immobile masked man for a few more moments, and then began his dash towards the desk.

From what had been an empty hand, a spiked, flat metal disk was thrown. "Don't," Scarecrow hissed as the barbs sliced and sank into Haythem's upper arm.

The unanticipated shock of an unfamiliar sort of pain brought a screech and a flow of crimson creeping down the white fabric of his banyan. Haythem froze, half of the distance covered to his desk, but enough of it covered to offer him a small touch of comfort while simultaneously frustrating and disappointing him.

Perhaps one more try would get him to the taser.

"What…is that…?"

Haythem did not need to follow the line of the man's raised arm to know where he was pointing. Anyone in Hebanthe Falls coming into this room, seeing that vision for the first time, would react the same way. "Haven't you ever seen the sky before?" he replied snidely, grimacing as he pulled the throwing disc from his arm, as though it was a sight he enjoyed every day…as though the Scarecrow was somehow inferior for never having had the opportunity to view such beauty. Though he had only been into the Levs once, the day of the woman's capture, Haythem knew from SCAM and ICD footage that world was perpetually dark, lit by neon signs, alglamps on the corners of streets, and the alglamps or fluorescent filament lighting within homes and vindis.

His flippant remark was his mistake. They were barely across his lips when Scarecrow leaped the distance between them as if flying, likely a series of steps but done so unexpectedly and swiftly that Haythem barely saw them before he felt his feet kicked out from under him. He landed on his back with a loud ooof of air and the crack of his head against the floor. Rather than attack again, rather than end his life the way Haythem expected him too, the Scarecrow loomed over him as if in triumph and looked up at the sky once more.

With slow, deliberate, careful movements, the wires and tubing were disconnected, the mask he wore removed. What did it matter if the Founder saw his face? Either one or both of them would not leave this room alive. What did it matter now?

He fleetingly hoped that the panel was open, that perhaps he could, just once, breathe real air, as he and Venn had dreamed many times of doing together. But there was no real air, only the recirculated, filtered air of the Uppers, and he realized with disappointment that what he was seeing was through the window. Black specks occasionally darted past, birds flitting here and there in search of the next morsel, a nest, or perhaps security from some threat below.

Birds. Living, breathing, flying birds.

Outside.

Haythem's attempt to crab backward away from the distracted vigilante was halted by a foot planted in his chest, pinning him in place, the Scarecrow not as distracted as he seemed. Their proximity, and the absence of the mask, gave the Founder the opportunity to look at the man who had dogged him for two years. Beneath the bulk of his protective attire, Haythem wagered him to be slight of build, not the hulking menace so many Crows reported, and his tousled blonde hair and whiskey brown eyes, days of stubble across his chin and the dark circles of fatigue beneath his eyes gave him the look of an everyman. Hardly the sort Haythem expected to assume the role of savior of the masses. More the sort of man found behind a desk or vindi counter. There was nothing, at a glance, about the look of him to fear.

Rather than express the apprehension and anxiety that clawed in his breast, which eased a little now that he saw the man's unassuming, normal features, Haythem forced a smirk and snorted, "I thought you would be taller."

Rhyd did not rise to the bait. Unlike the man beneath his boot, Rhyd had seen the Founder's face thousands of times, in prodcast after prodcast aired to the masses in the Levs in the ongoing effort to promote the Kemways' divine right to rule and to support the laws and teachings set down by the Doctet, the Voices of Faith Talkers, and the Kemways themselves.

"You too." Face to face, the Founder was not as tall or imposing as Rhyd expected a man with a god-complex to be. In fact, he judged the Founder to be slightly shorter than he was, though heavier built and broader at the shoulders. The man's dark hair was more disheveled and unruly today then Rhyd had seen it before, raked back from its usual slicked down styling by fingers of frustration, and his turquoise eyes darted wildly about as the man searched for anything he could use as a weapon, any means at his disposal that might gain his freedom from the one who held him down.

Held him down, Rhyd thought bitterly, the way the Kemways and Doctet had too long held down the citizens of the Levs whose labor made life easier, possible, for those living in the luxury of the Uppers.

"I want arrest records. I want to know what you did with Venn."

"Who?"

Rhyd applied more pressure beneath his boot and Haythem began to cough and use both hands to try to remove the man's foot from his chest. Rhyd did not budge.

"You know who I'm talking about. Venn Weyer!"

A flicker crossed the Founder's eyes, an acknowledgment and hint of recognition that the name brought to mind. He remembered that performance now. Weyer's first as principal cellist in Hebenon's primary orchestra. Now that he remembered that, he remembered this man's face as well, the man with whom the cellist had spent so much of the after party, and with whom he had eventually left. A friend? A brother? A cousin? A lover? A husband?

Now that he saw Rhyd, now that he knew Weyer's name, how could Haythem not have connected the rise of the Scarecrow so soon after that particular arrest? Then again, many arrests were made every day. Some came to his attention, most did not. Some he ordered, some were done at the discretion of Grainger and the Crows. Why should he have connected the two events? It had been, as he recalled now, just another accusation of treason, another traitor arrested among so many, another who said too much, a man with an addiction who spoke out of line one time too often. Perhaps it had been only once. Perhaps he had not spoken out at all. But there were reports, reports that were always heeded without necessarily investigating their truths. He remembered hating the decision at the time, hated ruining such a promising career and depriving Hebenon of Weyer's brilliance.

But laws were laws. There were no exceptions.

How could Haythem have known that the choice he made that night, after the music's final notes died away and the last reception guests had drifted home, would be his own downfall and undoing?

"I don't' know," he snapped indignantly, hoping to cover up any of the thoughts that might have been visible on his face. "I don't keep track of where everyone…"

"But you do keep records."

The men stared at one another, the pressure on Haythem's chest increasing with each moment he refused to answer. Finally, he could no longer cough for the crushing in his lungs and he feared that his ribs would break, so he bobbed his head in reluctant acknowledgment.

"Then find him." Rhyd pointed at the Echo on the desk and began to remove his foot. Though gasping for much-needed air and to clear the discomfort in his chest, Haythem grabbed Rhyd's calf with both hands and twisted, pulling the Scarecrow off his feet, causing him to land heavily where Haythem had just been lying. The Founder, however, was no longer there, having scrambled out of the way and to his feet as Rhyd came down.

Haythem laughed, feeling confident now that he had brought the vigilante down on his own, something his Crows seemed unable to accomplish. But Rhyd turned in that fall like a cat and sprang to his feet, charged with his head and shoulders down so that they caught the Founder across his already bruised chest. The force thrust Haythem back against the desk, knocking some of the items to the floor with a crash. The Founder wrapped his hands around the vigilante's throat, squeezing, trying to force him away to allow him to get around his desk to the stashed weapon.

If he could just get that in his hand, the Scarecrow did not stand a chance.

Rhyd smashed his forearms against the sides of Haythem's, the protective plating and padding in his coat and suit adding force to the blow. The death grip around his throat was broken as the Founder howled in agony, but Rhyd's action also revealed a weakness that Haythem had not noticed before.

Scarecrow's hand was bleeding and, it seemed he was making an effort to protect that same wrist.

Haythem rolled to the side, sliding out from beneath Rhyd's slighter body, reaching for a stylus that had rolled across the desk but had not fallen to the floor with so many other items. When Rhyd reached to stop him, swinging with his other hand to catch the Founder in the jaw with his gloved fist, Haythem recoiled. But the stylus was in his grasp now, and the metal nib was thrust deep into the area of the bleeding puncture in Rhyd's other hand.

Rhyd twisted away, stumbling, blinded momentarily by the pain, and Haythem caught him beneath the ribs with two balled fists. There was enough power behind the punches to drop Rhyd to the floor, gasping for air, wishing now that he had left the mask on. It would have at least provided the oxygen he needed to continue unimpeded.

It was enough of a break in the fight for Haythem, now spitting blood and wiping it from his nose, fighting the sharp pains that shot up his arms from his fists to his shoulders, and regretting that those punches had likely added to whatever damage the Scarecrow had done, to pull the taser from beneath his desk and aim it at Rhyd's head.

"I have had enough of…" he began with a snarl.

The office door slid open again, this time more unexpected than the last. Haythem spun sideways, his aim now on whoever was coming through the door. Rather than look to see for himself who was there, who had offered that precious gift of distraction, Rhyd jumped to his feet and over the desk as two successive shots rang out. Fire burned through his leg, above his knee, as he slid along the edge the metallic white surface of the desk and brought the Founder down with him, sending the Echosys crashing to the floor. The unit shattered and Rhyd's next cry was one of frustration, outrage, and pain.

*

The corridor felt to Tox like it stretched out indefinitely, as if it would never end, but neither Tamner nor Lash showed any inclination of slowing or veering off into any of the possible directions they were offered. None of the doors were closed here, revealing posh rooms with lavish furnishings and decorative artwork of a sort that would not hold up well in the pervasive damp of the Levs. She had no time to look, to enjoy, and her still-blurry vision made a close inspection of details impossible but maybe, she thought as she continued to follow the men at the front, she would see it all again on the way back.

There was nowhere else to go at the end of all of this but back.

The first door into the Factory East shaft was not closed and sealed as Tamner had feared, giving him hope that someone still remained in Upper 23, someone who still intended to evacuate but had some other priority to see to first. The Founder, he wondered. Or Grainger. Assuming that Grainger would be with his officers in the Levs, it made the Founder the most likely possibility, and Tamner fretted about how he could get these people inside, and keep them inside if he had to face the Founder to do it.

Only the fact that the sealed Factory doors would not open until the threats were past might save the lives of those he had been charged with protecting if they could get inside before the Founder arrived and discovered them.

Agnys, no longer carried, clutched Lash's hand and looked back over her shoulder repeatedly, hoping to see Rhyd and Zara running to catch up with them. She did not understand where they had gone, where she and these others were going, why it was taking so long to get there, but she did understand, without any explanation needed, that they were seeking safety and, as Rhyd had promised, home.

It did not seem likely, however, that home could be in this direction.

Passing through a tall, wide arch, its door still retracted as it waited for one final input from the individual who would seal it behind them, Agnys stopped, her hand pulling abruptly free of Lash's as she stared around her with wide eyes and a mouth formed into a silent, excited O. There had been little time that day to study the details of panels of lights, buttons, levers, and screens, to make note of anything except stacks of hemp bins, some full, some empty, before she disappeared behind them and into the vent that had started her journey Below. But she had snuck glimpses of it before, on previous trade visits, and the sight was familiar enough for her to recognize where they were. She snagged Maemi's hand as the woman stopped beside her, pointed into the unopened vent shaft near the floor and then towards one of the two opened passages beyond them. She did know where the other open passage in front of them led, but the one she pointed to, that one made her heart skip with joy.

"Home."

Maemi's eyes, however, gave no more than a flicker in the direction the child was pointing and no thought yet to what Agnys meant. She, like the others, was staring at the six Crows in front of them, officers fully armed with poppers, buzzers, injectors, and thumpers. Maemi and Tox moved together to shield the girl, and Lash stood in front of them as if he could protect them all.

Only Tamner approached the officer with no expressed fear. His genuine expression of relief made every other adult in the group frown and tense for the betrayal they now expected.

"Doctor Tamner," one of the Crows said mechanically, the voice retaining a feminine edge despite the efforts to mask it. Whoever was behind that mask, they recognized the Doctet scientist from the numerous times the man had come into this room to check the instruments that monitored the Outside conditions, and may well have encountered him elsewhere.

Without seeing the individual's face, Tamner could not say.

"Shouldn't you be with the others?"

In the west, Tamner thought bitterly, where his family already was he had no doubt. He kept his feelings from his face and instead of answering, asked a question of his own. "Aren't you evacuating too?"

"Captain sent us here. We're waiting for him."

Not the Founder then, Tamner thought with both relief and concern. The Founder would have been an obvious problem, but the Captain of the Crows would not be much better. Tamner could not guess what that meant in the course of the night's events, what was happening in the Levs, but he doubted this information boded well for Agnys, or Lash, or the Lev residents he had brought with him, and possibly not even for Tamner himself since he had failed to kill the parah child as commanded.

Maybe Grainger did not know about that order.

"Who are they?" The four with Tamner clearly did not belong in the Uppers, were sweaty, disheveled, and dressed, for the most part, in the filth and stink of the Level's mist. One of them looked as if she had been beaten almost to death. It was a miracle, from the looks of her, that she was on her feet.

Clearing his throat, hoping he did not sound as nervous as he felt, Tamner replied, "Test subjects." It was both a good thing and possibly a bad thing that none of the officers recognized Lash. Some might have shot him on sight, others might have understood the importance of this man's existence. "I was told to keep them alive at all costs...Founder's orders. They have been tagged for release to evaluate the data their chips send back."

Maemi and Tox looked at one another, none of them appearing to know what that meant, what release indicated. The women assumed he meant a return to the Levs.

Lash, however, knew it meant something different, but he could not, under any circumstances, allow others to know that he knew.

Beaked heads turned towards one another, but none of them spoke. Tamner held his breath, knowing the lie was a gamble but feeling he had no other card to play. He had sent others Outside for such data missions before, and others had been sent without his approval or knowledge, some simply as punishment for perceived crimes. Invariably the sensory data chips stopped sending not long after their deployment. Tamner had taken that as an indication that the subjects had found ways to disable them, possibly even remove them, whereas the Founder interpreted the failure to be due to the hostile conditions of the Outside and the subsequent deaths of the subjects.

He likely never thought about those people. Tamner on the other hand, spent many sleepless hours wondering what had become of those condemned to that world.

"We were on our way here when the power cut," he added as an afterthought. We were stuck in the lift. See…here's the tag…"

Hoping his risk was about to pay off, he pulled Lash's arm up and was relieved that the man still bore evidence of the tag he had previously worn during his years working on the shell, relieved that the X through it, which indicated he was a political prisoner, was easily recognized, thankful that the officer examining the circular crisscrossed indentation could not tell through the filters of his mask eye-pieces that both were old tags instead of fresh ones, thankful that Lash had tucked his popper into the waistband of his trousers when he first saw the Crows in the room.

He was also thankful, though surprised, when Lash reacted to Tamner's unspoken thoughts. He swung his arm up, catching the female officer beneath the chin hard enough that the Crow flew back into the officer behind her.

The women had lowered, hidden, but not put away their weapons, and thankfully, the Crows had not noticed them. A firefight ensued, with no one certain who fired first, the Crows fighting in the open while Tamner and the others took refuge behind the hemp crates. Luck was with them, for no other assistance came for the Crows, and after several exchanges, when the poppers and injectors fell silent, the Crows lay scattered around the room, some groaning in discomfort and pain, those struck with injector rounds beginning to either twitch or were curled into murmuring balls of moaning leather.

What none of them were grateful for, however, while they disarmed the Crows as the first of the shuffling horde began to arrive at the storage room, was the fact that, whatever happened now, they might well be disciplined for treason should they ever be caught and brought before Founder Kemway and the Doctet.

Tamner knew that he, and any of those with him who might have family elsewhere, would be lucky to ever see those people again.

Tamner waved his group into the left tunnel, the one Agnys had pointed to, that she remembered from many days ago. "This way." The others did not know where it led, but he did. That knowing terrified him.

Agnys pulled on Lash's hand and tried to make the group run with her. She knew where home was now and was determined to reach it as quickly as possible to escape the birdmen, escape the frightening chaos of the great metal nest. At the tunnel entrance, she paused to drop the only thing she carried, a marker meant to lead Rhyd to her, to allow him to find her again as he had promised.

❧*❧

Zara squawked in alarm, unable to prevent the shots Grainger took the moment they passed through the antechamber door. Nor could she prevent the fall of the Echo from the desk. She was not fast enough, and the only thing she had to fight with was the portable Echo. Unthinking of the consequences, she swung it, connecting with the Captain's arm hard enough to force him to drop the injector he wielded. The blow snapped the touchpad in two in a shower of sparks and hissing pops and made Grainger stagger. He did not strike her, which she expected, but rather pushed her away and stalked across the room with the popper in his other hand primed for another shot.

"Eblan," he swore, looking down at the men behind the desk. Rhyd was already struggling to his feet but his bleeding leg buckled and he leaned on the desk, his injured arm and hand, now bleeding again, wincingly holding up his weight on the corner as he clutched his thigh with his gloved hand.

On the floor beside him, at Grainger's feet, Haythem Kemway stared at his security chief with wide, glazing eyes, his hand clutched around the injector he had yanked from his shoulder. He could not be certain if that shot had been errant, if it had struck him instead of the Scarecrow, or if he had been the target himself. Never having touched Hebanthe Falls' drug of choice, he had no personal knowledge of the effects it could have. As his muscles began to twitch, sending spasms through his limbs, undermining his control of his body, he opened his mouth to hurl harsh words and insults at Oliver Grainger.

All that came out was a thin layer of pink-tinted froth.

A siren sounded, a steam whistle blaring from two levels below that gradually bled through the vents and shafts and open stairwells to seep into the room where they stood. Cause enough for alarm, but Grainger had already witnessed the damaged doors between the levels of the Uppers. If the Scarecrow had done that, had found Kemway here, those now penetrating Upper 21, whoever they were, would find their way here soon enough as well.

The Uppers had been breached by more than a vigilante and a dancer. Grainger could hope it was his officers tripping the alarms as they returned, but he was not going to bank on that.

"Go. Factory East is still open," Grainger growled, yanking a syringe from the inner pocket of his jacket, pressing it against the Founder's neck and depressing the plunger.

Rhyd did not know what Grainger had done, whether he was saving the Founder he had not meant to drug or if he was killing the man. But Rhyd did know that his objective, his reason for coming here, was not yet complete. The Echo from Haythem's desk, however, was in pieces on the floor, and Zara, who had reached him now and was helping to steady him on his feet, had placed her destroyed Echo T2 on the desk near his hand.

With the Founder either dead or drugged, unable to give Rhyd what he had come for, and the equipment to hack the Upper Hub for the information he sought now badly damaged, there was no way he would ever find Venn.

Leaning heavily on Zara, Rhyd's heart broke all over again.

Grainger saw the look on the blonde man's face and though he regretted whatever had caused that pain, he did not regret what he had done. Hebanthe Falls had to change if it was going to survive and thrive. And change it would, now that he had taken Kemway out of the picture.

He did not know how, but he would deal with the Founder's family later.

He shoved the syringe back into his pocket so no one would find evidence at the scene of this incident, staring at Zara the whole time.

In another lifetime, he would like to have known her better. Longer. Now, memory was all he had. All he would ever have. It was probably better this way, he sighed with resignation, but he wished it could be otherwise.

"Can you find your way?"

She nodded without looking at him, afraid to meet his gaze, and steered the hobbled man towards the door, pausing long enough to pick up the hood Rhyd had discarded. Whatever her feelings or thoughts might be concerning Captain Grainger, he would never be allowed to know.

❧Chapter 31❦

The wailing siren continued, a painful droning that seemed to drag them backward as if drawing them again to the Levs, clawing at their heels to keep them caught in the Uppers as Rhyd struggled to keep up with the pace Zara was setting. It was less the alarm having that effect then it was the knowledge that somewhere, perhaps in the Core Tamner had spoken of, perhaps in one of the factories Rhyd might never access, Venn might be waiting for him. The single hope he had to hold on to was that, ahead, somewhere, was Factory East, and maybe, if luck favored them both, Venn would be there. The thought kept him from retreating to the depths of Hebenon, to the familiar world he knew, to the shadows and a bottle or two of Zaolei, kept him struggling steadfastly forward.

"Stop a moment." He had nearly tripped over a fallen man, a streeter, a Heb addict, one of the many scientific test subjects he had freed judging by the condition of his bald hed, emaciated body and clothing. He leaned heavily against the wall, wishing for his mask and the oxygen source it could provide, debating the wisdom of consuming any of the painkillers he still carried.

Remembering how they had affected his senses the last time, he chose to endure the pain instead. But he still wanted the oxygen to ease his straining lungs.

Zara took the opportunity to bind Rhyd's thigh with a strip of material torn from the fallen man's clothing. The more they moved, the more he bled, and after the trail she and the others had followed earlier, and what had been left on the Founder's floor and desk, she feared that the loss of much more was going to be the death of him.

"We should reach them soon," she murmured, talking to keep Rhyd positive, attempting to shift his focus onto something other than despair. If there was time, if they found a hall terminal or Factory East had an Echo she could access, she would search for the information Rhyd had come for, search however long she had to in order to find Venn's location, Venn's fate.

By his unchanging, pained expression, however, Rhyd appeared to feel such an effort would be a futile waste of time. She could not believe he had given up. That was not the sort of man Rhyd Ballard was.

Returning to the pressing urgency of reaching somewhere safe, in case those breaching the Upper were foes rather than friends, in case any of them were to see his face, his attire, and learn the truth about the Scarecrow, she assisted in pulling him back to his feet and started them moving again.

What, she wondered darkly, would happen to Hebenon now, with or without the Scarecrow's help?

❧*❧

The shaft seemed longer than she remembered, now that the multiple checkpoints and protective doors were all open, now that there were no hemp carts lined up between them, now that there were no people from the village heaving bundles of harvest plants and crates of plant products from cart to crate and then accepting whatever payment in kind the birdmen offered. She remembered her cousin, six years her senior, explaining how to mark off distance by the passage of familiar trees, boulders, streams, houses, or any familiar landmarks she could pinpoint, but with each open doorway they passed, the tunnel looked much the same, with nothing to differentiate any of the steps they took from the others.

There was little light here, only that provided by the lightstick Maemi had stolen from one of the fallen birdmen. Agnys was beginning to despair of ever finding the door, ever finding the way out.

Then, unexpectedly, in the lightstick's beam, the path came to an abrupt end. Squeaking with excitement, Agnys released Lash's hand and pushed to the front of the group as Tamner located the control panel at one side.

Not even Lash knew how to open this door. Tamner was their only chance of doing so.

"Don't open…" cried Tox, a lifetime of learning warning her that whatever was on the other side of that door would surely kill them the moment Tamner opened it.

But the child was proof of something else out there, and by the time Tamner produced his Pass and slid it through the reader, following it with a sequence of characters entered on the keypad and his spoken "Rafe Tamner," it was too late to protest.

And, Tox realized, Outside might be the only place left to go.

What difference was there if they died here or out there?

The door, rarely used save for the periodic trades, groaned when the lock released, and Tamner, with Agnys' hand on the latch underneath his, held his breath anxiously as he pulled the door open to the outside world.

He prayed all of his sensor readings, all of his data collection, all of his years of research, had not been wrong.

Light spilled into the passage around them.

Haythem Kemway sat in his white, high-backed chair, slumped awkwardly to the side, glazed eyes staring across his now tidied desk, not acknowledging the presence of the other man in the room. He did not turn his head and his eyes did not follow the movement as Grainger one by one twisted the knobs on the wall that opened the six view panels that encircled the antechamber, view panels that no one except the Founders had opened since the birth of Hebanthe Falls six hundred years ago.

Grainger doubted any of those subsequent Founders, after Duncan Kemway, had dared to look at the horrors believed to exist outside.

He took no time to study the view himself until every one of the panels was retracted. What the windows reveal beyond, the sunlight, the sky, the lush green of the hemp crop and the forest at the mountains' edge, the blue-black of the sea, were unlike anything the Captain had ever thought he would see. He wondered, with awe, on the heels of his previous suspicions, listening to the strangled sounds from the throat of the man at the desk, how many Founders had dared to look and had kept this sight, this knowledge, hidden from the people they lauded over.

Haythem, it appeared, had certainly done so.

"No more," Grainger said to the air, to the man behind him in his blood-stained banyan, to those from the Levs who wandered the corridors of the Uppers seeking, demanding, answers.

Haythem moaned again and his head lolled down upon his chest as if heavy with defeat.

❧*❧

Bodies, some moving some not, littered the storage chamber, where popper pellets had bit into walls, into the sparking, hissing Echo terminals and the controls mounted on the surfaces around them. Broken crates littered dried hemp leaves and plant dust on the floor, and the hands of the gear-driven clock on the wall ticked an unmoving passage of time, a stray pellet having lodged into the clock's face, protruding enough that the hands were unable to click past it. By Zara's reckoning, that put the others in this room nearly fifteen minutes ago, but where they had gone next she could not guess, for either tunnel seemed equally likely. Without the schematics she had been following earlier, she had only been able to come this far by memory of where she had last seen Tox and the others.

Rhyd peeled away from her, eyes trained to notice small details catching an out of place hint of gold on the floor at the entrance of the left tunnel. Shuffling stiffly, he studied the grooves in the floor which stretched away into the passage, grooves of a similar width as the carts in the room behind them. Carts used, he believed by the scattered debris, for the trading of hemp. That meant this tunnel could only end at one place. Squatting to investigate the shimmer of metal caused a pulling and tearing in his injured leg that made him wince and lose his balance, but he had the object in his bloody hand now, a familiar chain that still held the warmth of the body who had last worn it.

Using the curvature of the wall to brace himself, he fought to his feet one more time. "This way," he grunted, staring into the darkness.

"How do you…?"

"Listen." He held his hand out to her to reveal the pendant clutched in his bleeding palm. From further down the tunnel, shuffling and groaning could be heard, though nothing could be seen. He and Zara looked at one another. The horde of test subjects, the injured, drugged, and tortured captives he had released, was still moving, which meant that, with little conscious thought of their own to determine a path to take, they were following someone. There was, to Rhyd's knowledge, no one to follow except Agnys and the others. Following to where was the question. Zara presumed their companions were heading to Factory East; Rhyd believed differently, believed the grooved tracks held the answer, but he was not certain he was prepared to meet what awaited at the end.

If he was to fail, to die without finding Venn, he might have at least earned the glimpse of the world Venn should have been there to experience with him. Then again, did he have the right to discover whatever was at the end of this tunnel without Venn at his side?

Far away, from what Rhyd presumed was the end of the tunnel, the end of the darkness, light blazed. Between them and it, a mass of swaying, faltering shadows paused, blinded by the brilliance before pushing onward with renewed vigor. It was not the light, however, that pulled Rhyd forward, struggling through his body's pain with the surge of renewed resolve that empowered him to shuffle faster. It was the smell of sweet, fragrant air that carried with it the bitterness of the mass of unwashed, decaying bodies in front of them yet could not be ruined by those heavier scents. It was the air, and a child's squeal of either delight or horror, that drove him, so that now Zara was the one struggling to keep up.

Elbowing through the weak throng was easy, as none offered resistance or fought back. His pace quickened, his limp growing more pronounced as he hurried but he did not let it stop him. Drawn like a fish to a baited hook, with Zara now clutching his hand anxiously, he reached the front of the mass. Without their bodies to help keep him upright, he stumbled, but Zara caught him up, steadied him, and pulled him forward. The half circle hatch was open, the Outside was beyond it, and two familiar women were silhouetted there, things of beauty he had not thought to see again.

Nothing, however, he thought as he reached them, could match the beauty and splendor of what spread beyond that open door. A dusty trail worn into the earth by innumerable years of feet and carts traveling up and down the gentle slope, wound through autumn fields of what remained of the year's last harvest. Rhyd guessed autumn by the gold and crimson hues of the leaves of some of the trees he could see in the distance, trees that formed a gradual blanket spread at the foot of mountains whose white-capped peaks spoke of early snow at the higher elevations, peaks that reached towards the pale blue morning sky. Rhyd knew it was morning by the sun's position, even though he had never seen the morning before. This was East, where the sun was said to rise, and there it was, the fiery globe hanging low on the horizon.

Tendrils of blue, tiny rivulets of life, snaked through the fields, either bringing water to them or else draining water away into the churning surge of the four rivers that had given Hebanthe Falls life and protected her, it was said, for six hundred years. A short turn to his left allowed a glimpse of the twin West Factories out of the corner of his eye, and to his right, beyond the reaches of Hebenon's Levs and the walls of Factory East Two, and a derelict, abandoned Factory East One, the green and gold land spread into a deeper blue than that which extended above them from horizon to horizon in every direction. The sea, he wondered, a stab in his chest robbing him of breath. The great weeping sea…and Venn would never get to see it.

A collection of six dozen or more small structures dotted the landscape between the fields, the four rivers, and the forest's edge. They were too far away to determine their composition, but their existence eroded the myth that those who lived on the Outside, the parah of legend, had been stripped of all traces of humanity except the ability to farm in the centuries after the fall of man. The buildings were there to prove otherwise, buildings and human shapes that rose up from the gleaning, tools resting on their shoulders, arms and hands shielding their eyes, beholding the humans who had emerged from within the metal nest. Humans…not birdmen.

From the midst of those in the field, a youthful, high-pitched voice shouted his name. Rhyd could barely see her above the drying hemp stalks but eventually found her by the waving of her hand and bobbing of her head as she jumped up and down to get his attention. But it was the shadow of a shape beside her, familiar even at this distance, that tore Rhyd's heart from his chest and the breath from his lungs.

He ran, impeded by his limp, stumbling but struggling to rise again in haste, certain that his eyes were lying to him. But the other was running too, leaving Agnys behind, ignoring the plants he trampled in favor of the miracle he had been given. When they reached one another, the differences of years, the pain of injuries, the misery of loss and longing, evaporated in their embrace.

"Little angel," Rhyd whispered, perhaps referring to the man who spun him around with joy, perhaps referring to the child who had, by some divine hand, brought them to this place, together again.

All along she had known.

"Whiskey," Venn laughed, his voice hoarse and heavy with relief. "Chocolate…"

He saw it then, but too late. Between the arches of the tunnel, a Crow appeared, one of the fallen who had found the strength to pursue those who dared to expose Hebanthe Falls to the poisons of the Outside. A crack split the serenity of early morning; beneath Rhyd's already bloody hand, red spilled forth. Venn lurched, stared into Rhyd's eyes in shock for the fraction of the time it took him to whisper, "Rhyd…" Then he slumped against Rhyd's chest, his head on the blonde man's shoulder as Rhyd lost his balance and fell.

A roar of rage and despair echoed into the distant mountains and was swallowed by the thunder of Hebenon's falls.

❧EPILOGUE❦

The sun sank over the purple-shadowed mountains, silhouetting the chugging stacks of the trio of factories which pumped and belched with activity night and day, guaranteeing the continuation of the efforts Duncan Kemway had struggled for long ago. The rising moon glinted silver off the blanket of snow that covered the fallow fields, but spring would come in time, bringing with it the new green shoots that were due to erupt from soon to be plowed fields. The swift-moving waters of the great rivers continued their eternal churnings on their way over the precipice into the collection basin that in turn spewed it on towards the distant sea, endeavoring to eat away at the edges of the six-hundred-year-old city in the mist.

The great paneled windows were open now, affording Oliver Grainger a view that no other governing officer, to his knowledge, had beheld in the years before him. Men and women, like a trail of wary ants, came and went in the distance, some going into the city to work, to shop, some daring to venture into the world outside for the first time. With chaos now the ruling force in Hebanthe Falls, it was a slow development, and most were still afraid. But Grainger believed the effort was worth taking, the effort to find a balance to preserve both Outside and Inside and help both to thrive.

If humanity was to survive, they had to spread their wings, leave their metal nest. Mankind was not meant to endure in a damp cage in the Falls. People needed the air. They needed the sun. They needed solid earth beneath their feet. They needed swift rivers and pulsing seas and the rain and snow that fell from above. They needed to be free of fear, free to grow. This coming back into the world, Grainger believed, was what Duncan Kemway and his fellow founders had intended and hoped for, for humanity, all along.

But always some returned, and that was needed too, for the hub of manufacturing and culture, such as it was, beat in Hebenon's wounded, struggling heart. Someday, perhaps, the layers of metal and plastic that had kept a portion of humanity alive for centuries would be stripped away, an empty relic no longer needed for mankind's survival.

That day, Grainger believed, would be a long time in coming.

The people in the Falls were not ready for that. They were still afraid of the unknown and afraid of the tales of horrors outside they had been told since childhood.

Silhouetted against the rising moon, on the cliff overlooking the sea, one man watched the light shimmer across the gently rolling waves, his coat clenched to his chest, a shield against the winter wind. Troubled, unsettled, he let out a sigh when the second man trudged up the incline and wrapped his arms around his waist. Rhyd closed his eyes and dropped his head back against the other man's shoulder. Thanks to Tamner, Venn lived. Venn was safe. And Rhyd had had time enough to heal his own wounds.

But clenched in his fist, a metal disk pummeled smooth by prolonged manual effort, a spade and crossed swords etched into it with matching care and effort, spoke of truth his still-weary body and soul had yet to process. It was a token that meant little to anyone else.

To Rhyd, it meant only one thing.

Whiskey-brown eyes fluttered open as he lifted his head, and for a moment they locked with the chocolate ones of the man behind him. They should be happy here. They had the earth, the sky, the sea. They had music again. They had Agnys, who had brought them together and was a constant source of joy. Most importantly, they had each other. Rhyd intended never to abandon Venn again.

But the Scarecrow's lure was too strong.

And some things remained undone.

This was something Rhyd needed to do.

This was something only Scarecrow could do.

For somewhere in the heart of Hebanthe Falls, if this rumor held true, Skelter lived.

THE END

(The Scarecrow will return…)

❧GLOSSARY❧

afatottari: grandfather fucker (Icelandic)

andi: androids; artificial humans made most often for the sex trade and as dancers. Sometimes used to perform other undesirable duties

bilger: those who work on dehumidifying systems

bozhe moy: my god

buzzers: tasers used to stun victims.

chrono: watch, time telling device, often with built-in comms

comm: communication device; there are many varieties available.

chushi: another term for bilger; those who work on dehumidifying systems. sometimes used as an insult.

crowed (being): being snitched on, ratted to the Crows, turned someone in to the authorities or someone who was turned over

crowing: snitching

Crows: police/military force, someone not to be trusted; a snitch

crucksake: a combination of Christ and fuck sake, one of the more common swear terms.

deks: holodeck suites used for recreation, vacation, and educational purposes, since there is nowhere else for those in the City to go.

denki: those who work on heating systems

Doctet: Hebanthe Fall's Council of 10 that works in conjunction with the Founder to run the city

eblan: dumbass (Russian)

Echosys (also XCO/ Echo): computer system used throughout the city. The current model is the 237 as they are frequently redesigned and built every 5 to 10 years. There are four basic models:

w (home view screens)

d (public view screens)

p1 (personal Echos)

t2 (portable tablet echos)

All are linked to the city's Hub at the time of manufacture. They are customizable and can be, illegally, removed from the Hub network.

filt: breathing filtration system

Hebenon: 1) name of the drug produced by official sources, intended as population control for use by the Crows but long ago made available to the public after its addictive properties became known; 2) The nickname Hebanthe Falls gained after the rise of the drug in the streets. The word Hebenon was taken from the Shakespeare play Hamlet due to the similarities in side effects experienced by its users.

Heb: the injected form of the drug Hebenon.

Hebbies: the drug Hebenon in pill form

heizer (also denki): those who work on heating systems

herpa: (from Japanese for helper) pastors, men of religious faiths outside of the Church of the Founder.

Hub: the central broadcasting & computer system in the city.

ICD Images: still images captured with an ICD by passersby.

ICD: Interpersonal Communication Device

injectors: air guns that fire needles laced with Hebenon

kistama: A derogatory slang title given to the Founders; from kistama tama: lord of donkey balls

Levs: refers to any of the lower 20 city levels. Houses most businesses and most of the population of the city.

libbing: making it up, ad-libbing

menasvodnik: a manager of dancers and sex workers; a pimp

parah: a corruption of the word pariah, used for those 'humans' who are living outside of the Hebanthe Falls in the world polluted by mankind's failings.

poppers: air guns, firing small synthetic pellets.

prodcast: broadcast productions aired through the Echosys, ranging from news, to sports, to entertainment and educational subjects.

qinai: dear (Chinese)

quatsch: nonsense, rubbish, garbage

SCAMs: security cams used for monitoring public behavior. There are no known SCAMs in the Uppers, although it is believed the Founders have employed them in both their private offices and residences and in the Doctet meeting chambers.

shed: facility out of which shaft crews work.

skolper: sewage worker. sometimes used as an insult.

source: the center of all material goods and food distribution.

spener: those who work on plumbing

stingers: needles fired by injectors, laced with Hebenon.

streeter: those living on the streets

swiver: someone who owns a food/beverage serving establishment or who serves food or drink; a bartender, waiter, waitress

tapper: computer hacker

Talkers: priests of the Voices of Faith established religion.

thumper: police stick used for beating prisoners to subdue them.

ticks: currency points used for the acquisition of food and supplies and services. Distributed by the Doctet on a predetermined scale.

tinger: someone who takes things, thief, vagrant living off of others

Vapors: Maemi's club/bar

vindi: vendors, shops, diners

Voices of Faith: the 'religion' supported by the Founder and Doctet which supports the Kemways divine right to run Hebanthe Falls; they produce prodcasts angled toward religious faith, community cohesiveness, and Kemway support

XCO: (also Echo/Echosys): computer system used throughout the city. Current model is the 237 as they are frequently redesigned and built every 5 to 10 years. There are four basic models: W – home viewing system; D – public viewing systems found in vindis and in a variety of other public places; P1 – personal desk units; and T2 – portable tablet units. All are linked to the city's Hub at the time of manufacture. They are customizable and can be, illegally, removed from the Hub network.

Zaolei: algae whiskey

About the Author

Unsatisfied with 'how the story ends' as a young reader, Tamara took on the challenge of crafting endings to the tales of others to better suit her vision of the world. That desire to mold reality into how she imagined it should be, gave birth to a life-long fascination with the written word, and its capacity, particularly through realms of fantasy and science fiction, to foster an understanding of the people, events, thoughts, and emotions that make us who we are.

A long-time resident of Clearlake, California, after a life that took her back and forth across the country, Tamara is owned by a pack of papillions, a pride of cats, and an eclectic arsenal of films she enjoys in her off-moments.

Hebenon is Tamara's seventh novel.

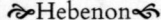